GOOD FAITH

GOOD FAITH

JANE SMILEY

RANDOM HOUSE
LARGE PRINT

*The Library of Congress has established a
Cataloging-in-Publication record for this title*

0-375-43277-9

www.randomlargeprint.com

FIRST LARGE PRINT EDITION

10 9 8 7 6 5 4 3 2 1

This Large Print edition published in accord
with the standards of the N.A.V.H.

GOOD FAITH

CHAPTER 1

THIS WOULD BE '82. I was out at the
Viceroy with Bobby Baldwin. Bobby
Baldwin was my one employee, which
made us not quite friends, but we went out to the
Viceroy almost every night. My marriage was
finished and his hadn't started, so we spent a lot of
time together that most everyone else we knew
was spending with their families. I didn't mind.
My business card had the Viceroy's number in the
corner, under "may also be reached at." Buyers
called me there. It was a good sign if they wanted
to see a house again in what you might call the
middle of the night. That meant they couldn't
wait till morning. And if they wanted to see it
again in the middle of the night—well, I did my
best to show it to them. That was the difference

between Bobby and me. He always said, "Their motivation needs to be tested, that's what I think. Let 'em wait a little bit."

Bobby was not my brother, but he might as well have been. Sally, his sister, had been my girlfriend in high school for about a year and a half. She was the first person I ever knew who had a phone of her own. She used to call me up and tell me what to do. "Now, Joey," she would say, "tomorrow wear those tan pants you've got, and the blue socks with the clocks on them, and your white shirt, and that green sweater I gave you, and I am going to wear my blue circle skirt with the matching cashmere sweater, and I'll meet you on the steps. We'll look great. Have you done your algebra problems? When you get to number four, the variable is seven, and x equals half of y. If you remember that, then you won't have a problem with it. Did you wash your face yet? Don't forget to use that stuff I bought you. Rub it in clockwise, just a little tiny dab, about the size of the tip of your pencil eraser. Okay?"

I had been short, and now I was tall. I had been skinny and quiet and religious, and now I was good-looking and muscular. It was Sally Baldwin who brought me along, told me what to wear and do and think and say. She was never wrong; she never lost her patience. She created me, and when she was done we broke up in a formal sense, but she kept calling me. She was smart and went off to Smith College, and I was sure she would get everything organized there once and for all. I went to Penn State. In April of my freshman year, Sally was killed in a car accident outside of Boston. I had talked to her two days before. "Now, Joey," she had said, "it's okay to see a woman who is almost thirty, but you don't say that you are dating her, you say that you are *seeing* her. Seeing is much more sophisticated than dating, and it doesn't lead to marriage."

I went home for the funeral. It was as if the Baldwins had been eviscerated. All they had left were Felicity, Norton, Leslie, and Bobby. That didn't seem like much without Sally to move them along. Betty, their mom, couldn't act of her own free will. The funeral director, Pat Mahoney, had to seat her here and stand her there and remove her from this spot and place her in that spot. Gordon seemed better, almost vigilant in a way, though my mother said he would never recover and maybe he never did. Bobby was ten then, nine years younger than I was. Gordon came up to me afterward and asked me how I was doing. He was concerned, the way you always get at funerals, and I couldn't help telling him that I wasn't doing at all well—I hated college and was terribly homesick anyway, and now there was this stunning thing that was the end of Sally—and the next thing I knew he was offering me a job and I was taking it, and I went back to pick up my stuff at Penn State two days after the funeral, and I started working for Gordon the following Monday, which I certainly would not have been invited to do if Sally were alive and my girlfriend or fiancée because Gordon didn't like to be bankrolling everyone in the whole family, especially not sons-in-law.

My dad used to wonder what the Baldwins' real name was. They weren't like any Baldwins he had ever known. Gordon was loud and affectionate. Hey, honey, he always said, no matter who he was talking to. He ate out every night. He had three or four restaurants he took everyone to, owned by his poker buddies, I think. He played poker twice a week, high stakes. These games had been going for generations. For a living, he bought and sold things. For a while, it was antiques; for a while, jewelry; for a while, cars; for a while, expensive fixtures out of houses and restaurants and hotels that were being torn down. Once in a while he would hear about some hotel in the city that was going under, and he would come home with a truckload of dishes or silver that carried a hotel monogram. One year, his barn was full of pink silk chairs and settees from the lobby of a hotel in Montreal. Another year he got a thousand commodes. That was the year he persuaded everyone who bought a house from us that "you got to have one more bathroom than the number of bedrooms. It's the wave of the future." Always land and houses and dairy-cattle breeding stock. One thing leads to another; that is, houses lead to commodes, and then commodes lead to houses, which lead to land, which leads to dairy cattle, which lead to cheese, which leads to pizza pies, which lead to manicotti and veal Parmesan, which lead to wine, which leads to love, which leads to babies, houses, and commodes. That was Gordon Baldwin in a nutshell.

My father, who didn't like anything to lead to anything else, because of sin, couldn't decide whether the Baldwins had originally been "Obolenskis" or "Balduccis" or "Baldagyis." He took solace in the fact that we were Stratfords, always had been Stratfords; there was no misspelling of the Stratford name since the Middle Ages. The Baldwins had come to town after the war. That was all anyone knew; and for all that Gordon had gotten rich and locally famous, and he, Bobby, and everyone else in the family talked and talked, where the Baldwins had come from was something they never talked about.

Anyway, I could hardly keep my eyes open, though it was only midnight, early for a Baldwin, and Bobby was wide awake. He was drinking and playing craps for pennies with a builder we knew. The bar was about half full. It was a Wednesday. I said, "See you at ten."

Bobby said, "See that, a five and a three. That's eight."

"Bobby," I said. "Ten! I have to show a house at ten-fifteen and I want to be sure you're there before I go."

"Ten," said Bobby.

"Ten in the morning."

"In the morning."

"Morning is when the sun is in the sky and you don't have to turn on your headlights."

"Got you. Roll 'em." He looked at me and smiled. He looked just like Betty. I shook my head. As I passed next to the table right behind where we had been sitting, I saw a guy look up, look at me. I went out into the parking lot.

The parking lot of the Viceroy backed up on the river, the Nut. My condo was in a development in a smaller town upriver, Nut Hollow. Instead of getting right into my car, I walked down to the river and had a look at the moon, which was shining round and bright. The river was black and glassy around the circle of the moon for just a single long moment; then the wind came up and ruffled the image. I saw there was a woman squatting at the base of a tree, about ten yards from the river. When she turned at my footsteps, I realized it was Fern Minette, Bobby's fiancée. She stood up with a big smile, wiping her hands on her jeans. Fern was about twenty-seven or so. She and Bobby had been engaged for four and a half years. I said, "Well, it's Fern! What are you doing, Fernie?"

"Cat entrapment."

"You're trapping cats?"

"Well, my cat. He got out of the car when I took him to the grocery store Friday." She pointed to a cat carrier with its door open, just barely visible, in a cleft up the bank from the river. "I put things in there. Liver. His toys. Last night he went in, but when I moved away from the tree, he ran out again." She sighed.

I said, "Bobby's in the Viceroy. Maybe he would help you. He's not doing anything productive."

"You can't help with a cat. A cat can't be herded, a cat has to be attracted. I just can't figure out the thing that would do it, and as the nights go by it gets harder. You should go away, anyway."

"Do you stay out here all night?"

"Till two. Then I come back at six. Go away! He might be watching me and making up his mind!"

I got in my car and shut the door. When I turned on my headlights, Fern waved, then hunkered down beside the tree. The strangest thing about Bobby and Fern was that they had actually discussed marriage. Neither one was the sort of person you could imagine having any life plan that would lead to regular hours, a house, and then children who accepted them as parents.

Bobby was still on my mind when I got up to go to the office in the morning, probably because I was annoyed in advance that he would be late and I would have to rush to my appointment. It was a sharp but clear spring morning, not quite to the daffodil stage. The sky was a cold blue-gray, but the grass had greened up on the hillsides, and it seemed like you could see each blade shining with chlorophyll. It was the sort of day where houses look great, especially brick houses, and I had a brick house to show, one with a big front lawn and a newly blacktopped driveway.

The surprise was that Bobby was at the office, in a jacket and a tie, and he had the Multiple Listing book out of his desk, wide open to the listings in the high one-hundreds. In those days, that was the back of the book and there were some nice houses there, houses up in Rollins Hills with five and six bedrooms and Sub-Zero refrigerators. I remember I showed a house up there with its own little sauna/steam room. The buyers and I stood in our shoes in the bathroom, turning the seven dials and staring into the little wood-paneled cubbyhole like we'd never seen running water before. Anyway, Bobby was deep in the Rollins Hills listings. As soon as I walked in, he said, "Guess what! This guy in the bar last night, he's moving out from the city. I'm taking him out this morning, eleven-thirty. He wants to see seven houses today and seven tomorrow, and then he's going to pick. You should have hung around, but I'm glad you didn't. He was this—"

"Dark-haired guy in a gray jacket?"

"Yeah."

"That's funny. He looked up at me when I was leaving."

"People always look at you when you're leaving the Viceroy. They're looking at you in disbelief."

"They're looking at you in shame, Bob. Anyway, did you see Fern? She was out there trying to catch her cat."

"She's never going to catch that cat. That cat has been trying to escape for five years. You know, when she moved into her apartment, that cat had the vermin cleaned out in a month. Here he is."

A Cadillac pulled into our little lot and eased between my Lincoln and Bobby's new BMW.

GOOD FAITH

Baldwin Development bought a fleet of cars every two years, always whatever some crony of Gordon's was just getting into. After the New Year, Rollins Hills Motors had gotten the BMW franchise, and Stu Grade had sold Gordon six BMWs over a poker game. Bobby's was red. The local sheriff had been informed that Bobby's was the red one.

The guy who got out of the Caddy was very smooth looking—creased tan slacks, expensive-looking white shirt, Italian-cut jacket, tasseled loafers. He pocketed his keys and threw his sunglasses down on the seat of his car, then glanced around for our door. When he saw me looking at him through the plate glass, he broke into a smile. There was no one with him. House deals without women put you out into unknown territory sometimes. That was especially true in those days, when most buyers were families moving around the county, to nicer houses, or out to the country from the city. But Bobby needed something to do with his time, and I thought an iffy client was better than any one of his usual six activities— sleeping late, going to the Viceroy, going to the doctor, going to the dentist, doing repairs around his own place, or calling Gordon and asking for something to do. It was this last that had resulted in Bobby's employment at my office. Bobby was well-meaning, and even smart, but he was a danger to himself and others simply because he couldn't use any sort of tool or even do anything outside of his normal routine without hurting himself or getting sick. If it wasn't a broken toe from stumbling over a stack of weights at the gym, then it was poison ivy all over his face from taking Fern on a hike, or some sort of food poisoning. Gordon said to me, "That kid could put his eye out with a hammer or break his leg with a screwdriver. Real estate is the safest place for him." And it was. But I didn't think he would be any match for this Marcus Burns, to whom he was now introducing me.

My clients were, or would soon be, waiting. My clients were careful buyers, the Sloans. I made a living in real estate by keeping track of what a buyer wanted and doing research— going to every open house, calling other agents, visiting model homes, just in general mastering as many features of as many listings as I could— but you couldn't get ahead of the Sloans. What they wanted to know about every house they looked at, even the ones they didn't like, defied preparation. They had been looking for four months, not an inordinately long time, but they had seen every house on the market in their price range and now they just waited for new listings. Usually, at some point you gave up on people like that, because you knew they would never buy. The one thing that made me think the Sloans would eventually go for something was their conviction that something valuable or even precious was out there. The more I assured them we were on top of every available property, the more worried they got that we were missing one. I thought the tension would eventually become too much for them to bear. Needless to say, they were prequalified in every way. The mortgagor was dying to lend them money.

They were standing in front of their Toyota at the house, a Dutch Colonial that had just come on the market. The neon-bright sloping lawn was framed by the driveway and scattered with darker shafts of daffodil leaves; a few blooms were out on the brow of the hill in front of the house. The weathered brick and black shutters contrasted with the brilliant weather just as I had hoped, and I could see that Mrs. Sloan was opening up. But Mr. Sloan, who distributed office equipment in the tristate area, said, "Needs tuck-pointing."

I hadn't missed that, but I hadn't spoken soon enough. Nevertheless, I filled in. "Not right away. Two years from now." I followed them up the front walk. She was about thirty-five, with red hair that curved around her head like a cap and pale, easily flushed skin. She was not pretty but oddly attractive. I tended to take her side when she disagreed with him, especially since he was not very appealing—short and emphatic. He opened the front door with a slight bump, and entered as if daring the place to sell itself to him.

It was a center-hall floor plan, living room to the left, dining room to the right, kitchen behind that, family room behind the living room, nice enclosed porch across the back, and four bedrooms and two baths upstairs. There was another half bath off the kitchen. Wallpaper everywhere, parquet floor in the entry hall. The house was what people liked in our area, more compact than expansive, with a heavy well-built feel about it.

It is arrogant to assume that you know what will fulfill another's needs—every expert on how to live from Jesus Christ to the Monday Afternoon Businessmen's Lunch Group of the Nut County Board of Realtors agreed on that. Even so, I knew that this Dutch Colonial, just like three-fourths of the houses I had shown the Sloans, would fulfill their needs. Houses are houses. If you had a lottery to assign houses of appropriate sizes to random families, it would do no worse and no better than those families did themselves in finding abodes, because the accumulated human wisdom about dwellings is sufficient to satisfy dwelling-related human needs. But no. Mrs. Sloan sighed in the kitchen, her spirit that was uplifted in the garden now depressed. Mr. Sloan found his suspicions confirmed—in addition to tuck-pointing, there would be replacement of the carpets and a new refrigerator. Making a low offer wouldn't solve these problems, it would only convince the Sloans that they were settling for less than they wanted. As we went to our cars, cordial in every way, I wondered if I would return their next call. I was single. There were other clients.

As I was getting into my car, Mrs. Sloan said suddenly, "We should put our house on the market. I think we're doing this backwards."

"Honey—" said Mr. Sloan. They had talked about this. She was enlisting me in a family disagreement. I said, "There's no one way to do it. You want things to mesh, but—"

"I just feel that if we had the money in hand for our house, things wouldn't be so complicated."

"I never think it's a good idea to burn your bridges behind you," asserted Mr. Sloan.

"I need something to happen," said Mrs. Sloan.

I said, "We can put your house on the market any time you like."

As I drove down the driveway, I looked in my

rearview mirror. They were sitting in their car, arguing. It was a pleasure to drive away.

I had been divorced for a year by then. My wife left me, I always said, as a result of terrorist activity. What happened was, we were in Barcelona in 1969. We'd been married two or three years by that time, and every year we went to Europe. She loved to shop, so we were strolling down the Ramblas, I think it's called. We turned into a side street and went into one shop, heard some popping noises, came out, looked around, didn't see anything. We went into another shop, and she got kind of into the back of it. I went out into the street, then into a shop around the corner. From there I could hear louder noises, and when I came out a few minutes later, I saw smoke and heard sirens. I went out into the middle of the Ramblas to try and see what was happening, and suddenly policemen and police cars were everywhere, and they were herding us all away from the shopping district. I could see the end of the street where Sherry had gone into the tile shop, but I couldn't get to her, and she wasn't visible. I said a few things in Spanish, but it was no use. They pushed us back and cordoned off the street, and then, literally, there were bullets in the air.

I didn't know what to do and didn't have the fluency to ask. I went back to our hotel and got the concierge to call the police and a hospital or two, but of course there was nothing to learn; everything was still happening. I went to our room, but that made me nervous, so I hung around the hotel lobby for a while, and then I made the mistake that was fatal to our marriage. I went into the bar and ordered a drink. Sherry appeared in the doorway at exactly the moment I was raising the glass to my lips. I admit there was something about it that looked excessively casual, especially since my clothes weren't disarranged or anything. Our marriage went on for nine years after that, but to the last day she would append to every argument, "And for another thing, when there was all that shooting in Barcelona and people were being killed, *you* were in the hotel bar ordering a stinger! Why weren't you out looking for me? That's something I'll never understand!" That was always the last word.

Sherry was still around. She had taken the money she got from our marriage settlement and opened a restaurant across the Nut, in Melton Township, called L'Auberge Normande. It was not the sort of restaurant Gordon took everyone out to late at night, so I never saw her or heard about her, but around Christmas she had gotten a three-and-a-half-star review in the *Nut County Reporter,* complimenting her especially on her crème brûlée and her pork medallions in Calvados.

Sherry had spent the years of our marriage complaining about local cuisine, devising ideas of her own, trying to persuade me to find her a location and make an investment in her cooking skill and business acumen. I resisted. Anyway, now she was gone, and we had nothing to do with each other. We'd had no kids, no dog. It seemed to me as I drove away from the arguing Sloans that there hadn't even been a marriage—only, perhaps, this woman I knew who didn't quite fit in with the Baldwins, my real family.

On the way back to the office, I passed Bobby and Marcus Burns in the red BMW. They were turning right out of Maple Glen Road, which I thought was interesting. Maple Glen Road had a couple of lots being developed by one of my builders, Gottfried Nuelle. Gottfried Nuelle built in the mid two-hundreds, and all his houses, two at that time, had been my listings. Marcus Burns saw me and looked at me, even in that brief moment when I passed. Bobby did not.

• • •

GOOD FAITH

When I ran into Bobby at the Viceroy that night, he was both secretive and self-satisfied. I plied him with beer, always an easy thing to do, and he revealed that Marcus Burns had very much tried to conceal his interest in Gottfried's most imposing production, a four-bedroom Queen Anne that had been on the market for seven months. This house was Gottfried's pride and joy. At first he'd considered moving into it himself, though that contravened his dearest commercial principle, which was that the workers can't afford to purchase the products of their labor. The lot was a beautiful acre that swept down from the house to a small stream, over which Gottfried had built a bridge. It had a wraparound veranda; Gottfried had sited and designed the house to preserve three of the old maples that Maple Glen was named for. But the greatest pleasure of the house was a subtler one. About a year before, Gottfried had found a guy who did wood moldings, the sort of decorative relief designs that they used to do in plaster. He was a young kid, not more than thirty, and his last job had been repairing and replacing decorative woodwork at a state capitol somewhere out beyond Chicago. How he got to our neck of the woods and how Gottfried got hold of him I never knew, but he put him to work in this house for four months. The kid lived there; he got up every morning and made and installed crown moldings in every room. He was a scholar, too. He didn't just do what Gottfried liked. He decided what period the house "referred to" and then carved moldings from that period. He was a quiet guy, like a lot of carpenters and joiners, and that just made it all the easier for him to ignore Gottfried. The result was elaborate, elegant, and expensive, and Gottfried had been complaining for months that our local clientele didn't have the class to appreciate the house. Nevertheless, the kid was now at work on another of Gottfried's houses, because Gottfried just couldn't let him go.

"You know," said Bobby, "I set it up perfectly. It was the fifth house of the day, and we went from there over to the place on King's Creek, where that woman has junk all over the place, and she sits there while you're going through the house and watches you to make sure you don't steal anything from her 'collection.' He wants to see Gottfried's place again tomorrow with the wife."

"A wife is a good sign."

"He didn't even blink at the price."

"Did you tell him how long it's been on the market?"

"He didn't ask."

GOOD FAITH

"He will." After all, asking how long something's been on the market is the buyer's first obligation.

I should say about Gordon, whom I had known almost all my life and worked for forever, that his idea of a good deal was unvarnished and old world; he wanted to make sure he took unfair advantage of everyone he negotiated with. In bridge, he trumped you; in poker, he bluffed you; in Scrabble, he used every tile. He haggled at all times and in every situation. When he took everyone out to dinner, he haggled with the waiter about the bill, not just about the tip. In fact, if the waiter took ten percent off the bill, Gordon would sometimes add something to the tip, but not always. When he saw a sum of money that he owed, he discounted it by 20 percent automatically and paid that. If the clerk pointed out to him that he owed more than the sum he had laid on the counter, the haggling began. Beyond that, he didn't mind giving away far more than he ever saved by bargaining—he was not a miser by any means—he just viewed every price as a starting point, and his greatest regrets had to do with having been suckered, as he thought, from time to time over the years. In years of doing business for and with Gordon, I had been had more times than I could count and then received the difference, or more than the difference, at some later date, in another form. You could say what Sherry had said, that Gordon Baldwin lived to swindle others, but most people around the area, like me, didn't take offense, just hit him up later for a loan or a donation.

In a more timid and less successful form, Bobby adhered to the same principle. It didn't matter to him how much money he made on a deal, just as long as he made one percent, or one tenth of one percent, more than the other guy. I knew Gottfried would sell for ten or more percent off the asking price (not without ranting and complaining—Gottfried liked an energetic face-to-face negotiation of exactly the sort that Bobby, who had also been had by his father over and over, detested). Not too long before, Gottfried had gotten a buyer in a corner at a closing and threatened to grab him by the jacket and push him out a (ground-floor) window. As long as Marcus Burns didn't force it, I knew Bobby would do the easiest thing and make a full-price offer, but I was curious to see whether Marcus Burns was going to force it. "So," I said. "What's this guy do?"

"I guess he was an IRS agent. Can you believe that? Anyway, now he's an investment counselor at that new office in Cashel Heights, that Merrill Lynch office. He knows the tax code cold."

"How did you find that out?"

"Well—"Bobby shrugged."I guess he told me."

And that was all we had to say about Marcus Burns for several weeks.

CHAPTER 2

I WOULD PROBABLY STILL have been
married if Sherry hadn't acted to unmarry
me. All through our last year together, she
would say, "Are you happy, Joe? What do you
want?" and I would say "Well, yes," and "I don't
know. This is fine." And it was. My mental life
was pretty clear. I would say, "Are you happy?"
and she would say no, but then she had never
been happy, in the sense of being satisfied or generally pleased. Not being happy was one of her
good points. Not being happy led her to try
things, like gourmet cooking. When I met her,
she didn't know how to bake a potato. Every year
of our marriage the food was different and better—roast chickens with onions and lemons
stuffed inside and herbs crushed all over the skin

were followed by roast chickens with herbs and onions and lemon peel ground up and pushed between the skin and the meat. Mashed potatoes were followed by roasted potatoes with olive oil and rosemary, and then she discovered how to boil the potatoes a little and then roast them so that they were crunchy and buttery on the outside and melting and soft in the middle. I always called our house "Hog Heaven." I was the hog. She liked sex, too, and keeping the house neat, not to mention having it look just right. One year I painted the living room five times, and only Sherry and I could tell the difference, but we could tell and we thought it was worth it. Another time, she bought an antique chandelier for the dining room, and I spent days and days gold-leafing it. It was frustrating and painstaking work. The gold leaf was like sheets of ash, that delicate. But when I was done, the chandelier looked graceful and expensive, as if she had paid a thousand bucks for it, rather than forty-two. When my mother said, afterward, "You know your father and I don't care for divorce, Joey, but between you and me I never thought she treated you like you deserved," I was surprised. She had just been Sherry, that's all, someone who rubbed some people the wrong way. But my analysis hadn't worked in the end, since we were no have made the most of on my own. But maybe my business acumen wasn't so bad after all, because I'd done pretty well in the year since the divorce. Even with the uncertainty about interest rates, I'd sold a lot of properties, and I had also bought two acreages for development—a forty-acre farm near one of Gordon's farms and a thirty-four-acre piece with a nice old house on it that I could easily imagine living in myself, subdividing the acreage into five-acre parcels to pay for the renovation the place needed.

But it was not with these things in mind that I went out to the Viceroy a couple of weeks later. It was with nothing in mind, as usual. When I got there, I looked around for Bobby. The Baldwin I saw, though, was Felicity, laughing with a group of people I didn't know over in the corner. Felicity was a year younger than Sally, which made her a year younger than I. She was married to Hank Ornquist, who worked for the State Parks Commission. They had two teenage sons, maybe seventeen and eighteen. I saw them two or three times a year, here and there. Felicity always did what she now did when I caught her eye, she got up and came over and put her arms around me and gave me a sisterly kiss. Then she put her head longer married. And of course, Sherry had angrily predicted I was going to miss her (why angrily I don't know, because I predicted it too—it wasn't something we disagreed on), but the way I missed her no one had predicted. I didn't miss the food or even the sex and I didn't miss the house, which she got, and all the things in it that I had built or fixed or done up; I missed the attention I had paid her, the time and effort that took, and the pleasant and happy feeling I used to have of being sure that everything with her was okay for the time being.

The divorce lasted a long time and cost a lot of money because I had made a lot of money all through the seventies. Every time the lawyers settled on some numbers, Sherry would agree too and then come back a few days later with revised figures. She had a lot of confidence in me, I have to say. She thought my relationship with Gordon Baldwin was going to turn into a windfall that the simple act of divorce would exclude her from. I spent several years trying to demonstrate how small-time I was and would always be, while my estranged wife spent the same period of time trying to prove what fabulous business acumen and wonderful connections I had, connections she alleged she had cultivated for me, that I couldn't on my shoulder in a friendly way and pinched my cheek. She looked more like Gordon than Betty. She had long curly dark hair and a cheery smile combined with a sharp-eyed gaze. I kissed her back and put my arm around her waist. But our friendliness wasn't backed up by a close acquaintance. More than Sally or the other three, Felicity had always set herself a little apart from the family, marrying someone entirely unlike Gordon, for one thing—Hank Ornquist was about as untalkative as a guy could be. For another, Felicity kept her holidays mostly at her own house—they would show up Christmas morning after breakfast, or leave Thanksgiving dinner to go to Hank's parents before the pie was served, when Sherry and I, not even related, would have to be sent home after midnight. So when Felicity, with her head on my shoulder, whispered "Oh, Joey" in my ear, I spun my head to look at her in amazement. She laughed. "Oh, Joey!" she said aloud.

"Oh, Joey, what?"

"Oh, Joey, I saw you come in, and you were so wrapped up in business you didn't even look around and see that four women were watching you."

"Which four?" I must say I was doubtful of this, but on the other hand she didn't have any reason that I could see to be flirting with me. "You're teasing me."

"That blonde at the end of the bar."

"That's Carla King. She's a Realtor, trying to figure out whether I'm doing any business tonight. So she doesn't count."

"Okay. Let's see. Oh, there she is. That other blonde coming back from the bathroom."

Laurie. I said, "That's Laurie. We had an unfortunate experience about a month and a half ago. I'm sure she was watching me to see if my manners have improved."

"What did you do?"

"Well, I was a little drunk."

"And?"

"I believe she made the case that I had been discovered by her dog-walking neighbor at six A.M. peeing on her—that is, Laurie's—flower beds. And that might have been true, because I did leave Laurie's house before daybreak that day, and it may be that I was trying to avoid awakening her prematurely by not using the bathroom, but I thought that dog was just an excuse for the guy to be out patrolling the neighborhood when he should have been home in bed. Anyway, Laurie doesn't count either."

"Okay. That girl over there."

Someone I had never seen before, pretty, but

who looked about eighteen. "She's a kid. Doesn't count for at least a couple of years, and only then if she's interested in me because she mistakes me for someone close in age to herself and does not see me as a father figure."

"Do I count?"

"Were you watching me, Felicity?"

"Always do."

I looked around the bar.

"Hank's away on business."

I turned the barstool so that we were face-to-face. I said, "Who are those people you're with?" but I meant, What exactly is going on here?

She said, "The woman in the red sweater is someone I went to college with. She came down from the city for the weekend. Those are her friends who came with her." I think she meant that there was more going on than met the eye.

"Are they staying with you?"

"They're at the Blackbird Inn, that new B and B out on Route Five." And then she licked her lips. I continued to be astounded. I put my hands on her shoulders and eased her off a step, then looked at her again. She looked steadily back at me, smiling slightly, her eyes alive and her cheeks flushed. I said, "Always do?"

"Always do."

"Is my jaw dropping?"

"Oh, Joey, you are such a dim bulb. I've been flirting with you for a long time. Don't you have any instincts?"

"Not according to Laurie." We looked across the room at Laurie. Then I said, "Felicity, do you think my condo is burning down?"

And Felicity said, "I don't know. Let's go check." She laughed again and put her hands together in a gesture of excitement that I knew well. It was perfect in a way—she was utterly familiar to me and yet completely mysterious. She said, "You go out to the parking lot. I'll sit down with my friends for another ten minutes, and then come out. You keep an eye out for me, and then when I get into my car—it's the silver BMW?—you drive out of the parking lot and I'll follow you."

I knew exactly what she was getting at. I said, "You know, Fern might be out there. Did you see her? I think she's still lying in wait for her cat."

"That's okay. You speak to her; then, ten minutes later, I'll speak to her. Fern doesn't put two and two together until you tell her to." She went back to her friends. I watched her for a moment and then finished my beer and left.

Twenty minutes later I was heading down Hardy Well Road, and in my rearview mirror I could see the headlights of the last person on earth I had expected ever to make love to, and I knew we were going to make love, and I had no doubts, as if I had been simply waiting for it to happen.

Those moments, when we were parking our cars and getting out and fumbling with keys and I was directing her to the door of my condo at one in the morning, were maybe the time in my life when I felt the most purely young. There was none of that grinding sense of getting through the various stages of an acquisition project that I often felt when I was flirting. No strategy, no trying to figure anything out. I didn't even touch her or take her elbow—no first moves that would lead to a goal. Rather, the air was damp and fresh-smelling, the grass was growing a few feet away in the darkness, trees rustled their new leaves all around us. The stars pressed down on us so we didn't have to look up to sense them. My condo intended to take us in; all I had to do was find the key. It was Felicity who touched me. She slipped her arms around my waist and pressed her head briefly against my chest in a manner I recognized intuitively as ecstasy and at once shared.

I had never kissed Felicity, not on the lips. How amazing was that? What an oversight!

GOOD FAITH

Now I poured kisses into her, and her lips, which were perfectly warm and cushiony, found a place just inside the circle of my own and nested there. We kissed and kissed. I could feel the palm of her hand glowing against the back of my neck, her fingers pushed up into my hair. My hands were somewhere—the small of her back, her cheek. And I could feel my cock pressing against her belly through our clothes, coats and all. But really there was only kissing, the dark house we made by pressing the portals of our lips together, so spacious and fascinating a place that our whole selves could go right in there and live.

Of course the kissing melted into something else, but there was no desire as I had formerly known it: that is, no imagination of anything to come, just a sensation of joined movement. The condo was cold. We kept our clothes on and pressed ourselves into each other. I was aware of her size—not that she was big or small but that she was new—new shape, new weight against me, new fragrance. It was exciting. I found my way through the layers of her clothes and my clothes to her skin, which goose-pimpled in the cool air, and so we slid under the comforters and then I slipped inside her, still kissing, always kissing. I heard her crying out and cried out myself. It was the cries that seemed to make me come, not the other way around.

The room was dark. I turned on a light. Felicity said, "Joey Stratford! I recognize you!" Then she embraced me around the chest and laid her head there, so I couldn't see her face.

She was laughing so merrily I started to feel remote and dizzy from it all. Finally I said, "Well, Felicity, you have just given me the surprise of my life."

"Didn't you think I was capable of such a thing?"

"I still don't. My assumptions haven't quite caught up with reality here."

"Oh, Joey."

"That's what you said to start all this, as I remember. You whispered 'Oh, Joey' in my ear."

"Wasn't I bold? I was so bold. Bold as brass, my mother would say."

"What *would* your mother say?"

"I don't think we'll ever find out, Joey."

"Okay."

I had never made love to Sally—we were too young—but I had kissed her over and over, especially gentle kisses on her face, planted like a delicate grid over her cheeks and forhead and lips. When I kissed her lips, she didn't kiss me back, but let me explore her quiet lips with my own. She said it made her feel as if she were something precious. After she died, I got out an old photograph of her and kissed it in the same way, to make myself feel that she had been loved, loved by me as best I could. Now it happened that Felicity kissed me in just that way, carefully, setting one small kiss right next to another, and when she came to my lips, I lay still while she worked over their contours and then down my neck. When she was done, she sighed and lay back quietly. Her hand stroked my arm, up and down. She was bold indeed. She touched me without shyness or embarrassment, or what you might call a sense of proprietorship. I had never felt anything like it. She sighed again.

I said, "Are you okay?"

"Right as rain." We were silent and still. Her hand came up and pushed her thick dark hair out of her face. She spoke softly and sleepily. "What time is it?"

"After two."

"Oh, not that late."

I laughed at this very Baldwin sort of reply.

"What do you have to eat around here?"

Ten minutes later, Felicity was wrapped in my bathrobe, frying up cheeseburgers in the kitchen. I was sitting by the breakfast bar in my jeans and a T-shirt, watching her. She did it just the way a woman with a husband and two teenage sons would, slapping the meat around almost unconsciously, peppering it but not salting it, toasting the bread I had scrounged up in lieu of buns, finding onions and tomatoes and lettuce. She said, "I could eat both of these after that. You know, I always thought it was so strange that people would go to sleep after sex. I always want to get up and at least eat a good meal. Going to the grocery store. Now that's a very sexy thing to do after you've been getting it on. All the food looks so appetizing." She flipped the burgers and hummed a little tune, took the second batch of toast out of the toaster. She said, "So, now tell me why you asked if your condo was burning down? That was such a funny line, Joey. You are so funny." She pressed the burgers with the spatula.

"Just a come-on. It popped into my mind."

"Pure genius." She smiled.

She put the burgers on a couple of plates, arranging the vegetables in neat rings, looked in the pantry and found some potato chips, did it all efficiently and gracefully.

I said teasingly, "Thanks for the burgers, Mom," and put my arm around her. What I was really doing was getting inside that force field of honest pleasure again. Then Felicity got up, went over to the cupboard, and rummaged around. She came back with Tabasco sauce, sprinkled it all over her burger, and set it down. "Want some?"

"I don't need any of my own. I can feel yours inside my nose."

"Those Tabasco-sauce people own something called a salt dome."

"What's that?"

"Oh, it's a geological formation where there's a big pool of oil deep in the ground, then there's a cap of salt over it. You can extract both, I guess. Tabasco sauce is just a sideline business with them. Their real fortune is in oil. Daddy always said that if any of us ever ran into a McIlhenny, marry him or her quick. But we didn't." She finished her burger, not without looking at it appreciatively, then ate her chips, licked her fingers, and sat back. Now was the moment to ask her what we were doing, what it meant, what she thought about it, what was next. Instead, I ate my own hamburger. I was not entirely motivated by uneasiness, or fatigue, or even indecision. Right in there with those heavy hesitant feelings was something lighter and more expansive. Along with my knowledge of all the things that could go wrong here, there was a caroling inner voice that kept repeating, What could possibly go wrong?

I cleaned up the plates, and we went back to

bed. It was bright day when we woke up. While I was rolling over, just beginning to appreciate the sunshine, Felicity bounded out of bed, pushing her hair out of her face. She was smiling and stretching, saying, "Oh, Joey, that was nice. Thank you. I feel much better," and I was wondering in what way she had felt bad, and then she took a big deep breath, sat on the bed, kissed me in a sisterly way on the cheek, and said, "I have a million things to do before Hank gets home." I was listening for any sign in her voice of fear or regret, but there was none. She got into her clothes. She was very boyish in her way, casual but confident about putting on this and stepping into that. She had slim hips, a small potbelly, and small breasts, long arms and a long neck. Her body was sexy in the same way that the whole experience had been sexy—a fluid combination of maternal, girlish, and boyish, not like anything I'd known before.

I said, "You know, Felicity, this sounds strange, but I think you're the only mother I've ever slept with. Some of them went on to be mothers, of course."

"We'll have to talk about that sometime, Joey. That's a very bad sign with regard to your level of maturity."

"Do you think so?"

GOOD FAITH

She kissed me again. "No. Good-bye. I'm leaving." On the way out the door, she said, "By the way, Daddy seems to have solved that tax problem he's been having. Thank you thank you." She blew me a kiss and was out the door.

CHAPTER

3

ON MONDAY, Bobby presented me with an offer from Marcus Burns for Gottfried Nuelle's most expensive house. It was a full-price offer, but there was one contingency: that Gottfried would fence the road frontage with something appealing, like split rails. It was a smart contingency. The property would look better for it. If Gottfried had done it in the first place, the house might have sold more quickly and for more money. But it was a contingency that would drive Gottfried crazy, implying, in his view, that the property was less than perfect. When I went over to Maple Glen to present the offer, I was careful. I clapped him on the back. I was extremely enthusiastic. I exclaimed that it was a full-price offer with an early closing, only one small contingency.

Gottfried, who was feeding electrical wire into a hole while someone two rooms away pulled it, shouted, "Stop! Wait a minute! Now." He looked at me for the first time. "What contingency?"

"Split-rail fence along the road frontage."

He stared at me for a long moment, then shouted, "Dale! Get in here!"

Dale, the young kid who did all the moldings, entered from the kitchen. Gottfried said, "That Maple Glen Road house. Split-rail fencing along the road."

Dale shook his head.

"No," said Gottfried.

Dale went out of the room.

I said, "What do you mean, no?"

"No split-rail fencing. It's an aesthetic abomination."

"Excuse me?"

"That's a Queen Anne. Now, in this part of the country, the vogue for Queen Anne houses was in the late Victorian period, say 1890s. You didn't do split rail in those days. Split rail was more rustic, a pioneer thing."

"They aren't insistent about the split rail, they just want a fence. If there's a style that would—"

"They thought split rail; that's what they *saw* there."

"I don't know that, Gottfried. I can't remember how the idea of split rail came up, actually. What sort of fence would *you* put up there?"

"I wouldn't put a fence up there. I didn't put a fence up there, so if I didn't, I wouldn't."

"It's a full-price offer. The house has been on the market since the first of September."

"I'm going to move in there myself."

"You don't want to do that, Gottfried. That way lies bankruptcy. That's what you always tell me."

"No fence."

"How about a hedge?"

He looked at me, leading me to believe that a hedge was unspeakable. I glanced around the room. Gottfried was putting in flooring, which was wide pine boards of random lengths, nice and knotty. One of the knots caught my eye— it looked exactly like the head of a bird with a long beak and a wary eye. He said, "It pains me to say this, but have you noticed the way that slope on Maple Glen Road curves up from the road there? It's a beautiful thing. It always reminds me of a woman's ass. I laid sod there, you know that? Because I didn't want to wait to have that nice feeling that I got when I approached that house from the west. I'm a cheapskate, but I didn't want to wait for the grass to grow." Gottfried's favorite wrong idea about himself was that he was a cheapskate.

I said, "You know, I've sold seventeen houses for you over the years. Every one, I've had to pry it out of your hands even though you were bitching at me for months that the carrying costs were killing you."

"A guy who wants to put a fence around the swell of a woman's buttock doesn't deserve to live there."

"He loves the house. It's the only house he wants. He thinks it's perfect."

"Perfect for what, entertaining? Showing off? I guarantee you, this guy's an egomaniac. Mark my words."

"You haven't met the guy, Gottfried."

He turned on me suddenly and shouted, "You want to make this sale? *You* put up the fence. I don't ever want to see that house again, though. Out of your commission, a God-damned white board fence, clean and straight-forward, no split rails. I won't pay for it, and I won't build it, and I won't even look at it, but I'll sell the house at full price to this bozo be-cause the bank's got me by the balls! Do you know what my life is like? I worry every night about carrying costs, and then you take some guy out there and bingo, you got fifteen grand that comes right out of my pocket! What are you coming around to me for, asking me about this shit? Dale!"

"Then you'll take the offer?"

"You build the fence and I'll take the God-damned offer!"

I went over to the worktable and laid out the papers. They were already flagged for signatures, flagged in yellow, though they might as well have been flagged in red. I handed Gottfried a pen. He managed to sign the papers without tearing through them, but I knew he would rant around for the rest of the morning. Fortunately, Dale, the only guy working with him that day, was impervious.

When I first met him, Gottfried was a shop teacher at the middle school, building houses on the weekends. When I listed his first house, he was amazed and gratified to have made it to the selling stage; he was utterly polite with me, almost obsequious. But that vanished when he met the buyers. They did not meet his standards; no buyers ever had. But he had made a fortune, his houses were famous, magazines took pictures of them, commercials were filmed in them. I was his only listing agent. Sometimes we socialized, and once, over a beer, he had loosened up and told me that when his family was escaping the Huguenot purges in France, they had changed their name to Nuelle because Nuelle meant *nothing* or *no one.* He'd looked at me and said, "Think about that, Joe. Think about running off to North Dakota or somewhere and changing your name to 'Joe Nobody.'" For whatever reason, after he told me that, I didn't take his rants personally anymore. Nevertheless, I was more than relieved to flee with the signed purchase agreement in my hand.

I got back to the office, planning to give Bobby the papers right away before Gottfried Nuelle could find me and recant, but Bobby was nowhere to be found. I put the agreement on his desk and hand-printed a note saying, *Get this to the buyer asap, before the seller changes his mind.* When the phone rang, I was tempted not to pick it up, but I did anyway. If you are a Realtor, you have to answer the phone; that's the first rule of business. It was Gordon Baldwin, not Gottfried. That put me in a better mood right there. Gordon was my main builder over the years, and his market was much different from Gottfried Nuelle's. Gordon bought farms. He had been buying farms for twenty-five years. He had a farm-buying pickup truck, an old International Harvester with what sounded like a tractor engine under the hood. He also had farm-buying clothes, not quite

overalls and a straw hat but almost. He also had
a farm-buying lingo. One of his many connections would tell him that some farmer was getting old and didn't have any farming children,
or that some kids who lived in Portsmouth had
inherited the family farm, and he would get on
the proper costume and go talk to whoever was
in a state of landowning flux. Often enough he
would come back home with an oral agreement to buy, and then I would follow up on the
deal with the paperwork. By the late seventies,
Gordon had quite a few farms, amounting to
several hundred acres in all, some of them con-
tiguous, some of them close to town, some of
them way out in the middle of nowhere. Those
were the farms where he kept his cattle. One
piece of property, some 120 acres, was a development about ten miles from West Portsmouth
that Gordon had been building on at least since
I got into his business. It was called Glamorgan
Close. My father thought this name was ridiculous; the acreage was open, almost flat at the
front, rolling more steeply toward the back. My
father never tired of pointing out that, on the
one hand, a close was a stabling area, and, on
the other hand, there was nothing "close" about
Glamorgan Close and nothing Glamorgany, either, since there wasn't a Scot anywhere in the
vicinity.

GOOD FAITH

Glamorgan Close had had several phases. Phase One, near the highway to Portsmouth, had inexpensive three-bedroom houses with small front yards, large backyards, and three styles, the Maryland, the Virginia, and the South Carolina, which had a larger front porch, labeled in the brochure as "the veranda." These houses, which were on straight streets (Kinloch Avenue, Glengarry Avenue, Kirkpatrick Avenue), were a quarter mile from the elementary school Gordon had talked the county into and a mile from the Kroger's shopping center. Phase One was a big success. Behind Phase One was Phase Two: Stuart Way, Robertson Way, and Ivanhoe Way. Phase Two featured three-bedroom houses also, but with two and a half baths and a bonus room. Phase Two styles, the Sonoma, the Mendocino, and the Santa Rosa, had somewhat larger rooms than the Phase One styles, lots of wood and beams, decks off the back, and a little bit of a view. The ideal couple who moved with their first two toddlers into the Virginia would find themselves, ten years later, entertaining junior high schoolers in the bonus room of the Sonoma, the deck of which could easily support a hot tub. If the couple did extremely well and maintained the integrity of their assets by not divorcing, Gordon was ready for them with Phase Three, the Greenwich, the Hastings, and the Ardsley: four bedrooms, four baths, master suites with sitting rooms, screened-in verandas, center-island kitchens, and mother-in-law apartments. These properties (Blacklock Circle, Praed Circle, Tartan Circle) were larger and had better views than those in the other two phases and, in fact, looked down on the other two, but at this point the ideal couple was expected to finance the down payment of their eldest child and his or her spouse in one of the Phase One houses, which now had mature landscaping and the individuality born of age and idiosyncratic property ownership.

This was Gordon's vision of life, even if he didn't say so—you made your way and populated your vicinity with your offspring, who then dropped the grandchildren off at your house whenever they felt like it. Phase Three was essentially complete now, some twenty years after groundbreaking for Phase One. There was still some land, though not much, and Gordon was going to start Phase Four when he could get around to it. Glamorgan Close was not Gordon's only development, but it was the one that had established him in the Portsmouth area. Selling houses in Glamorgan Close was as simple as putting a notice in the paper that one was available. They were reasonably priced, well-enough built, and perfect examples of my basic belief about housing and the corollary, that what people really like is a simple canvas to fiddle around with. Gottfried Nuelle couldn't stand anyone to fiddle with his houses, but Gordon relied upon his buyers to transform the uniformity of his developments. Gordon had some ideas about Phase Four, and he wanted to talk to me about them.

Gordon's other developments were smaller and less philosophical, and he also built commercial properties. If one of his cronies wanted to open another restaurant or put in a miniature golf course with six waterfalls and a merry-go-round, Gordon would do that. He had sold one farm ten years ago, way out in the country but at the busy intersection of Highway 12 and Hardy Well Road, to Bert Milstein and then built a Colonial-style shopping village that specialized in shops that sold one thing: door handles or table linens or fudge. The security guards wore knee pants and the waitresses wore long skirts and frilly décolletage, and the center had succeeded against all odds, partly by hosting nonretail events, like chamber music groups and pig roasts, and partly by hosting craft fairs and swap meets. It had become a very successful fake village and Gordon loved it—it was not at all the sort of place he would ever shop, or even go, but exactly the sort of place where he could sell high what he had bought low. He couldn't believe how the small shops and upscale décor put people in the mood to pay through the nose, but he had a little antiques shop there, which Betty ran with a friend, and he stocked it with whatever he had found here and there. One year they made a huge amount of money on gilt-framed mirrors that he got out of a hotel in Buffalo. Another year they had fifteen golden oak washstands and a rack full of silk kimonos from prewar Japan.

At any rate, I got in the car and drove over to Gordon's in a happy mood. Phase Four would be simple and fun. Gordon would build them, and Bobby and I would sell them. One of the ways that Gordon kidded himself that he wasn't supporting Bobby was that he only discussed his projects with me, and Bobby did all his sales of Gordon's properties through me as the broker.

Of Gordon, my mother always said, "Well, I never thought he was a handsome man, though obviously some people do." Some people did; he looked like a movie star of a certain era, Tyrone Power, say, whose looks not only change but become outmoded. In his early sixties, he was florid and jowly, and his dark pomaded hair had failed, suspiciously, to thin or recede. He had big shoulders and big hands but he was actually not a large man; I was an inch or two taller and outweighed him by maybe fifteen or twenty pounds. What he had was ease of movement. When he opened the door for me, put his arm around me, propelled me across the foyer into his office (shouting the whole time for Betty to come out and say hi and bring me a beer), it was his dance. His touch and his presence felt like they were infusing grace into me. In his office, which was pure 1970—orange shag carpet, a long low window looking out on their back acreage, which featured a man-made pond with a swimming raft and a rope swing hanging from the limb of a big oak—he had the plans for townhouses spread out on his desk. At first, say just for two or three minutes, I forgot that Felicity had put us in a new and strange relationship. He was just Gordon and I was just Joe and we were about to do what we had done so many times—build and sell and drink and eat and talk and shout and curse or celebrate as the deals rolled by. Then Betty came in with the beer.

Betty was about sixty then. I suppose when I first met her she was in her mid-thirties, and of course she had changed. Sally had adored Betty. What she always said was, "My mother was a legendary beauty, you know. None of us girls will *ever* be as beautiful as my mother. Daddy says that's evidence right there that the theory of evolution is wrong." Then she would laugh, so pleased that she was lucky enough to be Betty's daughter. I liked beautiful women as much as anyone, and I had seen quite a few over the years who possessed a more perfect surface than Betty, but she had a thoughtful and yet entirely untormented quality that I had never seen in another person that made her beauty open, contented, and unsullied. Of Betty, my mother always said, "She's a very nice woman, Joey. Between you and me, he's lucky to have her." That was my mother's highest compliment.

She came right over and kissed me, put the beer in my hand, closed my fingers around it with her own fingers, and said, "Here's Joey! Aren't you looking handsome, Joey! I've been missing you," and even though Felicity did not look like Betty, in Betty's presence I felt it as a physical jolt that Betty and Gordon would not in the least appreciate the new turn my relationship with their family had taken; Gordon might understand it as a general feature of male behavior, though he wouldn't like it, but Betty, I thought, wouldn't understand it at all. Nevertheless, I returned her kiss, and maybe I did so with more enthusiasm than usual. I had always appreciated Sally; now I appreciated Felicity too.

Betty said she was going to the supermarket, so Gordon came over and danced her to the door of his office. She looked back at me over his shoulder; her smile and her wave were sophisticated but intimate, implying that while nothing much surprised her, she was happy anyway.

Then he propelled me toward the plans. "Now here it is, Joe. Good American-style townhouses, nothing fancy. Three buildings, thirty units in all, eighteen two-bedrooms, twelve three-bedrooms. Look at this elevation, now: simple pitched roof, clapboard siding, white trim, cream siding, black doors, and black shutters. They're going to go along the street like this, but a little set back. You know, when we went down to South Carolina at Christmas, I went over to this plantation they had outside of Charleston, it was called Forbes Plantation, one of those big old places, but it hadn't been burned down by Sherman, you know. Even so, one guy couldn't afford to keep it, not in this day and age, so they turned the whole thing into condos, did a nice job too, didn't change the exterior at all. I think they got eight units into the main building and then maybe four or five into the outbuildings and the slave quarters. Anyway, here was the great part." He moved his finger across the bottom of the elevation. "They made sure to keep the old gardens, front and back, and I'm telling you, these folks who live in this place, it's like living in a park. So that was what made me think it was time to get on with Phase Four up there, because just a bunch of townhouses is nothing; I wasn't interested; but now I see we can retain control of the property and have beautiful gardens all around. That piece there faces southeast, so they'd have flowering trees and roses. Don't you love it? Little playgrounds for the grandkids, and some gardening areas for the old Italian guys who want to put in a few tomatoes. I'd live there myself if Betty could stand it. But she can design the garden. Or Hank could. He does that sort of thing."

I said, "Hmm," self-consciously.

"So! Here we go! What day is today, March what? Oh, yeah, twenty-ninth. Now, see, we got all the roads and sewers and everything here, from the other three phases. They staked it out last week, so we just got to wait a couple of weeks to break ground."

I said, "What sort of price range are you thinking, Gordon?"

"Something nice, you know, something friendly. Forty-nine-nine for the two bedrooms, seventy-nine-nine for the threes. But they've got an association fee, of course. Fee simple once you're inside the house, but got to pay an association fee as soon as you step down off your bottom step onto the walkway. And see, back here, a little parklike area—that's the latest thing, common areas. Pool, maybe, or, better, an indoor lap pool that you can swim in all year round for the exercise. We'll see. Milstein, he built himself one of those, and now he comes to every game with his hair wet. And he drinks water all the time. Jack, you want a beer; Nathan, you want a beer; Gordon, how about a beer; and then, Bert, you want a glass of water? I swear. But I see it coming, Joe."

The plans were simple: slab foundations, parking spaces instead of garages, but rather large rooms. If there was one thing Gordon knew about real estate, it was that you could trim a little off the necessities and add a little to the space, and make the place look open and desirable. I said, "How about vinyl siding? That would save you money all around, and they can't paint it. You don't want these places all looking different ten years down the road."

He said, "You know Frank Lloyd Wright, Joe?"

"Not personally."

"Well, he was a big deal—still is, for that matter—but when I was just getting into this business I used to read about him whenever I could, and he did a thing I always thought was funny. He designed the chairs for his houses, but he made sure they were uncomfortable, because he didn't like people sitting down, so he'd put in this furniture that looked nice and fit right in, but you couldn't stand to sit in it for more than ten minutes, so you'd get up and walk around, which he wanted you to do so you would admire the place, I guess. Anyway, that's a perfect Frank Lloyd Wright idea: sell 'em the house, but give 'em siding they can't paint! Ha!"

"Vinyl-clad windows, too, and you ought to put in crank-out casements rather than double-hungs. For some reason, all my buyers lately want them. And they're cheaper to install." I was getting excited. Thirty units was a good number. I could think of three possible buyers already. "May I take the plans to show around? You know the Rebarcaks on Robertson Way? They were asking me to find them something smaller."

"Presolds! That's what I need. You know, if the foundations of the first building are in by June, you can do a muddy-shoe walk-through of the samples in mid-July. I got my best crew free; they can get these places up in no time.

GOOD FAITH

You know Larry, who runs that crew, Larry Svendsen? Back in the sixties, when he was just married, he made a bet with that old guy, Lombardo, that he could build a whole house in a month, from staking out to turning the key. He did it, too, twenty-nine days and five hours. Three bedrooms, two baths, split-level. The electricians would be right behind the framers and the sheetrockers right behind them. One guy was putting up the moldings, and the painter was painting them right next to him. He finally had to yell at the guy to back off long enough to let him nail them down. Lombardo walked through and paid Larry a grand right on the spot. And Milstein made book. I bet five grand changed hands when the buyers moved in."

"I think it looks great, Gordon. You lay out the gardens and put in annuals and turf, and that's not much money out of pocket, but it makes the place look great; then over the fall and winter you put in the trees and perennials, and by this time next year it looks like people have been living there for years."

Gordon grabbed me by the shoulders and planted a big kiss on my cheek. He said, "You know, Joe, how old I am?"

"You're sixty-three, Gordon."

"Here's the deal. A lot is the world's most

boring thing. I love to look at farms and buy farms and all that, but when I've got one, and it's been surveyed into lots, my heart kind of sinks. But then we get to this point, where we got the plans and we know how fast the buildings are going to go up and the people are going to get in there, and I feel great! I feel sixty-two!"

We laughed. I finished my beer. Gordon turned and looked out the window, then turned back to me. I had a feeling he wanted to say something unaccustomed, but to be frank, given the sudden appearance of Felicity in my life, I didn't want to hear anything unaccustomed, and so when he turned back and offered me another beer, I shook my head. I bent down over the desk and began to roll up the plans. "Are these the ones I can take? I'll show them to Bobby if you want."

"Nah. He and Fernie are coming over tonight, Betty says. I'll show him. But wait a minute, Joe. I got this other deal too. That's what I really wanted to talk to you about."

Deal was a safe word. I said, "What's that?"

"You know the Thorpe property?"

"Salt Key Farm?"

"That's the one." Gordon raised his eyebrows. "I got it."

I whistled. Salt Key Farm was hardly a farm.

GOOD FAITH

It was a five-hundred-and-eighty-acre estate, owned by the wealthiest family in the eastern half of the state. They had properties all over, but Salt Key Farm was something of a jewel. The Thorpes were railroad money; train-coach makers and engine builders. But the decline of railroads had meant nothing to the Thorpe fortune; over the years, the money had become self-generating. At any rate, Jacob the Fourth and Dolores Thorpe, who were probably in their eighties, lived much of the year at Salt Key Farm, with servants and horses. The houses, a main house and two other houses, and the barns, for mares, stallions, weanlings, hay, and so on, and the fencing were all simple and elegant, built on a grand scale. I said, "Did you see inside the house, Gordon?"

"Sat right in the paneled study. You haven't ever seen anything like this paneling, Joe. Split maple, book-matched, the edges just melted together, no moldings to hide any flaws. Pegged floors. You know how, before the French Revolution, the Queen of France had a little toy farm that was a sort of rich people's version of life in the country? Well, this study was a rich people's version of simplicity. He showed me the barns. All the horses' stalls were tongue-in-groove golden oak, chevron style."

"Why in the world would they sell, Gordon? They can't need the money."

"I don't think they need the money. My guess is, they had some big argument with the kids. Those Thorpes are like that. Always a big argument. John Thorpe, I guess he was Jacob's uncle, he made a will in 1910 that put all his money in trust for generations yet unborn. Everyone then alive, even the babies, had to be dead before they could distribute the money. There was a piece in the paper about it when the last one died a year or so ago. Anyway, the old man called me up the other day and asked me to come over. He said he wanted to sell me Salt Key Farm, and what I did with it was up to me, except he wanted it advertised and put on the market for six months, so the relatives could see it. If any of them want to buy it, I'm supposed to put some sort of deal-breaking contingency on it. But I guess that's your department."

"Did you talk about developing it?" I said.

"Well, he must know I'm a developer. But let's pretend I don't know what I might do with it. It's not like anything else. He said he'd looked around and decided I was the only guy who could afford to buy it. I said, 'Well, appearances are deceiving, but it is quite an opportunity.'"

GOOD FAITH

"I can't believe they want it developed."

"Well, let's put it this way: He offered to sell me the property. I didn't say, 'Mr. Thorpe, I'm going to put thirty houses on this farm,' and I don't know that I am. I could live there with all my kids and their families, and we'd never see one another if we didn't want to."

There was a time before my divorce when I used to drive around and fantasize about owning this property or that one, living with this view or owning a particular house. I was pretty rich, and I thought I was going to be richer, and the county was my own buffet. Wheeling and dealing would, I thought, get me any dish on the table, if I wanted it enough. Any dish on the table but Salt Key Farm.

Gordon went on. "What he said to me was, he wanted to list it for five million and then after the relatives had seen it and maybe tried to buy it, he would sell it to me for our agreed-upon price, which is high enough as it is. They want to move to Florida. I'm telling you, Jake Thorpe didn't look good and Dolores Thorpe looked worse. She came to size me up too, in that toney polite way that covers everything up."

"How much?"

"Two and a half million."

Back in '82, nobody I knew, including

Gordon, had ever even heard of pricing a house at two and a half million. Now it was my turn to raise my eyebrows. This did not seem like Gordon's sort of money.

"So," he continued, "I guess you're the listing agent. You go out there and do the paperwork for the sale and put together the pictures, and we'll put in on the market like the guy said and see what happens."

"I feel like I'm a little out of my depth, Gordon."

"Well, son, that means it's time to swim!" He laughed, but I could see he was a little intimidated too, probably by the seller's idiosyncratic motives as much as by the size of the deal. Phase Four of Glamorgan Close had a better feel to it—simple, straightforward housing for local citizens so that they could enjoy, or at least get on with, their lives. Nothing eccentric that could somehow backfire. Gordon put his hands in his pants pockets and cocked his head. "Here's the question I ask myself. Why did he really call me? Why would he think I'm the only guy around who can afford it? My specialty is buy it cheap. I've never spent any time with the guy. Our social circles not only don't intersect, they don't even recognize each other." He shook his head. "Now, there's two sayings. Both of them are true. One is, 'Don't look a gift horse in the mouth.' That's what Betty says. The other is, 'If it seems too good to be true, then it is.' That's what Felicity says. I mean, you can tell this shook me up a little, because I never ask their advice, do I? So, what the hell. He's an old man and maybe he's a little addled."

He handed me Jacob Thorpe's card. I looked at it and put it in my pocket. Why not? I thought. I said, "When do they want to relinquish possession?"

"October first."

"Six months?"

"Well, they got a lot of stuff to move out of there." He looked at me and grinned. "And he wants to be around for the scandal with the relatives."

"What if some unrelated buyer shows up and actually wants to pay five million for it?"

"I looked up the tax assessment. It was assessed in 'sixty-five at seven hundred and fifteen thousand. It's never been on the market. The market is going up now that interest rates are down a little. You put together a purchase agreement that's good for six months. If anyone shows an interest, we'll put up the money and close the deal. Here's my opinion. The value of

the place is completely in the eyes of the be-
holder. If some guy beholds it and wants to pay
me five million dollars for a property that I can
get for two and a half, I say take it!" He threw
back his head and laughed at the absurdity of
the idea.

I said, "People sell property for all kinds of
reasons. But what if you have to come up with
the money? Have you talked to Bart?" Bart was
a vice president at Portsmouth Savings and
Loan, the biggest and best-financed S and L in
our neighborhood. I'd had good luck with him
over the years; I liked him and he liked me. If I
had well-qualified buyers, I sent them to him,
but he and Gordon, though they had a good
business relationship, didn't mix very well.
Gordon thought Bart was too short and Bart
thought Gordon was too "New York."

"Not yet. I thought you could do that, just a
preliminary chat. I mean, he knows us. But
twenty percent down is half a million. That
could be something that takes a little discussion. He trusts you. And we've got six months."

I nodded.

"So, you want to stay? I guess we'll go to
Minelli's for some spaghetti. Felicity and Hank
are bringing the boys over."

I shook my head.

GOOD FAITH

Now Gordon came right up to me. "You keep Bobby out of Salt Key Farm for now. He's bound to do something to screw it up, even if it's just running his car over the outside lighting or falling down the steps. I want this deal to go smooth as possible. You do the paperwork and I'll give you your three percent, but that means you keep Bobby busy on something else."

I nodded. Three percent of $2.5 million was seventy-five grand. If by some piece of luck we ended up selling the place for $5 million, of course, 6 percent of $5 million was $300,000. That you could make that kind of money brokering real estate seemed so amazing I didn't know what to think about it.

On the way back to the office, I detoured past Salt Key Farm. The longest side of the property ran along American Legion Road. White board fencing in double rows traced the contours of the pastures, which were a thick mature green. Fruit trees had been planted in the aisles between the fences and, carefully pruned, looked oddly Japanese, the way the dark trunks twisted within the clouds of blossom. It was late afternoon, and grooms were leading some of the horses to the barns. I didn't know too much about their horses, but some went to the racetrack, I thought. One dark figure was fixing a line of fence, hammering a board to a post, and the horses nearby were standing at attention, shining in the sunlight, their ears pricked, watching him. There was a pasture for mares and foals not far from the road, and some sort of feed had been thrown into their trough. They were lined up with their tails to the road, their heads down. For a family estate, Salt Key Farm was unusually visible from the road, but then, when the place was built, American Legion Road had been a dirt track. Where the residences had once been visible, the Thorpes had put up a high stone wall, which I soon passed but looked at with renewed interest. It must have been ten feet tall, faced with beautiful local sandstone the color of peaches. Against the green of the pastures, it glowed like an early sunset. Instead of continuing down American Legion Road to County 169, I turned at the farm gate onto Dixon Road and continued past the sandstone wall, which ran for maybe two hundred yards, also planted with flowering trees—dogwood and redbud, which would soon be in bloom. Underneath these, a meandering track of daffodils, tulips just beginning, and iris still dormant. Outside the wall along this little-used country road but clearly maintained by the Thorpes, this border amounted to a private garden, dedicated to the enjoyment of very few—not really even the Thorpes themselves but just those who happened to make this turn, neighbors and passersby. I had never seen it before. It was daunting to think of this property coming into Gordon's hands, our hands.

It's funny what happens. One time Sherry and I had some friends who spent two years remodeling and decorating their house, which was a small brick three-bedroom in Callaway Village. Good schools, nice neighborhood: a real jewel box. When the husband was transferred to Texas suddenly, I put it on the market. Every room was just so—wallpaper, carpets, curtains—including the basement bathroom, which was done entirely with a Nittany Lions theme. I showed that house a hundred times; everyone said it was so cute. I got one single offer, from a childless couple. The wife was blind. So much for redecorating. Very few buyers want something that is incredibly beautiful or well-done. They seem to feel they are just not up to it, somehow.

Nevertheless, the privilege of becoming familiar with Salt Key Farm was a privilege I was glad to have, especially since I didn't have to pay for it. I couldn't imagine what Gordon would do with the place, but it was just the sort

of gamble he liked. Of course, he liked every
sort of gamble.

Back at the office, I saw that Bobby had picked
up my note and the papers. His desk was clear
except for a manila file folder labeled BURNS,
M. On my desk was a note from him: *Call
Sloans, 856-3245, 2 P.M.* It was after five now. I
picked up the phone but then, instead of calling, I put it back on the hook and went over to
Bobby's desk and opened the cover of the
Marcus Burns file. Right on top were his tax
returns from '79 and '80. I picked them up and
looked at them. Name, Marcus Burns; spouse's
name, Linda Burns; gross taxable income,
$125,678 and $102,345, about $30,000 each
year from her. She was a teacher. They had
lived in Hempstead, on Long Island. He had
been, as he said, employed by the IRS. He also
had investment income, capital gains, and interest income. He owned his own house and
deducted $10,000 mortgage interest. He used
both his cars for work, depreciated them, and
deducted mileage. He took a large sales tax deduction, because he lived in New York, and
claimed seven dependents, including himself
and his wife. At the back there was an oil de-

pletion allowance deduction. The forms ran many pages. In '79 he had paid $15,935 in taxes, and in '80, $13,986. I picked up the mortgage application just beneath the tax forms. He was now employed as a financial advisor and investment consultant, with some work as a free-lance tax specialist on the side. His estimated income for 1981 was $135,000. He was applying for a 90 percent loan, $25,000 down to be realized from the sale of his previous home. His payment, at 12 percent interest, would be about $2,000 per month. He was prequalified. The expected closing date was June 1. I stacked the tax forms and the mortgage application together and replaced them inside the folder. He was, to all appearances, fully capable of buying Gottfried Nuelle's pride and joy and raining income upon this office. In addition, I didn't think he needed my help (my taxable income for 1979 was more like $72,000) to pay for his fence. I went to my typewriter and tapped out another note:

> Tell buyer if he doesn't buy Gottfried intends to put the house back on the market for ten thousand more, since present price doesn't cover his costs to date. Quibbling about the fence probably will kill the deal.

This was actually a good idea, and if Gottfried hadn't thought of it, I would certainly suggest it if Marcus Burns made a fuss. Ah, I was in a wonderful mood. I decided to call the Sloans in the morning.

CHAPTER 4

BY EARLY MAY, I had Salt Key Farm
advertised everywhere—*Town and Country, The New York Times Magazine,* even
The Blood-Horse and *The Chronicle of the Horse,* as
a working horse-breeding establishment. Jacob
Thorpe, or rather his assistant and his housekeeper
and his stable manager, were friendly and cooperative about photographs, and I had a six-page foldout brochure printed up with something like
twelve or fifteen views of various aspects of the
property, including the paneling in the library,
which was, as Gordon had said, a work of art or, as
I said, "the work of master craftsmen, whose skills
have long since vanished." I saw Jacob Thorpe
once, and he was friendly and apparently sane;
he had sparkly blue eyes, a rather abstracted de-

meanor, and feathery white hair that stood up around his head. He sat down with me at a dining room table that had the depth and shine of honey and signed the purchase agreement, which gave Gordon four months—until the end of August—to come up with $250,000 and gave the Thorpes until October 1 to vacate. It was all very friendly. When I told him I was taking photos for Gordon's sales brochure, he beamed with apparently sincere benevolence, and said, "Well, you just go about your business, and we'll help you in every way possible." He patted me kindly on the shoulder. If Gordon hadn't told me his aim was to goad and provoke his relatives, I would never have suspected such a thing. At one point, while I was photographing the kitchen, he stood behind me for a while before he said, "Frankly, son, I thought things were going to turn out differently for me, but they didn't." And then he sighed and left the room.

I listed the property at five million. The calls were few but themselves priceless: Did it have a bomb shelter? Did it come furnished? Were the horses included? I got a call from a resort hotel conglomerate looking to construct a luxury spa. I got a call from a European businessman looking for a place to put his mistress—she was an English horsewoman; was there a flat spot on the property for a helipad? I got a call from a woman asking me brusquely who had authorized the listing (this must have been a relative; she didn't give her name). I got a call from the state, asking if Mr. Thorpe would consider donating the property for a historical museum with a farm theme—typical farmhouses and outbuildings from all eras would be brought from around the state and reconstructed on the property, and people would be hired to impersonate figures from the past for tourists and school groups. I got several calls from California. All those callers seemed to think the 580 acres was cheap at five million and would ask me repeatedly about whether the place had any water. I sent out about a hundred brochures. The activity never got past fielding phone calls.

As soon as I put the first ads in, I went over to Portsmouth Savings and sat down with Bart MacDonald. Bart was a tiny guy, not more than five foot three or so, and slender, but he had the casual manner of a much taller man, which no doubt resulted from his years as a boxer at South Portsmouth High and Portsmouth State College, where he was undefeated in his division and something of a legend. He still went to the boxing gym in Portsmouth four times a week, he had told me, and lifted weights in his basement the other three days. He could bench-press 210 pounds. He was affable and easygoing with clients, especially first-time clients; he had a wife who was six inches taller than he was, and four big kids. All in all, I considered him one of the most successful men I knew.

Portsmouth Savings had four branches that all looked alike, classic Colonial: red brick, white trim, columns, elegant draperies. Everyone I knew had had an account at Portsmouth Savings for years. I had one myself, a passbook account with five or six thousand dollars in it that I added to whenever I had an extra small commission. I always thought I would use it for a house at the shore someday or an emergency with my parents.

Bart didn't seem ebullient, but he was friendly. He had run a marathon and come in in the top twenty-five. Business was good in spite of the economy. There was a moment of silence, and then I couldn't help grinning. I said, "I've got these ads coming out. I wanted to get to you before you see them. Thorpe is selling Salt Key Farm to Gordon Baldwin."

Bart frowned at once.

I said, "It's a beautiful piece of property."

"No one's going to want to see that developed, Joe."

GOOD FAITH

"I might just turn it right around. I wanted to tell you, though, before you had a heart attack at the price." I told him Thorpe's scheme. He shook his head skeptically. I continued. "Well, we can go elsewhere for the financing, but I wanted you to be the first to know."

"How soon do you need the money?"

"Six months."

He got up and closed the door to his office, then came back and perched gravely on the edge of his desk chair. He said, "I got word this morning that there's about to be some changes around here."

"Management?"

He nodded toward the next office, which I knew to be the office of Frank Perkins, the president of the thrift, and mouthed the word *out*.

I said, "Doesn't he know?"

"He knows, I know. Nobody else. The board gave him two weeks this morning. I don't know anything about the new guy, but he's got something of a reputation as a shark. Thirty-seven." Bart was in his fifties. I drew my chair toward him and leaned in. I thought we were good enough friends for me to say, "What about you? Did they—uh, pass over you?"

He leaned even closer to me. He said,

"Thank God they did." He shook his head and put his finger to his lips. I sat back. I have to say I was surprised, because we never heard a single rumor about Portsmouth Savings. He said, "Anyway, bring me the papers before you go anywhere else. I'd like to see them, and there's a long lead time."

"And we could sell it to someone from California and get rich."

"I'd like to be in on that too," said Bart.

I decided afterward that his gloom had nothing to do with me or the farm. He had worked with Frank Perkins for seventeen years, a nice man who was on every charitable board in the county. Frank had brought Portsmouth Savings through the Carter years intact. It was just another example of how you never knew.

In the meantime, I had three units of Glamorgan Close, Phase Four, presold, one two-bedroom on Mary Crescent, a three-bedroom on Elizabeth Court, and another three-bedroom on Anne Court. The buyers had seen the plans, walked around the property, and put a little money down. I had promised that they would be walking through the models by the first of July and picking carpet colors and paint shortly thereafter. I advertised Phase Four in the

GOOD FAITH

Marlboro County Shopper and the *Portsmouth Herald*.

Felicity had called me at the office several days after our first encounter, asked how I was feeling, apologized for perhaps taking advantage of my good nature, and said she found the idea of a closer friendship with me very appealing. She was utterly matter-of-fact. She said, "You know, I do what I want most of the time, and I don't investigate my own motives very well, but I do recognize that the world we live in requires me to cover my tracks as the price of freedom. I'm willing to do that. Hank says I am a building block of nature: can't be controlled, can't be divided, can't be understood, can only be observed." Right then, standing in my office, listening to her voice and gazing out the window at my picket fence and the traffic passing on the other side of it, I had a true experience of freedom, which I can only describe as a physical sensation of release without any previous sensation of tightness. I felt myself breathe and smile without knowing I had not been breathing or smiling. There was nothing I was obliged to do about Felicity.

I said, "I would like to observe you more closely myself, Felicity."

"There we go. Agreed. Days and times random, possibly infrequent, though."

"That's fine." And it was. That was our contract. Sometimes lunch, sometimes a chat on the phone, sometimes a visit in the office when Bobby wasn't around. Once she came along when I went out to look at some houses, and that was the best time, driving around the countryside in perfect weather for four or five hours. We didn't stop or visit any beauty spots or do anything romantic. We lunched on sandwiches and Cokes that I bought at a country deli, and we conversed: Sherry, Bobby, her sons, Sally, Gordon, Betty, the job she had had until the place (a framing gallery) had closed and she hadn't bothered to find another one. She had a knack for telling funny stories on herself—how she bought a bikini without trying it on, and when she went to wear it she put one leg through the waist and another through a leg hole, and then when she pulled it up, she couldn't figure out why it was so tight and lopsided until she came out of the locker room and one of her sons told her she had it on sideways. How when she and Hank had been dating for over a year, he shaved his beard, and his chin had such a dimple in it that she screamed before she could stop herself. And she knew this other guy who had broken his jaw in a motorcycle accident and then grown a beard while it was healing, and five years later when he shaved it, he didn't recognize himself in the mirror, but he had to grow his beard back anyway because the doctors had rerouted his facial nerves and he couldn't tell by feel or by looking in the mirror what part of his face he was shaving. "Things are so funny," she said. I thought how like Betty she was, knowing and yet good-natured. And so it went as we drove from property to property, an idle conversation of such richness and pleasure that I felt happy about it for four days afterward. And from time to time she said, "Oh, Joey, how is it that you are so irresistible?"

After that I had occasion to drive past her house twice. I knew the place, had passed it from time to time over the years without realizing that Felicity and Hank lived there. It was a rambling frame house, white siding, black shutters and trim, screened-in porch with chairs visible through the screening, a low table with a flowering plant on it visible too. Turfy yard; the garage was the old barn. It looked like the fields formerly belonging to the house had been annexed by the neighbor, who had them planted in something that was just coming up. Sherry and I would have considered that it looked a little run-down and needed work, but as a setting for Felicity, it partook of some of her charm. It made me think there was something to be said for not painting the living room over and over, for letting a few things accumulate. The life Felicity and Hank and Clark and Jason lived on Nut Hollow Road involved sports equipment lying in the yard, a light on in an upstairs window when all the cars were gone, a half-full wheelbarrow next to a flower bed, a sweater draped over the porch railing—many things going on, some of them not finished, tasks put off in favor, I am sure, of something more interesting. What would have seemed careless to me a year ago now seemed simply evidence of movement. How much of my life had I spent in erasing all trace of activity, all trace of my own presence? Was that what I wanted to do always? Suddenly my condo seemed odd to me. I could live in it my whole life, and my existence there would not register.

On Mother's Day, Bobby fell down the church steps and sprained his ankle. I knew because he called me to ask me to hold open the house he had advertised for that afternoon. It was a ranch style in Farmington, so I drove past my parents' house, the same brick house I had grown up in. Three bedrooms and one bath upstairs, with a sleeping porch off the back, living room, dining room, kitchen, and entry hall downstairs, a modest house whose only claim to distinction was the arch over the front door and the two windows facing the street. There was a honeysuckle arbor in the side yard where my father liked to sit in summer and a swing set in the backyard that I had played on as a child. It was two blocks from the elementary school and a block and a half from our church. It had a one-car garage, and all we ever had until I bought my first car in high school was one car, a Buick. I went to school in the winter and church camp in the summer and my parents lived entirely within the circle of the church, where my mother volunteered and cleaned and my father passed the collection plate, always putting his own tithe in first. The minister came to dinner regularly, as did missionaries home from missions abroad and relatives on both sides, but all my cousins were much older than I was. My parents never raised their voices, never disagreed, read aloud to each other from the Bible, and discussed salvation every day along with the price of tomatoes and chicken or the problems of the neighbors or what had to be done to keep up the brick house and the small yard. They never spoke of buying things or needing money. They prayed aloud many times every day, not only at meals. They were strict but they were not gloomy—my father had a wealth of stories that my mother enjoyed hearing, and he also sang funny songs in a mellow baritone while my mother played the piano for him. When people came to the house who were gloomy or dour, my parents would disapprove afterward; they couldn't understand anyone who considered God or salvation in the least frightening. Now sin, that was fearful, but to be fully committed to the Lord's path, that was a source of perennial joy, which one was obliged to display as an example of glad service to the Lord and the sure expectation of everlasting glory. After I left home, I never knew anyone who had fewer ups and downs than my parents. They were very neat, like me, and it could be said that after forty-five or fifty years they too might leave no trace of themselves in the house they had lived in, but that was good—the best possible evidence that they were not of this world to begin with.

I was in the office the next day when Felicity showed up with a bag of hamburgers and fries. It was the first really hot day of the year, and she was wearing linen shorts and espadrilles. Her hair was pinned up casually and fell in sweaty tendrils over her collar. It was almost too hot to eat, but the hamburgers smelled good. She set them out on paper towels on Bobby's desk. She lifted the top of the bun off mine and showed me the underside. She said, "Look at that. See that crispy rim there? This is a great bun. Aren't you hungry? I almost got another one to eat in the car on the way over. And these seasoned fries. I told the waitress to be sure they came out of the fryer and into the bag so they would be perfect by the time I got here. Oh, God!" She put two fries into her mouth.

"How's Bobby?"

"Safely ensconced on his sofa with a cooler of Cokes next to his right hand and the TV remote in his left. My father brought him some take-out veal piccata for dinner last night and some take-out bacon and eggs for breakfast this morning. God forbid he should miss a meal."

"Is he on crutches?"

"He would be, but the last time he was on crutches—remember? when he fractured his heel going down into the basement to turn out the light—anyway, that time he went to the movies at the Odeon Plaza in Portsmouth with Fernie, and when they came out the whole floor of the lobby had just been mopped, and the crutches went right out from under him and he hit his head against the refreshment stand and Fernie had to call an ambulance so they could monitor him at the hospital all night. Remember that?" She took a bite of her burger. "Crutches are just too dangerous for him. We're catering to his every need on a round-robin basis, all except for Fernie, because my mother thinks—"

"Your mother is afraid that if Fern really comes to understand what married life is going to be like—"

"She wouldn't marry him in a million years! Exactly. Eat! Eat! I brought you iced tea with mint and lemon to cool you off."

We ate. As always, a meal with Felicity was savory, delicious, and almost silent. I noticed the crunchy onion and smooth tomato and juicy meat, as well as the crisp edge of the bun and the lightness of the fries. If I'd been alone, I would have eaten and been satisfied—I was a hungry sort of guy from a family of big eaters—but I would have been reading something, or talking on the phone, or getting ready to go out. Felicity did only one thing at a time.

While she was balling up the papers and stuffing them into the bag, I put my arm around her waist. She put her hands on my shoulders and smiled and said, "Do you have appointments this afternoon, then?"

"There's a house the Sloans want to see. I'm going to meet them in Nut Valley."

"What time?"

"Not till three."

She threw the remains of the meal into the wastebasket and then let down the blinds and closed them. The room had seven more windows and a door, and she went around to each one and did the same, until we were in semi-darkness. She locked the door and turned the OPEN sign to CLOSED. Then she went into the back closet and rummaged around. She came out with a parka, two raincoats, and an exercise mat, and laid them out in the middle of the floor, between Bobby's desk and mine. Then she sat down on the arrangement she made and began to untie the ribbons of her espadrilles. This took maybe two or three minutes, but I watched it like a kind of performance: her pale shirt and shorts and long legs, made longer by the wedge sole of the espadrilles. She had Gordon's grace of movement, long arms, long fingers, such dramatic hair. I pushed back my desk chair and went over to her.

She looked up at me, smiling. She said, "I was going to go have my hair cut, you know—my hairdresser is right in this mall—but then I got into your aura or something; maybe it's your bodily fragrance, but it has this effect on me. I start looking at your face, and the way your eyes are so bright and your eyelids are kind of droopy, and then your eyebrows have this wing sort of shape, and then I start looking at your nose, which is very smoothly big and beaky, and pretty soon your hand is there too, and I love your hands, you have these long knuckly fingers."

By now she had pulled me down onto the clothes and was stroking my face with her own two hands, touching each feature as she named it. She lowered her voice, not so that others wouldn't hear, but so that I would hear more clearly, and went on.

"And then there's the bonus of your personal apparatus. Well. I can't say I knew what I would find there, but I am very appreciative of—what shall I call it?—its objective aesthetic charms: you know, size and shape and texture." She inhaled slowly. "There. Now feel that." I did. She was running her thumb and forefinger very lightly up either side of the shaft of my cock. "That is just not like anything else on earth, so silky and delicate." She licked her lips. "Mmm. Just so nice."

I put my hand in her hair and began kissing

her while she arranged herself, pressing her stomach against me, then unbuttoning my shirt and hers, pressing her breasts against my chest. Soon enough we were naked; the room was cool from the air-conditioning, but Felicity was warm. When she kissed me, when she put her arms around my shoulders and her legs around my hips, I was contained in a delicious embracing glow. I went deep inside her and she squeezed me, decidedly and rhythmically, all up and down the shaft. Then she angled her hips slightly to the left, then to the right, all the time murmuring, "Ahhh, ahhh." I opened my eyes. The room was brighter. Her eyes were closed. She spread her hands over the cheeks of my ass and pressed. I closed my eyes. We kissed and made love in this way for a long time, but the only way that I knew time was passing was that I began to feel my heart pumping faster. Her fingers slipped up and down my back, to either side of my spine. Suddenly she started trembling violently, gripping me hard into her and pressing her mouth into mine. When her trembling stopped, I felt myself swept into coming not a buildup like I was accustomed to, something aimed for and cultivated, but a much more sudden and overwhelming sensation that seemed to empty me out. She pressed her head against mine.

A moment later, she said, "Oh, honey, you were screaming."

"I was?"

"What will they say next door?"

"I don't know. Were *you* screaming?"

"I was calling you God."

"I suppose they'll say Joe's been saved at last, then."

We caught our breath. I handed her my shirt to wipe off the sweat we had made. I laughed again when she sat up and started with her toes. Everything about her delighted me.

After a moment, we lay back on the clothes. She rolled into the crook of my arm and I pushed her hair out of her face. I yawned, but I wasn't tired, only relaxed. She said, "I'm going to meet that woman for a drink today."

"What woman?"

"Linda Burns."

"Who's that?" It had been several weeks by that time since I had looked over Marcus Burns's tax returns.

"The wife of Bobby's friend Marcus. They went out with us—Thursday night, I guess it was. We went to Mercados."

Mercados was one of Gordon's favorite restaurants, truly out of another era. They served large plates of pretty good old-fashioned Sicilian food, but the menus had no prices. If they knew you, they gave you one price; if they didn't, they gave you another price, much higher. Strangers were not encouraged to return, but friends ate practically for free. I yawned again. I was still a little disoriented from the direction my afternoon's activities had taken. The Sloans and the ranch-style three-bedroom with three-car garage on a corner lot that we were seeing seemed very very far away. I realized Felicity was still talking about the Burns woman. I said, "Do you have your own friends, Felicity?"

"Of course I do. I have lots of girlfriends."

"What do you do together? I mean, Sherry didn't have many girlfriends. She thought women were irritating."

"She thought everyone was irritating, honey. She was so jealous, I didn't know how you could stand it. She was always herding you and guarding you and telling you what to do."

"Maybe she was."

"Daddy always used to say after you left, 'Isn't that one a full agenda?' and Betty would say, 'He would have been perfect for Sally.' And then everyone would sigh." She looked at me mischievously. "I would say to myself, 'More perfect for me.' Wasn't that utterly wicked?"

"Have you been planning this for a long time, Felicity?"

"Well, not planning. Just being open to opportunity."

I gazed at her. She looked friendly and receptive.

She went on. "You know, a couple of years ago, I was going in the door of my house with a bag of groceries, and I just happened to look down at the basket we keep by the door for shoes and sneakers. We started doing that when the boys were little, so I wouldn't have to be looking for their shoes all over the house whenever we had to go somewhere. Anyway, this time I looked down, and all their shoes were so big! Then, a couple of days later, I had this vase Mom gave me, and I'd put some star lilies in it that I had bought. So I set it on the mantel and stepped back, and I was looking at it, thinking how pretty it was, and a football came over my shoulder and smashed right into it and all the pieces and the flowers fell to the floor."

I said, "Oh, Felicity!"

She said, "Oh, it wasn't a tragedy or anything. I was shocked in that moment, but then it was a revelation! I thought, *I live in a frat house and it's okay with me.* My boys are very independent, and so is Hank, and I thought, *What am I doing, holding some kind of candle up here for traditional family life when my family doesn't even see it?* So I started living like they do—getting up every morning and saying to myself, What would be fun today? and then going out and doing it. I'm telling you, the house doesn't look great, but everyone is a lot happier. I don't think any of them even realized the degree to which I was nudging them to conform to an ideal I didn't even know I had. So that's what I mean by being open to opportunity. Many desires have gone through my mind over the years about lots of things. I'm almost thirty-nine. And while I haven't *planned* to pursue any of those desires, I remember them perfectly well when the opportunity presents itself." She looked at me for a moment. "So there you are."

"And here you are."

"Not for long, I suppose, if you have to go show a house. Linda Burns loves that place. When are they moving in?"

"Closing is in a couple of weeks, I think. I'm hoping Bobby is up and about by that time."

"Oh, who cares! He's safer in his house."

In spite of the darkness and the CLOSED sign, I heard a knock on the door, then another sharper knock. I looked at my watch. It was not beyond the Sloans to come and find me if I was late, but I wasn't late; I still had over an hour before I had to meet them. Felicity and I looked at each other and hunkered down, but there was still another knock, this one very insistent. I pulled on my jeans and shirt and went to the door. Through the blinds I could see two men standing on the porch. They looked like brothers, one slightly taller and heavier than the other. The shorter one was bending down and peering at one of the for-sale photos I had in the window, and the other, I saw, was looking at me.

I opened the door and said, "Yes?"

"Oh, I knew you were in there."

The other one stood up. He said, "We're going to buy this house." He put his finger on the window glass over the photo. I went out on the porch and looked. The house in question was a beat-up Colonial on Main Street in Deacon. It was big, but two hundred years of remodeling had not done it any favors. About ten years before, for example, the current owners had covered the old clapboards with aluminum siding and boxed in the decorated soffits. "A lot of work" didn't begin to cover what it would take to get that place together. And the price was high.

The taller one said, "We've already been over there and looked in the windows. I mean, the ones we could get to. The shrubs were monstrous. It was right out of the Addams family over there."

I said, "Central location."

"May we come in? It doesn't matter what

you were doing in there. Believe me, we've seen it all."

I looked in the door. Felicity was dressed and sitting at Bobby's desk. She had kicked the clothes we'd been lying on back into a corner and turned on a light. When the two men followed me in, the shorter one said, "Oh, hi! What a surprise! I'm David and this is David. You must be Joe's wife, right? Nice to meet you." But it seemed by our glances and our smiles that we all knew Felicity was not my wife.

I cleared my throat and attempted to become more businesslike. The shorter man said, "Your belt is unbuckled."

I buckled it.

"All better now," said the taller man.

They were David John and David Pollock. Felicity introduced herself, and they drew up chairs near hers. David Pollock was the taller one. He said, "Well, Felicity, have you seen this house in Deacon?"

"Not really. I can't remember it."

"Want to go over there? I'm sure Joe would be happy to show it to the three of us, especially since we've practically bought it already."

I recollected that I was legally the seller's agent and said nothing. David John looked at me. "I'm sure the place is sordidly run-down."

The other David: "Abominations to be uncovered on every floor. That's why Joe is keeping mum, right, Joe?"

"I can show you several promising properties."

"Joe, we always buy on impulse. We drive down a road or a street and we say, 'Time to buy and that's the one.' Then we snoop around; then we call the Realtor. Five years ago, we bought a house in a town we had never been to before and moved there three weeks later, all the dogs, all the objets d'art, all the canned tomatoes and pickled peaches."

"We made forty percent in sixteen months on that one. Of course, that was California, but still."

"Our instincts are famous," said David Pollock.

I reached into a drawer and pulled out purchase offer forms.

"But let's say we see it anyway," said David John.

"Felicity," said David Pollock, "you have great hair. Let's go in our car."

The two men drove an Oldsmobile Toronado, from the sixties but perfectly maintained, upholstered in the brown leather of library sofas. Most of the roomy backseat was taken up by two dogs. "Marlin Perkins, here, is a rat terrier," said David Pollock, "and Doris Day is a simple but elegant bichon frise. Scrunch together, girls." He got in beside the dogs, who moved together for a moment until the spotted one arranged herself in his lap. He stroked her ears. "Marlin is a female too, but she just looked so much like *him* that we couldn't resist."

David John slipped into the driver's seat and we swooped away, down Highway 12 at eighty miles an hour and around the curve into Hardy Well Road. Felicity had her hand on the dash, but she looked cheerful and sassy in her shorts and shirt. It was eight miles to Deacon. Riding with these guys was like taking a spaceship.

The listing—103 Main Street, Deacon—looked even gloomier than I had remembered. Knowing the owners wouldn't do it, I had set up a yard maintenance schedule, but they were only cutting the grass every two weeks and recently there had been a lot of rain. The few flowers in the beds were awash in weeds. Dandelions bloomed all over the front yard. But John and Pollock were undaunted. "Yards are the easiest thing!" John exclaimed. "Oh, my God! We'll have that yard tricked out in a week or two."

"Of course, the best thing is that we aren't selling our place in the city. This is our first second home! Can you believe it? The start of a lifetime of weekending, two venues, Friday drives from the city, talking about the weather all the time, breakfast Saturday morning! My God, we'll be right out of *The New York Times Magazine*. The sunlight coming in here and just sort of angling across the butcher-block table."

We walked through every room. The two men, I noticed, spoke extravagantly, but they scrutinized the place very carefully and didn't miss any of the dry rot or the deferred maintenance or the structural wear and tear I knew was there—the place had been on the market for almost a year. David Pollock even reached up suddenly, when we were surveying the backyard from the back porch, and pulled off a piece of siding. I didn't stop him. What was underneath was better than what was on top, and he saw it and liked it. The house was listed for $89,900, a kitchen and two large rooms down, four bedrooms, a bath, and a sleeping porch up. They offered $81,000, closing as soon as possible. That was at least $4,800 to me, listing agent, buyer's agent, and broker, for a very short afternoon's work, and I was sure the seller would take it because the property was starting to deteriorate.

After they signed the papers and left me the number of their hotel, I walked them to their Toronado. David John said, "We always work with the listing agent."

GOOD FAITH

"And we have so many friends," added David Pollock.

"With so much money!" exclaimed David John, with a laugh. They got into the car, arranged the dogs, slammed the doors, and laid rubber as they turned into the road.

"Oh, Joey," said Felicity, "I have had so much fun this afternoon!"

In the end, I kept the Sloans waiting for an hour and a half.

CHAPTER 5

BOBBY CONTINUED to play it safe at home, so I was the one who walked the Burnses through Gottfried Nuelle's pride and joy for a final inspection. When they arrived at the house, where I had been busily making sure that Gottfried didn't show up, I was surprised that they seemed utterly unfamiliar to me, perfect strangers. It was odd, because they had been on my mind. Although I hadn't been paying much attention at the time, I had come to know that Burns and Bobby were friends, that the couple had gone out with the Baldwins to Mercados, that Felicity intended to cultivate Linda Burns. It was hard to tell why.

What I noticed now about Marcus Burns was

that he was very neat, almost formal. Even though the weather was hot, he was wearing a light blue shirt, a navy blue tie, and a sport coat. The shirt collar had a starchy sheen and lay smoothly against his neck. The cuffs emerged a half inch from the sleeve of his jacket. The jacket itself, a nubbly buff-colored weave, also looked as crisp as if he had just taken it off the rack. I looked down at his shoes. Tan loafers, as smooth around his feet as if his feet were shoe trees.

He was younger than I was by five years, I thought. Most people who were that much younger than I were baby boomers—casual about dress at the very least, usually wearing jeans. But it was more than expense and style that struck me about Marcus Burns, it was that he gave off the air of being cleaner and better cared for than a man could do for himself, as if he employed another man to do it for him. He was good-looking, too, with a quick smile, an open face, and an easy manner. He was not the sort of guy who, I thought, would appeal to Gordon, or even to Betty. He looked too finished. Gordon liked people who were either loud or eager or a little shaggy, even a little hapless. His cronies were the last guys who could be called smooth. Their characteristic pose was gripping their poker hands, yelling about something, and squinting to avoid the smoke of the cigarettes that were dangling from the corners of their mouths.

Linda Burns was taller than Marcus, nicely dressed too. As we went through the house, she tended to run aground here and there, standing for a long moment with a cabinet open, staring into it, or leaning her elbow against the wall, gazing out the window. Marcus and I walked briskly, inspecting Gottfried's work and talking about it as critically as possible (which wasn't very); she dawdled after us, almost silent. Burns was affectionate with her and eager with me. He clearly liked the house very much. In the foyer, for example, he squatted down and ran his hand across the pegged floor, then sat back on his heels a little and surveyed the woodwork: a dark chair rail and a beautiful staircase with turned spiral balusters. On the newel post, Gottfried had set a beautiful wooden globe. The grain of the wood glistened all around in tawny and chocolate striations. Burns ran his palm around it with a sigh.

The striations were repeated in the steps, even though, no doubt, they would eventually be carpeted. I said, "Look at these steps. Gottfried builds everything to be seen, even the things he knows are going to be covered." The steps were a perfect example of Gottfried's idea that beauty didn't cost much; he had taken a few minutes to look through the boards available for stair treads and had chosen interesting ones. "How hard is that?" I could hear him rant, as if I personally had dared him to overlook something.

Burns went up the stairs, sliding his hand up the banister, and turned around on the landing and looked down at me. He put his hands in his pockets and grinned. Linda was wandering around the living room. She said, "Our furniture isn't nice enough for this place," but she said it dreamily. Then she said, "We can get rid of it all."

Normally, the buyers do their last inspection to make sure they know what they're getting and that everything has been completed to their satisfaction before the closing, but when I heard Linda's voice from the living room say, as if to herself, "I hope we live here forever," I figured they were satisfied.

Later, when we went outside to look at the grounds and the garage, they were practically swooning, their arms around each other's waists, smiling. It was like accompanying someone on their second honeymoon. I moved off a little.

The Burnses' house stood on a rise facing southeast. The front yard sloped down to Maple Glen Road, and the backyard sloped somewhat less to a little rill that ran off the hump of a good-sized hill to the north. There was a good view down the long valley of the Blue River, a tributary of the Nut. A series of hills crowned with maples receded into the purple distance. One neighbor, across the road, was visible, though the windows of his house were hidden by foliage. The other neighbors, who really weren't too far away, could not be seen, and a small shopping center at the crossroads of Highway 12 and Maple Glen Road was hidden by a curve, though it was less than half a mile distant. A child, if the Burnses had one, could easily and safely ride a bike to the shopping center and home again. Selway was about five miles in one direction, and Lesterville, which had nice restaurants, two gas stations, several bed-and-breakfasts, and a short shopping street, about three miles in the other. We weren't far from Darlington Shopping Village, either, if they were in the market for luxuries rather than necessities. In other words, the house had just about everything. I could almost but not quite see myself having lived a different, possibly wiser life, a life that would have led me to this house. I was no less capable than Marcus Burns of appreciating it, and maybe somewhat more capable of taking care of it. As a rule, I was not an envious sort of person—didn't dare to be, in fact, because my parents had always been quick to note and punish covetousness (along with bearing false witness, taking the name of the Lord in vain, and every other commandment-breaking act)—but I thought I could have slid right into a bit of petty longing if I hadn't been feeling very good.

So I was standing there, feeling benevolent and avuncular, when Marcus Burns came up to me and said, in an easy and friendly voice, "What about the fence?"

"What about it?"

"There's no fence."

"Well, no. I told Bobby to make sure you saw that the seller had rejected the fence contingency before you accepted the counter offer." I remembered thinking that Marcus Burns could certainly afford a fence.

"I understood the problem was with the style of fence, but that the seller agreed to a white board fence rather than a split-rail fence."

"The seller was more positive about a board fence, to the degree that he was willing to sell the house knowing that a board fence might someday be erected along the road, but he didn't agree to put one up."

"Oh." Burns seemed surprised.

"I'm sorry if Bobby didn't make the seller's position clear. I have the papers in the car. My advice to you is just buy the house and put up the fence you want."

"Nuelle's house that he's building now has a

fence, a split rail. I saw it when I drove by there a couple of days ago."

This was true. Gottfried's current project had recently manifested a split-rail fence, and he could certainly have gotten the idea from Burns, though of course the style of the house was Colonial, not Queen Anne. I said, "I understand your position, Mr. Burns, but this is something I wouldn't really bring up tomorrow at the closing. Gottfried is kind of a volatile guy. To tell you the truth, at our last closing he tried to throw the buyer out the window."

Burns laughed. This entire discussion had been a genial one. He was friendly, and I felt rather warmly toward him even though I'd hardly had a thing to do with him. He put his arm around my shoulders and bent his head toward mine. He said in a low voice, "Is he a big guy?"

"Big enough when he gets his dander up."

"You don't think he would be amenable to, say, arm-wrestling for a fence? We don't plan to move in for a couple of weeks." He smiled again. "Just a minute. Do you mind? I want to discuss this with my wife."

Linda Burns was standing in front of the house, her head tossed back, looking up at the façade and the long veranda that crossed it. Burns went up to her and put his arm around her, turning her away from the house and away from me. After a moment, I saw her lay her head on his shoulder. Then they turned and regarded the front of the property along the road. He stretched out his arm and made a gesture. Then they walked back up the hill to me.

She said, "Let's ask the builder again about the fence. I'm sure he'll prefer to accommodate us."

"In my note to Bobby when this issue came up, Mrs. Burns, I told him that Nuelle intended to put the house back on the market at a higher price if this deal didn't go through, so what that means is he's already thinking that he sold the house for too little as it is. He'll be pretty annoyed to take even less."

She said, "The confusion seems to me to be a middleman confusion. I mean, even if we look at the papers, and even if we talk to Mr. Baldwin about it, the reality stays the same. We asked for a fence and thought we were getting a fence, and here we aren't getting a fence even though we're paying full price. I said to Marcus that it seems to me it's like going to the store and bringing home a gallon of milk, but when you get home the milk is sour."

"You did sign the contract, Mrs. Burns. I'm sorry if you didn't read it."

She spoke quietly, sadly, shaking her head. "Okay. Okay. I hate that when you get into the you said / I said / you said / I said. Maybe this is the wrong house for us. Maybe this is a sign. Honey, you can deal with these things better than I can." She gave Burns a squeeze with the hand on his arm and turned and walked away. He looked after her, then he turned to me and said, "She loves this place. I don't know."

"You have a lot of money in this place already. You put down ten percent of the purchase price. That's twenty-five grand right there."

"Oh, I think she's just disappointed. I wouldn't worry about it." We watched her get into their car. "I'll work on her tonight."

"Excuse me?"

"Well, it's delicate. She likes things to fall into place just so, from the beginning. Have you ever heard the expression, 'Things begin as they go along'? She's very touchy about beginnings. Obviously we wouldn't give up twenty-five thousand dollars for the sake of a fence that would cost maybe five or six hundred."

"Closer to a thousand, depending on the contractor, but of course."

"I'll talk to her. That's all I can do. I'm sure it will be fine. Bobby, of course, isn't very experienced. I'm sure that's been a problem for you from time to time. But he's a good kid." We started down the hill toward the car. "And we met his two sisters the other night. Linda liked one of them very much— let's see—Felicity, it was. They've had lunch a time or two since then. They've been thick as thieves. I'll bring that up too."

When he got into his car a few moments later, I was feeling jealous more than anything else, that Linda Burns had seen more of Felicity since Monday than I had.

When I got home, I called Bobby a couple of times, but there was no answer. I reviewed my options. I could drive over there, but it was a long way, and if he wasn't there, a drive could be futile. And what would I do when I got there? The Burnses had signed the papers, had initialed the clause wherein they acknowledged that the builder would not put in a fence. If Bobby had misled them in some way, then it would have been orally, and chances were he wouldn't remember it. I was annoyed, but the deal was a solid one, a legal one, and a good one. Best to eat something and put it out of my mind, which I did.

In the end, given the fence problem, I decided to do the closing myself rather than leave it to Bobby; Gottfried Nuelle customarily took a bit of managing anyway. In the first place, he was always annoyed that he was in some title company's office rather than on the job. He didn't like the feeling that a job was unsupervised. One time he had gotten home from a closing to discover that his workmen had put in a slate floor backwards. The pattern in the slates that Gottfried had designed was installed right to left rather than left to right. He subsequently convinced me that the result was disconcerting, like seeing backwards handwriting, rather than soothing, the way it was meant to be. But he also hated for the workmen to be idle, so he began every closing in a frame of mind that was only exacerbated by actually meeting the buyers. When I picked him up for this one, though, he was pretty happy. Over the weekend, he had found a forgotten bin of black walnuts from several years ago in the back of his workshop. He'd spent a few hours Sunday morning driving back and forth over them in his car, crushing them. He'd then scooped them into five-gallon containers and added linseed oil, producing what he called "the stain of the decade." He planned to apply it to the dining room paneling of the house he was building. As we drove into the parking lot of the title company, he said, "I did this before, you know, but these walnuts are so old, nearly fermented. It's a much richer color than with fresh walnuts." Then he clammed up.

The Burnses were waiting for us. No Bobby.

GOOD FAITH

Marcus and Linda both waved happily, and Linda came to my side of the car and put her hand on my arm when I opened the door. She said, "I am so excited. This is such a dream come true for me. I feel like this house was built just for me. You're Mr. Nuelle? You are such an artist. I feel like even if I had told you what I wanted, it couldn't have come out as nice as it has, because I wouldn't have known what I wanted as well as you did! Isn't that amazing? Thank you very much." She took Gottfried by both hands and looked into his face with great emotion. He looked startled but pleased. Even Gottfried could be softened by flattery.

Marcus Burns was a little more reserved but, it seemed, no less happy. He introduced himself enthusiastically to Gottfried, and Gottfried scrutinized him but seemed placated. We were shown into the conference room at the title company and asked to wait a moment or two for the closing officer. Burns caught my eye and gave me the high sign. I relaxed. Once again the two of them looked perfectly turned out; he had on a pink shirt with a pale glen-plaid jacket, and she wore a yellow linen dress with white around the neck and sleeves. We sat quietly. I sensed Gottfried as a dormant volcano beside me.

Linda said, "You know, Mr. Nuelle, I am so sorry for the confusion."

"What's that?" said Gottfried.

I sneezed, which is probably why I didn't pay attention to this little exchange. At any rate, by the time I'd blown my nose, Gottfried was sitting forward, staring at Linda Burns, who was plowing ahead, though timidly. "It seems like a small thing," she said. "A few feet of fence is all, and yet I see it as the finishing touch. I mean, what if I went to the store and bought a birthday cake, and the cake was wonderful and the frosting was all creamy and rich, and it had beautiful red roses on it, but it didn't have *Happy Birthday* written on it? Or, really, what's more like it is, it had *Happy Birth* written on it, but you'd left off the *day* part. When I got it home, it couldn't be used for a birthday, could it? No matter how great it was, no matter how good it tasted, it really couldn't be used for what I'd intended it for."

I said, "Maybe that's not quite an appropriate comparison, Mrs. Burns. The house is completely useful—"

"Well, the analogy is not about usefulness really, Mr. Stratford. It's about getting what you pay for. About wanting something to be complete before you enter into a contract. I just want everything to be perfect, and I don't feel that it is."

"You don't?" said Gottfried. I knew he was thinking about the floors, the moldings, the kitchen cabinets. *Perfect* was the perfect word for her to use, since he prided himself on perfection.

"No, I don't. My husband and I spoke about this last night for a long time, and he, of course, was willing to settle, but I just wanted to appeal to you, Mr. Nuelle. I know that Mr. Stratford is being quite uncompromising about this, and holding us to the letter of the contract and all, and I certainly wouldn't want to lose twenty-five thousand dollars, but I have principles, and I want a split-rail fence along the front edge of the property."

"Split-rail?" said Gottfried.

"Yes. That's what seems right to me."

"Split-rail in front of a Queen Anne?"

"Yes. If I'm going to live there, that's what it's going to have to be. I told my husband last night before bed that I would compromise, but I was up all night about it—and about the tile in the powder room."

"The tile in the powder room?"

"Oh, yes. That's going to have to come up right away. I can't even go in there."

"The tile is off white. Very neutral," I said.

"It is *shiny*."

I looked around the table. Gottfried was red in the face, Linda Burns was staring down at the table but pressing ahead, and Marcus Burns was looking at her with an inscrutable half smile. Just then, Mary Lou, the closing officer, came in with the papers, saying "Good morning, Gottfried, Joe. You must be the Burnses. Okay! Everything looks in order here. The mortgage is approved, of course. I spoke to the savings and loan this morning. Shall we—"

Marcus Burns stood up, held out his hand with a ready smile, and said, "Good morning to you! Beautiful morning."

There was a long pause, and then Linda Burns said, "As I was saying—"

"That's enough for me," said Gottfried.

"Oh, good," said Linda Burns. "Then we're agreed about the fence. Split rail, along the front. I'm so happy. I think if you get it in there within two weeks, it will be fine. I don't want to rush you, in spite of the confusion. We'll just forget about that." She smiled forgivingly at me. Ah, she was pretty and agreeable-looking, but I don't think I'd ever had a buyer who seemed to me as crazy as she did at that moment.

Gottfried put his palms down on the surface of the table and pushed his chair back. The closing officer turned to look. I thought I might just not say anything, might just let this deal fall through. The Burnses wanted this house—she wanted it more than he did—and Gottfried had been moaning and complaining about the building loans for months. It was their deal, and each of them stood to get the thing he or she said they wanted. But in about two seconds, Gottfried was going to walk away, handing back the down payment and letting this crazy woman off scot-free. Did I really want to exert myself in these people's behalf? In the end, what did I care whether she ended up with her dream house or Gottfried got his money? At the moment, my part of the commission didn't even matter to me, sizable though it would be. But I said it anyway. I said, "Wait a minute, Gottfried. Please?"

"I told you before," said Gottfried, "about that fence—and you brought me in here? You let this thing go on like this? What do I pay you for, Stratford?"

He paid me for exactly what I was about to do. I said, "If you'll pardon me for saying so, I don't see why questions of personal taste would have to be deal killers. I happen to know what you've paid to the savings and loan, Gottfried, to keep this house on the market. If we list it again for ten thousand more, it could take longer to find another buyer than that amount would repay you." Linda Burns was nodding. "Your new house is almost finished. Put that on the market for ten thousand more and get rid of this one. That's my advice."

Gottfried's face was stone at my advice, but at least he wasn't purple.

Then I said, "I'll tell you what, Mrs. Burns. This is a house, but it is also a work of craftsmanship and art. If you didn't think so, you wouldn't want it. I don't personally think the analogy of buying something at the grocery store fits here, for several reasons. I have never seen a house that suited one person perfectly suit the next one perfectly. If all you are talking about is a fence and some tile, you have fewer disagreements with Gottfried's taste than ninety-nine percent of the people I see in a year. But frankly, do you expect to find another house that you like this well? Where there are only two things you want to add or change? Most buyers I see intend to gut the place they are moving into. You are paying top dollar here, but the fact is you will have very little to do. Some people pay top dollar and then top it off with many many more dollars to make it the way they want it."

Linda Burns wasn't looking at me, but Marcus was smiling and nodding.

"I don't know, this may be your second or third house, but I've sold lots of houses and I think this is a good match, a very good match. Gottfried is the best builder around. Besides that, I don't think anyone will be happy if this deal falls through."The title officer nodded and then raised her eyebrows, just subtly, as if to say, How many times do we have to go through this?

"I can't get over it," said Linda Burns.

I spoke soothingly. "What can't you get over?"

"Well, I can get over the tile, but I can't get over the fence. I just can't. I think it should be included."

I said, "Fine. We'll make a separate agreement, leaving Gottfried out of it, and I will see to it that the fence is put in."

"You shouldn't have to," said Linda Burns.

"Well, actually, I agree with you, but Gottfried asked me what I get paid for, and I suppose helping the deal go through is it."

She sniffed. After a few quiet moments, the closing officer began sliding the documents across the table to each of the parties, and then, after another moment, they began to sign. I figured the fence would cost eight hundred bucks. Maybe I would split the cost with Bobby.

The room was quiet for a while. All parties acted chastened and reluctant, but they did sign. And when they were through signing, one by one, they sighed deep relieved sighs, and the whole deal started to look inevitable, the way done deals do.

I got up and went to the bathroom. On my way back, Marcus Burns met me in the hallway and clapped me on the shoulder. He was all smiles. He said, "Hey, man! That was great! I couldn't believe it. I thought she had him, and we were going to be traipsing around to open houses for another six months. And you know, I'll tell you something. At every open house she would have said, 'I'm sorry we missed that other house.'" He shook his head, but affectionately, kindly. "She's just this way. Once the whole thing is over, she loves it and can't even remember what the problems were, but getting there puts her in a panic. Her mom's the same way. Anyway, thanks, man. I owe you."

I thought I'd done a good job too. As I was driving away, I ruminated pleasantly on my special talents as a Realtor: no, I wasn't passionate about houses; and, no, I wasn't quick and instinctive; and, no, I wasn't a natural salesman like, say, Jack Dorfman at the Century 21 office. Jack had been a linebacker for the Pittsburgh Steelers long long ago. He had gotten out of football and into real estate before turning thirty, but he was rich and also a legend. If a buyer showed the least little interest in a house, he—or she—was guaranteed to have bought it already. Jack Dorfman just put that looker on a train and sent him down the track—next stop, closing. I never knew if it was an instinct for who could buy or subtle bullying, but he never let them off the hook and frequently pointed out at Realtors' gatherings that if they changed their minds later, there was a whole other sale to be taken care of.

Anyway, I wasn't like that, but, I told myself as I drove away that afternoon, I was good at shifting the balance when things began to go sour. I was even—well, you might say, eloquent. In short, I was so good at my job, I decided to take the afternoon off. I drove down to the city, where there was good food and music playing that night in about six different bars. I didn't tell anyone where I was going.

C H A P T E R

6

B Y THE FIRST WEEK of June, I had
three of those townhouses in Phase
Four presold, and I arranged to meet
the buyers out at the site so they could get a
look at how far along things were. Ever since
the Burns closing, I had had the golden touch.
The Davids, John and Pollock, had closed,
and a friend of theirs with more money and
more expensive taste was about to sign a
contract. I had six new listings and potential
buyers for all of them. I knew enough about
real estate to recognize the flow of luck. There
had been times when I'd done everything
except bury voodoo dolls in front of the office
just to get some business—that's what it had
been like in the Carter years, with interest rates

approaching 14 percent and sellers knocking thousands off the price and me taking a cut in commission just to make a place a little more affordable for the buyer. Now interest rates were down from that high, though not that much—what mortgages were costing now would have killed the market in 1974. I remembered when we used to see all those Vietnamese boat people scrambling to climb onto those rickety boats back in '79. Well, it still seemed to lots of buyers that the boat was leaving the harbor for the last time; better to get on at any price than wait for rates or prices to go down. Realtors had lots of truisms at their fingertips, about how the price of land sometimes stabilized but never declined, about how you might pay extra for the mortgage or extra for the house but it was always going to be one or the other, about how the supply of (1) good land, (2) lake frontage, (3) prime locations, or (4) terrific older houses (built, always, of finer materials, with better workmanship than available today) was limited. The lesson of every rule was buy now if you possibly can, or buy up, or take a second job. Whatever boat you were trying to get on was steaming away to the promised land, and we Realtors had the tickets.

The buyers of the presold townhouses on

Anne and Elizabeth and Mary considered themselves lucky to get in on the ground floor. God only knew what the prices would be like when the places were finished and everyone in the world who wanted in would be banging down the gates.

I hadn't been out there since April, and Gordon had done just as I suggested: put in some temporary flower beds full of nasturtiums and marigolds, along with some turf. The streets were done, and they looked bright and smooth, the way new pavement does. Gordon had even put flower boxes on the mobile home where he had the office.

I got there early—it was about 9 A.M. on a breezy June day—and the air was fragrant with the scent of roses and lilacs from across the road along the fence that defined Phase One. The office was locked and I didn't see Larry, so I went out on my own and took a look at the site. The foundations were in. I stood back on a little rise and looked at the picture they made: the concrete outline of each unit, including the median walls between units. The eye is always deceived by empty foundations—the surrounding landscape makes defined areas look small. But there was something else about these walls that didn't look right. I stared at them for a moment, then realized that the formed concrete was twelve inches thick, rather than eight, and that about eight inches from the top there was a four-inch set-back. The setback ran all along the fronts of the units and also around the chimney foundations. The only explanation was that Gordon had made up his mind to add brick facings up the façades of the units as well as brick chimneys. I looked around. There was no brick in evidence.

I heard the sound of a truck and went around to the mobile home. Larry was just getting out of his Dodge. He was a paunchy, cheerful older guy. He had a clipboard in hand and a Cater-pillar cap on his head. He waved happily and came over to meet me.

"Look at this!" he said. "Moving right along. Weather's been great!"

"I've got some buyers coming for the muddy-shoe walk-through."

"Well, it's like walking through a damn meadow out here. This is a fucking vacation!"

"Glad to hear you're happy in your work."

"I've been hounding Gordon to put these units up for three years."

"What's the deal with the setback?"

"Well, you know. They got a load of brick from somewhere like Quebec City. Brick out of the street. They're bringing it down in a couple of days. I don't know where they're go-ing to put it. Probably be hell to work with. You know—myself, I like a nice new brick, sharp edges, uniform color, looks great, but Gordon won't look at a new brick anymore. I showed them some brick I could get for half the cost of these Canadian bricks."

"Them?"

"You know, him and this other guy."

"Nathan? One of the poker buddies?"

"Nah. Young guy. Good-looking. Younger than you. I don't know where he found him, but they're thick as thieves."

I knew who he was talking about before he even finished talking. "Well-dressed?"

"Like a Wall Street banker every day."

"Burns?"

"That's the one."

I estimated, depending on the cost of the brick, that the units had just risen in price. I said, "I thought this phase was low-ball all the way, nothing extra."

"Oh, there's plenty of extras. They canceled the vinyl-clad windows and ordered some wood-framed windows from this place out in Iowa. And they told me to find the tile guy, because they were changing the kitchen and bathroom flooring from linoleum to some kind of Italian tile."

"I've got brochures at the printer that have certain prices on them."

GOOD FAITH

"Well, my advice, you'd better stop the presses. These improvements ought to add twenty grand, if you ask me."

Let me say I was in a good mood that morning. The weather was gorgeous and my luck was flowing in a way that seemed permanent, maybe even a law of the universe. Therefore, while Larry talked, I nodded. No two ways about it, the units were definitely going to be nicer, not just good taste but expensive taste. Looking back, I would have to say that that's when the eighties began, as far as I was concerned—the first week in June, 1982, when modest housing in our rust-belt state got decked out with Italian tile. The fly in the ointment, I realized, as I heard two cars drive into the gravel parking lot and saw them park next to mine, was that my presold clients were not going to qualify for them. The two-bedrooms I had priced at $49,900, the three-bedrooms at $79,900. That meant about an eleven-thousand-dollar down payment for the one, a fourteen-thousand-dollar down payment for the other, and an income of more than twenty thousand a year to qualify for a mortgage. If Gordon's new plans added twelve or fifteen thousand to the price of the smaller unit and fifteen or twenty to the price of the larger unit, my clients would have to have an income of just over twenty thousand a year at the old price but almost twenty-five thousand a year at the new price. For the larger unit, a yearly income of twenty-four and a half thousand was sufficient at the lower price, but almost thirty-four thousand was necessary at the higher price. And as they got out of their cars and approached me, big smiles on their faces, I realized that asking almost a hundred thousand dollars for a townhouse unit in a development was an impossibility. Could not be advertised, could not be sold. It was an absurdity. But if Gordon didn't price them that high, there was no profit to be made. I remember thinking that whatever Marcus Burns was telling Gordon—and why would he be telling Gordon anything to begin with?—between the two of them they clearly had no idea what they were doing with these townhouses. I was sorry. I had been so busy with my own clients and Felicity (and that was a problem too, because obviously I had been avoiding the Baldwins out of guilt), I had failed to do my job for Gordon and make sure he knew what income niche he was in with these units. I wanted to call him right then, but of course here came the DiGenovas and right behind them the Monahans, and I had some explaining to do.

The DiGenovas were young and the Monahans were old. Mrs. DiGenova was carrying a baby on her hip, which Mrs. Monahan moved toward immediately. I saw her lean down and smile at the child and hold out her finger, which the baby grasped. Mrs. DiGenova laughed, then glanced at her husband. Mr. Monahan hung back for a moment. The Monahans didn't have children of their own. He was a machinist in Portsmouth. Their income was $23,000 per year. I had helped them fudge a bit on their asset-and-debt ratio in order to qualify for the mortgage. Mr. DiGenova taught math at the high school. He made $17,000 per year and supplemented it with summer school teaching, another $5,000. Mrs. DiGenova had a typing service. She made $5,000 a year. They qualified for the old price of the three-bedroom unit, but not the new. They weren't fudgeable in any way that I could see. As I shook Mr. DiGenova's hand, I began thinking of other properties I knew that might work better than this one.

The baby had let go of Mrs. Monahan's finger, and she had begun to walk around inside one of the foundations. She called out, "Oh, this seems so spacious! I can't believe we could be in by September!"

I saw Larry coming toward me again. I made a little gesture to wave him off and he turned on his heel and went back inside the trailer. In a few minutes, all four of the clients were wandering around, stepping over the foundations, standing in various corners and trying to imagine what the finished product would look like. Pretty soon, Larry came to the door of the trailer again, stood there for a minute, then came over to me. The four of them, who had only asked me where the front doors were, where the back doors were, and where the advertised garden space was, were on him in a second. It was an enlightening encounter. When could they choose the carpet colors? Well, actually, said Larry, there would be a choice of pine floors, hardwood floors, or carpet. There were several pricing options. How were the bathrooms going to be outfitted? Simply, I thought. Pedestal sinks, shower-tub combinations. But no, said Larry. Tiled shower stalls and separate tubs. He-and-she sinks were the newest thing. Everyone was smiling. Tile? In every master bath, he disclosed. "I love tile," said Mrs. Monahan. "We have linoleum now, but my sister in California has tile all over the place."

"Holds up over the long run," said Larry. "These places are going to be real investments."

Mr. DiGenova took the words right out of my mouth. "Too bad the neighborhood isn't a little nicer."

I kept smiling, and I did not let myself nod, but he was exactly right. Phase Three, the expensive phase, was a good ways up the hill from us. Phase Four looked out for the most part on

Phase One, in which there might not be a single tile, a single divided light window, a single hardwood floor. Phase Four had been meant to fill in the last bits of the property with some quick moneymaking housing. I'd been a smoker once; now I wished I had a cigarette.

More questions: How about garages? Didn't look like room for those. No garages, said Larry. The buyers looked disappointed. Tile but no garages, I thought. Wood-framed windows but no garages. He-and-she sinks but no garages. Larry said, "They changed the façade, you know. Bricks from Quebec City, Quebec, up in Canada. Beautiful weathered brick."

"That will be very nice," said Mrs. Monahan. "My sister's place in California is all board-and-batten. You know, it doesn't matter how much it costs, I always think board-and-batten looks cheap. Brick, especially old brick, looks so nice."

We walked around for half an hour or more. It did not occur to any of the buyers, man or woman, to ask if prices would remain the same, and I said nothing. I saw them off.

I got in my car and went straight over to Gordon's. There were five cars in the driveway, four BMWs and a Caddy. Gordon, Betty, Bobby, and either Norton or Leslie. Norton lived in New Jersey, where he managed shore properties. Leslie was the prolific one; she had six kids and her husband was a hospital administrator at East Portsmouth Community Hospital. Through the window of Gordon's office, I saw they were gathered around the pond in Adirondack chairs. The visitor was Leslie; four of her kids were gamboling in the pond or hanging on the rope swing. Everyone was wearing shorts and light shirts except Marcus Burns, who had on green-gray slacks and a tan sport coat.

Everyone turned as I came down the lawn and shouted friendly greetings. Gordon got up and came to meet me, his hand out to shake mine. Betty got up too, to get me a beer out of the cooler. "Hot, huh?" said Gordon. "What a day. How ya doin', Joey?" He slapped me on the back. "See? Leslie's got the kids here! What a crowd. Look at that little Marcy! If she isn't the spit of our Sally, I don't know about it."

A tall slender eight-year-old with blond hair to her shoulders and a sassy look about her paused as she was crossing the lawn and gave me a sideways glance, then ambled on. "She does," I said. "She does look like Sally."

Gordon propelled me toward Betty, who exclaimed, "Look at us! We aren't getting a thing done today! You know Marcus Burns, Joey. Joey is like a son to us," she said to Marcus. Marcus stood up with a grin, and he, too, took my hand. I felt like I was supposed to be asking someone to marry me. Oh, yeah. Felicity. Ah, Felicity. I kissed Betty on the cheek, wondering if she had once been, or still was, as wanton as Felicity. Why not?

Bobby hadn't come into the office today, though he'd been back at work for over a week by then, hobbling to showings with a cane. He unwrapped his ankle every morning and displayed it to me, swollen and still a little bruised, though getting better, and now he leaned forward and began to unwrap his Ace bandage. I put my hand on his shoulder. He said, "No, really, it's interesting. There's this bump over the outside here that just isn't going away. I'm sure it's broken." He finished unwrapping his foot and dropped the bandage in the grass. "If you touch it in just the right way, and push it, it wiggles back and forth." He did so.

"I'm telling you," said Leslie, "you should have insisted on an X ray."

"I did insist on an X ray, but you know I was delirious with the pain, and maybe I didn't make sure that they X-rayed that part. I can't remember a thing at this point. But look at this! Give me your hand."

"Well, I'm not going to touch it. Ugh. I don't

want to touch your foot! But you should go back! Your feet are important—"

"Come on, touch it! Kiss it!" He lifted his foot toward her face.

"Mom!" called one of the kids.

How many times had I sat here like this in the last twenty years, listening to them tell one another what to do, tell me what to do, pass around the food and the beers, go into the house for more. This, right here, was Gordon's tax problem. He gave everyone what they wanted, and after making his own deals he didn't have enough left for the IRS. I had heard, a couple of years before, that he owed a considerable sum, let's say more than a hundred thousand dollars, and after that I was too intimidated to ask about it again. But hadn't Felicity said that, thanks to Marcus Burns, the tax problem was solved?

Marcus was still smiling. I said, "How's it going with the house?"

"Lord! It's perfect. Linda had all the furniture on the lawn for three days, walking all around each piece. The kids had to rescue some of their things under cover of night!" I laughed. He seemed so forgiving of her quirks. I said, "So you have kids. I haven't met them."

"Amanda and Justin. She's ten and he's eight."

GOOD FAITH

"How do they like the house?" I thought, only two? Who were the other dependents he had claimed?

"They like it. Justin came up to me the first night, after he looked around, and said, 'Hey, Dad. When are the owners coming back?' Then, when I told him this was really our house, he stayed up till two A.M. just staring around the room." He laughed at his own story. "They've met these kids too. Things are great around here."

"If you mean around *here*, this very place, then you're right." We grinned at one another, two lucky guys who'd managed to get in the door. After a moment, I began. "I had a couple of my buyers out at Glamorgan Close this morning—"

"Looks good, doesn't it?" He sat back expansively in his chair.

"To my mind, it looks too—"

"To tell you the truth, I'm glad I came around before they'd gone too far. I was able to persuade Gordon that he needed to spruce the place up a little."

"That's what I—"

"You know what?"

"What?"

"Out in L.A., where I was over Christmas, there's this new thing, the teardown. That's when they pay full price for a house on a lot and then tear the house down and build new. Perfectly good houses, too. So I said to Gordon when he showed me around out there, Don't waste your time building future teardowns. People are more picky these days."

"You have previous real estate experience?"

"None whatsoever! I've been working for the IRS since college."

He leaned forward and looked around, then shook his head. "I'm telling you, this is the eighties. Experience doesn't count anymore. It's just a drag on you, because if you make decisions according to your experience, you will have no idea what is happening in this country."

"Yeah?"

"Yeah. I quit my job last fall. I only waited that long because Linda wanted me to. I was ready to quit the day after the election."

"You were?"

"Yeah. That's what I was doing out in L.A. I went around the country, just reconnoitering. I went to L.A. and San Francisco and Denver and Phoenix and Chicago and New Orleans and K.C. and Seattle and here, interviewing for investment jobs but mostly listening rather than talking, and I'm telling you"—he shook his head in amazement—"Gordon and I have talked about this."

Gordon appeared behind him. He said, "What's up, you guys?"

I said, "Well, I'm afraid my presolds are going to be priced out of Glamorgan's Phase Four." I tried not to let this sound annoyed but rather conversational, as if I were merely concerned.

"How come?" said Gordon.

"Well, Larry told me about the masonry and the tile and the wooden windows from Iowa, and—what else? let's see—oh, the—"

"Working fireplaces?" said Marcus Burns.

"I guess we didn't get that far."

"How did we price those places?"

"Forty-nine-nine and seventy-nine-nine."

"I thought it was sixty-nine-nine and ninety-nine-nine."

"It is now," I said. "Even with that you'll be lucky to get out of there with a profit."

"You sure I said those low prices?"

"I sent you the brochure I had made up and all the ads I put in the paper. Didn't you get it?"

"Yeah, I got it. Maybe I didn't look at it."

"Gordon! I went ahead and presold three places because I thought everything was agreed here."

"I've been a little distracted—"

I stood up, better to get his attention and, maybe, to get a little out of Marcus Burns's earshot. I lowered my voice and moved a little ways off. Gordon followed me. I said, "You can't sell a townhouse for a hundred grand, Gordon. People who want to spend a hundred grand want to live by themselves, with a yard and a garage and all. A hundred grand just looks *bad*. Six figures. Where's the pool and the butler? This isn't L.A., Gordon."

"Who are your presolds?"

"A machinist and a high school math teacher. And a retired couple, the Rebarcaks. That's another thing. Even the houses up on the hill aren't going for a hundred grand, and they've got four bedrooms." Gordon looked at Marcus Burns, who came over, I thought eagerly, to join us.

"They haven't gone for a hundred grand in the past, but that doesn't mean—"

"Gordon, these kinds of buyers are nervous—"

"Mind if I put a word in?" said Marcus Burns in a pleasant voice.

"'Course not," said Gordon.

"Joe, think about your educational role here. You say these kinds of buyers are nervous. They are nervous because they don't know what's going on and they feel intimidated, but that's where you come in. Really now, can they go wrong here?"

"Well, you can never go wrong buying real estate, but—"

"Right, so your job is to give them true information. Of course they have expectations about what you get for a hundred grand. My wife had expectations about what she should get for two-fifty. But this day and age, they're getting something extra—it isn't really visible, but if they stop to think about it, they know it's there. Who have you sold houses to in the last couple of months?"

"Well, you. And a couple of guys bought an old place in Deacon."

"Outsiders?"

"Yeah, and they've got a friend." They were grinning as they watched the sun come up in my head.

Gordon said, "Look around you, Joe! Who wouldn't want to live here? Name me another place anywhere up and down the East Coast that is like these two counties we got here. What happened in the twenties? The railroad ran southeast from Portsmouth to Lawrence Valley, and that was what got built up. The area north and west of Portsmouth, especially these three valleys, got left out. So it's scenic and natural and there's deer and bobcats and badgers and even a bear or two up in the hills, and that's what people want now. They want to come down from New York and get that. How long does it take to get from Manhattan to the Hamptons?"

"Three hours," said Marcus. "Four to Montauk."

"There you have it," said Gordon. "You tell those presolds they are sitting on a gold mine."

"Second-home people don't want townhouses—"

"You don't think? How about when I put in the pool and the tennis courts? The garden plots? People don't all want leaky old farmhouses for the weekend, or farmers' markets and a long drive into town. Some of them just want a place kind of like a hotel that is appreciating while they're enjoying it." Gordon rocked back on his heels, thoroughly happy with this argument.

"You heard of a time-share?" said Marcus.

"I'm sure that's related to a teardown," I said.

"That's where you buy a condo for a certain number of weeks per year. They do it in Florida. What if we sold each townhouse to ten or twelve different buyers for twenty thousand apiece. They could amortize that, pay a hundred and eighty bucks per month—tax deductible, mind you— and have a month in the country every year."

"A month like February, for example?"

"Well, you have to work out the kinks, and I'm not saying that's the plan with Phase Four, but I'm telling you, house owning isn't like it ever was before in the history of the world.

Inflation killed the old world, and the population explosion is remaking it!"

"He's right," said Gordon. "You listen. He makes perfect sense."

"Just saying that the townhouses turn out to be something like that, who's your lender?"

"Blue Valley Federal Savings and Portsmouth Savings, to begin with," offered Marcus. I looked at him. He looked eager, open, and interested. He had certainly gotten the jump on me, that was for sure. I said, "That's okay. I mean, it's good. But what about my presolds? I guarantee they aren't going to qualify for the higher prices."

"So what?" said Gordon. "It's good to have people in there. Give them the prices you talked about, and we'll phase in the new prices. They'll be happy they got such a good deal."

"You can say that again."

I had promised to meet the Sloans at a house they had driven past and wanted to see, way out past Roaring Falls on Nicknock Road, a house I had never seen but which had a famous history. It had been built in the twenties by a movie star. Supposedly she had held great parties there, and movie stars and gangsters would come to hide out, so far away and unfindable was it. The owner had died in California in the forties, and the house had stood empty while her son and her housekeeper fought over it, and then the son had died in the middle of the dispute, by crashing his single-engine plane. The housekeeper, alleged to have caused his death by means of a ritual curse, had lived there until the mid-sixties, followed by her daughter, who had recently, according to the listing agent, died. She—the listing agent—said, "Well, whatever you think, you've got to see this place. You have just got to see it."

"Magnificent?" I asked.

"Not quite."

"White elephant?"

"Not quite. Just go see it."

"Won't last long at these prices?"

"Joe, it's indescribable. Just go see it."

I had never heard the Sloans this excited, and when I got there and parked behind their car and had my first look at the house, I thought they had gone crazy.

The house was made of, or at least faced with, limestone and set against a west-facing hillside. The road switched back twice as it approached the façade, and the place must have had twenty windows, all trimmed with red curved tiles, facing in the direction of the setting sun. There were two floors, the first floor jutting out beyond the second. The second floor had three balconies and a high roofline that peaked above the central one. There was a fourth balcony set into this peak. The hillside rose behind the peak of the roof. It was of no particular style—Spanish in the use of red tile but not really Spanish. More like what provincial movie people in the nineteen-twenties thought would look romantic. The approach was so steep that if the Sloans' children had bikes or roller skates, they would have to be discarded before they moved in.

The other Realtor had dropped the key by my office, so I joined the Sloans and we climbed the front steps and let ourselves in. It was, of course, late afternoon, and the westering sun made a glorious show across the floors and against the walls of the front rooms, a large living room and dining room, with a smaller paneled library tucked in off the living room. Behind the dining room was a breakfast room with a tall window facing south over the valley. The kitchen had old-fashioned appliances and several pantries, but it was pleasant too. Woodwork was everywhere, the sort you really couldn't find any longer, from virgin trees, in this case oak and, it looked like, beech. There were carpets, probably laid in the fifties, but we lifted up a couple of corners and saw good floors. Mrs. Sloan kept saying, "What *style* is this house? It looks Bavarian, or something, but feels Italian."

In the kitchen, there were red tile accents. In the dining room, there were heavy dark ceiling beams. I looked out the breakfast-room window. To the south, there was a nice garden, though a little overgrown. I was charmed, I admit I was; it was just the sort of house heirs would squabble over. Unfortunately, it was not the sort of house I could imagine people living in.

But the Sloans were infatuated. They ran their fingers over the woodwork; they looked out every window. Their usual whispering and bickering fell silent. He said, "This is some view." We climbed the staircase.

The listing sheet said there were five bedrooms and two bathrooms on the second and third floors. These rooms were not quite as appealing as the first-floor rooms. The bathrooms were twenties originals—small white hexagonal tiles, claw-footed bathtubs, white towel racks, minimal storage. But the Sloans thought they were charming. Mrs. Sloan said, "You know, I always liked those tiles. They aren't slippery. Lots of little edges for traction." The bedrooms were inconveniently large and empty-seeming, meant to be filled with lots of heavy furniture, but Mrs. Sloan said, "This has a very European feel. Remember when we were in Tuscany? That is what this feels like."

She went to the French door that led to the

balcony and turned the handle. It came off in her hand. I said, "The house is not represented as being in good repair."

"We know that," said Mr. Sloan. "A handle is nothing." This was the man who had been put off by tuck-pointing and older appliances. I felt my eyebrows lift. They opened the door and went out together onto the balcony. I looked up for some reason. There on the ceiling, swimming like large amorphous sea creatures, was a school of water stains. I went back and looked into the bathroom. The ceiling was not only stained, it was buckling and sagging in the northeast corner. I went to the other three bedrooms and glanced in the doors. The back bedrooms were okay, but the other front bedroom had the same extensive damage.

The Sloans reentered from the balcony. Mr. Sloan was, if possible, more delighted than Mrs. Sloan. He exclaimed, "I just can't get over this view! I can't imagine coming home from work every night to this! It seems too good to be true."

I said, "What sort of commute would this be for you?"

"Twenty minutes, tops. This place seems out of the way, but from South Cookborough, where my office is, it isn't that much farther than where we live now, if you take Lansing Road."

"Look up," I said.

They looked up.

"What's that?" said Mrs. Sloan.

"Water stains," said Mr. Sloan.

"They seem too extensive for water stains," said Mrs. Sloan. Their conversation was idle.

He said, "Let's go upstairs and have a look." I followed them up the third-floor staircase, which was rather steep but nicely built of dark oak. The third floor consisted of one large room to the south, the balcony outside the west wall, and a pretty arched window in the south wall.

I said, "Look up." They looked up. In this room, the water stains on the ceiling had merged at the south end into serious deterioration—crumbling, buckling, discolored plaster. They didn't say anything, just looked up and then looked at me. I opened the balcony door and went out, carefully, not quite sure the balcony was structurally safe.

The hillside fell dramatically away from the front of the house, and the sky billowed over a landscape of woods and clearings. Several farms were visible in the valley bottom along the road, with white fences and white barns and stone houses. Horses grazed in two or three pastures and cattle and sheep in two or three others. There was sweet corn coming up in three squared-off fields, but what was really impressive was the density of the foliage in the wooded areas. Mr. Sloan was correct in saying that we weren't that far from civilization—twenty minutes from Cookborough and fifteen from Roaring Falls, maybe twenty-five from Deacon—but we might as well be looking back a hundred years, so little had the view changed or the landscape been developed.

No less amazing, in its way, was the roof that lay immediately in front of the balcony, the roof of the second floor. It was red tile, of the sort you see in Mediterranean climates. Given the vertigo of the location and the slipperiness of the tiles, it must have been quite a feat to install it. It was no small expanse, either, since the house was long from end to end. It was not especially steep—perhaps the architect figured that the smoothness of the tile would help the snow slide off. Unfortunately, however, the roof was installed upside down, with the tiles running upward from the seams, and the seams, which had been cemented over, serving as miniature traps to catch every drop of moisture that had fallen from the sky in sixty years. And yet the tiles were beautifully laid, in neat lines and rows. Not a single one, from where I was standing, had fallen off over the years. I started to laugh, and the Sloans pushed the door open and joined me.

"What's the matter?" said Mr. Sloan. He was not a laughing sort of guy. I gestured at the roof. He said, "What about it?"

"Look at it."

"Looks pretty solid."

"George," said Mrs. Sloan. "It runs uphill."

"God, what a view," said Mr. Sloan.

Mrs. Sloan and I exchanged a glance. She said, kindly I thought, given their tendency to argue, "It's a spectacular view, honey. I've never seen anything like it."

We stood there appreciatively for several minutes, until it occurred to me that maybe the balcony wasn't built for three, and I went back inside. Now that I recognized the cause, I saw there was damage everywhere, behind the wallpaper and in the floor as well as in the ceiling. Certainly the structural beams of the house, if they happened to be revealed, would be rotten and soft. It was a shame, I thought. A lot of imagination and taste had gone into building the place. Yes, it was pleasant, okay, even inspiring, inside these rooms. You could readily see it—every season, even late winter, would be beautiful here, veils of fog drifting up from the valley, or low snowy clouds all around you, or the distant southern sun lighting up this house and no other. The site, of course, was a nightmare as well as a dream, but there are houses like that, houses someone or other devotes himself to, that are in a different category from most houses, which are built to serve.

The Sloans came in from the balcony. They were holding hands and he was smiling, as if she had just made a joke. When she saw him smiling, she sighed, I thought in relief, and we went down the stairs to the second floor. We strolled through those bedrooms one more time, glanced at the bathrooms. On the first floor, we paused in each doorway as if saying good-bye. By the time we were done, the sunset was enormous in the windows. We went out. I locked the front door and put the key in my pocket. I walked the Sloans to their car, and we stood by the right taillight, lingering just a moment because it didn't seem proper to rush off. I said, "You know, I think there's something coming on the market in the Blue Valley. I should know in a couple of days." This was not true.

They nodded. She got in on the passenger side and he went around to the driver's side, pausing once more to look over the roof of the car at the sunset and down the valley. The tops of the trees, the edges of all the leaves, were lit up by the long rays of the sun, and then, a moment later, they were not, and the trees looked dark and mysterious where they had just looked sparkling and alive. He got in, turned on the engine, and drove down the driveway, cautiously. In the winter, of course, they would have to park at the bottom and walk up.

CHAPTER

7

WHEN THE DAVIDS invited me to
bring Felicity by for a visit in early
July, they already had the siding off
and a garden planted. They were ferociously efficient and strong and fast. When Felicity and I
got there, they were stripped down to shorts
and work boots, and the whole time we chatted
and sipped beers, they kept working. We started
out in the kitchen, where they had arranged
dishes of olives and cheese and some good
bread from the city. As we talked, they ripped
the rotten and discolored linoleum and the un-
derlayment it was bonded to right out from
under our feet, all the time asking Felicity
about her marriage and me about my divorce,
and how had we met each other, and how often

did we see each other, and was this an open secret or a secret that would follow us to the
grave? I listened while Felicity responded.

"Well, you never know what's secret, do you?
People are tremendously revealing if anyone
bothers to look, but then hardly anyone ever
bothers to look. My idea is to look upon it as
my own business, and that way I have what you
might call a philosophical position as a basis in
case of the surprise factor."

"You mean, in case your husband surprises
you with an accusation."

"Or my father or my mother or one of my
kids. Frankly, I think the idea of its being my
own business is the only one my husband
would accept. That's the principle he lives by.
He's a very private person."

"Too private for you, I'll bet," said David John,
tearing up a three-by-four-foot piece of linoleum and plywood backing with a grunt and
tossing it out the open door into the backyard.

She glanced at me. She said, "I don't think it's
fair to Joey to talk about my husband in his
presence. It makes him feel uncomfortable."

"Does it?" said David Pollock to me.

I said, "Any kind of probing beneath the surface makes me uncomfortable here."

"Oh my God," said David Pollock. "We are
dedicated probers beneath the surface. How can

we be friends unless we can ask you anything and everything? Especially since we always tell all. For example, David was married. He married his high school sweetheart. They were all tremendously Baptist. You wouldn't believe what a scandal it was when he ran off with *moi*. Absolutely the only way to get over the whole thing was to talk it to death. His parents wanted to hide everything, from the boy aspect to the Jew aspect to everything in between. But we said, 'Oh my God, we've got to get this vermin out of the box and look at it till we love it,' and that's what we do. Marlene, his wife—she comes around."

"How did you meet?" asked Felicity.

"At a yoga class," said David Pollock. "Actually, a yoga class that Marlene signed him up for to get him out of the house."

"Marlene had hippie aspirations that we exploited shamelessly for our own purposes," said David John. "When I was in the navy, I wouldn't let her wear bellbottoms or tie-dye. I was very strict. So actually she likes me better now."

"So do I," said David Pollock. "Anyway, you'll see her sometime. She comes to visit."

"That sounds very nice," said Felicity. She glanced at me again. "I keep telling Joey that this is nothing about my life, only about how I can't get enough of him." Her arms snaked around my waist and she laid her head on my chest. I could feel in the way she melted against me that although her tone was light, her feeling was strong and almost frightening. I put my arms around her and kissed her on the top of her head. Both Davids looked at her for a moment. Finally, David Pollock ripped up another piece of linoleum with a long loud cracking sound and said, "I think she's serious." He tossed it out the door on top of the others, crossed to where we were, and took another sip of wine.

"Far be it from us," said David John, "to object to any sort of seize-the-day experience. My God! Look what happened in the last election! If that isn't a lesson for us all, then what is?" I laughed, but after that they didn't ask any more questions. Felicity had added something to our romance that was no longer simple, cool, or bright. David John continued. "Of course, it's one of life's imponderables, this passion thing. Joe seems like a perfectly decent person all around, but let's face it, he's not, on the surface, an obvious candidate for stardom." He grinned. A smaller piece of the floor came up with more difficulty, and then a larger piece. David Pollock set down his crowbar with a sigh, picked up a towel, and wiped his face. It was hot, and he was dripping with sweat. Hearing the Davids talk was not like anything else I knew, and if they didn't think I seemed worthy of Felicity's feelings, well, they were only echoing my own doubts.

The Davids didn't rest until the entire floor was lifted and removed. What was underneath was something of a disappointment. The original kitchen had evidently been much smaller; there was an area of nice pine boards about ten feet square, but the rest of the floor was plywood, probably put down during a remodel in the fifties. The two men stood with their hands on their hips, regarding the island of pine in a lake of plywood. The two dogs, who had been sleeping in the yard, appeared on the other side of the debris. The rat terrier paused for a moment, then picked her way across the old flooring, hopped over the doorsill, and came in. She surveyed the four of us, Felicity sitting on her stool, me sitting on the counter, and the Davids pondering the floor. She went straight over to Felicity and jumped into her lap. Felicity laughed. David John said, "Marlin Perkins is no fool, honey."

I said, "You ought to look in the attic. These old houses were originally taxed according to the width of the floorboards, so they sometimes put the wider ones in the attic where the tax man wouldn't see them."

"How do you get to the attic? I haven't seen a trapdoor," said David John.

"There's an opening in the ceiling of one of

153

the closets upstairs. I went up there once when I was listing the house."

It was getting dark, but we took a couple of flashlights into the attic. The attic was more of a crawl space, not a pleasant place, but indeed the floorboards were fourteen inches wide, a treasure trove of virgin pine. The Davids were amazed.

I said, "Look at it this way. When they built the house, they got random-width boards from the sawmill, because the sawmill just milled the logs, they didn't sort and size them the way they do today. All the boards cost the same per square foot from the mill, but some cost more after they were installed, because of the tax assessment, so you hid them away."

"This happens to us all the time," said David John. "When we moved into our place in the city, we took down these abominable white ceiling tiles and found beaten tin underneath. Mmmm. Yes! Look at those boards!"

It was eight when we left. We had meant to leave by six. I didn't ask where Felicity was going or what her evening plans were, but it was hard to let her go all the same, and I wanted to stand in the street kissing her face and tangling my hands in her hair, which she wouldn't allow, since we were right in the middle of Deacon and it was still very light. She put my car between us and the street and she held me off with her hand while reaching out with her left foot and tickling my ankle with her toes. She said, "I like them. They're new. Do you realize how long we've known most of the people we know?"

"Twenty or thirty years."

"Sally would not have stayed so close to the nest. She would have gone to live in a commune and marched in political protests and joined naked encounter groups, and now it's too late and all those things are over."

"I want to kiss you again."

"No, you must give me a friendly smile and shake my hand and tell me to say Hi to Hank for you, and I will."

And so I did, and a few moments later she drove off. That night I felt lonely in an unaccustomed way.

I can't say that the buyers for Phase Four, at the new prices, materialized right away, but I had so many other buyers I didn't care. The buildings went up, the places did look pretty good, and I didn't have time to worry. One day Bobby and I were sitting around the office talking about this and that, and he started bragging about how introducing Gordon and Marcus Burns was the best thing he ever did and it was going to make everyone rich, including me.

"How's that?" I said.

"The thing is, he knows how it works. You know, he sat in on the famous poker game a week or so ago, and he cleaned everyone out. He won four thousand dollars or something like that. Everyone was fit to be tied except Gordon, who was laughing, they said, even though he lost eight hundred dollars himself."

"I suppose they have to have him back now."

"Well, there's some argument about that, because they don't want to be cleaned out again."

"Was he cheating?"

"Nah. He told Gordon he remembers every card laid, for one thing, and can instantly calculate the odds of anyone having a particular hand. He said he's got this photographic memory plus an adding machine in his head. So anyway, it was a good lesson for them. And they can afford it. They were just pissed, is all."

"I would like to have seen that. Those guys think they're pretty tough."

"The thing is, when someone like Marcus Burns comes around, it makes you realize how local you are. I mean, me, I've been to Florida and back and forth to the Caribbean a few times, but nowhere special. And you haven't either."

"I used to go to Europe every year for two or three weeks when I was married. Don't make me out to be a bumpkin, whatever you say about yourself."

"But you know, I should have gone to college longer. If I'd gotten an accounting degree or a business degree, I would have more sense of what's possible."

"Marcus Burns would be the first to say that all the old rules have been repealed."

"You aren't kidding. Listen to this."

"What?"

"Can you keep a secret?"

Better than you can, I thought.

"You know how much Gordon owed the IRS?"

"No."

"Two hundred and seventy-five thousand dollars."

"You're joking."

"I mean, he's had back taxes since the sixties. He was going to have to sell the house and the farms and everything. Mom thought he was going to go to jail."

"Gordon?"

"No kidding. I mean, you know how he is. He goes out and buys something, and he pulls the cash out of his pocket and hands it to the guy, and they shake on the deal; then he can't remember how much he paid, and there's no record. And then he goes and sells whatever it is for whatever he can get. I think for all those years he was thinking that the IRS was just another guy he could make a deal with. At Christmas, Mom had him sitting in a chair in the living room and she was telling him they meant it and this was the government and all."

"I thought he looked a little on edge at Christmas."

"Now all that's gone. Marcus Burns. And I introduced them."

"What did the guy do?"

"He made a phone call."

"He made a phone call?"

"One phone call."

"He made a phone call to the government and they decided to forgo two hundred and seventy-five thousand dollars?"

"Looks that way. I mean, the night I met him and he told me he'd been working for the IRS but had quit to go into business, we got to talking about Gordon somehow, and he said, Well, maybe he could help, and then a couple of days later he and Gordon went into the office for about half an hour, and then still later, maybe a week, Gordon got a letter saying the government had miscalculated, and all this stuff about depreciation allowances and everything, and he still owes something, but I think he got a year's extension to pay, and what they plan to do is develop one of the cattle farms over by Deacon, because Marcus says the gay couples are going to transform Deacon and make it very upscale, and then everyone will want a place there, so the key is to wait about a year or two and then be ready to move." He leaned back in his chair. "He says gay couples always know what the next thing is going to be because they're much more attuned to issues of style than we are, and they have a network that starts in L.A. and San Fran and all the newest ideas get here faster through that network than through things like TV or newspapers, because TV and newspapers are run by old guys."

I digested this, thinking of the Davids. It made perfect sense to me, actually. I said, "Why would you tell family business to a guy you met in a bar?"

"Looks like pure instinct, doesn't it? In the first place, you don't meet very many IRS guys. They're always working for the government, and he wasn't. You have to take advantage of opportunity, and I did. Look how it worked out! I'm telling you, this guy is going to make us rich. He says the question is not about millions but billions."

"Bullshit."

"See? You're afraid to think big. We all are around here. I'm telling you, Gordon has his eye on him all the time."

"Why is that?"

"Isn't it obvious? Here's a guy who knows all the rules. He knows which ones you can break and which ones you can't. I mean, even if he doesn't say anything, you just watch him and do what he does, and there you go."

I thought of this conversation a few days later when a tall guy with an even taller shock of white hair walked into the office and said he wanted to have a look at Salt Key Farm. He handed me his card. His name was Bill Avery and his company was Avery Development, world headquarters in Asheville, North Carolina. Avery Development was one of the biggest construction companies in the country, maybe in the world. They built country club developments, with golf courses, clubhouses, and gates. I nearly registered a very uncool level of being impressed, but instead I said, "I am aware of your company, Mr. Avery. Welcome to the neighborhood." I glanced out the window. He was driving a big white Chrysler. "Let me call over there and set up an appointment."

The Thorpes were out of town, I was told, so

we could come over right now, which was fortunate, since Bill Avery wasn't saying anything and my mind was a blank. I offered him some coffee, which he turned down. He looked around the office, then looked back at me. I said, "Are you ready? Shall we take my car or yours?"

He said, "What is this, about an hour and a half from New York?"

"About that, sir."

"How come it's so undeveloped around here?"

"Well, the main line of the railroad went southeast of here in the early part of the century, and the mountains run northwest to southeast. Most people around grew up either here or in Portsmouth. I don't know if you've been to Portsmouth, sir, but some people consider it something of a blight on the landscape. You wouldn't think of it as a gateway to paradise in the normal course of events."

"I didn't go through Portsmouth. I came down through this town—what is it—Roaring Falls."

"That's a beautiful town. Shall we go? After we see the farm, I'd be happy to drive you around the area. The valley of the Blue River is wonderfully scenic, and the towns along the

Nut River are nice too. And there are some other properties available."

After we got into my car, he was more talkative. "You grow up around here?"

"Over near Portsmouth."

"What kind of business have you got here? How many Realtors in this office?"

"Just myself and my associate."

"Huh. How'd you get a listing like this farm?"

"That was kind of a fluke, Mr. Avery. It's our understanding that there is some conflict in the family. You've heard of the Thorpes, of course."

"Well, sure. They're like the Rockefellers in their way."

"Yes, they are."

For the twenty minutes it took us to get there, he looked eagerly out the window. When we passed through Deacon he looked at his watch, and then he looked at it again when we got to the farm. I said, "Salt Key Farm is actually closer to Aberdeen, but from my office it takes longer to go that way. My guess is that it's about thirteen minutes to Aberdeen from the gates of the farm."

He nodded. I pressed the gate call button, announced myself, and the gates opened before us.

We were there for hours. Bill Avery looked at

every building, inside and out, up and down. We drove down every driveway and tractor path. We walked the fence lines and climbed through the fences and took in the views from any number of angles. He picked up handfuls of soil, investigated rock outcroppings, walked along Salt Key Creek for a quarter of a mile. We started at the house and we finished back at the house, and he went through the place as carefully the second time as he did the first. He didn't say much of anything, since clearly I didn't know the property in the sort of detail that after almost four hours he did know. Finally, he looked at me as we headed to my car. It was like being questioned by a superior officer in the navy.

"How long would it take to close?"

"Well, the escrow situation is complicated, but the sellers are planning to move on the first of October."

"Have you had any offers?"

"At this price? No." Not at any price, actually. "This place is a little out of the price range of anyone around here. The fact that they are selling has been fairly big news."

"Place been perked?"

"No, but I have fairly detailed soil maps."

"Any contingencies on the sale?"

"No relatives."

"No relatives?"

"They don't want to sell it to anyone they are related to."

He laughed. "What about development?"

I licked my lips, thinking of Gordon. "I wouldn't talk about development unless they asked about it."

"If an offer were made by a developer?"

"Depends on whether that gets into the papers." This, in fact, was true. Gordon had been worried about things getting into the papers himself. "I have had some interest from the state for some sort of historical site or museum. They like that idea, but the state, of course, would prefer the property to be donated."

"Five million seems a lot for a farm that's stuck out in the middle of nowhere, nice as the property is."

"Well, I'll be honest with you, Mr. Avery, the five million is for the relatives. My guess is that the sellers settled on a price they knew none of the relatives would be willing to pay. Once the Thorpes have moved to Florida, I'm not sure what the thinking will be. I don't believe they've really come to terms with the idea that something different might happen to the farm. Mr. Thorpe must be in his eighties and his wife is about the same age. Their ability to grasp the various things that might happen to the farm doesn't strike me as all that great."

GOOD FAITH

"Gotcha," said Bill Avery. I took him back to the office by way of Aberdeen and Nut Hollow, through the Blue Valley. That took an extra forty-five minutes. I pointed out a couple of farms that I knew were on the market, but I had to admit they were smaller; one was a hundred and twelve acres and the other was two hundred and sixty acres. He didn't want to stop. By the time we got to the office, it was past dinnertime. I suggested a place in Portsmouth, we shook hands, and the big Chrysler disappeared down the road.

I went straight to Gordon's. Betty seemed thrilled to see me. She said, "Oh, Joey, we were just talking about you. Do you know the Websters? They have that wine store in the shopping village? Actually, they have liquor stores all over the place, but I love that wineshop. They both know everything about wine. Anyway"— she looked at me and put her hand on my upper arm—"I want to set you up with their daughter. She is just so pretty and alive! I'm so impressed with her. She's been living in Europe for five years, Spain, and she's been talking Spanish so long she even has a Spanish accent, can you believe that? Anyway, she was married to a Spanish young man who was very well off and upper class, but the marriage just didn't work out. No children—I think that was part of the problem;

they're Catholic over there, you know—and she said that the parents were never in favor of the marriage in the first place. Anyway, she's had a hard time meeting people, and you know everyone." She kissed me on the cheek and whispered in my ear, "And you're a good person to know anyway, if you catch my meaning."

I was all full of Bill Avery, so this idea didn't really gain my full attention. I saw Gordon behind her, heading for his office, and who knew who was inside; the driveway was full of cars, not all of them BMWs, so he could be hosting the poker game. "Of course, I would do anything you want, Betty, but you have to find out what this girl would actually like to do so I can plan something. I don't want to go it alone."

"She's very pretty and has so much to talk about, I'm sure you'll have a good time. She's just thirty."

I said, "Anything you say. I have to catch Gordon."

He was as impressed as I was by the name Bill Avery. "You know," he said, as he turned on the light, "I saw one of those Avery developments down in Texas, outside of Dallas, when we went down for that football game last fall. The golf course and about a third of the homes were finished, and they were nice, let me tell you, with a lot of brick and extra woodwork, the way they like it in the South—you know, you don't have one arched door when you can have two—the sort of thing you can do with cheap labor. No basements, of course. And all the financing was out of North Carolina, even though the place was in Texas. You don't think there's going to be all that money in North Carolina, but I guess so. Anyway, what did he have to say?"

"Well, we walked around the farm for almost four hours. He was a fast walker, too. I think we looked at everything, but the fact was, he didn't say much. We went through the house twice, from top to bottom. He knew what he was doing, I'll say that."

Gordon stared at me for a moment and then said, "Hold on." He went out of the room and returned with Marcus Burns. I told him what I had told Gordon. He lit up.

"Oh, man! Oh, man! I'm telling you, that place is a gold mine! You know, I've got this buddy back on Long Island, he builds furniture. He's been doing it for a hobby for a long time, supporting himself by building cabinetry in new construction. I mean, we're talking museum-quality tables and credenzas and things like that, made of all kinds of rare woods—he has this stash of rare woods, some of them forty–fifty years old, that's worth maybe a million bucks at this point. Anyway, he said to me six months ago when he got a commission for a fourteen-thousand-dollar table, 'You wait. I can barely afford to build this table for fourteen thousand dollars right now, but in a year, when I build it again for someone else, it's going to be a forty-thousand-dollar table. And then I'll bring out the really *good* woods!' That's what this farm is going to be like. We're shaking in our shoes about two point five million, and this guy Avery is wondering if it's worth five, but in twenty years it'll be worth forty, and there'll be a buyer, too."

Gordon looked at me.

"You know," exclaimed Marcus, "my mom was right off the boat from Galway, and she always talked about signs and wonders! Here's Bill Avery, just driving along, and he drives right into our lives, maybe the biggest developer in the world. You've got to call that a wonder, and therefore a sign. You said he didn't want to look at anything else?"

"Didn't even want to stop; I don't think he more than glanced out the window at anything."

"He's not thinking the way we do," said Marcus. "I guarantee you, Salt Key Farm is the only place in this area he can even *see*."

"I don't think we can lose on the Salt Key Farm deal," said Gordon. "How long's it been since we did the purchase agreement?"

"It runs out at the end of August," I said. "You've got to come up with a quarter million."

"I think we need get to Jim Crosbie and nail down the financing this week," said Marcus. Jim Crosbie was the new president of Portsmouth Savings and Loan. Once again, Marcus Burns had the jump on me. I was impressed.

"This is good. This is good," said Gordon. His voice was low. It was our secret. Gordon slapped me on the back as we went into the family room. I was happy and excited. That was a good thing, because the dark-haired woman standing by the window overlooking the back-yard was Felicity. She was pushing her hair out of her face and laughing. She put her drink to her lips and then lowered it suddenly and turned to look at me. She said, very naturally, "Oh, Joey! You must have sneaked around by the back! I didn't realize you were here. Hello, Marcus. Is Linda here too?"

Marcus shook his head. "Justin is sick. He's been sick all day, throwing up. I just came over to see Gordon for a moment. You know what he said? I was giving him some soup, you know, where he was lying on the couch in the family room, and he looked at me and said, 'Daddy, I am so sick, I don't know right from wrong.'"

We laughed.

"How are you, Joey?" said Felicity.

"Busy," I said.

"Are you and Daddy having some secret doings? I saw you sneak through, didn't I?"

Betty came over, handed me a beer, and pinched my cheek. She said, "Do you know Susan Webster, Felicity? Her parents have the wine store? What is she, about Fernie's age, or between Fernie and Bobby, maybe a year behind Bobby?"

"A blonde? She went off to France or somewhere years ago."

"It was Spain. Well, she's back. I thought Joey would be the perfect person to fix her up with. She's very sweet. She was with her parents the other night when we saw them at Mercados."

"Mom, she's like twenty."

"Not anymore. She's thirty. Joey's what, forty? At his age, thirty is just right."

Felicity put her arm around me in a sisterly way. She said, "I think Joey's better off single. Look what happened the last time he tried to get married."

Betty said, "Oh, Felicity, for goodness' sake."

Felicity pinched me hard right above the waistband of my slacks, but I knew I was not supposed to react. I continued to smile. I felt enveloped by the familiarity of her scent. Her dark hair was almost but not quite in my face. I seemed to want to bury my nose and mouth in it, whether or not this was a wise idea. She said, "Well, clearly Joey can't be trusted to choose on his own, because most second marriages end up with kids, and then—"

"We'll choose for him," said Betty. "Actually, you know, Jewish people have female match-makers. What are they called, yentas? You know why? Because men have no idea what makes a good wife. But women are never fooled by other women."

"That's right," said Felicity. "But that doesn't mean you and I will necessarily agree on every prospect."

Betty was giving me sidelong glances. "We'll take her out to lunch, sweetie, you and I. Okay?" She laughed as she walked away.

Felicity removed her arm and backed away a step. I knew it was necessary. I had a tremendous urge to pull her back, which I dealt with by putting my hands in my pockets. I said, "Max Raymond—you know, he closed on that house on Burley Road?" Max Raymond was the friend of the Davids.

Felicity nodded. "I heard that. I drove past that house the other day." She was better at this than I was and seemed her natural self.

Marcus Burns, who had moved off, came back. He said, "You had this virus, Joe? Amanda had it last week, and Linda had a touch of it too."

I shook my head. Felicity said, "Hank was feeling a little under the weather this evening, but I didn't realize anything was going around."

She glanced at me, and Marcus Burns glanced at me. I realized I was standing like a post, a little glazed over by awkwardness. Finally, I said, "Bobby told me you sat in on the famous poker game."

"Oh, yeah." He grinned. "Twice now. I think the guys think I have some in with the cards, because they've run in my direction both times. I don't think I'm going to be invited back."

"I heard that," said Felicity. "I heard they put your picture up and then hung a cross in front of it and drove a silver stake into your heart."

"You know, when I was in the army, I got into a poker game with some officers and won a lot of their money, so they had to promote me to sergeant to try and win it back, because army regulations said officers couldn't play with enlisted men."

"When were you in the army?" I said.

"Right after high school. 'Sixty-five."

"Vietnam?"

"Yes, but I wasn't up near the front. I basically

was in charge of office supplies in Khe Sanh. My job was to get rid of all the letterhead that listed one guy in command when the next guy came along. You wouldn't believe how much paper I burned. Every commanding officer had to have a full supply of letterhead. Some of those guys weren't around for more than a month but they hated it, just hated it, if any orders or whatever went out under the previous guy's name, because you know in the army, the guy before you is cursed, I mean, even if he didn't die or anything, even if he just got transferred to a new command, whatever happened to him could happen to you if you weren't careful, so boxes and boxes of this cursed paper, out it went."

We fell silent, turning our beers in our hands. Maybe I was the only one who felt awkward, though, because Felicity glanced around in a languorous way and said, "Really, you know, my father and mother are very strange. Sometimes I think this house is like a circle of enchantment, and if I lived outside the circle I would see everything very differently." She turned to Marcus. "You want to know a secret?"

"Always," said Marcus.

"Joey is the real son. He's the *elected* son. My brother Norton, I don't think you've met him, he's got a terrible chip on his shoulder. He's got a list of grievances as long as your arm, starting with birth order and running all the way through the color of the free car he got this Christmas. His was black and he wanted blue. He used to punch my sisters and me in the stomach and actually try to hurt us. We all agreed he should have been, as my sister Sally used to say, drowned at birth. And Bobby is simply an idiot. He's a lovable idiot, but an idiot nonetheless. I personally don't know how someone like Daddy could get together with someone like our mother and produce two out of two bad males." Her eyes were sparkling, looking for Marcus Burns's reaction. "Joey, on the other hand, has no faults. He's smart. He's kind. He's careful but not stuffy. He has wonderful manners, and, of course, he's very good-looking." She grinned at me.

I said, "Norton has many positive qualities."

"Thank God he has them two and a half hours away."

"Do you think she's kidding?" I asked Marcus.

"I'm not sure."

"She is."

"I'm not." She put her arm around me again and gave me a squeeze. I squeezed her back.

"I'm off," she said. "Got to get to the grocery store before it closes." She made a kissing face toward me, crossed the room to the kitchen, and disappeared. Marcus and I stood there for a moment. Then he said, "So. What about Norton?"

"It's true that Norton wasn't very nice to the girls when everyone was growing up."

Marcus continued to look at me.

"He and Gordon don't seem to get along very well. I wouldn't say that Norton is a—uh, confidant of Gordon's. To be honest, he doesn't come around much."

He waited.

I said, "In my experience, Norton has a very hard time being patient. I would say that he is a little too ready to correct Gordon."

"I can't imagine Gordon would like that."

"He doesn't."

Marcus took a sip of his beer. Finally he said, "Well, I can't say I've gotten along with my dad all that well over the years. Of course, he's gone now, but I haven't used him as my model in trying to raise Justin."

I rocked back on my heels. I said, "When I was a teenager, my mother always used to say, 'If it wasn't for mothers, there'd be no fathers and sons at all.'"

"What does that mean?"

"Well, when she used to say it, I would think, What in the world is she talking about? but as I get older and look around more, I understand what she was getting at. But my father and I get along okay now. We agree to disagree."

"The subject of the agreement to disagree?"

"Oh. Religion."

He nodded. I nodded. We fell silent. Religion, in my experience, always brought conversation to a dead halt. On the other hand, I was quite sure, even though Marcus struck me as an observant person, that Felicity and I had escaped detection.

CHAPTER 8

EARLY IN AUGUST I got a call from George Sloan. It was about eleven in the morning, and I was doing some paperwork. Bobby had a client from somewhere between Pittsburgh and Denver—Chicago, maybe—who was looking at every house between $75,000 and $100,000 in Portsmouth and west to Conway, which was almost out of our area, so he had been busy for three days already. I had therefore seen Felicity twice and expected to see her again before the client left that evening. I picked up the phone. Sloan said, "That house still on the market?"

"Which one?" We had seen three houses in the last week, one of which I thought was a good buy for them, near Deacon and in a good school district.

"The one on the hill."

"I'm sure it is."

"I want to make an offer."

"I thought Mrs. Sloan was leaning toward the house south of Deacon."

"That's a very presentable house. She likes that house."

"But—"

"But I want to make an offer on this other house first, just to see."

"Just to see what?" I knew I sounded irritated.

"If they'll accept it."

"Believe me, they'll accept it. That house is a mess. I wouldn't risk it, if I were you."

"I'd put a couple of contingencies on it."

"What?"

"Leave the appliances. Have to have a buyer for our house first. Bank has to approve the loan."

"Those are hardly what I would call contingencies. Your house is going to be an easy sale. It's well located and well maintained. I'm not sure you'll be happy if you get into that project over there on the hill."

"It's going to be fantastic when it's all done."

"Maybe, but it's not a do-it-yourselfer. Those

damaged walls and ceilings are plaster. And the roof would have to come off completely."

"We could save the tiles. They're in good shape. They could just be turned around and put back on. That would save on materials."

"I'm not sure you can get those tiles off, Mr. Sloan. The way the roofer put them on, he filled the crevices with cement. That's why the roof looks so odd. I don't even want to think about how much that sort of rebuilding would cost. You shouldn't think of it as a remodel. You should think of the house as a site and foundation only." I spoke rather emphatically.

"There's nothing like it anywhere around."

"What does Mrs. Sloan think? A project like that—"

"We disagree a little bit on what direction to go."

"Oh."

After a pause, he said, "If it worked out, I think she would go along with it." He sounded wistful. "But I guess—"

"I agree that it's an amazing place, but you know, it wasn't a family house to begin with. It doesn't have a very happy past."

"That's true." There was a long pause. Then he said, "Okay. Well, we'll get back to you about the Cannon Road house." This was the one south of Deacon.

As I was replacing the receiver on the hook, I heard him say, "Wait. Wait a second."

I put the phone back to my ear. "Is there something else?"

"Can I go look at it myself? Without you?"

"I don't see why not. I'll check with the Realtor, but I'd be surprised if she objected."

"Okay. Let me know and I'll go by and pick up the key."

"You know, I don't think even that is a good idea."

He didn't reply.

There was another long silence, after which I said, "Okay. I'll let you know."

"I'll call you." So. It was *that* way. I said, "Okay. Call me after lunch."

Next day, Gordon, Marcus, and I met at Portsmouth Savings and Loan with Jim Crosbie, the new president, and Bart MacDonald. I hadn't seen much of Bart since the day Frank Perkins was fired, so I was surprised to see his normal easygoing manner changed with Jim Crosbie. He was—well, deferential. He acted *short*. Every gesture and glance showed that he looked up to Jim Crosbie, who was not only taller and handsomer but younger, close to my age. I had been in this conference room before. It was elegant and pompous, as if the Supreme Court had just vacated, but Jim Crosbie seemed to own it completely, rosewood table, crown moldings, and all. He had come from another one of those states between Pittsburgh and Denver, but I noticed that he spoke with almost an English accent and dressed soberly. In his sober way, he was glad to see Marcus and Gordon. After we were seated, he leaned toward me intently and said, "Tell me about Avery."

I told him.

"They did this in Houston. There was a big ranch owned by the Ward family. You know them?"

I shook my head.

"They're the Texas version of the Rocke-fellers." I wondered if every rich family was a version of the Rockefellers. "Anyway, for one of these prestige developments, the buyers like to know that they're living on the *Ward* property, so they build that aspect up, make a big deal, you know, redo the main house for a clubhouse but keep the flavor of the old place. It's a good idea. No one is going to have that kind of money again, but people who have new money want to feel at home in that sort of place. Girls making their debuts and all. Lots of parties."

I nodded. He sat back and smiled. I said, "He hasn't called back."

Marcus said smoothly, "He wouldn't, right away. They would be putting together the financing somewhere else, maybe in North Carolina, maybe not. Maybe with a big insurance company. They're always looking for high-level investments."

"This is a big deal," said Gordon. He cleared his throat. "Not, you know, local."

"It ought to be local," said Jim Crosbie. "Believe me, North Carolina is as local as you can get, until they decide to roll the dice. You'd be surprised where money can come from. People think, Oh, New York, L.A., but I think, Oh, Asheville, Little Rock."

"Little Rock," repeated Marcus. There was a moment of silence. Finally Crosbie said, "You bet."

Bart hadn't said anything at this point, but now he said, "We've gone over this Salt Key Farm opportunity, and I have to say that Portsmouth Savings and Loan is very excited about the possibilities here." He glanced at Crosbie. I couldn't help staring at Bart. This was not the tune he had been singing before Crosbie came along. Maybe he had learned the Frank Perkins lesson, which was—what? Better to be sorry than safe?

Gordon nodded. "I don't think there's a similar property in this half of the state. I've never seen anything like it."

"And you've seen almost everything around here," said Bart.

"At one time or another, I suppose I have."

Bart turned to Crosbie. "You know, over the years, Gordon has probably visited every farmer in the region. He keeps his eye on the obit column, for one thing."

"I like that," said Jim. "You know, I grew up in farm country, not like this but wheat country, and if I learned one thing it was that every time the farm passes from one generation to the next, there's a crisis. No way out of it. You can't have the right number of children, and they can't be the right sex. It's a funny thing."

"Good for us," said Marcus.

Everyone laughed.

"Now," said Crosbie to Gordon, "what sort of deal do you have with Mr. Thorpe?"

"I made the offer to buy, and he accepted, but I haven't put the money up, and he hasn't been pushy about it. Frankly, it's a lot of money, and I've been a little undecided. I had some things I was worried about in the spring." He glanced at Marcus, who nodded almost imperceptibly. "But maybe it's time to close the deal. What is this, August?"

"August tenth," said Bart.

"Well, best cast everything in stone then,"

said Crosbie, "so we can proceed. Any problems with the sellers?"

I said, "The sellers haven't really had anything to say about the proceedings since we signed the purchase agreement. I have the accepted offer on file. But I think this is something of a delicate situation. Gordon thinks the sellers don't care if the property is developed, but what I really think is that the sellers haven't actually thought about development, and if they did, they would—or let's say they could—back out of the deal. That's why we haven't had the place perked yet. We were going to wait to do that until the sellers had actually removed themselves. Fortunately, they were out of town when Mr. Avery inspected the property."

Crosbie said, "This doesn't surprise me nor, I suspect, does it surprise you, Gordon, with your long experience. It isn't unusual to have to go around the long way when you have a skittish seller. How old are the Thorpes?"

"He must be at least eighty," said Gordon.

A thought rose in my mind just as Crosbie answered it. He said, "I'll be honest with you. Portsmouth Savings would hate to see a sign in front of that place that says, Financing provided by Texas First National, or whatever. Makes us look small, and for various practical reasons, as well as reasons of pride, we don't want to look small. So, Gordon, we're willing to work with you on this. I'm sure there's plenty of profit in this project for everyone here."

We all nodded.

Crosbie turned to me again. "Obviously, the person to get this deal nailed down right now is Joe."

I nodded, but I said, "Mr. Thorpe did call Gordon to begin with, and he seems to want to sell Gordon the property. I'm happy to do the paperwork, but—"

"What we don't want is for Mr. Thorpe to get into a conversation with anyone about the future of the property and have second thoughts. I noticed the *Portsmouth Herald* ran a small article on the fact that the property is on the market. I really do think—"

"I should have closed the deal right away, or at least made the down payment," said Gordon, "but there were a lot of things going on at the time, and I didn't feel I could put the funds together, so I let it be."

"The funds are no problem," said Bart. "We've got the funds. This institution is prepared to put up the purchase price of the property, as well as the amount of the interest payments for one year and the fees."

I said, "I've never heard of a deal like that."

Crosbie smiled at me. "We think the farm is

actually undervalued at the price, and if it came into our portfolio as a result of foreclosure or in some other way, it would be a nice asset."

"I can't say I've had a tremendous amount of interest from prospective buyers."

"I think its value is long-term," said Marcus.

"I couldn't agree with you more," said Crosbie. It seemed like he agreed with Marcus about everything, so I guessed Marcus had cultivated him, which was fine with me.

"But of course, we have to have an ironclad agreement with the seller, and it's time to nail that down. My idea is that Joe should go out there and speak to the Thorpes, and then we should talk again if anything seems iffy. Tell him we're getting ready for the closing on the first of October, and you want to go over the paperwork."

"I should do that anyway," I said.

"All right, then," said Marcus and Crosbie together. I noticed that Bart was grinning, Gordon was grinning.

Marcus Burns showed up at my office the next morning. When he opened the door and stepped in, I said, "Oh, say, Bobby just left. He ought to be back before lunch."

"Great," said Marcus Burns. But he came on in with a smile and looked around. He stopped in front of the bulletin board and looked at the photos of my more recent listings. After a moment he said, "Here's Gottfried Nuelle's new place."

"Yeah. It's about finished. I think he was painting the porch railings when I was over there the other day. I put up the sign."

"Two hundred seventy-five thousand."

"I told him I thought he could get it. He started screaming."

"What was he screaming?"

"He was screaming that of course he could get it, why not two eighty-five; the place was perfect, top to bottom and inside out; what kind of idiot was I going to sell it to this time?"

Marcus laughed. "Well, he does beautiful work."

"As he would be the first to point out. He used to teach carpentry at Portsmouth State. He was good. But I think they breathed a sigh of relief when he became self-supporting."

"What's his wife like?"

"Well, interesting that you would ask. She's hilarious; literally, she laughs every time Gottfried opens his mouth. Over the years, I've had several theories. One of them is that she survives by convincing herself that he's always joking. Another is that he *is* always joking. And the third is that they are both crazy."

We fell silent, eyeing each other.

He said, "I want to pay you for that fence."

"The fence?"

"The fence along the road at my house. How much was it?"

"Eight hundred and eighty-six dollars."

"I'll write you a check."

"Why?"

"Well, it's been bothering me."

"It has?"

"Yes. It has. I have a little confession to make."

"What's that?"

"I want to clear the air."

"I never like the sound of that."

"Even so, I do. Here's the thing. I thought you were very kind to pay for the fence. I knew what was in the purchase agreement, and so did my wife. And we knew Gottfried Nuelle wasn't going to pay for the fence. So we thought we'd see if you would. It was kind of a game."

I looked at him. "What kind of a game?"

Here he smiled and said, "Say, do you mind if I sit down?"

I nudged Bobby's chair with my foot, and it rolled toward him. He sat down and stretched his legs, looking for a moment at the tassels on his loafers. Then he sighed.

Finally, he said, "I'm not sure, really. It's more that you seemed so cool and self-assured and unattached. I was kind of envious, and I'm sure Linda sensed it. So that was something we could get together around. I figured you would do pretty much anything to save the deal, and you did. But afterward we felt bad. I've been meaning to come in here for weeks but I haven't had the guts. After the meeting yesterday, though, with Crosbie, I figured if we're going to work together I'd better be up front about things and start fresh." He reached into the pocket of his jacket and brought out a checkbook and a pen. He made out a check for the exact amount, ripped it out of the checkbook, and pushed it across the desk. It was a check from Portsmouth Savings and Loan. I looked at it and set a paperweight on it.

I said, "Well, now, I don't know what to say, except for I don't know what to say. Thank you."

"It really started to get to me the other night when we were talking to Felicity. She so obviously thinks highly of you, and Linda is crazy about her." He leaned back in the chair and put his hands behind his head. "I'll be frank with you. This is not the sort of place I come from, this nice countryside where things just seem to work out right and everyone is more or less happy. My dad and mom stole from each other. Dad was always rummaging in Mom's stuff for the price of a drink and Mom was always going through Dad's pants for money for the milk-man, and both of them were always saying to us kids, 'Now don't be tellin' yer ma' or 'Don't be tellin' yer da.'" He shrugged. "That's no excuse, of course." He looked me full in the face. "I'll go one embarrassing step further and observe, 'You don't seem like the sort of person who comes from that kind of background.'"

"'Be not deceived; God is not mocked: for whatsoever a man soweth, that shall he also reap.' Saint Paul to the Galatians, chapter six, verse seven, to quote my father."

"And you would reply?"

"I would mumble, 'Sure, Dad, anything you say.'"

"They live around here, don't they?"

"Over in Farmington, in the house I grew up in."

He stood up and strolled around my office, looking at plaques and pictures and windows and doors. Finally, he said, "This place has some charm. Do you own it?"

"I rent it from Gordon. He owns the whole mall. But I've been here for years. I put up the paneling myself and urethaned the floors and generally made it look falsely Colonial. I even put up the picket fence, picket by picket."

He leaned forward in his chair and split the

blind with his fingers to look out the front window.

"Bobby told me you were working for the IRS."

Marcus looked sharply at me. "What do you think about that?"

"Well, Bobby said just the other day that you're a rare bird. He can't see any disadvantages in it."

"He's an idiot. What about you?"

"I don't see any reason to hold it against you right on the face of it." I glanced involuntarily at the paperweight and the check. Marcus saw me do it but said blandly, "I started with them right out of college. So, counting my service in the army, I've been a captive of the U.S. government for fourteen years. I'm just now breathing free for the first time maybe in my life."

I chuckled. "So how did you end up working there? I mean, with that sort of attitude."

He turned and crossed his arms over his chest. His jacket was so well cut it seemed to follow the contours of his shoulders. "Sure, and that's where all the fellas in the neighborhood signed up. It was a regular Irish Mafia there."

"I didn't know that."

"It's surprising how little anyone knows about the IRS."

"Afraid to ask, you know. Afraid to look, afraid to say a word."

This time he really laughed, but he nodded too. "I'll tell you something about the IRS, but of course you'll keep this to yourself."

"Yes, of course."

"Well, you know Gordon's little problem?"

"Not in detail but in general, yes."

"The first step was to get his file transferred to my old office. The second step was to put a call in to some of the boyos there."

"Then?"

"Oh, Jaysus, lad, you can't imagine what gets lost in that office!"

We laughed together. He returned to the seat by my desk. I tried again. "But why bother? You met Bobby in a bar."

"Oh, I don't know. Why not? Do you think twelve years with the IRS made me a believer in the social benefits of the tax code? I'm going to tell you something. You know what a card counter and number cruncher I am?"

"I've heard from Bobby, yeah."

"Well, the main thing about me is that I know the tax code backwards and forwards. It wasn't like I was bad at my job. I wasn't fired. I was a government bureaucrat, and I got exactly what I signed up for after college—a lifelong job and a steady income—except after a couple of years, after the death of my mother, say, I realized that a lifelong job and a steady income and sobriety were good but not best. And I started really looking at the tax returns I was going over, and you know what? I saw other sorts of lives there, perfectly legal lives, lives where the government backed a little risk, and the risk paid off, and it wasn't that these people were just making lots of money, it was also that they were having fun. And believe you me, the way things are going in Washington, there is going to be more fun, more more more fun than anyone has ever had since God knows when, because the tax code is transforming before your very eyes, and everyone is perfectly happy to see it happen."

"Well, Gordon is perfectly happy to see it happen, since his mastery of the tax code was totally lacking."

"Chaos! The auditors could come in and make absolutely anything they wanted of his whole career. In spite of myself, I was appalled. I mean, it's not like he has two sets of books. Most businesses have that. He has *no* sets of books. He has little slips of paper, most of which have been through the wash."

"He's had accountants. After a while he just says to them, 'Oh, don't worry about it, we'll see what happens. It'll be fine.'"

"And for years it was. But I'm telling you, even organized crime doesn't run like that. Most people in the world want to know how much money they have."

"Gordon just wants to know if there's enough. The answer to that question has always been yes, at least as long as I've known him, so he doesn't go on to the next question, which is, 'How much is there?'"

"Here's another thing. This isn't an IRS thing, just an accounting thing. Accountants are in the business of making sure the books balance. That's all. You could steal a company blind, but if the books balanced, the accountant would have done his job. I knew this case in Brooklyn where a company wrote off its whole inventory as scrapped—something like fourteen million dollars' worth of heavy equipment. They even shipped it off the premises, out to Jersey somewhere. Then they bought it back. They got a tax break for the loss, and a tax break for the purchase. But the books balanced perfectly."

"Huh," I said. "So what do you think about Crosbie? That was the first time I've met him. I guess he came in from somewhere out West."

"*There's* some books I'd like to get hold of," said Marcus.

"Portsmouth Savings? They should be in

pretty good shape. Frank Perkins was very conservative."

"I talked to Crosbie, you know. I took him out to lunch a couple of times. He was perfectly willing to talk. Saw me as a kindred spirit. They're getting ready to do some other kinds of business. He told me they're putting in a big new computer system that's going to take something like a year to get running, and until then they've hired some outfit from California to computerize everything. My guess is, they want to get out of the residential lending business altogether."

"How can they?"

"Don't know if they can at this point. And even if they do, I don't see Crosbie being the one to do it. He's been in the S and L business too long, shuffling papers this way and that. When there's rules to follow and auditors looking over your shoulder all the time, that puts a premium on thinking small. How old do you think he is?"

"Bart told me thirty-seven," I said.

"So he started out as a teller when he was twenty-two, putting money in a drawer and taking it out, and he's been thinking small for fifteen years. The S and L business has hardly been high-risk."

"God forbid," I said.

Marcus laughed, a loud hearty laugh. Then he said, "Look. Why don't you stay away from

Crosbie? I'll do the talking. This is a guy who thinks he's been around, and here he finds himself out in Hicksville. I'm not saying he's out to dazzle anyone; how can he? as you say, given all the rules and regulations. But if there's a deal to be made, he wants to be the beneficiary, and he thinks he will be, because Hicksville is Hicksville, after all. But all the hicks down in Hicksville were not created equal, were they, Joe?" He winked at me, and we laughed together. As he walked out, he drew my eye to his check, sitting on the corner of my desk, and he tapped on it with his forefinger and gave me a nod.

CHAPTER
9

WHEN I GOT TO the Thorpes' the
next day, I had all my paperwork in
order and a bank draft for a quarter
million dollars in my wallet. I drove through the
big gate and down the curving driveway to the
front of the house. The whole drive was shaded
with huge spreading trees that looked like chest-
nut to me and moved slowly and heavily in the
breeze. It was warm but dim, with a few rays of
sunshine lighting up the beveled-glass windows
on either side of the double front door. As I
walked up the brick steps, the door opened, and
the butler said, "Good morning, Mr. Stratford.
The Thorpes are in the study."

Neither Jacob Thorpe nor Dolores looked
well, but he, at least, was beaming very pleasantly

at me. I shook his hand and greeted Mrs. Thorpe, who said, "H'lo." Through the bank of French doors that ran along the south side of the room, I could see pinpoint white blossoms against the green of the hedge. We sat down at the table. I felt self-conscious as I spread out the papers, all neatly marked with flags for signatures. They acknowledged that we had a good-faith deal, and that Mr. Thorpe was in receipt of a check for 10 percent of the purchase price, and that the closing would take place on October 1. Paperclipped to the receipt was the check.

I was moving very smoothly, smiling and never pausing, so as not to give anyone an entrance for hesitation. I pulled out a chair and said to Mr. Thorpe, "Sir? Would you like to have a seat?"

The butler, who had been standing in the doorway, departed. Mr. Thorpe stood up shakily and made his way to the table, not without supporting himself on the backs of first one armchair and then another as he came. Mrs. Thorpe took out a handkerchief and blew her nose. Mr. Thorpe glanced in her direction and then said to me, "Maybe I should come to your office."

I helped him to the waiting chair. I said, "There's no need to go to the trouble, sir. We can do it right here."

He sat down. I handed him the pen and slid the

receipt with the check underneath his hand. His head and neck twitched, which I didn't understand until Mrs. Thorpe said, "Jacob." His head and neck twitched again; he was stopping himself from turning toward her. She said, "Daphne Lawrence said that even though you signed the papers before, we don't have to do this." He touched the pen to the line but didn't make a mark. She continued, "We can change our minds at any time. Mr. Stratford, that's true, isn't it?"

"Of course, Mrs. Thorpe. You don't ever have to sell your house."

Thorpe's pen was still touching the line. There was a long moment of silence. Finally he said, "I don't want to go through another winter here, Dolores. I'm too old for that. Last year I couldn't even get down the front steps for two months."

"I don't either, Jacob. I'm not talking about living here."

"This place makes me feel old." His voice was a bit petulant.

She didn't say anything. Still, he didn't move the pen. I said warmly, "Tell me what your place is like in Florida. Is it in Palm Beach?" I knew it was.

"Very spacious," said Jacob Thorpe. Mrs. Thorpe didn't say anything.

"When was it built? I've seen some very elegant places in Palm Beach."

"I've lived here for fifty-seven years, Jacob," she said.

"Yes, and in New York and Florida and England. Don't pretend that we've spent fifty-seven continuous years here, because we haven't. We talked about all this."

I got a picture in my mind of the way we had sat, the day before, around the table at Portsmouth Savings, grinning and eager, and in spite of myself, I said, "Maybe you need to talk about this some more, sir."

He looked up at me and laid down the pen. He sighed. Rather shakily, he stacked together the papers and the check and handed them to me. I was a little shocked at what I had done, and I knew I didn't know what to tell Gordon and Marcus and Crosbie and Bart. I took the papers. In the first place there was having screwed up the deal, and in the second place there was my injured pride in failing at the one thing I thought I could do, which was to shepherd a deal to its close. Thorpe stood up and put his hand on my elbow. We crossed the room. I paused beside Mrs. Thorpe, thinking he would sit down with her, but he squeezed my elbow and kept on walking. We made our way out of the library and into the entry hall. He propelled me all the way to the front door without saying a word. This allowed my regrets to build, but I didn't see any way out of my situation. I couldn't very well tell him he was bound by the deal, because he wasn't, and obviously the check, which might mean something to a seller who needed to sell, was meaningless to him.

I opened the heavy front door. The butler was nowhere in sight. It was still beautiful and shady in front of the house, and my car was right there. I turned to shake his hand. He said, in almost a whisper, "I'll come to your office. I'll come to your office this afternoon at three o'clock."

I looked at my watch. It was about eleven-thirty. I said, "All right, sir. I'll be there." I went down the steps and the door closed behind me.

I did an errand or two, picked up some lunch at a deli in Deacon, and stopped for a moment at the Davids' house. Only David Pollock was there with the dogs. He had removed the back door and was cutting a wider opening, for a French door to lead out onto a large deck to be covered by a pergola. Grapes. Local variety. Huge leaves. Very shady and elegant. Didn't the kitchen floor look fabulous? I nodded and smiled appreciatively and went back to my office.

It was hot. I closed the blinds and cleared my desk several times. Bobby, in whom I did not confide, was sitting at his desk reading *Runner's*

World magazine. I said, "I thought you had an appointment in Portsmouth at three-fifteen."

"Canceled. I'm going to try—"

Just then we heard a noise I will never forget. It was a quick, loud, clicking noise, rhythmic but fast. It may have lasted a couple of seconds or less, but it was so strange that we stared at each other and listened attentively. I said, "What in the world is that?"

Bobby set down his magazine.

There was a crashing *thunk* right outside. We both jumped up and ran to the window. I pulled up the blinds. A large black car—an older-model Lincoln, it looked like, black, with an oval-shaped chrome grille—had come to rest against the lamppost next to the sidewalk leading past my building to the rest of the stores in the strip mall. The front of the car had run along the picket fence I had built, popping the pickets off; that was the rapid ticking sound we heard. Pickets lay around on the grass, and the top stringer of the fence was broken in two. The amazing thing was the bottom stringer, a sixteen-foot two-by-four (I knew its dimensions because I had bought it myself), which had inserted itself like a skewer through the grille. Inside the vehicle, unmoving, was Jacob Thorpe. Bobby and I ran to the door of the office, and in a second we had the door of Thorpe's car open. The first thing I noticed was that the stringer of the fence had continued through the firewall and up into the cabin of the vehicle. It had missed Jacob Thorpe's head by three or four inches and poked a dent in the ceiling of the car just to the right of the interior light. The second thing I noticed was Thorpe's heavy breathing. He was alive, untouched, eyes wide, his hands still on the wheel. I said, "Mr. Thorpe?"

"Yes?"

"Are you all right, sir?"

"I believe so."

"Would you like to get out of the car, sir?"

"Not just at the moment, thank you."

I reached in, turned off the ignition, and sent Bobby in to call the police.

I took a step back from the car and surveyed the scene. Thorpe would have been coming from the northeast and probably had attempted a right turn into the parking lot on that side of the building, but possibly he didn't recognize the driveway quickly enough. At any rate, he had crossed about ten feet of grass and hit a large bush, then veered off to the right and gone straight down the pickets to the fence post, the lamppost, and another large bush, which by that time were sufficient to stop him. Everything was quiet for the moment. Cars passed; faces turned our way and stared. I didn't think Thorpe was in any danger because the back of the car was fine;

there were no fumes of any kind. I didn't want to take the responsibility for moving him. Bobby came out. I shouted, "Go back in and call an ambulance!" He went back in.

Thorpe said, "Oh, my. Do you think it's that bad?"

"That's for you to say, sir."

"Would you call my wife?"

"Is she at home?"

"Yes. 398–1836."

"You sound pretty good, sir."

"I have been startled, that is all." He turned his head and looked at the length of white wood right beside it. He said, "I suspect I have escaped serious injury by a very small margin."

"That's the way it looks, sir."

We heard sirens in the distance. Mr. Thorpe said, "Perhaps you could help me out of the car. I would like to enter your office and clean up, if possible."

"I would prefer it if you would stay where you are until the ambulance gets here, Mr. Thorpe. You never can tell." He nodded. After that, we became the passive objects of several operations. Two policemen, professionally unimpressed, went about taking down information for their report. The ambulance attendants arrived and got Thorpe out of the car and laid him on the grass, where they examined him briefly before putting him in the ambulance and taking him away, though without haste. The only thing wrong with him was that he had wet the front of his trousers in a large circle, which we all, including Thorpe, studiously avoided noticing. After the ambulance left, there was a lull, during which I called the number he gave me and spoke to the butler, and then the flatbed tow truck arrived, and the elderly car was hoisted up, still skewered by the fence stringer, and carried away.

After that, traffic picked up out on the street, as there was nothing more to see. It was about five. I reflected as I walked around the scene that I had expected to have a done deal by this time, the check safely transferred, the property one step closer to Gordon's possession. The scene of the accident was a mess: two bushes broken, grass torn up, fence posts smashed, and pickets scattered, not only on the ground around where the car had been but up against the building, out in the street, in the parking lot of the strip mall, even across the road. He must have been going pretty fast, because they had shot off like rockets and landed all over the place.

Bobby kept saying, "Wow, man! Did you see how the two-by-four went through there? He must have been scared shitless. Have you ever seen anything like that? Doesn't he have a chauffeur or something? I mean, wow!" He enthusiastically told the story to the police, the ambulance people, and the tow-truck people. When I was looking around afterward, I could see him inside on the phone, slapping his head emphatically. I suppose he was glad to have an amazing tale of misadventure that didn't involve himself.

Gordon called me about eight-thirty at my condo. He said, "How *is* the old guy?"

"Well, I called the hospital. They didn't keep him, so he must be okay."

"What was he doing over at your place? He signed the papers, didn't he? I thought you were going out there."

"I did go out there, but the wife was having cold feet. He was trying to get to me to sign the papers in my office when he ran into the fence."

"He hasn't signed the papers? You didn't get him to take that check?"

"Nope."

"I'm telling you, Joe, he's going to look at this as a bad omen. I can't count how many times I've had deals fall through because something went wrong, something completely outside the deal itself, but which the seller or the buyer saw as a sign and backed off."

"I know."

Marcus Burns called at nine. He said, "The

good thing is that you've got the signed purchase agreement from four months ago."

I said, "The bad news is that it's about to
expire."

"Monday."

"Monday."

"Gordon says there's trouble with the wife."

"She's backing off. My guess is that the problem at the beginning was between the father
and the kids, and she isn't so adamant."

"Or she understands the development possibilities better."

"Or that." One thing I liked about Marcus was
that he wasn't afraid to name the real problem.
Gordon, for example, was superstitious and
thought straightforward mention of a difficulty
evoked it and gave it substance. No doubt that
was why his "books" were in such chaos.

"I think you need to get out there tomorrow
or over the weekend."

"He didn't seem injured, just shook up. I can
call tomorrow afternoon and try to see him."

"You need to call anyway, to follow up on
the accident."

"I do."

"I wouldn't make an insurance claim for the
damage at this point."

"I hadn't even thought about that yet.
Gordon has insurance for the whole mall, any-

way. Usually we submit the claim, do the work ourselves, and Gordon pockets the difference."

"Thorpe needs to know you've been concerned about him."

"Sure. And I have. I mean, it was quite an accident. I can't get the image out of my mind of that two-by-four right up by his ear. If he'd bounced the wrong way, it would have smashed him in the head."

"Jeez."

"As far as I could see, he was untouched. Not even bruised. Thank God he was wearing his seat belt."

"Shit, yeah. Well, today is Thursday. The way I see it, we've got four days. We don't want to screw it up."

I said, "No, we don't."

I knew when I hung up that what he really meant was, We don't want *you* to screw it up.

Shortly before nine-thirty, the phone rang again. This time it was Crosbie. He was much sharper. He said, "I see we've got a small window here."

"Well, that's true."

"We talked about this Tuesday." I noticed that his posh accent had disappeared.

"Some of the complications were unforeseen. I had no idea that the wife—"

"Now that's something you should have

thought of, in my opinion. Everyone knows that not all parties to a deal are equally enthusiastic. I would have thought, with your experience, you would have foreseen that."

"I should have, I suppose." I tried to sound both relaxed and enthusiastic, as if I weren't getting a dressing-down.

"The rest of us of necessity work in the background. You, Mr. Stratford, are the interface with the public and with clients. I heard you had superior people skills."

"I think I—"

"But you have to use them when they count. Getting some guy and his wife to buy a bunga-low isn't the same as this sort of thing. Gordon, of course, has his loyalties, and well he should. He's done business in this community for forty years and those connections are vital, but at the same time, local is local and national is national. I want to feel that I can confidently play on a national stage and that the people around me are up to it. You know what I mean?" I noticed that his accent had returned.

"I do."

He hung up.

About five minutes later, the phone rang again. It was Bart. All he said was, "He wasn't threatening you, Joe. That wasn't a threat. It was just general principles."

I said, "Well, Bart, no one will be sorrier than I will be if I fuck this one up."

"Good," said Bart.

The next day, I sat around the office, looking out the window at the mess in the front yard, a mess even though I had picked up all the pickets and pulled out the posts and cut back the bushes and raked up all the debris, and I worried all day about whether it was too early to call the Salt Key Farm and inquire after Jacob. The problem was the butler. He would certainly answer the phone, and he was fully capable of answering my question as to Mr. Thorpe's state of mind and health. But if I asked him and he answered, how would Thorpe know I was concerned? How would I make the necessary connection? And then, of course, as the morning wore on, I began to worry that I was waiting too long. I thought of Thorpe sitting in his library, and it seemed to me that he was meditating on the fact that he had come all the way to my office, and been perhaps not hurt but certainly terrified, and all he got from me was indifference. Soon enough it was noon, and I still hadn't called. Every time I picked up the phone, the butler dilemma rose up in my mind and paralyzed me. I went out for some lunch, thinking I would be able to make a decision afterward. It was like the world had suspended itself, waiting for me to make up my mind and pass this test.

I got a ham-and-cheese hoagie and a Coke. Rather than go right back to the office, it seemed plausible, and even desirable, that I take a little walk, though the only place to walk was down the façade of the strip mall, which contained, in addition to the sandwich shop, a dry cleaners, a Kroger's, a frame shop, a fabric store, and a record store. I walked to the end of the supermarket and back, eating my sandwich and then rolling up the wrapper and carefully throwing it away, along with the Coke can. On the way back to my office, where I now went with resolution and a certain amount of fake speed, I let myself look in passing at the display of the afternoon paper that had just come out—the early edition, containing the weekend activities section. I thought how nice it would be to go down to the shore rather than stay here and deal with Gordon and Thorpe and everyone, and for a moment I was entirely unsurprised that Thorpe's name should appear on the front page of the paper. Then I looked again.

The headline read LOCAL LEADER SUCCUMBS: JACOB THORPE DEAD AT 79.

I took the paper off the stand. The article entered my brain right there and installed itself, word by word, permanently:

Attorney Jacob Thorpe, one of the most so-
cially prominent figures of the last fifty years in
this region, succumbed to heart failure in the
early morning hours Friday. Thorpe, who was
involved in a one-car accident Thursday afternoon, had been treated and released from
Portsmouth–St. Mary's Hospital early in the
evening and had returned to his home at Salt
Key Farm near Roaring Falls. As a hospital
spokesman confirmed, "Mr. Thorpe showed no
injuries from the accident. All tests were negative, and he was in good spirits at the time of release. He never lost consciousness at any time,
and his vital signs were normal for a man of his
age."

According to his wife, Dolores Thorpe, née
Allen (of Camden, South Carolina), Thorpe
ate a normal supper with her, watched some
television, and went to bed about a hour earlier than usual. He awakened in distress sometime after three in the morning. He was taken
back to the hospital, but doctors were unable
to revive him.

There was more, but no mention of me or my
office. His two children were listed, and his
clubs and other memberships, his family connections, the locations of his five homes (here,
Palm Beach, Manhattan, London, and the south

of France), followed by a brief history of the Thorpe millions.

I carried the paper back to my office and sat down at my desk and read it again. Then I opened a file drawer and took out the original signed purchase agreement and looked at it. I wondered if Gordon, Marcus, and Crosbie were going to go for the idea that it just wasn't meant to be, or whether they were going to get stuck on the idea that I had screwed up. I felt intensely guilty for agreeing with Mrs. Thorpe out loud that they could back out of the contract at any time. Of course they could, but I might have just kept my mouth shut. The fact was that even had they taken the money and signed the papers, she could still back out of it. Every real estate deal includes incentives to go through with it, but they are only incentives. I once had some buyers who were so indecisive that they gave up their down payment four times before actually getting to a closing. The house they eventually bought was the house they had reneged on the first time. They had to pay several thousand dollars more for it the second time, but at any rate they were happy at last and never looked back.

The phone rang. I looked at it while it was ringing, and counted the rings—eight. I was certain it was one of my three partners, if not all of them together. I set the paper down on the desk and left the office, turning the CLOSED sign out and locking the door. I got in my car and drove to Deacon.

The Davids were home. The Toronado was sitting in the shaded driveway, and the two dogs were sleeping on top of it, the terrier on the roof and the white dog on the hood. They lifted their heads and barked when I pulled in. I got out of the car and could immediately hear hammering from the other end of the property. I walked around the big car, past the flower bed, and toward the back of the house.

It was invigorating to see what they had accomplished in such a short time, especially since they only worked about two and a half days per week. The aluminum siding had vanished, and the cracks and breaks in the original siding had been filled and repaired. The kitchen was more or less finished; it was now a large airy room that looked less like a kitchen than a pleasant space where some cooking could easily be done. A deck with trellising on both sides and a pergola across maybe half of the top extended from the kitchen door. When I stepped up onto it, I could see them at work—only their backs—both were kneeling down, and the hammer blows were quick, expert, and purposeful. I shouted, "Hey! Hey, guys!" Silence. They stood up.

Their welcome was instant. Only then did I feel uncomfortable. I didn't have Felicity with me, and I had no reason for being here except for the fact that *here* was exactly the place no one would look for me. There was, of course, something I should be doing, but I hadn't the least idea of what it was.

"Look at this!" shouted David John. "The night before last, we looked at each other and said, 'screened-in porch!' and so we came down a day early and here we are, right off the living room. It just flows, yet from the street you can hardly see it. Twelve by twelve, so tiny, just a jewel." They had opened up an anteroom or closet of some sort off the living room and annexed an old pantry off the kitchen. Already they had walls taken down and openings cut for windows. David Pollock said, "We've measured for the screens and ordered them. They should be ready by next Friday. It's been slow, but things are shaping up at last."

"What's been slow?"

"This remodeling. Come in, the beers are in the refrigerator."

It was calming to watch them. They made big gestures and a lot of noise. They were not careful, as I would have been, but neither were they careless. They were making too much noise for conversation, and without Felicity there was no need for them to entertain. It was something like sitting around the frat house back in college. The afternoon progressed and declined, and I began to feel that it was okay, actually—the end of Salt Key Farm. It was more or less like having agreed to eat five pounds of roast turkey at one sitting, but then thinking better of it and pushing back from the table. This was what I really liked, selling old houses to decent people, people like the Davids or the Sloans, and then watching as individual lives developed in those houses. The truth of the matter was that Salt Key Farm had never been about that and would never be about that. Salt Key Farm was about some kind of stratosphere— people I didn't know and couldn't quite imagine living in a way that no one else around here lived. Maybe it was good or maybe it was bad or maybe it was the wave of the future, but I wasn't really interested.

The noise stopped. David Pollock said, "Was that the phone?"

The phone rang again. He went into the kitchen. David John said, "Would that be the happy Miss Felicity, the Felicitous Madame Happiness?"

"Only if she's calling from Virginia. They took one of the boys to college this weekend. I guess he's got some kind of job preparing the campus for the actual start date."

"And how are we?"

"We're fine. She came by Monday, I think it was. She—"

The other David came in from the kitchen and said, "It's for you."

He didn't say it was Felicity, but I went to the phone surprised but expecting that it was, so I was perplexed to hear a male voice on the other end of the line, laughing. He said, "How do you like that? I smoked you out! At last I've discovered what working at the IRS is good for."

"Marcus?"

"Marcus Burns, private investigator!" He laughed again.

"How did you find me?"

"You're asking me to reveal my methods? I don't think so, buddy. So. Meet me at Maxie's Diner in Deacon. Five minutes."

I hung up the phone.

In the dimming twilight on the new porch, the Davids were setting up lights. David John said, "You don't want dinner, do you? We ate a late lunch just before you got here, but we were going to go out for something around nine."

"No. Actually, I have a meeting right now." But I lingered for a few moments, trying not to go. Confession wasn't entirely my cup of tea.

Maxie's Diner had been recently refurbished. Always a traditional diner, now it was a traditional diner *trying* to be a traditional diner—everything was shiny and polished all over again, and the standard dishes Maxie's had always served were now displayed more self-consciously on the menu. Gordon had told me that Maxie's son Dean had gone to California, learned that his father's sort of diner was all the rage out there, and come home in the hope of franchising it.

Marcus was sitting at a table, his profile visible in the window. He looked out and saw me as soon as I drove into the parking lot. He waved, then signaled the waitress. He met me at the door, grinning. He exclaimed, "Man, I nearly shit when I saw the paper this afternoon! I said to Gordon, 'Gordon, you'd better sit down because otherwise you're going to keel over!'" He shepherded me to the table. We sat down across from one another.

"I couldn't believe it myself," I said.

He waved his hand. "Oh, I could. I mean, you can have that kind of life. I grew up with that kind of life, where just as you've got whatever it is you really want, it's snatched from your grasp. My dad and his brothers thought that was a fun way to tease the kids—you held something just out of their reach, like an apple or something, and got them to jump for it, and then when they snatched it, you grabbed it back and took a big bite out of it. Oh, how they laughed! If one of us kids cried, he'd get a smack on the head and the uncle would just laugh harder and take another bite. The only way the kid could get it was by walking away and pretending to be indifferent. Then the uncle, or Da, would toss it to you. Of course, you didn't want it by then. However, I don't have that kind of life anymore." He was scowling, but now he smiled.

"It's out of our hands as far as I can see."

"You've got a signed purchase agreement."

"It expires Monday. I guarantee you there's six lawyers hanging around already."

"So what? You weren't going to do anything illegal or unethical, were you?" He grinned.

"Of course not—"

"Why not? No, seriously. No, I'm excited. The lawyers don't make any difference. You know why?"

"Why?"

"Because we don't care."

"We don't?"

"*We* don't. You and I don't. Gordon does, Crosbie does, Bart does, but you and I don't. This is just a deal. Big deal, little deal, all deals are the same size. You know, my kid is a fan. He loves the Mets and he loves the Giants. He's always on this tremendous roller coaster. He always wants to know what some win or loss meant, why it happened, how it predicts the future. Every game has a size. If it's not an important game, then he can breathe a sigh of relief, but if it *is* an important game, he worries about it for days. Myself, I've never been interested in sports, so I say, 'Justin, there's no such thing as a big game.' He says, 'Okay, Dad; I understand, Dad,' but he doesn't."

"And so there's no such thing as a big deal?"

"Nah. One deal leads to another. Which doesn't mean you aren't going to go out there Monday and talk to the woman and try to get her to sign. I mean, really put your heart into it, really look her in the eye and *will* her to close that deal and walk away from that farm, but if she doesn't, then you are going to whistle as you go out to your car, because it doesn't matter."

My chest swelled with a deep comfortable breath that felt like the first really good breath I'd taken since Tuesday. And then another.

He leaned toward me. "You don't really care, do you?"

"Well, I don't know. This afternoon I was thinking—"

"Don't tell me. It doesn't matter why. Don't define why, because your definition is wrong.

You've got the feeling; whatever you think is the source of the feeling is just an interpretation. What's important is that you don't care. You can make that deal or not and walk out of there happy either way. Not *more* happy one way or the other, just happy either way."

"I never thought about it like that."

"All those buyers and sellers you've had over the years, did you ever really care whether they got any particular house?"

"Well, no. *They* cared—"

"Sure, but half the time you thought they were crazy, right?"

"At least."

"See, we're going to work together perfectly. I'm telling you, if you have the right attitude, you can make any deal work, because the thing that makes it work just comes to you, just floats into your mind, and you know it's going to work and you open your mouth and it floats out and it does work, but it doesn't surprise you at all. You think to yourself, I knew that."

"Well, yeah," I said.

"That's how it's going to be with the Thorpe woman. I know it. Now you just do something fun between now and Monday, and it'll all work out."

He slapped the table suddenly and firmly, and I felt revved up. I nodded.

Marcus looked at his watch. He said, "Okay. Got to get home. The kids are cooking hot dogs on the grill for the parents, and otherwise serving us dinner, and Linda says they expect a big tip. And because people don't live at the restaurant, they're sleeping outside tonight in a tent." He smiled happily, as if family life was the most fun life of all, and I wondered right there if maybe it was.

I went down to the shore late that evening and came home Sunday night. I spent the interim with a girl named Iris, from Delaware, who had several things to offer, none of them lasting but all of them pleasant. When I got home late Sunday night I went straight to bed, and when I got up Monday morning, I picked up my phone and called the Thorpe residence. I told the butler I would be there at ten-thirty to bring my condolences to Mrs. Thorpe and to complete our business. He said that would be fine.

There were four cars parked by the door. I parked next to them, walked up the steps, and knocked. I looked good, tan slacks and a white shirt. It was rather cool, so I had put on a jacket. The butler smiled and seemed nice when he opened the door. He showed me once again into the library. After a minute or two, Mrs. Thorpe came in. She was wearing a black dress and looked exhausted. She was immediately followed by two men and three women. She said to them, "This is that man, Mr. Dartford, who was hounding Jacob."

I kept smiling. I felt good.

She said to me, "Mr. Dartford, these are some people who are helping me. This is my sister, Mrs. Lambert. This is one of the lawyers. His name is Calvin Visser." She sighed.

I shook Visser's hand; I didn't recognize him. I guessed he was from out of town, New York, maybe. He said, "How can Mrs. Thorpe help you? You know we are getting ready for Mr. Thorpe's memorial service." He looked stern. "This is a very inappropriate—"

I kept smiling. It wasn't hard; I knew above all things just how inappropriate it was. I pressed ahead. "This shouldn't take more than a moment. As the purchase agreement expires today and the buyers are extremely eager, I felt I simply had to come out here and speak to Mrs. Thorpe about it for just a moment. Mr. Thorpe—"

"Was it your office where Jacob hit that wall?" asked Visser.

"Well, sir, he didn't hit a wall, as far as I know. He hit a picket fence, but yes, that's where he had the accident on Thursday. I was extremely sorry he had to endure that." I was looking right at Visser, but I could see the others out of the corner of my eye, staring at me. I said, "I was with Mr. Thorpe for at least an hour before he was taken to the hospital. He was lucid the whole time. Very alert." Why hadn't I, I thought, had him sign the papers then? There was a long silence. I kept smiling, but not insensitively—just a pleasant, neutral smile.

Visser said, "Dolores? What about selling this property? You don't have to."

I said, "No, Mrs. Thorpe, you don't. I was clear with you about that when I was here on Thursday, and now more than ever the choice is yours."

"Do you know," she said, "we had the most wonderful fox hunts across this property. Our huntsman, Rodney Lawton, was from England. He was from Leicestershire. I rode sidesaddle, just the way they do there. Rodney built the most beautiful fences, all brush, very forgiving. And then we would come in for breakfast. I enjoyed that very much. That was the best part of my life. I rode even when I was pregnant, the way they do in England; you know they are very bold there. Sometimes we hunted four days a week."

I said, "I've seen the hounds' kennels, Mrs. Thorpe. They're very nicely done."

"Of course, we'll never do that again. Jacob sold all the horses this summer, or sent them to Kentucky. He sent the racehorses to Kentucky."

I exchanged a glance with Mr. Visser. One of the visitors was staring at the books on the shelves. Mrs. Thorpe's sister was staring at Mrs. Thorpe. I said, "I'm sure you have wonderful memories of this place, ma'am."

She looked at me for a moment. Then she smiled and said, "Not really." It was an interesting moment. I had been thinking of her as an old lady, someone to be humored and cajoled, but maybe not.

The sister said, in a distinct Texas accent, "My land, Dolores, get rid of the place. This is a white elephant. Buyers for white elephants don't come along every day."

She glanced at me, amused, and I said, "That's true too, Mrs. Thorpe. At least as a general sort of rule." Everyone, including Visser, smiled or gave a little heh-heh sort of chuckle. The sister spoke up again. She said, "It's right out of *Citizen Kane*, Dolores. You know, at the end when they're throwing all his junk on the fire, all his collections and everything? Darlin', you're better off walking away from it, I'm telling you."

Visser said, "I don't think you should do anything too hastily, Dolores. A little caution is in order."

"Oh, for God's sake, Calvin," said the sister.

Mrs. Thorpe looked from one to the other, then at me. I said, "Personally, I am a cautious person, Mrs. Thorpe."

She sighed once and then brightened, as if out of long habit, and then said, "Do you have the papers with you?"

"I do."

"And the check?"

"I do, but the check would go into my firm's account, to be distributed to you at closing, which would take place, if you want to stick with the original plan, in about seven weeks."

"Marjorie is right. I think so. I feel better already. There are so many details now."

I took the papers out of my briefcase.

THE FIRST SET of townhouses in Phase Four approached completion, and for a while the three couples who had signed up at the lower prices were the only buyers. But I didn't think about it. I continued to advertise, emphasizing now one detail (brick walks and steps), now another (beautiful windows, blooming gardens), and suddenly, just before the first three couples were about to move in, I had all sorts of interest. I was over there every day or so, showing units. It didn't hurt that the Rebarcaks, the DiGenovas, and the Monahans were seen to move in—modest but pleasant-looking families, good neighbors, smiling. Of course, new potential buyers had no idea that the Rebarcaks and the DiGenovas and the Monahans had made the deals of a lifetime. I got offers and down payments on four other units in the space of three days, and Gordon came out two days later to see how things were shaping up. He buttonholed me the moment he stepped out of his car. He looked ebullient but smooth, his plentiful hair slicked back in a way my father would have found very suspicious. I was glad to see him.

"Look at this," he said. "It looks great. What a difference! It could've looked like 1949, but it looks like 1989!" We had changed the flowers in the beds; now it was marigolds and nasturtiums. The big trees over in Phase One were beginning to turn, too.

"It's luxurious, that's for sure," I said.

"People have a taste for that. You know what?"

"What?"

"People don't know their place anymore. That used to be a virtue, you know, knowing your place. That's why I never thought I fit in around here. I didn't know my place, and in fact, I'll tell you, Betty and I sometimes wondered what our place was, until I found a few guys like myself—you know, with some bad habits." He poked my arm and laughed.

I said, "Betty doesn't have any bad habits."

"She's got me, doesn't she? If she still had the

social pretensions she'd been born to, that would be bad habit enough, but lucky for me, social pretension ain't in her. One time when the girls were little, some woman asked her over to the country club—you know, over there in Blue Haven—and all those women made up to her that day: oh, she was new in town and weren't those girls so pretty, and why was Felicity's hair so dark when the others were blond—they were towheaded then. Anyway, you can't resist Betty, and they were all after her to join the country club, and then I guess they went home and discovered who Gordon Baldwin was from their husbands, and that was the end of that; so we dug the pond out back and put up the rope swing and all, and the kids had much more fun every summer than they ever would have at the country club; and they had plenty of friends too, which you will certainly remember—"

"I do."

"And anyway, one day I asked Betty if she felt out of her natural element, you know, and she said, "This is my natural element. Shade is my natural element," and she laughed that way she has. She has no regrets, I'm amazed to tell you."

"I'm sure of that, Gordon."

"Ah, well, she could have some if she would. But look at this place. This is a place where folks who've watched a lot of TV feel comfortable."

I laughed.

"No, I'm telling you. That's what Marcus says, and Marcus has it right. Now, I don't know where he gets it. I watch him sometimes, and I know he's just another mick; I don't care about the Italian shoes and the shirts and the car. *Erin go bragh* and all, a mick doesn't make anything of doing a little damage, a head butt in a bar fight or a knife in the ribs. But anyway, this place has got me going. I never trusted a mick, and I'm not sure I trust Marcus, but he knows what people want to pay for, and he knows it in a way I've never seen before, so I give him what he wants every time, waiting to see what the next thing he wants will be."

"I've had five buyers in the last five days."

"Just wait." Then he gave me both a poke in the ribs and a slap on the back. Then he said, "What will we get from this deal? A quarter million or something like that?"

"When they all sell, the gross might be as much as 2.6 million. I don't know what your profit is going to be with these . . ."

"What about you?" Gordon said.

"Well, I always plan for four, four and a half percent." That was going to be a hundred grand or so.

"Here's one thing Marcus is saying that I believe—we roll it all over into the company—"

"What company?"

"Salt Key Development Corporation."

"Yeah."

"And there's that tax advantage."

"You mean that tax advantage of having no income while you're on their mind, so to speak?"

Gordon grinned and nodded. Then he said, "I could have made a big mistake here."

"I guess."

That was the first I'd heard about Salt Key Corporation.

I didn't have to wait long. Pretty soon, I was able to advertise that the final few units were selling and this was the last chance to get into one of the "prettiest, most elegant complexes in the area, a ready-made neighborhood, and easy living to boot."

I showed the Sloans one of the hill houses, up on Praed Circle, a brick Colonial with a nice backyard but not much of a view. Those owners were doing what they had been assigned to do by the layout of the whole development—they were moving into one of the townhouses, something "smaller, more exquisite, easy to take care of, but sacrificing no amenities." The Sloans had now been looking for almost a year, and the Praed Circle house was like many houses they had looked at and passed up. Nevertheless, they were enthusiastic, no doubt partly because they got to see it and make an offer on it before it actually went on the market. As we walked through it, Mrs. Sloan kept saying, "This one won't last a day. Not in this market and this neighborhood. It's so obviously just right."

I had unearthed the jewel at last. We went back to my office. Mr. Sloan kept smiling and saying, "Yeah, I like it. I like it a lot." We got the listing sheet we had already filled in out of the file drawer. I said, "I don't want to get your hopes up, but some houses are selling above the asking price." We drank coffee in my office. There were some cookies Bobby had brought in that morning, and we each ate one. We laughed a couple of times about houses we had looked at in the last year: Remember that one with the bomb shelter and all the old canned food on the shelves? Remember that one where the guy had three boa constrictors in his bedroom? Human eccentricity. Here they had landed, safely in the brick Colonial mainstream, looking forward to that center-island kitchen and that screened-in veranda. They finished signing all the papers and I walked them to the door of my office and saw them off. As she got into the car, it came into my mind that I would like to have a strand of her red hair, to bury by the doorstep to the office as a good-luck charm, some little thing to sustain and nourish the great period I was having right then. I went back to where she had been sitting and looked around, on her chair and on the floor. A hair from that head would be unmistakable—red and about twelve inches long, floating some-where. But I didn't find one.

I was feeling very good when I got to the Viceroy that night. I stood at the end of the bar next to Bobby and Fern, who sat there playing trictrac for drinks, and surveyed the room. The fact was, I knew nearly everyone there, at least by sight or at only one remove. I had sold houses to several of them, sold houses *for* several others, gotten new clients for some of the contractors or lawyers. Right then I could see myself in the not-too-distant future, living the Realtor's dream, which is no office time, no open houses, no beating the bushes for buyers or sellers, just answering the phone and making calls, knowing the local housing stock and the locals themselves so well that anyone would au-tomatically dial my number if there was a trans-action to be made. That didn't mean I knew what I would do with my time—somehow my rather unappealing condo didn't fit into the fantasy—but on the other hand, among all those houses flowing back and forth, there would surely be just the one for me.

Bobby won a drink from Fern and went down the bar to get it, and I said, "Did you ever find your cat?"

"I sure did," said Fern. I was in such a good mood that I noticed how interesting she was— sturdy and solid but with the manner of an emphatic fourteen-year-old. Yes, they were well suited. She glanced toward Bobby, who was standing near the bartender. "But I never got him back. I see him from time to time, though."

"How come?"

"He's around. But he's wild now—or, rather, feral. There was this opening, but I missed it. Once they've established a territory, then they're just as likely to keep themselves on their own. I bet you didn't know there's a whole cat society out there. I mean, right around here. That's where I've been doing my work. But there are cat societies everywhere."

Bobby took his beer, spilling it a little, and headed back toward our end of the bar. He got to us. He set the beer down. He had been out of the office that day. Now he put his hand on his jaw. Fern said, "You should go home and go to bed."

GOOD FAITH

"But when I lie down, it's worse. The whole side of my head throbs."

"You had root canal a week ago," she said. "You need to get something stronger or an X ray or something."

"He said if the pain wasn't gone by yesterday morning, he would take another picture."

"But the pain wasn't gone by yesterday."

"Well, I'll go tomorrow." He drank some of his beer, but not enthusiastically—he took it in his mouth and swirled it around, then swallowed it with a gulp. Most of the time with Bobby, I didn't think about how he ran his life, but sometimes I found it unbelievable.

Just then I felt a fleeting pressure against the middle of my back and Felicity stepped up to the bar beside me. It gave me a jolt, all over my skin, as if I were being delicately electrocuted.

Over the summer, our friendship had achieved a balanced ebb and flow that I considered about perfect. It throve on secrecy and contingency. When she wasn't around, I thought about her almost abstractly, as an event that might or might not happen at any given moment but not actually a part of my ongoing life. When I was with her, all our dates seemed to string themselves together into a train of pure pleasure, and everything else I did seemed beside the point. It didn't matter—in fact, it was preferable—that our dates had nothing to do with the state of my own desires. Any wish or even longing I might have to see her produced no results; sometimes when she showed up it was actually inconvenient, but frustrated longing and inconvenience both ended the same way, in pleasure and delight. I was subject to a spell, I thought, and to investigate it would be to break it. I came to enjoy the secrecy especially. I would be standing in the checkout line at the supermarket, and the couple behind me would be discussing which movies they might see that evening, and there would be such an agreed-upon expectedness to their exchanges that at first they would depress me but then I would remember my Felicity secret and feel delivered from the ennui and the public quality of marriage. What it seemed to me that I knew that the whole world didn't know was a novel and unusual way to live that had no disadvantages, once you discounted longing and frustration—or, rather, balanced those feelings against unpredictable enjoyment.

Sometime in August, I had run into Sherry. I was not happy to do so, and I have to say that she caught my lack of enthusiasm. The smile disappeared from her face, leaving no trace, and I remembered how she could go from smiling to displeasure in no time at all. I said, "So, how are you?" But I didn't want her to answer. Having spent all that time with her, having made that life with her, suddenly seemed more than anything tedious, and not even because it was with her but because it was marriage. She said, "Fine. The restaurant business is very demanding."

"That's what I've heard."

"It's not just cooking. If it were just cooking, that would be one thing. That would be art. But all the other stuff is overwhelming. People don't realize that. They think it's just cooking."

"I think I always—"

"It's easy to burn out. What are you doing?"

"I'm renewing my driver's license. I have an appointment." I stepped past her. And, I had thought, I have a secret, and you may look hard at my face and wonder all you want but I will not tell it to you.

At any rate, I didn't have to see Felicity or even know it was she in order to buzz in her presence. My skin prickled with it. She said, "Here's Joey. How are you?" She gave me a sisterly kiss on the cheek and slipped her hand quickly into and out of mine.

Bobby said, "Did Mom give you that codeine to bring me?"

"Yes." She opened her handbag and took out a pill bottle, which she set on the bar. Fern reached across me and picked it up. She said, "You've had too much beer for that right now. Maybe later."

"There's something in there," said Bobby. "You know, Marcus said that sometimes when they are doing a root canal, the tip of the drill breaks off and gets stuck, and unless the guy takes an X ray before he closes it up, he won't realize it, and then they have to extract the tooth with some kind of major operation, and this was an upper tooth, so the infection can go right up into your sinuses, and then—"

"I've never heard of that happening," said Felicity. "There are three types of things that happen, you know. There's the *usual* thing that happens, that no one ever talks about. Then there are the things you hear about or read about that happen every so often but are *unlikely*, so they get into the paper, but you don't really need to worry about them; a good example of that would be kidnapping, say. And then there are the things that *never* happen, that *can't* happen, like what you just were talking about, and those sorts of things you don't have to worry about at all." She laughed happily. I knew the happiness was for me.

"Marcus knew someone it happened to."

"I doubt it," said Felicity. She turned to me.

I said, "The Sloans made an offer."

She pressed, with all apparent casualness, more closely against me, then said, "Big crowd tonight." Her fingers skated across my fly, went away, came back. She kept talking the whole time. "What did they decide on?"

"Dutch Colonial. One of those ones on Praed Circle that your father built ten years ago."

"It took them a year to find a house like that?"

"They seem enthusiastic. You know, I've given up trying to figure out what people"— she squeezed me—"see. Ah."

She grinned. She spoke in a low voice. "Have you ever been in New York, in a really crowded subway car, all pressed together, and everyone is avoiding your gaze and someone just feels you up?" She was smiling. "It's so dangerous, isn't it? I mean, I knew someone who had her purse opened and her wallet stolen. Anything could happen in a situation like that." She gave me a sidelong glance. "I always wait for the next car if the one that comes seems too crowded. But this just reminds me." She pressed her side against me again; then she leaned around me and said to Fern, "Did you get those books I left at Mom's for you?"

"I haven't been over there today," said Fern.

She squeezed me harder this time, and I stood quietly, looking down at my beer.

"Well, they're on the front hall table there. You'll see them." In a quieter voice, as if through a trick of producing two voices at once, she said to me, "I've missed you."

"Me too," I said.

"Show me that house in Deacon, on Fourth Street."

"That California-style bungalow?"

"Yeah. Tomorrow at ten. I saw those people moving out last week."

"They're in Vermont by now."

"Mmmm." She went back to her public voice. She said to Bobby, "Well, I've delivered, so I'm going now." She backed away from the bar.

I said, "Yes, you have. Good to see you."

She grinned. "You too. I don't see you enough, really."

Neither Bobby nor Fern looked up, so I allowed myself a smile. I could feel her track through the barroom and out the door. It opened. It closed. I knew where she was every step of the way, even though I was still looking down at my half-full glass.

At nine-thirty the next morning, just as I was taking the keys to the Deacon house off the keyboard, the phone rang. It was George Sloan. He said, "Has that house sold?"

"You put in the first offer, Mr. Sloan, and it was accepted. We should be absolutely fine."

"Not that one. The other one."

He didn't have to tell me. I said, "It's still listed."

"I want to go see it again."

After a moment, I said, "I think it's time to put that idea out of your mind, Mr. Sloan—uh, George."

"I went up there last night and stood on the front step, on my way home from work. It's only thirteen minutes door-to-door from work. It's twenty-six minutes to the other house."

"Even twenty-six minutes isn't a major commute around here. I—"

"Can you get the keys again?"

"Sure, but, say, you know. George." Felicity was enlarging in my mind. "George. Think of it—this house, I mean—as something you really want but shouldn't have. Something that is hugely tempting but not good for you. Something that will *hurt* you. Do you know what I mean?"

Surely he did.

I said, "Did you ever—ah, smoke?"

He said, "Yes."

"But now you've quit, right?"

"No."

"You know you should, though, right?"

"Well, sure."

Oh, I didn't want to be having this conversation. It was twenty to ten. "Do you ever calculate how much money you spend on cigarettes in a year? That's something that's supposed to help you stop, right?"

"About a couple hundred bucks."

"Well, this house is going to cost you, in repairs alone, about fifty or sixty *thousand* bucks."

"That's a lot of money."

"George, I'm going to be frank with you. You can't afford it. I've seen the financial statement you made out for the bank. You could get in there and pay the mortgage, but that's all, and that's not enough."

"Can I get the key again?"

"You call her. You've got the number."

"That's okay?"

"That's okay."

He hung up.

I got there at ten-ten. The driveway was empty and the house looked a little too uninhabited— the windows were shut tight and the kid I'd hired to mow the lawn was a couple of days late. There was a weekly shopper on the front porch, yellowed and flat, and the porch itself needed sweeping. All these annoyances vanished when

GOOD FAITH

Felicity's BMW rounded the corner and pulled up to the curb. She got out of the car with a wave, turned, locked the driver's side door, and came toward me up the walk, swinging her handbag. She was wearing a loose moss-green dress, about knee length, and sandals. Her hair was spread out down her back in a dark wave. I opened the front door of the empty house, and she stepped up onto the porch and held out her hand. I shook it. Her face was alive with playfulness. She said, "Good morning, Mr. Stratford. Thank you so much for showing me this house. I'm sure it will be lovely."

I said, "There's plush carpeting in the main bedroom."

"Let's have a look at it, then."

I closed the door behind us and heard the lock click. Morning shadows, crisp and cool, fell across the living room floor. The house was quiet, the way closed empty houses are. Even the hum of the refrigerator was missing. I said, "I feel snowed in."

She said, "Ooh, Joey. I feel indescribable."

We crossed the kitchen and entered the back hall, which was dim and close. She moved toward me and put her hand into my shirt. I put my arm around her waist and felt that she was wearing nothing underneath her dress. There was only the slip of mossy fabric over the smoothness of her skin. We stopped right there and began kissing against the wall of the empty pantry. She unbuttoned my shirt and opened it, then lifted her dress and pressed her breasts against my solar plexus. I whispered, "You are so undomesticated."

She whispered, "No one knows that but you and me."

I couldn't kiss her enough. Her lips fit with perfect softness inside mine. She didn't move them, but they were electric, and I seemed to feel their every little charge in my balls and my cock, which was pressed against her belly. It went inside her and she squeezed, and then pressed her tongue into my kiss and against my tongue. We seemed equal in this—I was pushing into her and she was pushing into me. It was painfully exciting. I lifted her over to the washer/dryer and sat her against it, then leaned into her. She began to cry out and I did too, at first kissing and then with our heads back and our mouths open. She hooked her ankles behind the small of my back. The heel of her foot seemed to dig into my lower spine, causing waves of sensation to move outward like rays. I pushed harder into her. I thought, She can take it. She can take a simple thing, the throwing off of all restraint. I had never known any other woman who could take that. I ran my hands down her sides and gripped her waist and she opened her legs even wider, anchoring her hands on my shoulders and coming all over me in a wet wave. Then it was my turn.

The next thing she said, in a low, pleased voice, was, "That took four minutes."

I laughed and said, "Is that good?"

"It was great. Wasn't it?"

"Of course. But why did you time it?"

"It didn't seem like four minutes, did it? It seemed like forever. I love that." She sighed and lay back across the washer/dryer combo. I eased out of her and she twisted her legs away, making a spot for me on the corner of the washer. She said, "This is comfortable in a way. Cool." She pulled her dress down and smoothed it, then lifted her hair off the back of her neck. I said, "The bedroom is nice, too."

"Look in my bag."

I pulled out a cotton sheet, single-bed size.

"I thought the carpet might be rough, but this is nice. Private."

"Old Realtor's trick."

She stretched her back and lifted her arms, then put her hands on my cheeks. "I wish I could roll over next to you now and just tickle you all over and chat about something. What do you think we would chat about if we were comfortable?"

"We'd probably complain. I'd probably complain. Or we'd gossip." I still felt enjoyably drained. "Maybe I'd add up money. I've made a lot of sales lately, especially over there with those townhouses. Maybe I'd lie there and talk myself into being rich."

"Daddy thinks those townhouses are a sow's-ear silk-purse sort of thing. Marcus just sits there looking quietly confident. Let's go lie down on the floor of the bedroom."

I helped her off the washer/dryer and led her to the back of the house, where she spread the white sheet over the thick champagne-colored carpet. We lay down. She said, "This room has nice windows. You know, I've lived in the same house for twelve years. I think everyone is moving but me. When the boys were twelve and thirteen, we could have expanded, but now it's time to contract."

"Is this chatting?"

"Yes, I believe it is."

"Maybe it will lead to second thoughts."

"On your part?"

"No. On yours."

She looked at me. She said, "It's okay for us to have no future. Two people having a future is more or less a habit, when you think about it. It's what you do in high school when you don't have any idea of what else to do. Look at Fern. The reason they can't get her to marry Bobby is because she has other things to do."

"Like what?"

"Study cats."

"Is that really something to do?"

"It is for her. You'd be surprised how little is known about cats. If you were chatting with Fern, she would have something to say. It would be about cats, but it would be something."

"You have something to say."

She ran her finger around my lips for a moment. "I'll tell you about me. I am a person who is interested, but I've never really pursued anything, so I'm still more *interested* than *interesting*. I changed my major six times in college, and then I got married instead of graduating. I mean, I've never—"

"I think you're very interesting."

"I know you do, but that's essentially reproductive behavior. When you smell my hair or want to fuck me because I have a certain demeanor, you are not really finding me interesting. It's not the same for me. I find you interesting because you're different from other men."

"I never would have thought that."

"I know. The funniest thing about you is that

you think you're an average guy. But you are *kind.*"

"Maybe I'm just not very, oh—"

"Ruthless?"

"Well, I was going to say smart."

"I don't know about that, but you do tempt me to find the limits of your kindness."

I tried to make a joke of this. "That doesn't sound like fun. At least not for me."

"Do you know that I'm *not* kind?"

"I haven't thought about it."

"I'm not. I am affectionate, though. And I like you very much. As much as anyone." She put her head back and looked at me. "You know I only use the word *love* in its most technical sense. Mother, father, husband, wife, sister, brother."

"You don't have to use the word *love* with me."

"It's better if I don't. There's no precedent, and it's too confusing."

Now the frenzy of our earlier coupling seemed distant. I wasn't sure why. I said, "Right now, I have to say, you are very *interesting.*"

"If I thought that was a laudable goal, I would be glad to hear it, but I don't. I am just enjoying myself." She kissed me.

"Tell me what's enjoyable about talking like this."

GOOD FAITH

"Well, it's not the same sort of talking we always do, for one thing. I mean, haven't you noticed that people always talk about the same things over and over? I look at my parents and hear them say the same things they've been saying for years to each other, as if they were in church or something. 'How was your day?' 'Could've been worse. Where do you want to eat tonight?' 'I don't care. Do you want me to cook?' 'You don't want to cook.' 'I can cook. I don't mind cooking.' 'Ah, why mess up the kitchen?' Then he kisses her."

"I've heard that conversation."

"Who hasn't? That's the Betty-and-Gordon conversation. The Hank-and-Felicity conversation isn't as long, but it's just as—you know. I'm not going to complain about him to you."

"I don't want you to."

"Linda and I were talking about that at lunch yesterday. When you start having a friend—a woman friend, I mean—one of the first things you always do is complain about your husband and kids. It's incredibly tempting. You make fun of them a little and you throw your hands around and you use a certain tone of voice, a very emphatic tone of voice."

"I know that." But what I really wondered was what Linda said about Marcus.

"It takes on a life of its own. You start getting

outside your own family and then it's hard to feel inside it again. You're easy to talk to, like Gordon."

"I don't have a lot else to offer, dear."

"I don't know if that's true."

"Are you upset about something?"

"No." She lay back on the sheet and looked up at the ceiling. "I miss Sally. Sally would have led the march *out of here*. I couldn't do it by myself. Anyway, I just want you to appreciate what a pleasure this is, to have no future."

"And nothing public."

"Exactly." She looked at me. "Do you miss Sally?"

"Not the way you do." I wanted right then to tell her that I loved her, but I didn't dare.

She nestled into me and I started kissing her again. The desire that had receded returned effortlessly.

Afterward, we folded up the sheet and looked around the house for a minute or two, and then we went out of the house, and I shook her hand on the step and we went to our separate cars without looking at each other.

SEVERAL DAYS LATER, Gordon, Marcus, Crosbie, Bart, and I met with Mrs. Thorpe and her lawyer. We signed the papers; they signed the papers. Salt Key Farm became the property of Salt Key Corporation, which was owned by Gordon (40 percent), Marcus (35 percent), and me (25 percent). I had agreed to put my two small farms on the market as a token of my interest. I thought they might bring about a hundred and fifty thousand together, but in fact we spent nothing; principal, interest for one year, and fees for the loan were covered by the loan itself. After Mrs. Thorpe and Calvin Visser had left, Marcus said to Crosbie, "Now, of course, we'll need another loan for preliminary development costs. Gordon and I were thinking that two-fifty ought to cover it for six months, maybe a year."

Crosbie nodded without turning a hair, and Bart said, "I'll see to the paperwork."

When we were walking to our cars, I kept glancing at Marcus and Crosbie chatting. As far as I knew, Marcus had nothing except a heavily mortgaged house and a job that paid on commission, but he carried himself importantly, and Crosbie nodded and laughed and made a big deal of him and stood there and waved him off when he drove away. I didn't know what to attribute this to, and in the end I decided it was genius. After all, everything he had told me had been right, hadn't it?

Marcus and I went looking for office space. This was Gordon's idea, Marcus told me, because he wanted the Salt Key Corporation to start out in an organized way. Marcus himself was keeping the books. The county was deep into autumn; every road ran through a golden tunnel of color that blazed up to a brilliant dome of blue. Autumn rains had returned the pastures and roadsides temporarily to thick green splashed with late flowers, and Marcus was in a good mood. I said, "I thought you had a job."

"I do."

"I mean with a firm: you know, the sort of job where you go to the office and talk on the phone."

"I do. But this I like better. You know, you can invest in anything now. It's like everything in the world all of a sudden turned into money, and whatever it is you just pass it back and forth and it's all the same. That's the secret."

We got to the outskirts of Deacon, and I pulled into the parking lot of a modest strip mall, built in the sixties. "No," said Marcus.

"Well, let's at least go in—"

"Why?"

I started the car again and backed out of my parking place. As we drove down Main Street, he turned his head back and forth. Part of the charm of Deacon was that it had gotten very ferny in the seventies—flower beds in front of every house, big old houses turned into professional offices rather than being torn down. Marcus said, "I've been thinking about Deacon. I'm not sure Deacon is the place. Too funky."

"Look at the foot traffic. Deacon is the most desirable commercial location in the county."

He turned to me. "Mercedes traffic is our kind of traffic." I laughed. "Mercedes traffic likes to park in a covered garage facility and enter a carpeted elevator to be lifted in silence to the top floor," he said.

"I've got to tell you that Gordon's projects generally work out of trailers or modular buildings."

We passed out of Deacon and drove along the river. Here it was quieter. The river was low and off in the distance, the crowns of the hills dark where the trees had dropped their leaves.

At Cookborough, I crossed the river and turned south on the interstate. We drove in silence until Marcus said, "Here's the deal. See that farm there?" He pointed to the right as we passed some red cattle with white faces grazing the side of the interstate.

"That's Gordon's farm," I said. "He's had that place for years, but the town never came out here."

"Not so far. But it will come out here if you make something for it to come to. You know how they settled the West?"

"The West?"

"Kansas, Nebraska, South Dakota. All the places that no one in their right minds would think of living in. Colorado."

"How?"

"I bet you think that enterprising farmers got land from the government at a dollar twenty-five an acre and built themselves modest homesteads, like *Little House on the Prairie*. Did you ever read *Little House on the Prairie*?"

"No."

"Well, when I was in third grade, we sat there for half an hour after lunch every day while Mrs. Judson read us *Little House on the Prairie,* and if you think a classroom of eight-year-old wops and micks and yids from Brooklyn could imagine what in the world she was talking about, you should have been there." He laughed. "Let's say she had difficulty maintaining order. Anyway, people don't go out and take a liking to a piece of raw land unless they're crazy. What happened all along was, the developers got the government to pay for the land being developed, and they got the banks to pay for the development, and then they got the farmers to buy in, once the farmers had a place to go where they could feel comfortable. Gordon's crazy to wait for the town to come to him. He has to build a place for the town to want to come to."

"It's at least six miles to the outskirts of Portsmouth from here. There's hardly even any housing developments out this way, just some trucking companies and that sort of thing."

"How old are you?"

I got a little defensive. I said, "Forty, actually."

"Here's a riddle. You know what was more important than the Cuban Missile Crisis?"

"The Kennedy assassination?"

"The Beatles."

"I was around for the Beatles."

"The day the Beatles got to the States, I skipped school with a couple of other guys and took the train uptown. We got off at the wrong stop and just walked around, looking for the Beatles. You can't believe all the kids that were there. It was like—oh, I don't know, water pooling around a storm drain, deep water, water from the whole neighborhood, enough water to sweep you away into the drain and down to the river. Anyway, by following the stream of kids, we got sort of to where the Beatles were. We never saw them, but we saw so many kids. I just never got over that."

"Never got over what?" We had passed the light industrial section and were driving through a part of Portsmouth that was seedy and run-down.

"Record buyers. Burger buyers. Blue jeans buyers. *Hmm mmm.* Customers. I mean, in this last election, everyone breathed a sigh of relief. Finally the sixties were over and the revolution had ended and something bad had happened to all those kids—they, or we, got our just deserts. We disappeared or grew up or something. The Carter years taught us the long-awaited lesson."

I had heard something like this from my parents, not specifically directed toward me, because I was, of course, a basically good boy with a steady employment history who was more sinned against than sinning, but nevertheless the date when a due sense of responsibility would begin to impose itself upon "young people" had been a long time coming. I nodded. I said, "That life is hard and success doesn't come easy."

"That's the lesson." He laughed. "But it does for some people. Oh, yes, it does. And here's the key. More people mean scarcer resources, scarcer resources mean inflation, and inflation means property and interest-bearing capital have a higher value and work has a lower value. It's as simple as that. Gordon is an interesting guy. He lives by simple principles—buy it if you can, drive a hard bargain, have fun, don't make enemies. He has a lot of personality that helps him ooze here and ooze there and in general keep himself spreading across the landscape, but on the other hand, he really doesn't know what he has. What's wrong with the other son, what's his name?"

"Norton?"

"Yeah."

I said, "Oh, he's a hothead. His problem is that he's already acted on his natural mean streak before he remembers that alienating people doesn't do him any good. He's always wanted to be rich, but he wants to inflict pain just a little bit more."

"That's not very cool."

"You know," I said, "Gordon is a warm and generous man and he's helped me and worked with me every day of my adult life, but he would take a poke in the eye before getting the short end of a deal, and Norton is like that. He just doesn't know where the deals end and life begins; he always thinks he is getting shafted, and Gordon has never let him think otherwise. I once saw Gordon beat Norton sixty-two times in a row at gin. And every time he rubbed it in, just a little. The tournament lasted—oh, three weeks or so. Norton never won a game."

We pulled up in front of the old Acorn State Bank building. I could tell that Marcus appreciated the grandeur of it, and in fact the building was more ornate than large. We peeked in the etched glass windows set into the large double doors and got a glimpse of the triangular lobby with all the old tellers' windows stretched along the base of the triangle. I took out my key and opened the lockbox. I said, "I don't think anyone's been in here in three years or more. Acorn moved out in 'seventy-two, I think. Then the Portsmouth County Credit Union was in here, but when the price of heating oil went up, they moved. I mean, look at those windows!" The lobby, where I had come so often with my mother when she brought me on the streetcar to deposit the week's receipts, reminded me powerfully of being a preschool child with nothing to do but say my prayers, obey my parents, and love God.

Marcus went behind the bank of tellers' booths and wandered around, a smile on his face. He rocked back on his heels and looked up at the ceiling. I looked up too. There was a faded scene depicted there—some men in a boat and a dim line of trees in the distance. He said, "That's Washington crossing the Delaware, I bet."

"I bet it is. It has that WPA look about it, doesn't it?"

He nodded and went through a door into the vault room. The big heavy vault door had been removed, as well as all the safe-deposit boxes and whatever else would have been there. I said, "This was our bank. We came here every Monday morning on the streetcar. My mother handed over her money and her passbook, and the same teller stamped her book and wrote something with a fountain pen. People stayed close to their money in those days."

"It sounds like an orderly existence."

"Order is my father's middle name."

"I would like to meet your parents sometime." He seemed sincere, though casual too.

"You would? No one ever says that. They're well known for expressing strong religious opinions without being asked, though always in the kindest of terms. My father and Gordon have agreed to maintain a cordial but extremely distant friendship."

He sighed. "Well, this is grand, but it wasn't what I had in mind."

We got back in the car and I pulled onto Essex Street. I said, "South Portsmouth might be more the ticket, but it's a little far from the farm."

"The farm is only the beginning. We don't want the corporation to be too linked in people's minds with the farm."

We drove for a while in silence, and then Marcus began humming a little tune that I couldn't identify. Maybe I'd been supposed to answer something, because suddenly he said, "What's the matter with you, Joe? How did you let yourself get roped into this?"

"What?"

"This development."

"I didn't get roped in. I mean, I've worked with Gordon for years, and then you came along."

"Crosbie is the real villain, you know why?"

"Why?"

"Because a big loan is an asset. All those deposits he's got, those are the liabilities, and those loans are assets. Crosbie's new. He came in to transform the savings and loan from money loser to moneymaker, and he's got to make the books look good, so he's making big loans, which go on the asset side and cover old loans that aren't making any profit. Was this whole thing his idea?"

"No, it was Thorpe's idea, remember? He didn't know Thorpe. And I don't think Portsmouth Savings has ever been a money loser. They're the biggest S and L around here. They got the first charter in the state way back when. They actually opened two branches a couple of years ago, when all the others were——"

"You know what I hate the most?"

"What?"

"I hate paying taxes."

"You do?"

"Sure."

"Well, everyone hates paying taxes."

"You know the simplest way to avoid paying taxes?"

"Obviously not."

"The simplest legal way that takes no cheating and no creative bookkeeping and passes every audit?"

"No."

"You live on borrowed money. You sell the property piece by piece to pay the interest and you keep borrowing more. Gordon's got collateral up the wazoo. That's how you got roped in."

"That's assuming that——"

"That the value of the property keeps rising. And it does."

"I don't know, what with interest rates so high—"

"It does. That's the lesson of the Beatles. More and more people who like things nice, who are educated and have good taste, are just starting to come into some real money. Families with two ambitious adults in the workforce instead of one. Gay couples. You know what?"

"What?"

"I'm hungry."

I laughed out loud. Just then we passed Cheltenham Park, an office complex that looked more like a private school: Colonial-style red-brick three-story buildings with white trim and fanlights above the two entrances. Marcus said, "What's that? Is that on your list?"

"That's incredibly expensive office space." But I didn't have to be told to stop. I turned into the parking lot.

He opened his door and got out of the car. His clothes fit in perfectly here. I saw with a sinking feeling that this was the place. I said, "Maybe they won't have any space, they're usually—"

But as we walked past the management office, a small elegantly printed sign in the

window read: LIMITED SPACE STILL AVAIL-
ABLE. We went in. The management office was
carpeted in pale Berber with a wheat-colored
Persian on top of that. The manager, a blond
woman with her hair pinned up, was very well
dressed. I cast Marcus a sidelong glance. I could
tell he felt comfortable here, and she could tell
the same. I said, "I'm Joe Stratford of Stratford
Realty. This is my client, Marcus Burns. Mr.
Burns is looking for office space."

The woman came from behind her desk and
held out her hand to Marcus. She said, "Mary
Linburg King, Mr. Burns."

Marcus gripped her hand with his right and
her arm with his left. He looked at her warmly.

She said, "What can I do for you, Mr.
Burns?" It was like watching two people get
married on the first date.

"First of all, show us around," said Marcus. "We
haven't seen anything really first-rate all day."

"Oh, believe me, Cheltenham Park is first-
rate."

"How many office suites do you have
vacant?"

"Only two. Businesses love it here. Two of the
best restaurants in town are here, too, Chez Mau-
rice is down there and Laguna is at the other end
of the building. Very upscale. But let me—"

"We haven't had lunch yet," said Marcus.

Inside the complex, the floors were marble, the walls had chair rails, the trim was elaborate and thickly enameled. The anchor store for this building was the Persian carpet store, which was spacious and beautifully lit. Carpets were piled everywhere, like treasure spilling out of a chest. They hung on the walls and from ceiling racks. Several of them had discreetly lettered signs saying, OWING TO THE DELICACY OF THESE PIECES, PLEASE DO NOT TOUCH THEM, BUT GAZE TO YOUR HEART'S CONTENT! Mary King spoke in a low voice. "The owner is quite a well-known expert." Marcus was beaming.

Next door was an art gallery. This was a smaller establishment, only one long room of white-painted, brightly lit walls. A display of prints and paintings of horses ran down one side and a display of black-and-white photographs ran down the other. There were two locked glass cases of antique jewelry. The proprietor, a tall woman with black hair, was standing by one of the photographs, inserting a price card into a wall mount. It read, *2000.*

Mary said, "Dana, this is Marcus Burns. He's looking for office space."

Marcus made an expansive gesture. He said, "Some wonderful works you have here."

"Thank you. The photographs are more in demand, but I have to tell you that the horse paintings are actually very good. Mr. Mellon's advisor was in here yesterday and said that Mr. Mellon might be in himself tomorrow. He doesn't come in unless there's something very rare."

"Paul Mellon?" said Mary.

"Oh, of course," said Dana. "I'm sorry. Mr. Mellon is a huge lover of English animal painting."

"Mmm," said Marcus. "I suppose you know that the Thorpe estate is changing hands?"

"He was killed in a car accident," said the art dealer.

"No, actually not," I said. "He had the accident outside my office and walked away from it. But he died that night of a heart attack."

"What a shame." Her face fell and then brightened. "But it would be great to have a look at some of their things." She gave Marcus a glance, and he gave her a glance back. Marcus shook her hand.

From the art gallery, we went to the first vacant suite of offices. They were on the second floor: a reception area, four nicely carpeted rooms, a bathroom, and a tiny kitchen area for making coffee. Marcus stood in the door and then shook his head decisively. "Not big enough."

"For what?" I said. "There's only one of you."

They paid no attention. We went to the other building. As we walked along, Marcus said, "So, Mary. What's the square-foot cost you're asking?"

She quoted a price I had never before heard in my life. Marcus said nothing.

The other building was anchored by an antiques store. We didn't go in. Mary leaned upward, toward Marcus, and whispered, "Only French. Not even Italian. I asked the owner once why he didn't have any Italian pieces, and he said, 'Too gaudy.'"

The second suite had six rooms arranged somewhat differently from the previous one. There was a front office, a conference space behind that where the coffee and refrigerator setup was, and then a corridor leading from there with two rooms off either side of it. The bathroom was at the end; it had a shower as well as a stool and a sink. As I followed the two of them from the front office to the conference room, Mary lost her footing. Marcus caught her elbow. When she was balanced again, he gave her a little squeeze, and she gave him a grateful smile. There was a brief moment of silence, at the end of which she sighed a very short and quiet sigh. Marcus did not move away from her and she did not move away from him. He said, "This is a bit better, at least for now. We could manage here for the first year or so. But, Mary, what has me really excited, and maybe persuades me to take this suite more than anything else, is what we could do for you."

"What would that be?"

"Let me ask you this question first: What business is your husband in?"

"He—um, he's a doctor, but I'm not actually married anymore."

"Well, you know," he said, with special kindness now, "I'm not going to congratulate or commiserate, at least for right now, maybe later, but that's perfect for my example here, because you can understand what I can do for you. You know the Thorpe property that we were talking about down in the art gallery?"

"Of course. I mean, I've never been out there—"

"I own it. I'm developing it. It's not going to be like anything this area has ever seen before. These four hundred houses are going to suck up Persian carpets and French antiques and fine art. You should see the house plans."

I said, "Four hundred?" They didn't hear me.

"Families like these—*women* like these—are going to need a destination for shopping and lunch and dinner and all sorts of things. Gold trading. Joe here said there's a gold-trading firm?"

"SAF Investments has an office on the first

floor. Actually, a bedding shop is talking about coming in. You know, Swedish down comforters and silk blankets."

"Perfect! And a fitness center would be great. Have you thought about a fitness center?" He poured an appreciative gaze down upon her that seemed to honor her personally for installing the bedding store. "I knew this would be perfect as soon as we drove past. I think Joe tried to call you, but we couldn't get through, right, Joe?"

"Yesterday I was calling around."

"But here we are and it's working out perfectly. I think I can offer you—" He lowered his voice and turned his back to me, but I heard him say "square foot" and then he said, normally, "As soon as one of the bigger suites opens up, we can roll over our lease. Here's what I want to do, I want to be here, right here, to oversee how this place develops into a mecca for our buyers. Something bigger would suit us better, but this is where I can make sure that everything comes together, you know what I mean?"

"Yes, but—"

"But you were told by your boss to get more for the suite, weren't you?"

"My boss doesn't actually have all that much to do with it. That's the rent."

Marcus stayed with her. Now he had his

hand on her elbow again, and he drew her gently toward him. I was not even sure she realized he was touching her. He was beaming and twinkling. He said, "It's not rented."

"No, it isn't."

"And you don't have a prospect, do you?"

"Not right now—"

"Let my company fly standby."

"What?"

"You know how they fill up planes when they've got seats to spare. You don't want to fly this place with empty seats, do you? One more firm moves out and you begin to look a little empty, right, Joe?"

"Yes. That's true."

"Joe's been in the real estate business for twenty-five years." And me only forty! "There's a moment when something elaborate begins to look white elephantish, isn't there, Joe? When people stay away because everyone else is staying away?"

"I don't think we've—" said Mary.

"This is a classy place, Mary, and that's an asset, but it's also a hidden danger, because it's intimidating and a little—well, sterile. Right, Joe?"

"That's a good word," I said. "Sterile is a good word."

"Class is an asset until it becomes uncomfortable. You want to have class, but you want it to be *welcoming*. It isn't welcoming if it isn't busy."

"I understand—"

"Do you? How about you yourself? Do you like to come to work in the morning?"

"Yes, I do, but—"

"But sometimes it seems a little lonely."

"I wasn't going to say that." She smiled. "But now that you—" He had her.

"Believe me. When Salt Key Corporation has been here a month, this place will never be lonely again. It's not just buyers who'll be parading in and out, it's investors too. And they'll be dropping in at the retail establishments just automatically. I'll tell you what. Rent it to us by the month. As soon as you've got a better deal with a lease, we'll move. No one loses with that deal, right?"

"No, but—"

He turned suddenly to me. "Joe, these offices are fine for now, don't you think?"

"I think—"

And back to Mary. "How about lunch? I'm starving."

Over lunch, he was delicately attentive, and she got happily self-conscious. I was amused but also impressed. He was a genius. I kept saying that to myself as if there were an argument about it.

GOOD FAITH

On the way home, he said, "I like women."

A few minutes later, I said, "So that office space is the one you want?"

"Don't let her raise the rent. If I were you, I'd go back there tomorrow first thing, while the deal is fresh in her mind."

"What is the rent?"

"I'll worry about it."

"We don't have any plans to show her."

"Aw, take something of Gottfried's. Not mine, maybe, but that new one you've got listed. That's pretty fancy."

"Cheltenham Park is a long way from the farm. An hour at least."

"I'll be here, you'll be at your place, Gordon'll be at the farm. That should work out. Those properties that are around here, those need oversight too. Actually, this is perfect."

CHAPTER 12

THE LEAVES FELL off the trees and Hank went to the University of Arizona for a land-use conference. Jason went to Virginia to visit Clark in college, and I was feeling flush. The townhouses in Phase Four were closing one after another like slamming doors, and another friend of the Davids had bought two places in Deacon, a large house and an even larger warehouse. He was a costumer in New York, and rental space for keeping the costumes had gotten too expensive in his West Side location. I had found him an old cold-storage facility that would be easy to convert to the perfect temperature and humidity for silks, brocades, satins, and chiffons, not to mention veils, crowns, scepters, swords, scabbards, and golden goblets. The collection, according to the Davids, was worth millions. Anyway, it was the Friday before Thanksgiving. I picked Felicity up at her place, and she threw her bag into the backseat and got into the car with the happy air of someone whose tracks are covered.

My car had a bench seat, so she scooted right over next to me and we began kissing at once, secure in the knowledge that no one ever came down her road. I have to say she was as uninhibitedly ardent right in front of her own dwelling, with the garden hose hanging over the railing of the front porch and a light on in a second-floor window, as she was in the most anonymous empty house. As we drove away, Felicity locked under my right arm, I said, "Why doesn't it get old?"

"The sex?"

"Yeah."

"Because I never get tired of it."

The weather was damp and overcast—umber and ochre November. The hillsides were dark with the tangled net of bare tree branches; closer to the road, we could see their trunks rooted in a thick bed of wet leaves. Felicity leaned against me and gazed out the window. From time to time, she kissed me on the shoulder or the cheek. At one point, she took my right hand off the steering wheel, turned my palm upward, kissed it, and then put it back.

The snow began about an hour outside of New York. It wasn't an unusual snow at all, at first. Each flake landed on the windshield with a tiny splat and was swept away by the wipers. The road was wet but not slippery. The roadside turf turned gray and then white, but the snow was fluffy and appealing. Felicity said, "I looked at the weather last night. It didn't say anything about snow."

"Very attractive snow, if you ask me," I said.

"I wonder if it's snowing at home. I suppose it will look very suspicious if the driveway is unshoveled by Monday."

"Don't you have friends in New York?"

"That woman from college I was out with the night I picked you up."

"Yeah. Just the sort of person to talk you into a trip to the city at the last moment."

"Absolutely. But I'll have to remember her name between now and then."

"Anyway," I said, "I'm sure it's not snowing at home."

"No, you're right."

The car was so warm and the company was so comfortable and I was so happy that it took a very long time for me to comprehend that the snow cover on the cars coming toward us in the southbound lanes had anything to do with us. Every time we came to a dead stop, we kissed until the car in front of us started moving again. At one point, for some undefined length of time, she spread her skirt across my lap and then flung her leg over mine underneath it. Then she hiked up the back of her skirt and pressed herself against my pant leg. She sighed and closed her eyes, rocking against me. After a moment, she murmured, "Have you ever gotten a blow job in a moving vehicle?"

"Not in a traffic jam."

"But on the highway?"

"Well, we pulled over."

"We didn't."

"That was very daring of you."

"It was daring of him."

"Hank?"

"Oh my God, no. My college cheating boyfriend. Driving around having oral sex was about all we did. He was a good driver, but he didn't have much to say otherwise . . . *mmm*." She continued to move against me while she was talking; it was very exciting. We approached the tunnel. Traffic intensified, with honking and jostling for position, but still I floated along on a sea of patience and only once thought of what this trip would have been like with Sherry, a prolonged exercise, for me, in calming her rotating pattern of annoyance, anxiety, fear, and boredom. Felicity removed her leg, turned around, and lay down on the seat with her head in my lap. Her deep-set and very dark eyes were peaceful, even sleepy. I felt a little discomfort—self-consciousness, I suppose— rise, take hold, and then subside. After that, her regard got to be a fact, a function of our situation together in the car. I looked down at her when I could, looked up at the traffic when I had to, stroked her face lightly with my thumb and the tips of my fingers.

The Hilton was bustling with happy conversation about the snow. In the lobby, though it wasn't especially cold outside, people were bundling or unbundling into or out of brightly colored down-filled coats and knitted hats and mittens and boots, as if they were just going out into, or just coming back from, long treks down snowy roads to crossroads grocery stores where the only remaining provisions were wholesome items like bread and milk and oranges. We got to the desk. The clerk acted delighted to see us, Mr. and Mrs. Joseph Stratford, who had made it at last. Adding to the festive atmosphere were the early Christmas decorations in the lobby—a tall tree decked out in silver and gold ornaments and clusters of poinsettia and holly. I kept my arm around Felicity, who yawned from time to time. "Long trip?" asked the clerk.

"Longest ever in my whole life," said Felicity.

Our room was small but comfortable, and while I was in the bathroom Felicity turned down the bedspread, took off her clothes, and climbed between the sheets. When I came back into the room, she was nestled into the pillows, yawning and stretching. She said, "This time yesterday I was busy with laundry and making veal broth for my mother and talking to Leslie on the phone and in general doing three things at once, and now I can't imagine doing one thing at once. Oh, your skin is cold. It's very refreshing." Her skin was warm and peachy-looking and I got as close to it as I could, putting my arms and legs around her and nestling my face into her neck and the curtain of her hair. "Oh," she murmured, "this is very nice. It's like being tossed around in the surf. I might as well give up and go under." She stretched against me for a few moments and then softened all over. I felt her sleepiness seep into me like the slow swirling of a drop of ink into clear water, and then, even though I had been planning in the bathroom to make love to her, I fell asleep.

It was twilight when I woke up. As I rose to awareness, I noticed that the window light was pearly and bright as well as bluish, and I lay there for a long moment, warmed by Felicity's embrace and simply appreciative of the unusual color of the light. It would be wrong to say that this was a fleeting moment, since everything about it impressed itself upon me—the color and the brightness of the window, the way the pinkness of the room's décor took on a kind of silvery sheen, Felicity's fragrance and quietness, the softness of her breathing, my own molasses heaviness.

Just then she turned away from me, and I got up and looked out the window. The glass was cool against my cheek, and there it was, 54th Street, at least three feet deep in snow, lit by streetlamps that were just beginning to come on and completely deserted. The snow was still falling—very thickly—in patterned gusts around the lamps and in a rich cold particulate fog everywhere else. As best I could, I looked upward. The undersides of the clouds were pinked by the reflection of the city lights, and the snow poured out of them in a deadening cascade that was very reassuring. I went back to bed.

Felicity turned toward me and, without waking up, I thought, put her hand on my cock, which instantly hardened. She smiled, though she didn't open her eyes, and rolled over and presented her beautiful round buttocks to me, and I entered her at once, and her hand went immediately between her legs and she stroked herself while I grasped her hipbones and pulled myself more deeply inside of her. In the twilight, I could see her buttocks press against me and then taper gracefully into the contours of her back muscles, which fanned into her shoulders. That was what I looked at while I felt her vaginal muscles pulsating around my cock, which was moving into and out of her. Here's what it was: The perfect relaxation of our whole bodies had concentrated at this one amazing spot and come together, and the effect then reversed itself, and the electricity of that spot gathered and spread out through the rest in hot waves and finally emerged in sound—the sound of Felicity singing out and me groaning, and then Felicity laughing and saying, "Oh, Joey, feel my hair. This is so amazing that my hair is getting hot." We sighed simultaneously. She said, "It's dark."

"Look out the window."

"Snowy?"

"Look."

She got up naked and walked across the

room—that was what I'd been aiming for—and pressed her forehead against the windowpane. She said, "Thank God we're stranded. Let's order room service before they run out of food."

And so we did. Two steaks, two baked potatoes with chives, sour cream, and butter, two Caesar salads, two shrimp cocktails, one Lindy's cheesecake, one crème brûlée, two glasses of wine, and a bottle of champagne and a fruit-and-cheese basket for later in case we needed to survive for the entire weekend on this one meal. It was a Baldwin sort of meal if ever there was one—no nuts and berries, as Gordon would say, and a side order of hot sauce in case anything was too bland for Felicity's palate.

We ate and showered and made love several more times and then turned on the eleven o'clock news. The subway was halted, trains were stuck between New Haven and Boston, the municipal buses weren't running, electricity was out upstate and in New Jersey, the tunnels were closed, Manhattan was deserted, people were urged to stay in their homes, surf on Long Island was licking the pylons of beach houses, trees were down, cars and trucks had slid off the highways, and estimates of damage ran into the millions. On the other hand, snowmen had mushroomed in front yards, children were sliding on cardboard boxes down hills, and the news team had a hard time maintaining their usual gravity. We turned off the TV, temporarily spent. She lay against me, my arm supporting her head. I gave her a squeeze and said, "It's nearly midnight, and I'm not at all tired."

"Me neither, but I always stay up till one-thirty or two."

"Doing what?"

"Reading. Darning."

"Darning?" Her face was so close. I gazed at the contour of her eye socket.

"Yes. Isn't that silly? I darn socks. That's my art. Daddy made us learn, because he always had cashmere socks, and he thought—"

"Your father wears cashmere socks?"

"That's his one indulgence."

"His one?" I kissed her.

"Well, you're right. Daddy has many indulgences. But he wears cashmere socks. He gets them from one of his cousins in England."

"Your dad has cousins in England?"

"Second or third cousins. We've never met them." This time she kissed me.

"That's funny."

"Why?"

"Oh, you know my father. He likes your dad, but he always thought *Baldwin* was short for *Baldassare,* or something like that."

"Bolechinsky." She lifted her hand again and pushed back my hair, then sat up.

"Yeah."

"Oh, the mysterious Baldwins. You should see Hank's parents, who are from Minnesota, trying to get a straight story out of Daddy. They've been trying for twenty years. 'So,' says Grandpa Ornquist. 'What grammar school did you go to, Gordon? We met this man, must be about your age, he went to Governor's Leasehold Boys Preparatory, and he said he remembered a boy in his class, Gordon Baldwin.' He's made it up, of course. And then Grandma Ornquist, who was a Harstad and don't you forget it—her mother and father were cousins, both named Harstad; what a relief *that* is for her to think about—she always inquires after Daddy's traditional family recipes: anything like, say, *kumla,* which are potato dumplings, or the sort of singed lamb's head she remembers her mother making for the family when she was a girl. But Mother just says, 'Oh, Gordon knows I wouldn't cook anything like that,' thus scandalizing Grandma Ornquist in two ways at the same time." She kept looking at me, her head on her hand. "Anyway, Daddy has cousins in England, but they aren't English, or at least the respectable ones aren't. There's a branch of Baldwins over there who've been doing things like touting cockfights and brawling with other members of the permanently unemployed classes for generations. Soldiers in the standing army, as Daddy likes to say. Our hardworking English relatives are from the Middle East. They're Lebanese Christians from Beirut. They have a tailor shop off Savile Row. They were very troubled when Aunt Delilah rustled up Jeremy Baldwin and threw herself away upon him. When Daddy's brother Simon was eighteen and Daddy was fourteen, the family sent them to America to give them a fresh start."

"I always wondered."

"Don't let on I told you." She flopped onto her back again. "I would hate for any information to get back to the Ornquists."

"Why do they keep it a secret?"

"Because people want to know. Daddy doesn't like people to know anything."

"Who do you think knows this stuff?"

"Me. My mother. The other kids. None of his cronies."

"Marcus?"

She glanced at me. "That's an interesting question. I'm not sure. Daddy has a really strange relationship with Marcus."

"Don't we all."

"Do we?"

"Maybe."

"You don't trust him, do you, Joey?"

"I don't know. I mean, in some ways. I guess I trust him not to blame me if I fuck up."

"But you wouldn't confide in him, would you?"

"I haven't told a soul about you, Felicity. I hardly ever say your name out loud. Do you trust Linda?"

"Do you ever trust an unhappy woman?"

"I don't know, do you?"

"No." She pulled the covers up to her chin, then went on, "But I'm like Daddy. I don't trust anyone." She looked at me and then at the ceiling. "No, not even you, Joey dear. Though you are the most utterly transparent person I've ever met and also the most well-meaning. But I especially don't trust women."

"Betty?"

"My mother is not a woman, she's a saint, but no, I don't trust her because her standards of behavior are different from mine, and she means them and she would use them against me if she thought she had to."

"How?"

"I don't know. But Leslie and I always agree that there are lots of things our mother doesn't need to know. Sally led the way. She used to stop us from volunteering information, just for our own good."

I got up and went over to the fruit basket and selected an apple; then I came back and sat cross-legged on the bed and cut it into four sections. I took the knife and shaved out the cores and set the quarters on the sheet. Felicity picked one up and bit off the end. I said, "Why is Linda Burns unhappy?"

"Well, she didn't want to move here—or there, I mean—in the first place. None of them did except Marcus. The kids hate the school and Linda is bored. She doesn't do anything anymore."

"I thought she was a teacher."

"She was, back on Long Island, but she didn't get a job in our school district, and Marcus told her he didn't want her to teach anyway. She feels like a slave to the house."

"I thought she loved that house."

"Well, she did love the grandness of it. I guess their house in New York was quite small. But she didn't realize how much dusting it was going to take. And Marcus wants there to be big gardens and nice plantings. I've been helping her, but you know she doesn't really have a flair for it." She shrugged. "But anyway, there's something about Marcus. He can do anything with Daddy. He can do anything with my mother. That's the surprising thing, but when he's with her, he's very funny and lighthearted. He makes a lot of jokes and she just laughs and laughs. And he's the first person ever who's willing to go swimming with her in the pond at night. They must have done that half a dozen times last summer. We're all late-night types, but Mom is the only athletic one, and she's always taken these ten-o'clock swims. The rest of us can barely tolerate athletic activity at the best of times. So she's crazy about him. And if Betty likes someone, then that person is fine with Daddy. But Norton keeps saying, 'Oh, he's from the IRS; oh, he's going to bust you.' He always sounds like he'll be happy if Marcus does pull out his badge and say, 'Gordon, I'm taking you in.'"

"Well, Felicity, the IRS is scary, but—"

"Norton is scarier? *Yes!*" She grinned. "Norton always thinks everyone else is going to do what he would like to do." She kissed me, then picked up another apple quarter.

It came over me how satisfying it was to be with her—her beauty and her lustiness were no more appealing than her familiarity. It seemed an unfortunate (though at the moment remote) paradox that the most comforting things about Felicity were also the most forbidden—her sisterlike position in my life, her knowledge of everyone I knew, and for that matter the womanliness that grew naturally out of the fact that she was someone's wife and someone's mother. I said, "I think you are a treasure."

"Do you?" She grinned again.

GOOD FAITH

• • •

When we looked out the window later in the
night, we saw that it was still snowing, the
streets were still deserted. I had a passing fear of
getting caught here and found out—what a to-
do that would be—but the fear had hardly
formed itself before Felicity summoned me
back to bed and wrapped her warmth around
me and began tickling and caressing my face
and head with her fingertips. She murmured,
"You look like someone whose face should be
covered with tiny kisses." She must have
worked on me for half an hour or more, until it
felt like all the layers of my skin had separated
from one another and lit up and the rest of me
had disappeared. I was dimly aware of falling
asleep, and then it was morning and I could
hear Felicity in the bathroom taking a shower. I
lay quietly. The curtains were drawn at the window and the covers were pulled up to my chin
and plumped around me. The room, I could
see, had been straightened a bit—my clothes
were hung up, my shoes were set together beside the door, the fruit basket was sitting in the
coolness beside the window, and the tray from
dinner had been cleared away. I looked at the
clock. It was after ten. I picked up the phone
and dialed the front desk and was told that the

subways were still not running and that only emergency vehicles were allowed in the streets for the time being. Yes, the hotel had plenty of food, and no, at least for a while, the hotel did not recommend sightseeing on foot, as all municipal buildings were closed and all the shops in the neighborhood as well. Snow? On the major streets and in Central Park it was drifting to four and a half feet, but in most places it was more like two and a half. I hung up and lay back.

I picked up the television remote, but Felicity came out of the bathroom before I had a chance to use it. She was smiling and naked, a white towel wrapped around her hair and hanging down her back. Her skin was flushed from the shower. I said, realizing it was true, "I missed you."

"You were so sound asleep. I feel wide awake today. It must be the sunshine." She went to the window and raised her arms to rewrap her towel. The sunshine fell across her breasts and belly and thighs and cast her shadow over the beige carpet.

I said, "Can I get you back into bed?"

"Absolutely. I mean, it's beautiful out there, but we can't get out the car and we didn't bring any boots, so we'll just have to live the sybaritic life." She rubbed her hair with the towel and gazed down at me with a smile on her face; then she bent down and pulled the covers off me. She said, "Ah. You are a hairy guy, Joey. It's very sexy. I just have one question. In the summer when it's really hot, does your body hair serve to wick away the moisture? That's what they say about dogs, you know. The undercoat keeps them cool."

I laughed.

"You know what?"

"What?" I answered.

She sat herself cross-legged on the end of the bed. She draped the towel over her shoulders and clasped her hands. She said, "There are several things I've been wondering about for the longest time."

I propped myself up on my pillows.

She said, "First you have to answer about the hair."

"Well, the hair does form a cushion between my skin and my shirt. My shirt doesn't cling to my chest or my back."

"That makes sense. Now, one time I had a dream that I was wearing a skirt, and I lifted it up and I had a penis, and not only that, it was erect, and I put my hand on it, and it felt wonderful and sexy and I was so glad I had it. I think that was the best dream I ever had."

"You're giving me a hard-on."

"Mmmm. Anyway, I wonder if it feels great every time you touch it."

"Yes. It does."

"I thought so, because one thing I've noticed about my boys is that they've always got their hands in their pants. They don't even realize it most of the time."

I pushed the covers back farther, to reveal my hard-on. Felicity licked her lips, but said, "Why do you have that?"

"Because you're sitting right in front of me with the sun falling on your breasts and your thighs and your bush, and you are drying your hair and talking about erections, and it's very exciting."

"Tell me about touching it."

"Well, it's right there where my hand is, which I always thought had to be for a reason. And I am right-handed, so of course I grab it with my right hand more than my left. I guess you would say that the right hand and the left hand have different functions. One is the grabbing hand and one is the supporting hand. My hand is fairly calloused, but that doesn't seem to be a problem." I began to stroke it, and Felicity's nipples got hard. She was gazing at me steadily now. "Here's what I like. I like that I can feel both sides of the engagement: I like that my hand can feel the smoothness of my hard-on, and that my hard-on can feel the—what is it? Oh, I suppose the security of my hand." Her hand went to her crotch, her right hand. She continued to stare at me. I said, "Any more questions?"

"I think so. But I can't remember them now. I want to have sex."

"Then I'll ask one. What is there about sex that you want to have?"

"I want to be penetrated. I want to feel some pressure in certain spots inside my vagina that I know you can reach." She turned around and lay back on the bed beside me and opened her legs. I got up on my knees and lifted her hips, put a pillow underneath them. The sight of her labia hardened me even more; I was so hard it seemed momentarily dangerous. She was still staring at me. She said, "I wasn't feeling sexy at all in the shower. I didn't care if we ever made love again, but now it's just washing over me." I entered her and she gave a sharp *"unnh"* and closed her eyes and raised herself to meet me and bring me in even farther, as far as possible.

I can't say that I had been feeling especially like making love either, but now we made love with a much grander passion than I'd expected, not as if we had spent the last twenty-four hours together, making love several times, but as if we hadn't seen each other in weeks, as if we couldn't get enough of each other, as if enough thrusting and enough kissing could not be had in this lifetime. Her head turned from side to side. I sucked one beautiful nipple and then the other, and then the first and then the other, and then I held her breasts in my hands and brought them together, and the whole time she was pressing her hands into my lower back and trying to get me deeper and deeper into her. Then we went back to kissing, and her mouth and lips were alive with hunger. I came with a prolonged shout, which I imagined shooting out of our window over the city, rising in a fountain of freezing drops, then shattering and raining down over the street in glittering crystals.

Felicity said, "That was the fuck of a lifetime."

After that, there seemed no reason to leave the room. In the room, Felicity was everywhere, her affection, beauty, and good nature surrounding me and reflecting my every glance. Outside of the room, I felt, she would diminish from a three-dimensional space to a point and then disappear, so it was very important to remain in the room.

Felicity said, "What if I don't have anything to say later today?"

"Then we'll just be quiet. Remember? I'm a single guy. Quiet is second nature to me."

She nodded. We were quiet for about five

minutes. Felicity sat up and put her feet on the floor, then rose gracefully and went across the room to the dresser, where two glasses sealed in cellophane were sitting beside an ice bucket. She said, "Did Daddy ever tell you he won my mother in a poker game?"

"No."

"Well, you know he didn't go to college. The fresh start financed by the English relatives didn't go that far. But he lived in Boston, where there were lots of colleges, and he bought himself the right kind of clothes—this was the thirties and anyway, the whole family's main article of belief was that all you really needed was the right clothes. So, Daddy would go where the college kids gathered and he would strike up conversations and get them to gamble. It was mostly cards, but he also made book on various sporting events and horse races. I think the Harvard guys thought he went to Boston University and the BU guys thought he went to Harvard.

"Anyway, my Uncle Norton had gone to Harvard from down south, where they were from, and he felt uncomfortable in Boston, so my father was like a godsend to him—whiskey, cards, horseracing, and going to strip clubs. So one day, Uncle Norton was way down; I think he owed

Daddy about a thousand bucks, and Daddy told him he wouldn't play cards with him anymore or take any more of his bets, so Uncle Norton showed Daddy a picture of Betty, and he said he wanted to play one more game; if he won, his debt would be cleared, and if he lost, Daddy could marry his sister. You know, Daddy will take any bet, and I think he thought this was just a joke anyway, so he played and of course he won, and Uncle Norton didn't even blink. He just started telling Daddy they would go down to visit the family for Christmas, and then he would arrange everything. That was going to be in about two weeks.

"The next thing that happened was that Daddy bought a house outside of Boston in a tax sale, and it wasn't a bad house and it was furnished. So now he had a house and he thought he was going to sell it and make a profit. Christmas came around, and they took the train down to Virginia, and Daddy had all the right clothes, and he resumed, just a little bit, his English accent, and he let on to my grandmother, who was an incredible snob, that his family had property in Kent, which they do, but he didn't say that the side of the family who owned the property wasn't the old English side. They got there a day before my mother did. Well, the day my mother arrived, she told my grandmother she had just gotten engaged to her boyfriend, who was a local guy from a long line of charming drunks, and this engagement was a possibility that had been terrifying my grandmother for years, because my mother had been seeing this guy since they were thirteen. So as soon as my grandmother found this out, she sort of set Daddy on Betty. Uncle Norton promoted it too, since he didn't want to lose his thousand dollars, so he talked up all Daddy's connections and told about the Boston house, and the long and short of it was that Daddy swept her off her feet and she broke the engagement with the charming drunk and they got married at Easter and moved into the house and Sally was born a year later and that was that.

"But Daddy was terrified to tell her the real story, and Uncle Norton was terrified too, so they kept it dark for months, but then after the wedding Daddy couldn't stand it anymore, and he went to her and confessed and said she could have the marriage annulled if she wanted to. But she just laughed, because it was fun and exciting and she hadn't really loved the other guy, and I do think she really loved Daddy, and this made him seem even less stuffy and less like her relatives at home, and that was how they got married."

• • •

After dark, we went down to the restaurant for dinner. On the way, we went out the doors of the lobby, just to see what it was like. It was cold and the sidewalks had crusted over, thoroughly unwelcoming. We turned and scurried back into the hotel.

The feel of the crowd in the restaurant was neither playful or innocently expectant—more like bored and irritable. At the next table, a waiter was telling a customer which dishes weren't available, and the customer was exasperated. Finally, he said, "Well, if I have to have chicken béarnaise, then I have to have it, but I would have preferred the steak!"

"We are out of steak, sir."

"You said that!"

I thought with satisfaction of the part we had played in eating up the steaks.

After we had successfully negotiated the menu—trout meunière for me and pork medallions with mushrooms for Felicity—our neighbor began moving his chair around irritably.

Felicity smiled at me. We felt so sexily superior to everyone in the room. Across from us, parents with four teenage children were sitting glumly at a circular table.

GOOD FAITH

Felicity's hand came underneath the corner of the table and took hold of mine; then she smoothed the inner seam of my pants with her fingers and squeezed my kneecap. I put my hand around hers and held it until the waiter brought our food. All around us, our fellow diners and, no doubt, hotel guests, seemed jarring and disorderly. Felicity looked at me, then hunched her shoulders. She whispered, "Let's run."

I motioned to the waiter, asked him to pack up the food so we could take it to our room, and a moment later, we were alone again, happy, eating naked in our temporary nest. I knew that within eighteen hours we would be on our way home, and the weight of that began to press against my sense of well-being, but only just. It was like the last hundred dollars in your bank account—enlarged by its contrast to the nothing that would follow, and so almost reassuring in its way.

We watched a late showing of an old Bette Davis movie called *Dark Victory* that I hadn't seen before but Felicity had. Bogart had a bit role, which seemed odd, like a sort of joke. We chatted idly about movies and movie stars and lay comfortably against each other. Then I fell asleep, and sometime deep in the darkness, I woke up from a dream that Felicity had been rude to me—irritable or brusque; after the dream was over, I couldn't remember exactly

what she said, only the hard look on her face—
and I woke up suddenly, very upset. She was
breathing quietly beside me, but when I started,
she woke up and said in a thoughtful tone, "Are
you okay, dear? Joey?"

"I had a nightmare." She put her arms around
me and kissed me on the temple, and I thought
how odd it would be if Felicity were unkind to
me, almost impossible, I thought, and surely that
was the result of not being married.

SUNDAY NIGHT I was awake all night in my bed in my condo, wondering what was going to happen between Felicity and me. There were plenty of things to worry about, perhaps especially the feeling I had that her attachment to secrecy was loosening and that at any rate a large part of her irresistible charm was that she was unpredictable. I had never spent time with any woman, any person, that was so enjoyable moment by moment as our trip to New York, but the lesson seemed automatically to be that such enjoyment was unsustainable and maybe even punishable (here was when I got up and turned on the TV for a while). Of course I wanted her to have had a good time too, as good a time as I had, and of course I knew she had, and the next thing after having such a good time would obviously be leaving the hospitable and friendly conditions of Earth as we knew it and entering the unknown vacuum of outer space, where anything could happen, and so it was best to not dwell on what a good time I knew we both had had, and so. . . .

Early Monday morning, when I finally gave up on sleeping and got up, made myself a cup of coffee, and called my answering service, I discovered I had seven messages from Gordon and four from Marcus. Gordon only said, "Call me." And Marcus only said, "Where the hell are you?"

When I got hold of Gordon at seven, he was not the least interested in where I had been all weekend. "They dug holes all over the place," he said. "Right where the engineer told them to dig; they dug ten holes at least. Took 'em all day. Water just sat there."

I had forgotten in my rush to get out of town that they were going to perk the farm on Friday. "That's not the only possible site, Gordon—"

"Yes, it is, because after they dug the percolation holes, they got the backhoe back out and dug some more deep holes on some of the other flat ground, and the clay layer came up to eighteen inches below the surface."

"There's five hundred and eighty acres of ground out there."

GOOD FAITH

"But between the wooded sections and the hills and the buildings that we wanted to keep for the clubhouse and the equestrian center and the golf course and all, there isn't much leeway. I'm telling you, you put that place back on the market at a moderate price and we can get out of this with our shirts. Remember how old Thorpe died on Friday the thirteenth? That was a sign." I hadn't noticed, but Gordon would have, and did.

"What did Marcus say?"

"Ah, he's got some idea. I just tuned him out. I got a feeling about this one, Joe, and it's not a good one. It's a run-for-your-life feeling."

"You know, when I had it on the market before, I hardly even had anyone look at the place."

"That was the price. I'm telling you, you put it out there at the right price, and someone will show up."

"Okay."

I got to the office at nine. The phone rang as I was hanging up my coat.

Marcus said, "Meet me out at the farm at three."

"I hear it didn't perk."

"I never expected it to perk."

"You didn't?"

"Nah. I had the engineer go over the soil maps with me weeks ago. There's clay everywhere out there. According to old records, that was always considered poor farm country. I guess that's why the Thorpes got it cheap for their horses."

"Gordon is freaking out."

"I know. I spent all afternoon Saturday trying to talk to him. Where were you, anyway?"

"He told me to put it on the market."

"He did?"

I could tell Marcus was genuinely surprised.

"Yeah. He said price it moderately and get rid of it."

"Can't do that."

"Why not?"

"Because the bank would be a little upset if we sold it at half the price they appraised it at."

I had forgotten about that.

"I mean, we can do it if we have to, but my opinion is, Gordon's just panicking. I always thought—" As usual, Marcus sounded relaxed and congenial. I remembered him telling me that there are no big deals. He went on. "I'm going to tell you exactly what we're going to do and how it's going to work and why it's going to work. I tried to tell Gordon, but he just wouldn't hear me, and finally Betty sent me home. She was nice about it, but she meant it."

"She's the one you've got to convince."

"No, you've got to convince."

"Why me?"

GOOD FAITH

"Aren't you the elected son?"

"I've heard that."

"Well, now it's your turn."

Salt Key Farm was carefully under wraps. The gate was padlocked. The flowers and vines and shrubbery, in addition to being dormant, of course, were cut back and banked with mulch. The blizzard had passed north, so the landscape still had the comforting brown look of late autumn. The drive had been raked of leaves; everything still exuded care, and that feeling would be an excellent selling point, but when Marcus's Caddy pulled up behind my Lincoln, I knew in an instant there was going to be no selling. He opened the door smoothly and seemed to roll out of the car and up the steps to where I was standing. He was wearing Timberland boots and jeans, a red wool sweater, and a black goose-down vest. He looked no less perfect than usual, his outfit was just from a different part of the magazine.

"So, listen," he said, taking my elbow and turning me so that I was looking west from the house. "My first thought was a sand mound, of course. There's a kind of dip in the elevation just past that line of trees over there, not far from the horse barns, where a sand mound would more or less disappear, but the guy—you know, Bob, the engineer—said no sand mound.

It doesn't perk enough even to support a sand mound."

"If we divided it into ten-acre parcels, they would qualify as mini farms and—"

"Shit, man! Can you see this place turned into mini farms? Talk about Dogpatch! Nah. We can't afford mini farms. In the first place, the whole back three hundred acres doesn't have thirty building sites and we'd have to put in miles of road and telephone poles. We're in too deep for mini farms, my man. Way too deep!"

"We're in way too deep for lots of things."

"You don't sound like a guy who hasn't had to come up with a single payment yet. You know who I met? The other night at a party for the investment firm I was working for?"

"Who?"

"Your ex."

"Sherry?"

"You got more than one? She gave me such a look when I told her I knew you and how."

"What kind of a look?"

"The look of a woman who let her meal ticket get away."

"Believe me, it was not without a fight."

"I'm sure not. She served our table herself, and when the guy next to me pushed his salad aside after she set it down, she pushed it right back in front of him."

I laughed and we went down the steps.

He said, "She's right."

"Oh, yeah?"

"Yeah. She let a big meal ticket get away."

"Sure. Well, keep it to yourself."

"Nah, listen. Did you see that place up the road, right by the intersection?"

"I knew that came on the market."

"Eighty acres and a couple hundred feet of road frontage or so."

"It's a nice farm. But we have a farm."

"We're going to put a branch of Portsmouth Savings on a couple of acres in there, along with our permanent offices, a small office building, a gas station, and a gourmet market. I don't know what else. Housewares are big. You know, pots and pans from France with copper bottoms. Dish towels from Provence. That sort of thing."

"Very nice, but it's not zoned commercial. They haven't zoned anything in this area commercial since the sixties."

We walked down the driveway, then veered off to the west until we came to a big field. You could still see the pockmarks of the holes they had dug and filled in when they were perking the place. Dry grass, very good dry grass, turfy and thick, whispered beneath our steps. I said, "This is such a beautiful place. It makes you happy to look at it, so I always wonder when

I'm walking around somewhere like this why the people who built and owned these places were never happy."

Marcus looked at me. He said, "They weren't?"

I looked at him. I thought he was joking, but his gaze was open and surprised. I said, "No, they weren't. Haven't you even seen *Citizen Kane*?" Actually, saying this gave me a chill. I suddenly remembered the way Mrs. Thorpe's sister advised her to sell this very place. "Mrs. Thorpe said she didn't have very good memories of living here."

"They're happy," he said. "They just don't tell the rest of us about it. You know, I knew this kid from my high school. He got a scholarship and went up to Yale. Anyway, he came home Christmas of his freshman year, and we were at a party. We were out smoking in the backyard. I'll never forget him turning to me and saying, 'Burns, you just can't imagine all the stuff they have at that university. You name it, they've got it. If the guys from our neighborhood knew what they had, there really would be a revolution.'"

"All right, but it didn't perk."

"Nope, doesn't perk, so no septic, not even with a sand mound. That means there's more opportunity here than we thought, because we're going to have to build a sewage plant.

GOOD FAITH

Now, you can build a sewage treatment plant for a hundred houses, and the cost is prohibitive, or you can build a sewage treatment plant for four hundred houses, and the cost is still prohibitive, but actually not all that much greater than for a hundred houses. But if you lay some pipe, you can link it up with your little shopping center and your other development a couple of miles down the road, a more modest development of, say, three-bedroom houses on quarter-acre lots. Two hundred houses there, four hundred houses here, the little shopping center—I think Jim Crosbie is going to go for it in a big way, especially when he realizes that with this deregulation of the S and Ls that Congress just passed, he can get a branch of his savings-and-loan out here before anyone else thinks about it. And they're going to let S and Ls develop properties now. It looks to me like they're going to let them do just about anything they want, and maybe you and I don't think Crosbie's the man to do it, but he does, so we work with him. I can deal with him. Say, where were you over the weekend?"

"This area still isn't zoned commercial. No one out here is going to want commercial zoning, either."

"Where's the mandated low-income housing in this township?"

I smiled. I said, "Gordon did that once, about fifteen years ago, when he was putting in Lawrence Hills Estates."

"Did what?"

"Told the zoning commission that he was going to put a trailer park in Lawrence Township, since there wasn't one—or any other kind of low-income housing either. They changed the one-acre minimum to accommodate his quarter-acre lots at the next meeting of the zoning commission."

"A savings-and-loan branch and a few tasteful and convenient stores and some office space would brighten the area up, is what I think. And with six hundred houses, there would have to be a school. That's always a lucrative project."

"Are you going to call this place Marcusville?"

"Phoenix Park. Look at this."

We had been walking in an arc from the house. The grounds were not exactly lawn and not exactly pasture but a cultivated, gentle slope punctuated by solitary spreading trees that had been shaped over the years to frame the view of the house. At the bottom of the slope, we entered an open glade that ran along a sizable creek. Marcus grinned. He said, "This flows into the Nut down from Blue Valley. I think we can also get into the water business."

GOOD FAITH

"You can't take water from the creek, Marcus. Then you get the whole state into everything."

"Maybe later. I'll look into it. Maybe I'll run into someone with an idea. But the main thing is not to let Gordon get cold feet at this point. You need to talk to him."

"Why me?"

"He doesn't quite trust me. He thinks I'm too glib."

"I don't know that Gordon listens to me. Mostly over the years I've listened to him."

"Shit, that's your advantage, man! All these years you've listened and learned, and now you've got an opinion of your own, something worth hearing, because you normally keep things to yourself, but this you can't keep quiet on, because you don't want this opportunity to slip away, right?"

"Well—"

"Shit!" He spun around. "You know what? I always know what's going on. When Justin was born, the cord was wrapped around his neck. We were in the delivery room, and Linda was breathing and all, and she hadn't quite gotten to—what do they call it?—the final push, and I was looking at her face, and then I looked down at her belly and I saw him in there with the cord tight around his neck, and I stood up and grabbed the OB by the shoulders and

shouted in his face, 'The cord is choking him!'
Thank God the guy just put her under and
opened her up right there, in like two minutes,
and sure enough. But I wasn't surprised. It was
as simple as reading a book."

"But that's not the same—"

"As what? As knowing what this place is going to look like and be like? As seeing our
money turn over and over and over until it's
worth billions?"

"Billions?"

"Billions."

"More than one billion? Because you know
even that Wal-Mart guy down in Arkansas is
only worth a couple of billion. And he's the
richest guy in America."

"It's all changing! I'm telling you, this time last
year I was reading income tax returns. It's like
reading the book of the future, to read income tax
returns all day. There's money everywhere! Money
money money! You know what they say at the
IRS? Reported income is like cockroaches. For
every dollar you see, there are a hundred more in
hiding. And it's looking for a home! Don't you understand how things work? There's a lot more
money than there are good investments, or even
investments at all, even bad investments. I mean,
you go to the racetrack and all these guys are plac-
ing bets. What does that tell you, first thing?"

"I don't—"

"It tells you people have too much money, even down-and-outers, even dedicated track bums whose idea of a day's work is finding a tipster who knows a guy in the barn. Money these days is like water. It can't stop looking for a place to go. It's filled up all the places it usually goes, and now it's lapping at the shore and seeking out other nooks and crannies. I always look at questionable investments, you know, to see how much extra money there is. Pretty soon, the people who have the money don't care what the return is. They can take a tax loss if the return is negative, and that's worth something too."

"But look at interest rates. If there was all that money, interest rates wouldn't be so high."

"I don't agree with that. That's what they tell you, but it's not true. My analysis of high interest rates has to do with the shakeout of the banking system. That's another aspect of too much money. The banking system is being flooded with money and all the investors, especially the institutional investors, like the Soviet Union—"

"The Soviet Union?"

"Sure. You don't think they aren't big participants in the worldwide capitalist system, do you?"

"I don't know, I—"

"Look at that house."

I looked up the hill at the crisp granite lines of the house, the windows across the front, the shrouds around the shrubbery, the graceful arching branches of the trees.

"It's so small. As long as you think of it as big or imposing or impressive, you won't understand what's going on. You can't be intimidated by what you see, or you won't think up anything new. If you're afraid of something, like a big number or whatever, then your mind sort of locks up and nothing else can get in there. You know that feeling?"

"Well, sure."

"What I think is that every moment of fear is a lost moment of imagining something new. You said that the state wouldn't go for the water plan. Okay. Maybe not; we can decide about that later. But If I look at the creek, and think, Oh, it runs all year round and runs pretty good, what does that make me think of, then, that might lead to another idea that the state wouldn't care about. All over the world except America, you know what they drink?"

"Wine?"

"Wine is good, but no, bottled water."

"Bottled water? Like seltzer?"

"Some fizzy and some not. It's a holdover from the spa days, when they thought the minerals in the water would cure things. We find a spring on this property—and we easily could, given the geology of this area—and I'm telling you, we've got Blue Valley Mineral Water in greenish bottles shaped like flower vases, and it's another fortune!"

I said, "You are so full of shit, Marcus."

The day after Thanksgiving, I found myself over at Gordon's. The festivities of the day before had sloshed over into breakfast, which had shaded into lunch, and there was quite a crowd, including Felicity, who I knew was there but hadn't seen. I had seen Hank and greeted him in a friendly way, without an undue sense of unease. Maybe Felicity's strict refusal to talk about him or about their marriage had had the intended effect. My relationship with him was exactly as it had always been, because I knew exactly what I had always known about him and no more.

Betty was in her element. While I was waiting, subtly, to get Gordon alone, I watched her with her granddaughters. Betty was beautiful, and you didn't think of her as a grandmother, but she had Leslie's four girls, the oldest about twelve and the youngest about five, sitting at the kitchen table drawing ball gowns with colored pencils. She was flipping pancakes. "That's very elegant, Renee. But do you really like black for a ball? Maybe a masked ball, but a wonderful Christmas ball in a golden palace? I don't know."

"How about navy blue?" said the twelve-year-old.

"Navy blue is for conservative little girls who will certainly end up in the Junior League in some secondary town like Hartford, Connecticut. I suggest midnight blue with some sort of silver trim. Peach, is your dress meant to be ankle length, darling?"

One of the middle ones held up her drawing and Betty looked at it, then flipped her pancakes. "Ankle length is very sexy, Peach, but you have to have just the right shoes. It's so hard to find the right shoes. You have to go to Paris. It's even hard to find the right shoes for an ankle-length gown in New York."

"I'll go to Paris, then," said Peach.

"Excellent idea," said Betty. "I'll go with you."

Peach smiled, perhaps at the thought of having her grandmother all to herself.

I was tempted to ask for something, just to be a part of the group. My mother, of course, did not have this sort of opportunity, though she would have liked to. When I was her only child, she had made something of being my mother, creating pear salads with faces and teaching me rhymes and games. But I had no children, and so our

GOOD FAITH

Thanksgiving the day before had been attended by my father, myself, my mother, and four ladies from the church, ages seventy-two, seventy-three, seventy-four, and eighty-six, who had nowhere else to go. Betty must have sensed me watching her, because she cast me a friendly glance over her shoulder, as if to say, If you would only listen to my advice, you would have everything you want, even the things you haven't got sense enough to want.

I went into the living room and once again gave Gordon the high sign. Bobby, idly massaging his calf, did not look away from the television, but Norton, who had brought his family to town for the long weekend, scowled at me without, I think, actually realizing it. Then he poked Bobby, who was sitting beside him on the couch, and said, "Move the fuck over." Bobby moved over. Gordon got up and cocked his head to motion me into the office.

He closed the door behind us softly, with a Middle Eastern touch, I thought, my view of him now colored by Felicity's revelations. "Ah, Joe," he said, and strolled over to the window that looked down over the back lawn. The summer furniture was put away and the pond was glazed over with a thin layer of ice. The rope swing hung from the tree and swayed heavily, describing a small circle in the otherwise invisible outdoor breeze. "You put that place on the market?"

"It's a bad time to put a place like that on the market, Gordon. Somebody gets out there for a look, and pretty soon he's saying—or she's saying, which is all the more likely—Where the hell am I? How much is it going to cost to plow the driveway?"

"Probably. Serves me right, anyway, having to do with old man Thorpe. I always said I wasn't going to be a sucker for the blandishments of the bourgeoisie—"

"You did?"

"Well, not in exactly those words." He smiled. "I'm telling you, those are the folks you sell to, not the folks you buy from. And it's hard enough to sell to them. If you do, then you know who they are. But he got me."

"Gordon, if we aren't putting it on the market, I think we should go ahead with our plans."

"Whose plans?"

"Yours, mine, and Marcus's."

"I don't remember having a plan."

This sounded very bad. I knew Gordon well enough to know that the very best way to get him to flee any situation was to give him the idea that he was being had. And his sense of whether he was up or down was entirely instinctive. He was a good poker player, but he didn't count cards. I sometimes thought he sniffed the air of the room like a dog and scented some sort of subtle change in his opponents as soon as they looked at a hand. I gazed at him. He was unhappy. The key was to make him happy. He drained his cup of coffee and set the cup down. I said, "Can I get you another cup?"

"Nah." He looked out the window. "Just don't try to talk me into anything I know better than."

I said, "Marcus thinks you don't trust him."

"I don't. I told you that. I never trust a mick."

"Well, you told me that, but you said that you trusted Marcus because he knows what he's doing."

"Did I?"

"Well, you said he knows what people want."

"That might be true." He reached into his back pocket, took out a handkerchief and blew his nose, and put his handkerchief away. Then he said, "But the other night he was talking to me, and I looked at him all of a sudden, and I thought, Who is this guy? I met this guy, what, six–eight months ago? And who introduced me to this guy? Bobby!" He blew air out between his lips, not quite spitting, and shook his head. "Between you and me and the wallpaper, Bobby is not such a great reference. And now he's here in my house in the bosom of my family. How the hell did he get here? I don't know. Just gave me a fishy feeling. I mean, everyone I know, I've known for twenty–thirty years."

I said, "Okay, let's leave Marcus out of this. I've got an idea. Who's that guy you know up in the city? Zack somebody."

"Zack Schwartz?"

"Yeah."

"What about him?"

"Why don't you have him come down here and look at the place. Doesn't he buy building supplies and fixtures for fancy brownstones and apartment buildings?"

"Yeah, among other things."

"Well, you've got a treasure trove of building supplies and fixtures in that place, even just in the barns and the outbuildings. Even just in the windows. You said it yourself months ago. Take the place apart and sell it piece by piece. I bet you could make back most of the purchase price, and then you could decide what to do with the land after." Actually, I had no idea about the market for things like leaded glass, crystal chandeliers, inlaid flooring, or book-matched paneling, but I happened to know that the market for rare woods was pretty good.

"Marcus is thinking that house is going to be some sort of clubhouse."

"But we set that aside. It's not going to be a

clubhouse if there's no club. I'm just saying this. We put the place on the market in the spring, when it's at its best. Who are we going to sell it to? Say some insurance mogul comes around and he's got some money to buy it, but when he looks at the gardens and the grounds and then walks through the foyer and the library and the kitchen, he's going to say to himself, 'This is more than I can take care of. Where do I hire the servants?' So let's say we sell off the fancy stuff at a good price, and then we have the leeway to figure out the best thing to be done with the land." Even as I was making my way through this murky idea, it was sounding almost plausible. "At least call him up and have him come down and tell you what's salable and what isn't."

Gordon was looking visibly perkier. "The real money is always in things you don't expect, like doorknobs. You know, once I bought a house in Portsmouth, nineteen-hundreds home or there-abouts, nothing special—I mean, no future on the National Register of Historic Places or any-thing like that—squeezed between a diner and a dress shop down on Henry Street. Anyway, it turned out that the doorknobs, of all things, were handmade in Hungary in the seventeen-fifties. Very historical doorknobs, made by some famous sculptor when he was an apprentice somewhere, and how they got to Portsmouth nobody knew, but there they were. I must have gotten twenty-five for them, and that was when you could buy a nice little house for twenty-five."

"Twenty-five thousand dollars?"

"Yup. A guy came over from Europe and packed them up and took them home."

"How did you figure out they were valuable?"

"Oh, I just had a feeling." He shrugged, but the fact was, I had hit pay dirt with that scavenging idea. There was nothing Gordon liked better than getting something for nothing. He stood up from the desk and stretched. He picked up his coffee cup and came around the desk, taking my elbow. He said, "Come on. Let's go see what everyone is doing."

When we opened the door of the office, Norton was standing right there. Without blinking or making the slightest small talk, he said to Gordon, "Did you tell him to put it on the market?"

"We talked about it," said Gordon evenly.

I said, "It's the wrong time of the year, right now, but—"

Norton scowled. Gordon pushed past him in a practiced way, and I was right behind him, but Norton put his hand on my arm and more or less stepped in front of me. I stopped. He said,

"Are you guys out of your minds? Has it occurred to you that this guy is an IRS agent?"

"He *was* an IRS agent. I thought that was
one of his attractions, Norton."

"Yeah, well, how about undercover investigation? How about this unreported commission
and this other unreported sale? Who says
he's doing what he says he's doing? My guess is,
he's been sent out here to—"

I stared at him in disbelief.

"Fine. Fuck. See what I care. But don't say I
didn't warn you."

"I won't." I started to ease past him.

"And another thing. You do something he
doesn't like, and that whole tax bill? Back bigger than ever."

"Maybe so." By this time, all I wanted to do
was get away from him. He had that effect on
people, always had.

Felicity was in the kitchen, looking rumpled
and sleepy. She smiled when she saw me and gave
me the expected sisterly kiss. She was wearing
checked pajamas and sheepskin slippers. Hank
was behind her, leaning into the refrigerator, his
back turned to us. He said, "I think I'll go out and
pick up a gallon of milk and a dozen eggs. It
looks like your mother is running out." I
thought, So this is it, this is how we go on, and
while he was talking and I was thinking this,

Felicity was introducing her fingers between the buttons of my shirt and tickling my chest, which was so dangerous and exciting that I stopped thinking entirely. By the time Hank had turned around, Felicity was yawning, her arms stretched over her head. She said, "Oh, honey, bring me back a Coke, would you? They're out of that too. Are you leaving, Joey?"

I spoke casually. "I'm going back to the office."

Hank said, "I'll walk out with you."

Felicity kissed him on the cheek, as she had just kissed me. She said, "Drive carefully, sweetie."

He nodded.

Of course, I could not help being hyper-aware of Hank as we ambled toward the front door. His nearness made me edgy. I gauged whether he was taller than I, better looking than I, younger or older than I in less than a second, and not voluntarily. I must have sighed. He said, "Something wrong?"

"What? Oh, no."

"You were breathing heavily."

"I was?"

"You were."

"Hunh," I said.

We opened the door and went out into the cold, me first, him closing the door behind us. All of a sudden, he said, "Hey."

GOOD FAITH

My heart jumped, and I felt the back of my neck turn to rock.

He said, "I want to talk to you about something."

"You do?"

"Yeah." He turned to face me. "Listen."

I wondered if he was going to poke me in the nose.

He said, "You guys really going to build four hundred houses on the old Thorpe place?"

I nearly fell down with relief. "I don't know. Depends on the waste-treatment situation. The place didn't perk, you may know."

"I heard that. But I also hear Bobby pushing Gordon to build a sewage plant last night after dinner, saying you were all for it and the other guy too. Marcus."

"We've barely talked about it."

"It's a shitty idea." He sniffed, and some of his too long, too lank hair fell onto his forehead. There was a moist quality about him that put me off.

"Maybe, but—"

"That whole end of the county should be kept as is. That end of the county doesn't need to be developed. Doesn't make sense."

"We don't know yet if it makes sense—"

"There's nothing out there! You want to put something out there that wouldn't naturally come there, that will have a lot of negative environmental impacts. I wouldn't even support a golf course. You know what kind of pesticide and fertilizer runoff you get with a golf course? And then four hundred lawns on top of that? Lawns disgust me."

"They do?"

He looked actually angry. I had never seen anyone angry about lawns before. "Yes . . . they . . . do."

"Oh."

"Now, Joe, we've known each other for a long time, right?"

Had we? I said, "Right."

"Why would you go out on a limb for something like this? I don't understand it. I've never seen you as a slash-and-burn developer type. I mean, you recycle. You sell old houses and then find contractors for people to help fix them up. I actually think that's an admirable thing, a type of conservatorship. I've often thought you do good work. Don't undo in a couple of years what you've spent almost twenty years building."

"Well, I—"

He put his hand on my shoulder. He said, "Sorry to lose my temper there for a moment."

"That's okay, I—"

"We'll talk again." He nodded and then trotted down the steps. I followed more slowly, watching as he went to his car, opened the

door, and got in. I have to admit, I was offended. All the way to the office, my thoughts
ran along Who-does-he-think-he-is? lines. It
was his manner that annoyed me, I told myself,
just that hint of self-righteousness, that idea that
he had exonerated me of slash-and-burn! It
went on and on, even though I knew perfectly
well that he had a right to his opinion and I
was sleeping with his wife to boot.

Back at the office, I called Marcus and told
him he had some time; Gordon was going to
think about recouping some of his investment
by selling off the interior of the buildings and
the house. Marcus said, "That's what you talked
him into?" He sounded nonplussed.

"It was a spur-of-the-moment argument. He
got happy, though."

There was a long silence. Then Marcus said,
"Well, I see your point. I do see your point. I
definitely want him happy."

CHAPTER 14

THE SLOANS CLOSED on their new house a couple of weeks before Christmas, and the folks they were displacing, the Meyerses, closed on their new townhouse half an hour later. It was a profitable morning for me, because still another buyer, this one a single woman who was a new dean at Portsmouth Junior College, was closing on a nice house in Farmington, not far from where my parents lived. That neighborhood, though modest, had held its value, and Dr. Montague paid $80,000 for a house that friends of my parents had bought in 1936 for $6,000. It was a successful morning all around: happy buyers, happy sellers.

Thus it was with some surprise that I received

a phone call several days later from Carla King, a Realtor with a big firm in Portsmouth. She said, "Joe, isn't this guy George Sloan your client?"

"He was. We closed Friday. They looked for—"

"You know that house Swallow Properties had listed?"

"The Hollywood place?"

"Yeah. Well, it's our listing now. I've had it for about a month."

"Good luck, it's rotten from top to—"

"He's still got a key. I don't want to have to change the locks; they're old and they're all brass and everything."

"Have you spoken to him?"

"Four times. He keeps putting me off. It gives me the creeps."

"I'll speak to him."

"I wish you would. He seems very strange to me."

"He does? I always think of George Sloan as Mr. Normal."

"Oh, no. No, no, no."

"Well, I'll call him. Do you have any nibbles on that place?"

"Maybe for a restaurant. There's a couple of guys down from New York. A chef and an investor. A *destination eatery* they keep calling it."

"They're going to need plenty of money to fix that roof."

"Oh, they've got two of the most profitable restaurants in the city, and a TV show. Money is no problem."

George Sloan's secretary answered and put me through to George. He answered in his office-supplies-distributor voice, very deep and a little hard. I identified myself. His voice softened and rose slightly. I said, "Mr. Sloan. Glad I got through to you. How's the move coming?"

"A week from Monday. I guess we'll be moved in by Christmas."

"You got a good deal on that house. I'm sure you'll like it."

"The kids are excited."

"I don't know if you remember that hillside house, the one with the upside-down roof?"

I waited for acknowledgment. It came.

"Well, they need the key back. The Realtor said you can just slip it in an envelope and mail it over."

"Yeah."

"Soon, though, or they're going to have to change the locks."

He didn't say anything.

"That place is going to be a bear if they have to change the locks. Very inconvenient."

Nothing.

"Here again, I'd have to say the former Realtor did you a favor by letting you go over there on your own, that's really not allowed, and probably she let you do that because she didn't think she was going to find a buyer, but now they've got some restaurant people down from New York who are interested, very interested, so it's important that you return the key ASAP."

"Yeah," said Mr. Sloan. Carla was right. A little creepy. Not tremendously creepy, as if he were entirely unlike himself, but a little creepy, as if the George Sloan I knew weren't all the George Sloan there was. "Yeah," he said, more loudly and firmly. "Yeah, I'll have my secretary send it over today."

Apparently, on Monday, the day of the move, George Sloan was not around to lend a hand, nor did he turn up on Tuesday, which was the day Carla King realized that the key had never gotten back to her, though it was over a week since my reassuring call, and on Wednesday, she called Mrs. Sloan. In the meantime, Mrs. Sloan had called the county sheriff's office. Everyone put two and two together, and on Wednesday afternoon, Carla, the sheriff, and Mrs. Sloan found Mr. Sloan camped out in the old house. He had a cot, a kerosene lamp, a little stove, and some other supplies. On Thursday, it was in the paper, which is where I found out about it. The article was titled, LOCAL MAN SQUATS IN HISTORIC HOME and read, in part:

There aren't many neighbors, but if there were, they might have reported ghosts, or at least odd doings in the old Horner House, which overlooks the Jamaican Valley from its perch on the side of Glass Mountain, west of Cookborough. George Sloan, of 456 Meadows Drive, Monhegan, has apparently been staying in the house from time to time for the last three or four months. He was found there Wednesday afternoon by his wife, Torey Hayward Sloan; the Realtor who lists the house for a local real estate firm; and Sheriff Andrew Slater. He had been missing from his own home since Monday.

The Horner House, also formerly known as the Glenwood Estate, was owned by silent screen movie star Marydelle Horner McCue, and was built in 1924. In its day, it was famous for the parties given there by Miss Horner, as she preferred to be called, and her New York friends. Marydelle Horner, known in her movie days as Della, the Darling of the Polo Set, specialized in movies about runaway rich girls and Palm Beach scandals, though she was actually born and educated in Denver, Colorado, the fourth daughter of the owner of a dry-goods store, before moving to Atlantic City in 1919, at age sixteen, in search of celluloid stardom. Her mentor was the famous German director, Mauritz Goffman. Her original name was Hilda Veck. Ms. Horner died in 1954, from the complications of alcoholism. There was some evidence of suicide, but her son, flyer Rolf Horner, forbade an autopsy. There was no evidence of foul play.

The Horner House then was the subject of a disputed—

I skipped down to the bottom of the article. The last paragraph read:

Mr. Sloan had little to say about his reasons for squatting in the house, except that he found the view restful and the situation a pleasant one. According to Ms. King, the Realtor, the Horner estate, which owns the house, will not press charges. She went on to say, "I understand the Sloans contemplated purchasing the house at one point, which I certainly believe, since it is a unique and historical house and very reasonable in price."

There was no mention of the upside-down roof.

What do you know? I thought.

My problem about Felicity had several aspects, which I had organized in my mind. One was that we had gone too far. The trip to New York had been too much fun and too intimate. If I hadn't experienced that, I might not now be ruminating obsessively about some way into the future for us both, in a manner that allowed not just sex but conversation, companionship, long hours together. The aspect that sat right next to that first one was that we could go no further now that we had gone too far. You didn't have to think about it more than a few seconds to understand the whirl-wind we would get into—I would get myself into—if Betty got to know, or Gordon, or my parents, or even Marcus—even Crosbie and Bart, for that matter. Imagine a group of friends and family sitting around an outdoor table, eating peacefully. Imagine the umbrella shading them. Imagine the pole of the umbrella going through the circular hole in the table and then into the patio. Imagine a stick of dynamite inside the pole. Imagine them laughing, and then imagine a trusted member of the family lighting the dynamite. I wanted to be that guy I had been in the fall, ready for anything, equally ready for nothing. If I could be that guy again, Felicity and I could go on as before, keeping our perfect balance between frustration and delight. She didn't call and she didn't call, and then she did. Bobby was sitting at his desk. The phone had a long tangle of a cord, and I took it into the storeroom and closed the door. Then I sat down on a box and stared at the way the black coil was pressed against the doorjamb. She said, "What are you wearing?"

"A big hard-on."

She giggled.

"How about you?"

"Jeans. No underwear. No bra."

"When are you coming over?"

"I don't know. On holidays everyone is around."

"Your brother is in the next room. He's listening outside the storeroom door, for all I know."

"Then you shouldn't refer to him as my brother."

"Do you have any nude pictures of yourself?" This was my solution. I had asked for them before.

She didn't say anything.

"Just to get me through the winter."

"If I say yes, you'll think I'm a wanton hussy, and if I say no—"

"You *are* wanton, Felicity. But—"

"I am with you. Anyway, no. And it's very sordid and exciting for you to ask. Thank you."

"I'll take some. Come over. I've got a Polaroid for taking pictures of houses."

"No, I want to present you with them." She giggled again; then the receiver went dead, the cord tightened against the doorjamb, and I heard "Shit!" from the office. I stood up and opened the door. Bobby was sitting on the floor. He exclaimed, "What the fuck are you doing with the phone, man? I nearly killed myself!" But it turned out that he just jammed a couple of fingers against the bookcase and bruised his forehead.

On Christmas Eve, 1982, I was almost forty-one years old. I could not see anything wrong with my life. I felt good: old enough but not too old and better than I had felt at thirty, still married then and, it seemed in retrospect, inured to keeping my head down and trying not to cause, or at least get into, trouble. In the past ten years my parents had given up on me, which was more or less a good thing. Though I didn't share their beliefs and I hadn't produced grandchildren, I was gainfully employed and we got along amicably. On Christmas Eve I took them a present, a plum pudding of just the sort my father recalled from his youth, wrapped in a cheesecloth soaked in brandy and accompanied by a jar of hard sauce. When I went into the dining room and set it on the table, we stood back for a moment, and then my mother put her arms around my waist and gave me a squeeze. She said, "You are always a thoughtful boy, Joey. Don't think I ever forget that."

I returned her squeeze. I knew that my thoughtfulness was not exactly cold comfort compensation for the other things, but maybe cool comfort. I was a disappointment but at least likable, and that was not unimportant to them. How many times had I listened to them deplore the way some of the children of their friends treated their parents—disrespectful, or inattentive, or argumentative. At least I was none of those things.

My father came in from the kitchen with a box of kitchen matches, which he set down on the table. Then he relieved the heavy dark pudding of its brandy-soaked wrappings, my mother lifted it carefully out of its box and placed it in the center of her Royal Doulton cake stand, and my father set it afire. After it was well lighted, and burning with a steady but almost invisible blue flame, he stepped back and took my mother under his arm, and they watched it with happy smiles on their faces. He gave her a little squeeze and kissed her on the forehead when it was all burned down and, supposedly, all the alcohol in the brandy had been dissipated. Then my father lifted his voice and exclaimed, "Thank You, Almighty Father, for this delicious and traditional treat, which reminds us simultaneously of Your bounty, of our son's kindness, of the abundant year just ending, and of the abundant year yet to come. It reminds us also, O Lord, of our loved ones who taught us of Your love and have gone before us into Your mansion, where they await our coming with the same eagerness that we await seeing them again. Tomorrow we celebrate the birth of Your Son, for whose coming we thank You, Father. Amen." He spoke without self-consciousness, because giving thanks was something he always did, as normal for him as asking a customer how he could help her or ordering a shipment of laundry soap and toilet paper. We said "Amen" and my mother brought out three leaf-shaped dessert plates. She said, "I didn't look for a celebration until tomorrow, but one found me anyway."

"I knew you didn't have any plans, Mom."

"Well, there was a service before supper this evening. We went to that, but the congregation is so small these days. When you were a boy, all us ladies were young, and there was more a sense of Let's-do-it-for-the-children, but now the sense is, The last thing any of us need is another slice of pie." She laughed.

"Frank should have a membership drive; that's what I told him," said my father.

I nodded. My parents' congregation was part of a sect that was peculiar but, more important, small. All of evangelical America was growing up around them without any effect on their church. The whole sect, around the nation, didn't number more than a few thousand, and most of the members, worldwide, were in Australia and the South Island of New Zealand. There were missionaries in South Africa, Kenya, India—everywhere in the British Empire—but as the empire shrank so did the sect. When I was a boy, we had missionaries to dinner all the time and success stories abounded: a small church built here, several souls saved there. The church was making headway against ignorance and self-indulgence. But even then, the stories got told, and the jubilation was expressed, and then conversation gave way to laments about what the larger churches could afford to do, especially the Catholic Church, the all-powerful, wealthy, strangling, popish, robot-creating, idolatrous octopus whose control of otherwise beautiful and populous places like Ireland and South America and Mexico would never be broken. The worst thing that could happen would be that our missionaries would soften some souls up for salvation, and then the priests would move in and win them away with the temptations of spectacle and secrecy and conspiracy and the easy alternation of sin and absolution. Not to mention the open promotion of sex and procreation for the express purpose of increasing the number of Catholics, who, of course, were then christened before they knew what hit them, and after that carefully robbed of free will through the rote learning of the catechism. My father hated the sin, though he loved the sinner—he really detested Catholicism the way only Orangemen could do, but he was a very sociable man, who was welcoming and helpful to everyone he met, O'Houlihans and Ferraros and all. He had been the same with me—kindly and loving, on the whole, but quick to use the rod for my own good. I often thought that, but for the accident of a warm and almost jovial temperament, which most consistently expressed itself in affection toward my mother, my father would have made a sincere and effective tyrant.

They were interested in current events, more interested than I was, but, as they filtered every issue through tests of faith, sometimes they took unexpected positions. In the election the year before, my father had ended up abstaining from voting altogether for the first time in his life, because the candidate he preferred, Ronald Reagan, was unclear about his religious background. How could he be Irish and not have a lot of Catholic back there somewhere? And if he wasn't or hadn't been Catholic, how come he wasn't more forthcoming about it? Didn't he care? But it was impossible that he didn't care; indifference to religion, as far as my father was concerned, was the greatest impossibility of all. However attractive he found the candidate, in the end he couldn't pull that lever for fear that the mind-shaping effects of early Catholicism were latent in the man. I remember him saying with perfect seriousness as the election approached, "Well, I hate to say this, but I would just have to meet him and judge for myself before I could vote for him, so I can't do it." Somehow, something that bothered others, and that I expected to bother my parents, that he was a product of Hollywood (and my parents abjured movies and did not allow me to see one until I was fourteen) didn't come up. Hollywood was something you could slough off; early Catholic influence was not. And my parents were suspicious of the Moral Majority and the other evangelical movements, too. "Baptists!"—my father would shake his head—or "If they really understood what John Wesley said, they wouldn't be flocking to that church!"

My mother set out three prettily embroidered napkins, and we sat down in our places at the dining room table. Things were a bit awkward, then, because in spite of the fact that we got along well enough—or, perhaps, in order to get along well enough—we didn't have much to say to one another. I heard the teakettle whistle and, with some relief, got up to make the tea. When I returned with the pot and the cups on a tray, my father was helping himself to another slice of the pudding, and my mother was well into hers. I set a cup of tea by each of our places and put the pitcher of milk in front of my father. I sat down again. My father asked me what I had been doing. I bragged a little about selling a lot of houses.

"I'll tell you what happens around here." He shook his head. "I've seen it more than once. Someone, or some group of people, suddenly gets a lot of money, the way people did in the twenties, say, and all of a sudden they discover this area, and it's beautiful and unspoiled, and they build a legendary house, and everyone around here thinks, Well, it's finally happened; we've finally been discovered, and it's all gravy from now on. But what it's really like is an extra-high tide. It floats things up onto the beach one time, but that's the only time. The tideline hasn't changed."

My mother was nodding. She said, "There's always a reason why some place is unspoiled."

"Too far out of town," agreed my father.

Since this directly contradicted our Salt Key Farm plan, I was tempted to argue, but I had yet to tell them much about the place, and anyway I had stopped arguing with them so long ago I didn't know how to begin, so I just sat there uncomfortably, watching my father pour milk in his tea and drink it down. The fact was, I had always preferred Gordon and Betty to my own parents, just as, according to Felicity, Gordon had always preferred me to his own sons. Maybe the real tragedy was that Norton and Bobby didn't prefer anyone to their own father.

But finally I said, "What do you mean, there's always a reason why some place is unspoiled?"

"Well, people do tend to spoil things, don't they," said my mother cheerfully. "They take the best places first, so what's left is naturally second best for some reason."

My father was nodding. They always agreed, so they had this habit of one nodding when the other one was talking. "Here's what I think," he said. "We can't live in paradise, because man is fallen. He felled himself with his own hand. Redemption doesn't take place in this world, Scripture says, so whatever looks like paradise can't be, and so it isn't. If we look for it to be, then we are deceived, and Satan is at work."

"More than you know," said my mother. Now they nodded together. I was having my usual feeling—whenever I found myself thinking that they lived in the same world I did, I was almost instantly disabused of that notion. I must have sighed a deep sigh, because my mother said, "That's right. But the lessons are all around us, if we choose to pay attention to them. More tea, honey?"

As I went down the front steps to my car, I wondered for the umpteenth time what would happen if one of them died. I had been wondering about this in one way or another since childhood—which one could I live without, did they actually have any existence apart from each other, who could I live *with,* what in the world had they been like before they met (he was thirty at the time; she was thirty-one, not young), would the survivor feel any sense of relief, or would he (she) just die? They, of course, would have answered that it was the simplest possible thing for one to go on ahead and receive the well-deserved jeweled crown, and it would be as a moment in eternity until the other one appeared. But could you have such a thing in a marriage as too much agreement? Would either of them manifest less righteousness if he or she *didn't* have the support of the other one once in a while? And, the oldest question of all: Would things be different, would *I* be different, if I were one of many, even of two or three? If there had been two or three to be holy and two or three to be prodigal, maybe I would have escaped notice altogether.

There was a late Christmas party at the Davids' place that I was headed for. I had hardly seen Felicity, only briefly one Sunday evening at Gordon's. The days went by. That was reassuring in a way, because it seemed like we were putting more distance between ourselves and that dynamite explosion, making more of an opportunity for a real solution to present itself. Driving from my parents' house to Deacon reminded me of another feature of my childhood—the safety of doing nothing, of nothing happening. My parents were always on the alert for sin, always ready to root it out, especially out of me. Categories of misbehavior were clear-cut and rather numerous. I could get into trouble without really meaning to, and my father realized this but punished me anyway, to give me something to remember the next time. He thought that if a memory of the punishment cropped up right at the same time as the temptation to transgress, I would stop myself. It was all a manner of systematic training. For whatever reason, this did not work with me, so there was always a period after I realized I had transgressed but before my parents found out. It was like being under a spell, so quiet and still, my parents so like themselves and me so like myself, yet lit up with the expectation of what was to come. Any stray word or action could break the spell, tip them off to the transgression, tumble us into the endless effort to drive sin out of me as it had been driven out of them. Over the years, I suppose, I had gotten to be a careful person. The Baldwins had made me more exuberant, but they hadn't really made me less careful.

But Felicity was at the Davids'. It was nearly midnight. She drew me into a corner and put her arm through mine and bent her head against mine and kissed me on the cheek and I was so happy to see her and feel her presence that I rang like a bell with the shock of good fortune. She whispered, "You know, I sent them skiing today. I said to Hank that the boys had been wanting to spend time with him, which was an absolute lie, and then I said to Jason and Clark that he missed them even though he doesn't say much about it, and so they were on the slopes for seven hours, and everyone came home, very happy and tired, to the turkey I cooked, and they were sleeping by nine! I was a tremendously good mom today." She kissed me right on the lips. The Davids' house was dark and filled with people I had never seen before. David John came over and put his arm around Felicity. He said, "No secrets, darling."

"I told you I drugged my whole family so I could come to this party."

"You could have just told them you were going to Midnight Mass. That's what Elena did." He gestured across the room. "How's Joey?"

I looked meaningfully at Felicity. "A little frustrated."

"Oh, my goodness. Do tell."

"He wants me to give him dirty pictures."

"Of you?"

"Not dirty," I said. "Just nude."

"Oh, the dirt comes later. Absolutely. Yes."

"But they're impossible to take!" exclaimed Felicity. "Have you ever tried to take a picture of your whole body? I bought an inexpensive Polaroid, but I couldn't get anything in. I mean, one shoulder that looks like a loaf of bread and a breast that looks like a mozzarella cheese. So I got my husband's camera, one that has a shutter delay, but then it felt strange setting it up and then running over and arranging myself on the bed and even stranger setting it up and running over and arranging myself on the dining room table.

And when I had a roll, I didn't dare take it to be developed because I had forgotten and put my face in." She was laughing.

"I want your face in. That's what makes it not dirty pictures." I was laughing too, mostly with delight at the thought of all her efforts.

"It's a much harder assignment than I thought it would be."

"I'll take them," I said.

"Oh, honey," said David John.

"Come to my condo."

She shook her head. "That's a half hour from here and I have to be home in an hour."

"Mingle," said David John, and then we had to mingle. Felicity stayed for maybe forty-five minutes. I watched her the whole time. She kissed me good-bye when she left, a full-on Felicity kiss that reassured me in several ways, and then I stayed till at least three, because I couldn't believe how many new people had slipped into our area without first stopping at Stratford Realty. I was very friendly and welcoming—a lot of them hadn't bought yet. I fell into bed later thinking I had done a good night's work in every way.

It snowed on Christmas Day, and I had a piece of luck. I was supposed to go to Gordon's late in the afternoon, but I stopped by my office on the way, to do paperwork for an hour. Even though the snow was cascading out of the sky, there came a knock on the door, and then Morris Levine walked in. Morris was looking for a five-bedroom house, and he wanted to buy before New Year's. I pulled out the multiple listings, and we found one—just one—five-bedroom house. It was south of Deacon, maybe seven miles from the office, and we drove there carefully; Morris had chains on his tires. I let us in with the key in the lockbox, and two hours later I had a signed purchase agreement—a perfect example, I told Bobby, when he didn't even show up for work on Monday (hungover), why Realtors have to be prepared to work holidays. "Well, yeah," he said, utterly without conviction. But by the time I had finished with Morris Levine, the roads were so snowy that I dared not go anywhere but straight home, and so I didn't see Felicity, which I had been counting on.

After that, two storms came right up the coast and turned inland, and a third storm came south off Lake Erie instead of going north, and the result was that I was preoccupied with shoveling and just getting by for almost two weeks. I saw more of my parents. I shoveled their driveway and walks five times in fifteen days and helped my mother with grocery shopping and a dentist appointment; she was terribly afraid of breaking her hip. Even if my father hadn't been at his store, I would have taken her around because, as she herself said, "He's got enough to handle in this weather with his own old age." On Sundays, I took them to church before noon and brought them home in the late afternoon. It reminded me of when they drove me to church when I was a boy. We took the same streets and made the same turns. The only difference was that I was not as sure as I had been that everyone going in the opposite direction was literally going to Hell. I didn't see Felicity at all. I came to think that spring would solve our insoluble dilemma or at least we would find ourselves going off together again once things picked up at the state park and Hank had more to do.

CHAPTER 15

IT WAS LATE JANUARY when I emerged from this familial cocoon. The weather had been clear for a couple of days. The sun was out and the roads were dry. Ice hung in the trees like glass beads. I was driving around, checking on my listings to make sure they didn't need any caretaking—that the driveways were clear and no tree branches had fallen in front of doorways. I didn't want any buyer's first impression to be that there was a mess to clean up. I had two listings in Portsmouth, and after the first one I happened to be driving past Cheltenham Park. I saw Marcus's car in the parking lot, so I turned around at the next intersection and went back to see what was going on. I hadn't heard much from him—

or from anyone, for that matter. My eagerness for Felicity had subsided a little too. I was just a guy doing stuff, not a billionaire in the making or a connoisseur of the erotic. It was boring, but familiar and not unpleasant. That was another pleasure of not being married—I could subside into dullness without bothering anyone.

I hadn't been to Marcus's office since he'd moved in, which struck me for the first time as odd. If I was his partner and his friend, shouldn't my presence be required more often? Perhaps I shouldn't be feeling like I didn't know even the most basic facts, like where was the place. Whose office was this, anyway, Salt Key Corporation or Marcus himself? I was suspicious and edgy by the time I actually found the door and opened it, and my first unmannerly question to the person inside was "Who are you?"

She looked up. She was a thin brown-haired woman in a blue dress, and before she had time to say anything, Marcus flowed out of his office with a grin and came around her desk. "Joe! This is so perfect, man. I just said to Jane, here, you've got to call up Joe at his office and see where he is, because there's so much going on that I need to talk to him about. God! I can't believe this weather! Where have you been, in hibernation?"

"More or less. Bosom of the family."

"Speaking of family, this is my sister Jane. She's helping me out."

Jane came around her desk with a big smile, holding her hands out, and when I went to shake hers, she slid smoothly up to me and gave me a hug. She said, "Joe this and Joe that. I was beginning to think they were putting me on, and there wasn't any real Joe to help me put my little brother on the right path."

"Jane Burns?" I said.

"Ah. I wish. Jane Johnson for now."

"Have you moved here?"

"Lock, stock, and dog. Three weeks ago to-day."

"Where did you come from?"

"Kansas City."

I laughed.

She said, "You must have been to Kansas City."

"No, I was thinking of something my mother said. Someone she knew came back from the Midwest, and she couldn't remember where, only that it was one of those places with slaughterhouses."

They laughed.

"So, Jane," said Marcus. "I'm going back to my office, and you show Mr. Stratford in to me." He sped into his office and closed the door.

A moment later, Jane called out, "Ready or not, here we come!"

Then she turned to me. Even though she was plain-looking, she had a humorous smile and a twinkle in her eye. She propelled me in front of her, opened the door, and said, "Mr. Stratford to see you, Mr. Burns. Won't you go right in, Mr. Stratford?"

She closed the door behind us.

Marcus leaned across the desk. "Jane is a genius, Joe. I couldn't believe it when she told me she was coming East. I begged her to come and work with me, even though she had already taken a position in New York. I won't even tell you what they were going to pay her to analyze third-world loans. Enough to buy an apartment by the Metropolitan Museum of Art. She was all set to sign the papers and I talked her out of it. She is really excited about what we are doing. Makes banking look like playing pattycake, that's exactly what she said. I mean, everything I know I learned from Jane."

"I didn't realize you had a sister."

"Well, she's five years older, you know; she was a senior in high school when I was in seventh grade, so she's always seemed beyond everything else. And then she moved out to the Midwest right out of college, got married and everything, so I've mostly viewed her as a legend." He leaned forward. "No kids. That's the bad part. She waited too long. And then he left her for a younger woman who he's already got pregnant, and they aren't even married! Good thing my mother isn't alive to hear that. Ugh. I can't believe that guy. I'd like to say I could see it all along, but I couldn't. I thought he was great. We've played golf plenty of times, no problem. I thought they were stuck together with Krazy Glue."

"She must be devastated."

"Well, she and Linda have had a few talks, but she's a monster for work. Just sets it aside and gets on with it. She is really on top of things, too. She knows all the new investment instruments, and how they work, and who's doing this and who's doing that."

"What are *we* doing?"

"Well, that property is still on the market, the farm by the side of the road that we talked about a couple of months ago. Time to make our offer. Crosbie thinks the whole thing is a brilliant idea, very visionary; even better than that, I discovered he's been in secret negotiation with an S and L in the western part of the state. I have to hand it to you, Joe. I didn't understand what Crosbie had to offer, but now I do, and it's exactly what you said. Lots of very conservative depositors."

"I've had an account there since junior high."

"Exactly. I guess this possible merger candidate has a better loan profile but iffier depositors and is dying to get into this part of the state. Anyway, the place is about to get a tremendous infusion of cash. He told me one of the nuggets he had to offer was this new idea. Even though the Salt Key Farm thing wasn't big to them, our plan for a sewage plant and the minimall and the more modest housing was like a golden apple hanging from the branch. No one else in the state is doing anything like this. You would have to go down to the DC area to find anyone who really understands the possibilities; that's what they told him. So the merger is waiting on some paperwork, and then there'll be cash everywhere."

"What did Gordon have to say?"

"He was pretty dazzled. Crosbie called him, so he called the guy in New York who was going to come and cart away all the good stuff and told him to wait. I think, outside the savings-and-loan and even outside the inner circle over there, we might be the only ones to know what's in the works, and we're all pledged to secrecy. The problem is working capital. It's almost February already. The first of April we've got to start on the roads and the pipes—"

GOOD FAITH

"Where did you get the permits?"

"Well, that's what I was going to call you about. The planning commission out there meets in eleven days—what is that, Tuesday, February eighth?—and I think you have to have your application ready before that meeting. I leave that entirely to you, since I don't know that side of it at all."

"What am I applying for?"

"Everything we talked about. Four hundred houses at Salt Key Farm, a golf course, a clubhouse and equestrian facility and bridle paths, the sewage treatment plant, and the minimall and two hundred dwelling units on the new property. I haven't mentioned the elementary school; I think it's best to wait on that for at least six months, but obviously we're going to need permits, and pretty fast, so there you go!" He was grinning enthusiastically.

I thought he was joking. The last planning commission meeting I had been to, in Deacon Township, they had talked for an hour and a half about whether the Washington Market should be allowed to enlarge its sign from four feet by twelve feet to eight feet by sixteen feet and eventually voted it down. They denied the post office another twelve feet of parking space. That took forty-five minutes and the testimony of thirteen citizens of the town. I said, laughing,

"And when would you expect to get the zoning approved?"

"Well, an April-one start date would mean approval, at least basic approval, in March. The March meeting is also on the eighth. I think twenty-five days would be time enough after that to get things in order. Gordon built those townhouses in about four months—"

"Which isn't the same thing at all."

"Larry built that house in—what, twenty-eight days?"

"Twenty-nine, but that was in the sixties. I've seen that house. It was a simple ranch-style house on a slab." It seemed he wasn't joking after all. I sat down, the way you always do when you are delivering unexpected bad news. "Look, Marcus. For a project like this, we are going to be going back and forth with them for months, maybe a year. It's not like we can go in there eleven days from now and come out with permits."

"You work on it. Don't be careful unless you have to. See what you can get away with. Dazzle them with the size of the project and the beauty of it. I'll find some plans somewhere. I've got the ones of my house here. I've been showing them."

"Are you crazy? Those are Gottfried Nuelle's plans, and he isn't going to be building these houses. It would take him four hundred years to build four hundred houses."

"Just to give the feel of that house. I never say he is the builder or these are the plans, but just for a sense of what it's going to be like. Jane thinks we should have a model of the whole thing, 3-D, like they do corporate headquarters and stuff. I don't suppose you know anyone who does that sort of thing? If you could have that ready by next week?"

He looked so excited and eager and well-dressed and businesslike that I hated to say what I had to say, which was, "I doubt it. Actually, I wish you would come to the board meeting and meet the enemy. It's not the way you think. These are people with jobs. They don't get paid much and they do it in their spare time."

"Maybe I should, but for now I've got too much else to do. Potential investors are parading in and out of this office. Jane is bringing some people in on the third to work up this investment idea we have. Out West they do it all the time. It's called real-estate trust shares."

"Did you tell Gordon you expected permits in the next two months?"

"Well, his attitude was the same as yours, so I didn't get into it with him." He came around the desk and sat down on it. He leaned toward me. "You're right. We should have gotten started on this in the fall, I admit that, but we didn't, so we are getting started on it now. Time flies when you're having fun. That's okay. Crosbie wasn't being swallowed up in the fall, that other property wasn't on the market in the fall, Jane was still married and working in Kansas City in the fall. Everything is fitting together just fine. Don't worry about it." He put his hand on my shoulder. "I'm telling you, Joe, we are never going to pay taxes again."

So I didn't worry about it. For one thing, he had the big suite, and for another, although there was no way to explain the challenges of the permitting process, one meeting would bring him right back down to earth, and there was no use worrying until he'd been to that one meeting.

I checked on my other Portsmouth property and went back to my office and called the Board of Supervisors for Plymouth Township, and—lo and behold—Vida put me on the agenda for the February eighth meeting, after Marie's Pink Poodle Dog Boarding Kennel, which wanted to add six more runs; the county itself, which wanted to upgrade the toilet facilities at the state park in the northern corner of the township—"That shouldn't take long," said Vida, "they'll rubber-stamp that one"—and the Darley Corners Garage, which wanted to take out one gasoline storage unit

and put in a newer one. "And that isn't volun-
tary. Mike Lovell would dearly like it if the
township wouldn't give him a permit. It's a big
job. But they're gonna stick it to him after all
this time. That place is an eyesore. So, you're up
after Mike, Mr. Stratford. I hope the weather
holds and the meeting isn't canceled." She
added that I would need to have a sketch plan
for the township engineer and the commissioners themselves a week before the meeting. That
would be four days from now.

I sat back in my chair and gazed out the window, thinking how maybe I was the only person
in the whole world who could appreciate these
two things coming together—the nationwide
quality of Marcus Burns's ideas and the sheer lo-
calness of Plymouth Township. As if my mind
was being read, the phone rang, and it was Hank
Ornquist. He asked me to have lunch with him
and, not taking the *no* I couldn't quite utter for an
answer, said he would be passing my way around
lunchtime and would stop by. I should look for
him a little after twelve. All I could manage in reply was "Okay."

After he hung up, I called Felicity, not even
thinking that he might still be at home, but sure
enough, he answered. The sound of his voice
when I had been expecting hers ran up the
back of my head like the point of a knife. I said,

"Oh, Hank. What time did you say? I was momentarily distracted."

"Just after twelve."

"How about more toward twelve-thirty?"

"I'll be there."

So I had thoughtlessly done myself out of "mistakenly" missing his visit.

Hank showed up. Why was it so easy for him to show up and so hard for her? I was drawing up my little plan of two phases of the Salt Key Farm project, the golf course and the clubhouse. I had a call in to Gordon's favorite engineer, who was supposed to get back to me after lunch. On my own I had decided it was best to break our plan to the zoning board gently, one step at a time. First the golf course and the clubhouse.

There was a knock on the door. I put my sketch plan in the drawer of my desk, and shouted, "Come on in!" Even the fact that he bothered to knock when there was a sign on the door that said WALK IN annoyed me, but I smiled and stood up and held out my hand and said, "Thanks for coming by."

"Oh, sure." He pulled out his handkerchief and wiped his nose. He said, "Sorry, we've all got colds."

"Really? That's too bad. I haven't had a cold in a year." I saw that I was going to be involuntarily posting evidence in my own defense throughout the lunch.

"Mind if we get something to eat? I'm starving."

"There's a sandwich shop over in the mall."

I held the door for him and turned the sign to the BACK IN A FEW MINUTES side. He walked out ahead of me. His pants were too short. His hair curled in a lank and unsightly way over the collar of his shirt, and its sleeves were also too short. His feet were very big, as Felicity had said. I couldn't stop looking at them. I said, "So, there must not be much going on in the—uh, state parks this time of year."

"Cross-country skiing. Snowmobiling. Snowshoeing. Helicopter rescue."

I looked at him: deadpan or humorless. Hard to tell. "Yeah?"

"We brought a fellow and his son out last weekend."

"Were they okay?"

"A little exposure was all. They got caught in that storm Friday night. They didn't quite have the equipment and supplies they needed."

We ambled on. I said, "You like that sort of thing?"

"Winter camping?"

"Yeah."

"Not much anymore. I used to take the boys

out, but then I broke my leg one time." I imagined Felicity catering to a broken leg. We entered the sandwich shop, and he ordered tuna salad and water. I ordered a double roast beef with cheese and extra pickles and a large Coke, a very masculine order I would have said, if I had been entirely honest. I paid.

"So," I began, as we sat down at one of the tables. "What can I do for you?"

He blew his nose, took a bite, wiped his mouth, took a drink of water. Was he good-looking? What had she seen in him and when?

"Jerry Taylor called me from out in Plymouth Township and told me you put yourself on the agenda for the next meeting."

"Jerry Taylor. Yeah, right. He's the township engineer."

"I was hoping it wouldn't get this far." He looked stricken. His forelock flopped forward again, so unappealing. I decided to stop noticing his hair, and said, "How many times have you seen Marcus Burns in the last year?"

"Every couple of weeks, either at Gordon and Betty's or at our house for dinner, I suppose."

"So what gave you hope it wouldn't get this far?"

"Marcus Burns spouts this and spouts that, but he doesn't have any idea what he's doing. Without you, he wouldn't get anywhere."

"I'm sorry?"

"Oh, he's just a bullshit artist. His type comes and goes. They don't usually do any harm, but if they get hooked up with someone who has a real plan, they're dangerous."

"And I'm the one with the real plan?"

"I think so, yes." He squared his shoulders.

"Well, Hank, I'm flattered in some ways, but I've got to beg off on this one. I think Marcus is pretty visionary myself. He's got a whole theory about what's happening with this administration and the country as a whole, and how that is going to affect this area, and I think he might be right, and his vision might be profitable for me and Gordon and for this area, for that matter."

"Felicity said you would put it off on him if I confronted you, but—"

"She did?" Then I recollected myself. "How would *Felicity* know?" Maybe that constituted a recovery. We stared at one another for a moment, then he said, "Well, she's known you longer than I have. I think she would call you a friend."

"I suppose." My reply, I thought, was a masterpiece.

"But frankly, I've been with the guy, maybe more than you have, and I've watched him pretty carefully, and I don't think he's got what it takes to come up with this—to get in with Gordon so far and so fast. And through Bobby?

Gordon is suspicious. It takes him a long time to warm up to people. I think I probably knew him for five years before I was convinced he remembered my name. Now he's putting up all his best pieces of property as collateral in various schemes? I doubt it." He took another bite of his sandwich. "You're the one he relies on; you always have been, though you can deny it all you like. I don't know your reasons, but I'm making my pitch to you."

"So make it."

He took a bite of his sandwich, set the sandwich down on his plate, chewed and swallowed, and turned the sandwich around a quarter turn. "You know what I think about Deacon."

"Why don't you remind me."

"It's overpriced and overdeveloped. In the last ten or twelve years, it's gone from being a real small town with actual people living on Main Street to being this plastic fern-bar souvenir sort of place. I can't even go to Deacon anymore. The traffic drives me crazy."

"Hank, fifteen years ago, Deacon had a population with an average age of sixty and everyone any younger was planning to get out. Now it's a growing little town. People are taking care of or improving the housing stock, for one thing, and even though some of the improvements aren't very tasteful, others are. The town finally has some money for street repair and services, God forbid."

"And higher assessments and a larger proportion of native residents who can't afford to live where they have spent their whole lives. But Deacon is done. I'm just telling you about Deacon to set the stage for the next thing. I've given up on Deacon."

I thought of Marcus Burns. I said, "Look, fifteen years ago people our age didn't have any disposable income; now they do. They're going to move to nice places like Deacon and redevelop them into the towns they want. It's a population explosion sort of thing."

"But you don't have to *lure* them there. You don't have to set up a beacon in the woods that says, *Come here, come here.*"

"And that's what you think we're doing?"

"Well, of course. A fancy golf course and a clubhouse, the whole idea of getting access to a famous estate." He sniffled again. "And it's at the wrong end of the county."

"It's at the end of the county where the estate is." I suppose to a developer, or at least a Realtor, that fact was self-evident, so I said it as if it were. Hank shook his head skeptically, as if the estate weren't where it was. I said, "It's not wilderness, it's farmland, and not very good farmland at that. It's more beautiful than it is good. When the Thorpes bought the land, they didn't buy it from prosperous, thriving, successful farmers, they bought it from people who were lucky to get rid of it, looked at from a farming point of view. What are you going to grow there? I don't think you have a leg to stand on, Hank. You can't say it's wild, you can't say it's highly productive, you can't say it's likely to be a state park or anything like that, because there's a state park only ten miles away. Jacob Thorpe is dead, the Thorpes are finished with the property and the area, and it's time it was put to another good use."

"The support network that would go into building and keeping up four to six hundred houses, a club, and the necessary shopping areas would be more than that end of the county could tolerate. The roads would have to be widened, there would be waste-management stress, and it has no purpose. It doesn't grow out of the local economy, and it doesn't make sense for the area as a whole. It's arbitrary." He rested his forearms on the table—pugnaciously, I thought—sat up straight, and looked right into my face.

"It's not arbitrary. It's where the land is. What would you do with the property?"

"Thorpe should have left it to his children. The daughter, at least, was eager to have it."

"A, he didn't, and B, that's what she says now, but why didn't she persuade him at the time?"

"He didn't like her husband, is what I heard. I think it's a tragedy. The whole issue could have just lain dormant for another generation, and that end of the county would have been able to find its own purpose."

I finished my sandwich, folded up the paper it had been wrapped in, and took a last swig of my Coke. I truly didn't want there to be hard feelings between myself and Felicity's husband. I pushed my chair back and smiled in a friendly way. Finally, I said, "It's not always clear what the highest and best use for any piece of property is. This one has been beautifully cultivated for fifty years or more. There's a nice garden and beautiful buildings and pastures and lawns. I could make the case that in order for it to be kept in cultivation— kept up, even, given its size—more than one family has to contribute to its maintenance. It's like when Sherry and I were in England a few years back. Those estates that the nobility were able to use two hundred years ago their descendants now have to turn into hotels and amusement parks or give them to the government to maintain as museums."

Hank shook his head.

What did I learn about Felicity from watching him? At that moment, I thought, the property could come and go, the scheme could come and go, the billions could do what they pleased, if only I could figure out how her exuberant and affectionate soul had come to be joined with this stubborn and slightly uncouth guy, how she had gotten caught in what she called the "frat house." I sat back and grinned a big friendly grin, heaved a "well-that's-that" sigh and said, "So, if you're heading home, say hi to Felicity for me. I guess Clark is back in college, huh?"

Hank looked at his watch. "Actually, he and Jason went for a day of skiing. I guess they'll be back late tonight. Then he goes. I've got to be in Portsmouth at two. I have three meetings this afternoon. What with all the snow, there's a lot of stuff we need to catch up on." He shrugged. "I've got to admit, I get a little cabin fever this time of year. That helicopter rescue was kind of fun, though of course we ought to charge them for the helicopter time, since if they'd been prepared. . . . Well. State services cost money. We're always begging for such little bits of money. Anyway." He pushed himself back from the table.

From the window of my office, I watched Hank turn east toward Portsmouth and then jumped in my car and drove immediately in the opposite direction, toward their house. I did not call ahead.

GOOD FAITH

Whoever was there or not there, I would deal with it. I was a Realtor. At any time of the day or night, I could be driving down any road in the county on perfectly legitimate business.

Felicity's road looked especially scenic. The leafless dark branches of the encroaching trees opened upward toward the bright sky, and the plowed snow along either side of the blacktop was as clean and billowy as clouds. Sunshine poured down. Red barn here. Green barn there. Two furry ponies eating hay by the side of the road.

Felicity's house looked peaceful, dappled with moving patches of light. The front porch was gently subsiding away from the house. I hadn't noticed that in the summer. One car was parked in the driveway, her car, the BMW. The driveway was not meticulously shoveled, the way my parents' was and the way my office was. Bluish tire marks snaked over areas of flattened snow. I opened my car door, but then I just sat there for a moment, hoping her face would appear in the window and she would wave me inside. It did not. I got up out of the car and closed the door. I went to the front, stood on the porch, used the knocker, and pushed the doorbell. No answer. Then I used my knuckles. Quiet. I went off the porch, traipsed through the snow, went to the back door, knocked, peered in. Chairs were pushed back from the table. One pair of boots stood by the stove, and another had been pushed under the table. There was a plate on the table, and a fork on the plate. At the exact moment I was thinking that maybe there was a side to Felicity that I didn't want to see, a side that contrasted to her beautiful free side but that was inextricably linked to it, I heard her voice in my ear, saying, "What are you doing?"

I jumped. "Looking for you."

"I was in the barn." She was cocooned in a navy blue goose-down coat, her hair hidden under the torpedolike hood and her hands in her pockets. I put my arms around her shoulders and kissed her on the forehead, but I could tell she wasn't happy to see me. I said, "Hank said he was going to be in Portsmouth all afternoon, so I seized the moment."

"Hi." She softened a little and smiled at last. After a moment, she turned her face up and kissed me, but her hands were still in her pockets. She said, "How was your lunch?"

"We agreed to disagree. Who do you agree with?"

She looked at me for a long moment and then softened a little more, reaching up and kissing me again. She said, "Not you, dear."

"You don't think we should develop the farm?"

"Now that you ask, no."

"Oh." I almost asked why not, but I didn't. I knew why not. They were married. They talked about things. They had opinions together and shared interests. I couldn't keep myself from looking around—stoop, door, driveway, car, the white bulk of the house looming over us, property (an acre or two? more?) spreading around us. This was not what I had been looking forward to. I said, "I've been missing you."

She shook her head.

I tried again. "May I do some pictures? I have a camera in the car."

She stared at me, then said, "The house is a mess. I don't want you to go in there."

"Let's go somewhere." I unsnapped the two snaps on her hood and pushed it back a little, so that I could see her hair. She didn't stop me, but then she pulled it forward again. We kept looking at each other, until finally I accepted that I had done just the wrong thing. In other circumstances, with someone else, I would have said, *I love you,* because it seemed to me that I did, but hadn't she told me love was a technical term for her, reserved for others? And if I told her I loved her and she didn't reply, would I not do something very odd, like start to cry? It seemed like I would. I suddenly felt very sad, as if I might start to cry anyway, and so I gave her a little kiss on the forehead and turned and went down the steps to my car and got in and drove away, and while I was retreating down that road, I thought that this wasn't the way that I had thought we would go forward after our trip to New York, but after all, it was the most logical, so logical there was really nothing to say about it.

I tried to reach her the next day, and then there was another storm, and then it was Monday, the day before the sketch plan was due, and the engineer and I were working feverishly on it. In the morning I was to take it to Marcus and Gordon for their comments, and then I needed to get it duplicated and in to Vida by five. Axel Tinker, the engineer, was an old friend of Gordon's and was doing me another in a long line of favors—the first favor had been going out there on Saturday, even though the snow was knee-deep, and snow-shoeing around for three hours trying to put what little you could see together with a de-tailed site plan of the property. The second fa-vor had been working for a few hours on Sunday. The third favor had been not yet even mentioning his fee. Now he was well into the fourth favor—working after hours—when the phone rang. "David Pollock here," said the voice when I answered.

"Hey! I thought you guys were snowed in up in New York."

"Someone wants to see you."

I glanced at Axel, who had known Felicity since she was a child and certainly had attended her wedding and knew to whom she was and was not married. I said, "I'm working late on—" But I knew where her loyalties lay. I interrupted myself. "How late?"

He turned away from the phone to mumble something and came back to me. "Curfew is at ten tonight. A certain someone is on the alert, though not for anything in particular. But my guest is watching her step these days."

"Gotcha." It was seven. We had planned on working all evening. Now Axel was looking at me. I said, "I'll see."

"We'll put a candle in the window, darling."

"Right." I hung up. I said to Axel, "Something's come up."

Just because Axel was accommodating didn't mean he was not irritable. He gave me a sixty-year-old-man look, but I braved it and was motivated to say, "Two more hours ought to about do it anyway, don't you think? It's just a sketch plan."

"I like to do things right."

"I know you do. That's why Gordon relies on you."

"He does."

There was a silence. I sighed. I said, "Well, we'll see where we are at nine."

"I told you, you're not asking for enough. You're not preparing them, and they're going to be put off by later surprises. You've got to put some houses on the plan, around the fairways of the golf course and on this long hillside here, where they've got the view. And the treatment plant needs to go in too, at least a small one. You can add on to those in a modular way. Here's a spot by the creek that's kind of out of the way."

"I don't know that they're going to go for lots of houses right now. I'm afraid of too much density."

"Well, the zoning out there is for two-acre lots. Do that and put more in later."

I looked at my watch. Axel said, "We can put this off a month. That's fine by me."

And so I didn't see her that night, because I was intimidated by Axel. I sat there with Axel Tinker until after eleven, watching nine o'clock come and go and feeling it as a certain kind of inevitable pain whose source had been there from the beginning. My father would have had all sorts of expressions for it: chickens coming home to roost, getting what you deserve, making your bed and lying in it, maybe this will be a lesson to you. We talked about the sketch plan; we added in this and that; I arranged to take the plan over to Marcus and Gordon the next day and discuss it with them and then find Axel and put in changes, if need be. And when we closed the office and Axel said, "Well, I think we've done a good job here," I nodded and thanked him and shook his hand, but the fact was he cared more than I did. I got into my car, I think it is safe to say, a different person from the one I had been when I arrived at the office that afternoon.

CHAPTER

16

O N THE DAY of the meeting, Gottfried Nuelle called me and said that he wanted to go with me that night. I said, "What?"

"Don't you *what* me. I'm already fit to be tied that you didn't tell me you bought the Thorpe place. I've been looking at that property for twenty years. I saw it go on the market, and I saw the price they put on it, and I was waiting."

"What were you waiting for, Gottfried?"

"Well, I was waiting for the goddamned price to go down, what do you think I was waiting for? I'm not an idiot."

"So, just out of curiosity and without offending you, I would like to know how you know about the planning commission agenda."

"Vida's husband is my wife's cousin Buck."

"Vida."

"The woman who put you on the agenda, Stratford. What's the matter with you?"

"We've got lots of people going already."

"Good, then I won't have to sit near that asshole."

"Which asshole is that, Gottfried?"

"The one you sold my beautiful house to."

"Marcus."

"Him. Yeah. You fix it up so I don't have to sit next to him, and I'll go with you. I won't say a word."

"I'll believe that when I see it, Gottfried."

"Watch me." He hung up.

I didn't see a way out of this, given the fact that I had two houses of Gottfried's listed and I had spent a lot of money advertising both of them. I also didn't see that I absolutely had to get out of it. Gottfried was an interested bystander, he had been building upscale houses for a long time, and maybe he would have something to say or offer that would be of value. Gordon didn't actually like Gottfried, few did, but he respected him and he was a more-the-merrier sort of guy anyway.

Even so, it made me a little uncomfortable—though not nearly as uncomfortable as the actual meeting. We filled an entire row at the back of the general purpose room of the township hall: Gottfried next to me, me next to Gordon, Gordon next to Jane, and Jane, at Gottfried's insistence, next to Marcus at the other end. Jane was very friendly with Gottfried, almost, you might say, uppity. As soon as we arrived (the three of them had gotten there before us), Jane marched right up to Gottfried and took his hand. She said, "Well, you must be Mr. Nuelle. I'm impressed. You're surprisingly young. I thought of you as some sort of ancient craftsman, you know, ninety years old and still fitting stones, no mortar, just the thinnest seams."

"I don't do stonework, ma'am," said Gottfried.

"Well, that's just an example. Excuse me for running on. But my brother's house is maybe the most beautiful new house I've ever seen. He's hardly worthy of it, being such a Philistine and all. Would you mind showing me some of the others?"

"Joe here can do that, ma'am. I don't show my own houses."

They went to their places and sat down. Everyone sitting in the rows in front of us (maybe ten people) turned to look around. They gave Marcus and Jane extra-long stares because they were beautifully dressed, Marcus in a gray suit and Jane in a black cashmere outfit, as if they had a big city date after the meeting. It was hard to tell if Jane had flattered Gottfried or offended him, but he did keep his mouth shut for the next two hours, and that was astonishing enough.

The poodle woman was wearing pink, the theme of her establishment. She had hair from the 1960s, ski pants, and rubber boots, the sort you never saw anymore, that were made for wearing over high heels. They had fur around the tops. She wore a big smile and lots of lipstick, but when it came to pitching her dog runs, she mowed them down with facts, presented very rapidly. There were five commissioners, and she locked her gaze on each one in turn as she discussed dog and cat populations in the county, animal control possibilities (as a favor to the county), waste management, dog shows, the American Kennel Club, neutering programs, and general dereliction of animal control duties on the township's part. She had seen a dog pack herself, crossing Roaring Falls Extension, numbering sixteen animals and led by two basset hounds, and if we didn't think basset hounds were capable of feral behavior— well, we had another think coming. They passed her six dog runs 5 to 0.

The commission had decided to pass the state park facilities without meeting, so that left

Mike Lovell. It was only seven-thirty. Marcus leaned around Gordon and caught my eye, tapping his watch happily. Gordon looked a little dozy, and Gottfried was monumentally quiet. After the pink lady, everyone in the front rows turned around and looked at us again.

Mike Lovell shuffled to the front of the room and stood in front of the table of commissioners like a recalcitrant schoolboy. From her place at another little desk, Vida read aloud the permit status: "'Gasoline Tank Installation permit for Michael Paul Lovell, Darley Corners Garage, 261 Grass Hill Road, Unincorporated Area, Plymouth Township. Permit applied for the removal from said property of one gasoline tank, thought to be leaking—'"

"I don't think it's leaking," said Mike.

"Where is Grass Hill Road?" whispered Marcus to Gordon.

"'And disposal of said tank. Tank to be replaced by newer model of similar capacity.' What company is doing the removal, Hank?"

"Don't know yet."

One of the township commissioners said, "When we met about this before Christmas, Mike, you said you'd have something lined up by the new year."

"Well, I ran into a little trouble."

Another commissioner spoke up. "This has

been on the agenda every month since the summer, Mike. That tank has got to come out."

"They'll take it out and see there's no leak, and then that's going to be a waste of my money. Here's the deal. I think if you folks want it out, you ought to pay for it."

"It says right in your operating license that you have to 'oversee your equipment and make sure it is in good repair,'" said the first commissioner.

"My dad got that license."

"Well, yes, he did, but when you took over the station, you were supposed to know what was in it."

"Well, I didn't, and now I'm stuck. This whole thing is your idea. If that woman down across the road there hadn't complained, this never would have come up, and now you're believing her and not me. I say the tank isn't leaking, and there's nothing wrong with the woman's well water."

A woman in the front row stood up and said, "It stinks to high heaven. I've been getting water from up at the state park now for ten months. I ought to sue you. You know what it's like, to have to go get every drop of water you drink and wash dishes in? It's no picnic. The lab said there's benzene in the water."

"That doesn't mean it comes from my tank. That tank is no more than ten years old—"

And now Marcus Burns raised his hand. One of the commissioners noticed him and said, "Yes?"

"Do you mind if I ask where Grass Hill Road is?"

"The property in question is on the northeast corner of Plymouth Village, where Grass Hill Road crosses K Street."

"Thank you," said Marcus. Next to me, Gottfried rolled his eyes. But Marcus was not finished. He said to the woman, "Do you mind if I ask your name, ma'am?"

The woman's head swiveled in our direction. She said, "I'm Suzannah Saylor."

"Thank you," said Marcus.

I turned to Gordon and whispered, "Don't let him buy any more property." Gordon nodded.

A third commissioner said, "Mr. Lovell, this issue has already been decided. We can't keep arguing over the same facts."

"Well, take my license away. Then where's everybody going to get gas or get their cars fixed? Will they drive to Cookborough or Deacon? That's a twenty-mile trip for gas. You know how many times a week I look under somebody's hood, knowing I'm not going to get paid for my time? I jiggle this or I fiddle with that so the driver can get to the dealer and have it fixed. Or I sell somebody a buck or two's worth of gas so they can fill up over by the highway. You think it's worth it to me to go into debt so I can keep doing that?"

Marcus shook his head. Gordon put his hand on Marcus's knee.

"What about last week? I was out in the cold jumping somebody or other at the crack of dawn every day. And I pulled you out of the ditch, Vida, when you slid there on Rose Creek Road."

"I did pay you, Mike, but I'll thank you again."

"You're welcome."

There was an uncomfortable silence—which Marcus Burns filled.

"I take it that you're an independent proprietor, Mr. Lovell?"

"Yeah, I am now. We had Esso before, but the franchise expense wasn't worth it."

"So where do you get the gas that you sell?"

"Well, what happens is, a guy has a load for, say, a Texaco station down in Deacon or somewhere, and if the place can't take it all, he brings the rest out to me, and I get it for a good rate."

"Very interesting," said Marcus.

I leaned around Gordon and whispered to him, "No, it isn't!"

All this time, Mike Lovell had been treating Marcus's questions as annoying intrusions upon his efforts to persuade the township to let him off the hook, but now he turned around, looked Marcus full in the face, and gave each of us the once-over in turn. He leaned toward Vida and muttered, "Who are they?"

"The company that bought the estate."

"Yeah?"

She nodded.

The second commissioner said to Marcus, "You got any more questions? Anyone?"

"Not right now," said Marcus.

The commissioner said, "We do need to move forward on this matter, Mike."

"Well, the ground is froze, I can't get the damned tank out of there right now anyway."

Suzannah Saylor said in a rather loud voice, "This is ridiculous! I don't want to be poisoned!"

The commissioners looked at one another, and then one of the ones who hadn't yet spoken said, "I move that the permit be granted to Mr. Lovell, and that he be given until April first to remove the tank. After that, if the tank isn't removed, I move we notify the county and leave the issue to them."

"April first!" exclaimed Suzannah Saylor. "I'm supposed to monitor my well every week until—"

"Now, see, I'm not sure I can get it done before April first. They could be backed up at the company—"

"Excuse me," said Marcus. "Do you mind if I talk to Mike outside for a minute?"

And that was how we came to have a lease on an existing gas station in the village of Plymouth, five miles from the farm down a rather bumpy road and not, at least in any obvious sense, our business. Marcus took Mike Lovell outside and told him we would pay for the tank removal and reinstallation and help him pay for his franchise renewal, and all of these things Mike communicated to Vida and the commissioners when he came in from his conference with Marcus. Mike Lovell was all smiles and came to the back of the room and shook hands with each of us in turn, and when he went up to talk to the commissioners one last time they were all smiles too. Only Suzannah Saylor, possibly feeling that Mike Lovell was undeserving of such bounty, said, "I can't believe this! This guy is a notorious polluter! He should be fined! But as long as that tank's out of there, I don't care who takes it out!" She glared at us as she left the room.

It was now close to eight-thirty. Several of the commissioners got up from their seats and left the room. A few moments later, I could see them outside the window, in the lee of the front stoop, lighting cigarettes. The poodle lady and a couple of others took the opportunity to depart, and those remaining, Mike and three or four more, still sitting in the front of the room, stared at us a few more times. The commissioners returned.

Vida announced that we were here for preliminary consideration of the development of Salt Key Farm, and that the sketch plan we had submitted included a golf course, a clubhouse, a modular sewage plant, fifty to a hundred houses, roads, sidewalks, et cetera. I was perfectly familiar with what we wanted, or at least what we were admitting right now that we wanted, and it sounded like a lot to me.

The commissioners stared at us, I assumed in disbelief, for a few seconds after she finished talking. Then one of them said, "Who's who, please?"

I said, "On the end there is Marcus Burns, next to him is Ms. Jane Johnson, then Gordon Baldwin"—two of them nodded—"whom you already know. I am Joe Stratford. We're the developers."

Vida leaned over to the commissioner closest to her and said, "Gottfried Nuelle." But Gottfried kept his mouth shut. They looked at us for a moment, and we looked at them. Then they opened up the plans. I stood up and went forward.

After a moment, they looked up at me, and I

said, "Naturally, the most important thing to us is maintaining the look of the estate as it's always been."

They remained impassive.

I said, "I don't know how many of you have been in the house recently." No response. Possibly none of them, ever. "The house is a beautiful example of the work of Hunter Reston, who was a prominent New York architect in the period during and after the First World War. He specialized in rather traditional architecture but used very elegant detail; for example, the book-matched paneling in the library and the dining room. He also designed the gardens."

Still nothing.

"We would carefully refurbish the house and renew the gardens, which are actually in excellent condition." My voice began to frog up, no doubt because of the freezing response I was getting. I wanted to turn around and look at the faces of my associates, to see some signs of encouragement, but I went on, my voice getting higher and higher. "Our view is that the property is a valuable part of the history of this area, but unlikely to find a buyer who can by himself maintain . . . excuse me"—I cleared my throat—"maintain it in its present condition, and so the centerpiece of our plan is an eighteen-hole golf course and the retention of the house as a clubhouse for the course."

No golfers in this group.

"Um."

Now there was a question. "A private club?"

Now I could feel Marcus's presence behind me, and I said, "No, public course, public access to the club—"

"Yes?" He called on someone, and I turned around.

Gordon said, "Last year I was down in North Carolina, where they have those famous courses. Pinehurst. You been down there? They've got seven courses. Anyway, the locals play for twenty bucks a round and the tourists play for a hundred."

At last, a response. All five of the commissioners smiled. Gordon continued.

"When they get a famous golf tournament in there, that's hundreds of thousands of dollars for the local economy. Joe?"

"I think some form of public/private mix would work best in this situation." I cleared my throat again. "You'll notice that we've asked for acre-and-a-half lots, though in this township, lots are three acres. This is because we don't want to break up the grounds. Theoretically, we could put one hundred ninety-two houses on the five hundred-and-eighty-acre property without asking for a zoning variance, but"—I cleared my throat again and paused for a moment—"our real interest is in making sure that the community has a say in what we do, and, let's say, agrees with what we do, because, of course, Salt Key Farm is and always has been an asset belonging to the whole community"—how was that again? I thought to myself; the only people around here that Mrs. Thorpe knew were her house servants and her stable hands—"so we would like to cluster the houses together on smaller lots, leaving plenty of open space—some cultivated, some in pasture, and some for—ah, wildlife. The Salt Key community aims to maintain the historic values of the farm, while adding to them by making the farm more accessible and useful to the general region."

The commissioners stared down at the plans again, passing them back and forth and turning pages. Behind me, Gottfried shifted position and crossed his legs the other way, then pulled out his handkerchief and blew his nose. The commissioners looked at him. I stood quietly, waiting for more questions. One of the commissioners who hadn't yet spoken said in a quiet voice, "I see you got a waste-treatment plant here. Does that creek run all year around?"

Behind me, Marcus stood up, and in a moment

he was beside me. He said, "I'd like to answer the questions about septic, waste treatment, water, all of that. We expect to have a modular state-of-the-art plant, expandable at any time that we need more capacity. We expect to set a new standard for environmental protection in this area. Now I think my friend Mr. Lovell's dilemma illustrates some interesting features of the world of the future. Ms. Saylor, who unfortunately left during the break, came into the region from outside—what, about two years ago? I believe she has some sheep and is planning to start a boutique wool farm for upscale knitting supplies? Very interesting, and I would be glad to discuss further the market possibilities for specialty goods, but Ms. Saylor has left. Anyway, folks coming from outside have a certain belief or, you might say, picture of a place like this, and that is that it is pristine and unpolluted, because, you know, it looks so pretty, so when they get here, they are all the more disappointed to discover that many years of what you might call an unnaturally depressed local economy has resulted in some corners being cut with regard to environmental concerns, and while we around here might understand that sort of necessity, others don't. So we at Salt Key Corporation have addressed that concern by designing—and I can show you the design if you would like me to, though I don't have it with me—this, as I say, state-of-the-art facility to, essentially, make the waste products of the development vaporize—it's really amazing what technology does these days—and of course this plant will be accessible to the surrounding community, should that need arise." He paused, then grew confidential. "This part of the plan, by the way, is my particular passion. And I will oversee it myself." Ah, he was grinning. They were grinning. I glanced behind me. Jane was staring at the floor, Gordon was staring at the ceiling, and Gottfried was staring at Marcus. He went on casting this spell, and then he fell silent and one of the commissioners said, "Looks expensive to me. And you're talking a lot of effluents. There's got to be an impact report, and I don't know what all. You got this plan to Jerry Taylor, didn't you?"

"Yes, sir," I said. "Mr. Taylor had the plan the same day you did."

"He's got a terrible cold and laryngitis," offered Vida. "He called me today."

"So he's not here. You folks are going to have to come back next month; that's the first thing. But I do want to say that I think everything on here looks expensive."

"Sir," said Marcus, "I assure you. There is plenty of money."

"Well, you don't have to assure me, since we'll see the letter of credit."

That was where they began talking like this

was a done deal. There's always a moment at any meeting like this where the tone changes from *no* to *yes*. It may be long before they have a discussion or actually vote, and even before the commissioners think they've seen everything and even begun to make up their minds. Before that moment, whoever wants it has to work to make it go; after that moment, whoever doesn't want it has to work to stop it.

Gottfried blew his nose again. I saw Vida look at him and give him a little smile, and I heard him clear his throat. But he didn't say anything. Now there was a longer, rather more awkward, pause after which the first commissioner said that he and his colleagues needed to have some time alone. So our group stood up and, since the township center had only one room and a couple of rest rooms, we went out onto the porch where the commissioners had previously been smoking and stood there. It was cold.

"God in heaven, Marcus!" exclaimed Jane, as soon as the door closed behind us. "Can't you stop lying? I nearly fell out of my chair at all that shit vaporizing into thin air. State-of-the-art indeed! You are shameless!"

Marcus shrugged and wrapped his muffler more tightly around his chin. "Someone, somewhere, has some modern technology, and I guarantee we'll find it. It's easy to find. It's only a lie if it doesn't exist. It isn't a lie if you just don't know right now what it is."

Jane shook her head.

I said, "I'd like to know about the plenty-of-money part."

Marcus burst out laughing and slapped me on the back as if I had made a tremendous joke. I laughed too; I couldn't help it. But he didn't actually answer my question, because the door opened and Vida called us back in. They wanted to ask about the time frame we were looking at. Marcus dipped his head graciously and said, "Well, that all depends on you. Things are in place on our side. All the ducks are lined up in a row, and we are ready to move."

"Well," said the main spokesman of the group, "we are drawn to several features of the plan, including the golfing facility, assuming you are aiming at real quality, tournament-style quality. So we'll want to know who your course designer is going to be. And we like this part about retention of the house and the gardens, especially the gardens. I understand there are several varieties of old and rare plants on the property, which we think should be cataloged and preserved. You know, old Thorpe was something of a collector. Vida, has the heat gone off in this room? It feels very cold now."

"Might have, Mr. Nickles, it's after eleven."

"Well, we'll hurry then. Now, we don't often have to deal—or may never have had to deal— with anything like this, but we like it, at least for now. Pete, here, has some reservations, but we know Gordon, and we know Gottfried, and so, young man"—he looked right at Marcus—"we are going to advise you that we think it's okay to go on with this, though nothing's official yet until Jerry Taylor gets out there and really looks the place over, and he's not going to do that in the snow, so you'd better put yourself on ice for a bit. And now, if no one has anything to add, I am going to have to leave, because the chill in here is giving me some problems." And he got up, put on his coat, and went out. And so did the rest of them.

My phone rang at 6:30 A.M. Wednesday, which meant it was Gottfried, since that was when he got up and began his business day. As soon as I picked up the phone, he said, "I want to build those houses. I know just what to put there, something that will fit in nice with the big house. And I want to go into that house today, if you can get out there. Dale wants to see it, too. Dale's as excited as I've ever seen him. You know he refurbed the wooden moldings and paneling at the statehouse in Nebraska before he came here. And he was thinking of going to England and Germany, but now this has come up. He'd stay here for this."

"Dale is an unusual person," I said.

"Well, you think I don't know that? I give Dale just about everything he asks for. My wife says that if Dale wanted my kidney, I'd give it to him, and she's just about right."

"The thing about those houses, Gottfried—"

"Now you're going to palm me off with some mealymouthed deal. I knew you would, Joe. I knew when I found out about this, and you didn't tell me first thing, that there was something going on and you weren't going to tell me; you were making other deals without me."

"Gottfried, when did you ever tell me you wanted to build hundreds of houses at once? Didn't you always tell me you are a craftsman rather than a building contractor? Aren't those your very words?"

"I've had my eye on the Thorpe place for thirty years."

"Since you were seventeen years old? Yesterday you said twenty."

"Yes. It's been a very long-term thing. I'll meet you out there in half an hour."

"It's dark."

"They got lights. I'm bringing Dale with me."

"Gottfried, I'm still in bed. I haven't eaten breakfast yet."

"You got some woman with you?"

"Is that your business?"

"Well, if you don't, what are you waiting for? You can stop at McDonald's on the way out. They're open."

"I don't want to meet you out there. I have partners. We have to talk about things. I don't make decisions alone."

"I've already talked to Vida."

"This morning?"

"Yeah, and she said the main reason they looked favorably on your plan—and don't think for one moment they are fooled by that asshole and his sister; what was she wearing? I couldn't believe it; she looked like she was going to a party—was because I was there. Gordon Baldwin just gets by, you know. Everyone knows he has some shady deal going on, but he hasn't been caught yet, so he gets by. Me, they trust. So because I was sitting there and everyone knows me and I've been doing good work around here for thirty years, they gave you the benefit of the doubt."

"That's not what it looked like to me, Gottfried."

"Well, Vida has forgotten more last week than you'll ever know, so believe it."

"Why are you yelling at me at six-thirty in the morning?"

"Because I'm trying to goddamn wake you up and get you to smell the coffee."

"Okay, but I want to tell you one thing once and for all."

"What's that?"

"You keep running Marcus down—"

"So what? He's a jerk."

"Only so this. You hate everybody who buys one of your houses, so you're not proving to me anything about Marcus in particular. It's you who's the crank."

"Yeah, well, just meet me out at the Thorpe place."

Finally, the reason I got up and put on my clothes and went out and started my car in the freezing dark and let it warm up so I could drive out there on the coldest morning of the year with only a cup of coffee in me was I knew if Gottfried really *really* wanted the Thorpe property, he could afford, just barely, if I were to sell his houses I had listed, to buy it, and if he bought it the commissioners would agree to anything he wanted to do, no problem, and it would keep him busy for twenty years and get Gordon out of a deal that he was still a little reluctant about, and furthermore it would return me to the sphere where I felt most comfortable: selling houses one at a time, not owning property and developing it.

Dale was duly impressed. Dale was a forgettable, round-shouldered, bearded, silent guy with a knitted hat pulled down over his eyebrows and overalls and well-oiled Redwing boots and cotton gloves on, but Gottfried followed him around the Thorpe house, and Gottfried stared at everything Dale stared at, and then I stared at it too. Dale whistled and hemmed and nodded and said, "Mmm-hmm," like he was tasting something, and touched things and got up close to them and peered at them, and when we had finished looking at the library he turned and shook my hand and said, "Thank you for showing me this, Mr. Stratford. This is quite an education."

"It's not very elaborate."

"It's simple," said Dale, "but it's not easy. Here's what they did. They made all these panels and moldings by hand, with hand planes. That way, if anyone made a mistake, it would only be a thirty-second of an inch mistake, and he could rub it out, no problem. This is beautiful, painstaking work. It's always harder to make something simple look right than to make something elaborate look right. I'd much rather spend a week putting together leaf moldings with ridges and beads and all that than spend a week making a straight chair rail with a square edge and, let's say, a groove down the center."

They looked at the floors and the banisters and the cabinetry and the picture moldings and the window casings and the windows themselves and the interior doors and the exterior doors and the baseboard trim and the window trim and the hinges and the drawer pulls and the bathtubs and the sinks and the sink fixtures and the lighting fixtures and everything else. It was almost noon by the time they had had enough. I was yawning so much I had to go outside in the cold and walk around.

When they were done, they walked me to my car. Dale said, "This house was built around the First World War?"

"Yes. I'm not sure of the exact year."

"I like it."

Gottfried broke into an honest-to-God grin.

I said, "It's a beautiful house."

"Here's what I like about it. Now, normally, I'm not much into eclectic. I saw this house once out West that was parts of seven different kits put together. Seven different styles. There was Gothic and Greek Revival and I don't know what else. I considered it a personal affront, that's how much I hated eclectic. Go

ahead and shoot me, but I did. Now this—this
is eclectic too; I see that—but what the guy
did, the architect, was he simplified every element of every style that he drew from, so
there's a kind of squareness in some of the
rooms that just gives you the feeling of something Greek, and that flows into something a
little more vertical, that gives you just the feeling of the stick style. He knew how big it had
to be, and he knew how self-important the
family was, so he gave it a little museum-type
grandeur, mostly in the size and the propor-
tions, but he also knew it was, you might say,
their farmhouse, so he rusticated it by smooth-
ing it all out and giving it real grace. Just grace.
Myself, I don't think it ought to be furnished
or used—let the elements be seen—but most
people like to make use of a building, so I say,
let them, if they own it." He sighed deeply and
generously and went on. "Gottfried and I,
we've got just the picture on what to do with
the houses that are going to go along the golf
course. What you do is break out the different
styles of this house, and you intensify each one
just a little—not much but enough to catch the
eye a bit—and then you offer the prospective
buyers one or two of each of the different
styles. I identify four offhand; I can tell you
what they are another time. There is some

variety in the development, but it all flows together. You won't get some Tudor monstrosity staring down from the top of the hillside at everything, but at the same time, you won't have a hundred little versions of the clubhouse dotted all around. That's what you should do."

"Genius," said Gottfried.

He was right. He was exactly right, and I was going to feel some residual guilt when I stole that very idea and gave it to our future builder, whoever he might be. What I said was, "I like your ideas, but you were there at the meeting, Gottfried; it's going to be months until we can break ground, and the clubhouse and the golf course come first, and after that the sewer plant, and you know how long that's going to take, so what can I say?"

Gottfried stared at me without speaking, knowing for once that I had him, that practicality and wisdom were on my side, and no amount of ranting and raving would change, or quicken, our course. He nodded. They got into Gottfried's truck and drove off, and all I could do for a few minutes was stand there, staring after them in relief.

CHAPTER 17

AN EIGHTEEN-HOLE golf course requires a hundred and eighty acres, but two hundred is better. This was the first thing I learned when Marcus and I began driving around and visiting golf courses in March, when the ground reappeared. I had played golf maybe half a dozen times over the years, mostly at a public course outside of Deacon called the Dawson Club, but not really a club at all. Marcus passed by the Dawson Club without a second glance and went straight to the Cookborough Country Club. The whole way out there, he told me about golf. "I hate golf," he said. "I told you I hate sports, but even more than sports I hate golf, but I've played golf a hundred–two hundred times

over the years, and every single time has been enlightening."

"It takes so long," I said. "I don't see how
anyone with an actual business to run can get
the time in."

"Or a family to raise. But do you ask your buyers why they have such oddball tastes? No. You
just hope to find some house that will appeal to
them. Same with golf. Now what we're going to
do is look at all the courses in the area, and we're
going to make our course more challenging than
eighty percent of them. When all those golfers are
living in all those houses and staring out their
windows every day at the third hole or the
eleventh hole or whatever, we don't want them
grinding their molars in frustration. Maybe
there'll be one hole, say the ninth, the last hole on
the front nine, right by the clubhouse where no
one can see it, that is the most challenging hole in
the county. But all the other holes will beckon
them outside. Nice plantings, contoured fairways,
good views."

At the Cookborough Country Club, he drove
in the gate with a wave to the guard, pulled up in
front of the pro shop, and parked in a reserved
spot next to a golf cart. It was a nice enough day,
but no one was playing, and there was still snow
in the shady spots. The greens had begun to turn
green, but the fairways were still brown. The

door of the pro shop, which had a CLOSED FOR THE SEASON sign in the window, opened, and a man in a sweater and a jacket came out. Marcus went right up and shook his hand. "Hi. You are?"

"Ray. I'm Ray."

"Hello, Ray. I'm Marcus Burns, and this is my friend Joe Stratford. I'll tell you what we're doing. We're building a golf course! First one around here since 1949. What we want to do is see what's needed. You know, what would fit in. What would be an addition to the area's present facilities. Are you the pro?"

"Nah."

"Do you play?"

"I been playing. I'm not very good."

"Well, Ray, what do you like about this course?"

"I don't know."

"Just one little thing, the littlest thing you can think of. The first thing that comes into your mind."

Ray looked at Marcus. After a moment, he said, "I like the crick across the fairway in front of the green on the sixth hole. You get the ball in that crick and you're sunk, but if you put it on the other side, you've got a pretty good approach to the green and a good chance of making a birdie."

"Would you mind showing us that hole?"

GOOD FAITH

Ray looked at us again, then said, "I guess not. But it's a ways from here. Get in the cart."

We piled into the golf cart, and Ray wheeled us expertly down the winding blacktop path, past several tees and several greens, in and out of a few stands of trees, past sand traps and forlorn benches and ball washers. When we got to the sixth hole, we got out of the cart and stood on the tee, staring down the fairway toward the green. Sure enough, the sharp cut of a creek, wider than it looked from where we stood, angled across the fairway, which sloped gently upward on the far side. We stared at it for a minute.

Marcus said, "What's par for this hole?"

"Par four."

"How many times have you birdied it, Ray?"

"Maybe half a dozen."

"I'm impressed," said Marcus. "Why don't you show us the rest of the front nine on the way back to the pro shop."

"Well, all right," said Ray. And we wound our way, into the chilly wind this time, back to where the car was parked. When we got out of the cart, Marcus took out a notebook. He took down Ray's name and gave him his card. He said, "Now, Ray, you call me if you have any more thoughts about how this course plays, okay? What I'm interested in is the average player, you know, average but experienced. Okay?"

"Yeah," said Ray.

We stopped for something to eat, which I had noticed Marcus never failed to do—he always got even more sociable over food—and we went on to the Marque Valley Country Club, where Marcus got into a chat with the guy doing maintenance on the sprinkler system for the putting green at Deacon Hill. His opinion was that the best course in the area was the Preston Mountain Resort course.

"I've never heard of that one," I said.

"No one has. That's the most exclusive club in the state," he said.

Marcus's face lit up. "Where is it?"

The guy drew us a map. It was down a road I had driven any number of times, between Nut Hollow and Roaring Falls. I said, "Well, I thought I knew this area."

"You know what?" said the guy. "When I've got to go over there, they meet me at the gate and escort me to the work site, and when I'm done they escort me out. One of the caddies told me that when his shift is over, if he leaves something at work, he's not allowed to go back and pick it up."

Marcus was beaming.

GOOD FAITH

"You know who I saw there a couple of years ago? Paul Newman. Paul Newman the movie star."

I said, "Around here?"

The guy shrugged. "The security guard over there told me he comes here all the time, and that other guy too. What's his name? Oh. Sylvester Stallone. Rocky. There's movie stars and CEOs all over that place."

Needless to say, Marcus picked me up at noon the next day, and we headed straight for the Preston Mountain Resort. We drove in his car—or, rather, I drove his car—and he sat in the backseat. Hatchcock Road was the sort of road they put into autumn travel brochures, pleasantly curving between rustic fence lines with leafy red mature maples bending together above. In the middle of March, the trees were bare, wet, and black, and the roadway was lined with puddles and dirty patches of snow, but there was nothing unbeautiful about it. Exactly 4.8 miles past the intersection with Nut Hollow Road, there was a paved driveway off to the right that swung around a thick stand of evergreens, and—what do you know?—when we drove back there we found a split-rail fence line, a nice stone gatehouse, and a closed gate. I eased to a halt and Marcus whirred down the automatic window behind me. I sat quietly. As soon as the guard approached, Marcus said, "Has Mr. Newman arrived yet?"

"Excuse me?"

"I'm to meet Mr. Newman here, and I'm afraid I'm late."

"I haven't seen anyone this morning, sir. Who is Mr. Newman?"

Marcus smiled knowingly, then said in a low voice, "You know, Paul Newman the actor." He looked at his watch. "I was supposed to be here at twelve-thirty, but I got delayed in Portsmouth on my way from the airport." The guard cleared his throat to speak, but Marcus interrupted him. "Have you heard from him? I'm on my way to Florida, and he promised to meet me here so I could see the place."

"What place?"

"The club."

"The club?"

"Have we got the wrong place, Joe? Sir, isn't this the Preston Mountain Resort?"

The guard looked around.

Marcus adopted a tone of convivial concern. "Mr. Newman drew me a little map, and I was sure I could find it, but maybe it's farther down the road. We're looking for a private club called the Preston Mountain Resort. I'm Marcus Burns. I do business with Mr. Newman, and we were planning to meet at that club because Mr.

Newman is proposing me for membership, but he said it was so secret that even the neighbors don't know right where it is, so I suppose we're really screwed if his map is wrong." He kept smiling in a friendly way.

The guard heaved a sigh, gazed at Marcus for another moment, then said, "This is the club, but members always call ahead, and no members have called for this morning. Maybe you should wait here for Mr. Newman."

Now it was my turn. I got out of the car and took the guard over to one side. I said, leaning close and whispering, "I don't think you should make Mr. Burns wait in the car. He's had a long trip from Paris." To Portsmouth? But the guard didn't notice that. "He's not really the kind of guy who waits in his car for movie actors. Or for anyone."

"Who is he?"

"Have you heard of Horizontal Technologies?"

"No."

"How about ABM?"

"I've heard of that."

"He *is* ABM."

"And he doesn't want to wait?"

"He's not *used* to waiting."

He went into the guardhouse and picked up the phone. I got back into my car. Marcus kept smiling. I watched the guard. He nodded and shook his head and nodded some more, and then he came out with a doubtful look on his face, and before he could say anything, Marcus held out his hand and put a folded-up twenty-dollar bill up the guy's sleeve and said, "Thanks so much for your help." While the guard was pulling it out, he said, "Go on, Joe. Up to the clubhouse." And so we did. He said, "Who did you tell him I was?"

"You heard of ABM?"

"What's that?"

"Well, I believe it stands for antiballistic missile, but he'd definitely heard of it. I said you *are* ABM." We laughed all the way up through the woods.

The club was laid out on a big piece of ground that sloped upward first, and then gently downward into a shallow bowl, then upward again toward the northeast. The buildings were made of logs in that northwoods style they loved at the turn of the century. It was in the deluxe-summer-camp architectural family, somewhere between Yellowstone Park and a cluster of cabins, one of the few architectural styles that is impossible to remodel and even, on this scale, to tear down. It looked like an entire virgin forest from somewhere out in California had been brought here. The grounds had an old-fashioned air also—more lawns than gardens, and the few gardens were very formal. The dark logs of the buildings gave even the air and sky the austerity of a pine forest. The Thorpe place, by contrast, had grace and human scale in addition to grandeur. I had a moment of appreciating what we had before two security guards in their golf cart approached us. Marcus said, "Turn right."

I turned right. In a moment we were cruising along beside the golf course, and Marcus was staring at it avidly. He said, "Don't look. Just keep going and do what I say." I kept going. The road curved around the lake. I turned right again, and went between a couple of fairways. I turned left and went up the hill behind the main lodge. Marcus said, "Speed up just a little." I did. "Turn left." Now we were at the beginning of the back nine, which stretched up the hill and had beautiful views of the lodge and the perimeter of trees and the valley beyond, toward Roaring Falls. Maybe I had seen this place from a plane sometime over the years. It still seemed amazing that I had never heard of it. Then the road eased around the back side of the mountain, and I saw that the property had another hidden valley with no road access other than from the lodge. We passed the outer holes of the back nine, probably thirteen, fourteen, and fifteen, which wound around a man–made lake. Marcus said, "Pull over here."

I pulled over into a service road, behind some bushes, and a few minutes later I heard the golf cart go by. Marcus said, "Now go." I pulled out and drove in the direction we had come from, and soon we were at the top of the hill again, looking down toward the lodge and the gate. Marcus was laughing. He said, "Now they're actually after us. I don't think they believe in Mr. Newman! Let's get out of here."

I could see a more direct route to the gate, and I went straight for it. Marcus said, "They're right behind us. That golf cart is going pretty fast." I sped up. At some outbuildings, I turned toward where I thought the gate was, and sure enough, there it was. The guard was standing in the middle of the road and the gate was closed. Marcus said, "Slow down, but don't stop." He rolled down his window and began waving the guard out of the way. A moment went by. "Keep going," said Marcus. Another moment. And then the guard stepped to the side of the road. He just stepped. He didn't actually look afraid, but only as if he had decided not to chance it. Marcus leaned out the window and called, "Thank you so much, Lloyd! You've been terrific!" And then the gate opened, whether of itself or because Lloyd opened it, I have no idea. We sped around the blind curve and out onto Hatch-cock Road, where I made a right turn and zoomed toward Roaring Falls. We were laughing and laughing. Marcus climbed over the back of the seat into the front and said, "Oh, God, I feel about fifteen! Wasn't that a kick!"

"What a depressing place!" I exclaimed. "I can't believe a guy like Mr. Newman spends much time there."

"Nah. For sure he doesn't. I've heard of places like that. It used to be where people like the Rockefellers and the Morgans brought the wife and kids and sat around for the month of August, planning world wars and fomenting counterrevolutionary movements. I bet there was a train station somewhere close by—"

"There was one in Roaring Falls."

"—and they had a branch line for private cars that went right up to the lodge there. But I'm sure all they do now is the men gather for some kind of secret meetings where they swear allegiance to one another. My bet is, it's owned by some secret society, you know, something like one of those Princeton eating clubs or Yale senior things. What else would you do in that lodge besides dress up in bear suits and howl in a ritualized manner against the hoi polloi and the Jews?"

"I didn't even see the golf course."

"I did. Not bad, but very old-fashioned. Wide fairways, big greens. The length is probably the challenging thing. Dogleg here, dogleg there. Ours is going to be much nicer than that one. Have you heard of Pete Dye?"

"No."

"Jack Nicklaus?"

"Well, of course."

"One of those two."

"One of those two what?"

"Is going to design our course. Only one in the neighborhood, maybe in the eastern half of the state, though I'm not sure about that. "I've had Dye's people on the phone. They're very interested." He started laughing at my obviously terrified reaction.

"How much? What did Gordon—"

"It's not that much more for a famous designer than some schmuck, and it's worth it from the beginning. For one thing, all the golf magazines talk about it, and so buyers begin sniffing around for properties as soon as the guy gets on board, and anyway—"

"Anyway, nothing but the best."

"Oh, yes!" exclaimed Marcus. After a moment, he said, "Crosbie insists on it. I was on the phone all last week. He knows an S and L in Oklahoma somewhere, can you believe that? And they're doing some golf and condo development in California, near Pebble Beach somewhere, and as soon as they hired Pete Dye, the price of the lots doubled. This little S and L, you know, Okie State Savings, one branch. They're rolling in it. Crosbie's eyes were green when he was telling me about it. You can't believe how I cultivate this guy, Joe. It's hardship duty."

"I believe you."

"Anyway, Pete Dye, Jack Nicklaus, Dwight David Eisenhower. You've got to get a designer all the golfers have heard of."

At Roaring Falls Road, we turned toward the village, and as soon as we got into town Marcus said, "Here, I'll buy you lunch. Wow! I can't believe that! When that guard looked at me, I didn't know what I was going to say. You know, I still carry my IRS ID card in case it might come in handy."

"Winning by intimidation?"

"Oh, yes! But that didn't seem, I don't know, it just didn't seem cool. So I just opened my mouth and out it came."

"Well, you were a piece of work, as my dad would say."

"I still want to meet your parents."

"Oh, right."

We got out of the car and went into the Frog Prince, a lunch place that did a lot of weekend business, and when we sat down, he said, "But you're the genius. I was really stuck. I thought he was going to make us sit there until Paul Newman pulled up! I loved how you just kind of took him aside, very confidential, and gave the guy the true picture of my worldwide importance!" He threw his head back and laughed. Then he leaned across the table and looked right at me. He said, "You know, Joe, a lot of this would be like shoveling snow if it weren't for you. I don't feel that anyone, other than you, can really see what I'm getting at here. Everyone thinks so small. Linda quizzes me every day about how it's going. I mean, I know she can't help herself. When we came out here, she was worried about the risk. She always thought at least we had her job to fall back on, *blah blah blah,* and now we don't have that, and you know the mortgage payment is something of a stretch for us, so I've got to say there's a little refrain for every day. When she's having a good day, it's 'Things are really working out, aren't they, honey? You were so right! You really can't get anywhere without taking a plunge. We don't want the kids just thinking we always played it safe all their lives, and set them such a, I don't know, *unenterprising* example. I mean you have to show kids how *they* can be through how *you* are.'" He sounded exactly like her. He smiled.

"Then, on bad days, it's much more straightforward. 'I just have a bad feeling about this. It isn't going to work. Your sister had a worried look on her face today, and when I asked her what was wrong, she wouldn't tell me, so I know there's something you have to tell me, so you'd better get it over with and we'll deal with it somehow.'" He shook his head. "Anyway, Joe, that's just one example. You're the only one who just goes on, gets things done."

"Well, I—"

"You know, it kind of amazes me that you have settled for this. I mean, I don't want to sound like I'm running down your life or any-thing—"

"But you are."

"Well, yeah. I am. But, you know, only in comparison with your potential."

We laughed.

"No, really. You've got a lot on the ball. Everyone likes doing business with you. People trust you. I mean, I can't tell you the number of times I've said, Well, one of my partners is Joe Stratford, and they can't help themselves, they breathe a sigh of relief. I mean, two or three of them, yes, it's 'Oh, that's Daniel Stratford's boy,' and I guess your father is famous in his way too, but there's lots of others that are more like, 'Oh, I bought a house from him once,' or 'He bro-kered a deal I did once.' You know. I mean, I can't tell you how valuable that is in a place like this just for getting off the ground."

"Well, I've always tried to—"

"But it could be more. I mean, I'm not saying it's not good, it is good, no two ways about it. It's an absolute good to be respected in your community. But let's face it, it's a small community. Opportunities are greater elsewhere."

"I was married until two years ago, don't forget. Sherry—"

"Oh, the famous ex-wife! Didn't I meet her? Oh, yeah! Madame Chef!"

"I believe that's Ms. Chef to you, buddy."

He grinned. "But she's ambitious. I mean, pork medallions in Calvados, *clafouti*, crème brûlée. That's *très français*."

"It was a long approach to the pin, let's put it that way. She added ambitions one grain at a time. For most of our marriage, she repainted and furnished our house. One year we repainted the living room four times and the only people who could tell that the shade was different were us."

"Exacting. So maybe the man of the house did a lot of, you know, catering to the—oh, the queen?"

"Well, there was that. Though I didn't see it as that at the time. I just saw it as her ideas being a little more intensely held than mine, so why not?"

GOOD FAITH

Marcus looked carefully at the menu, took a couple of sips of water, and said, "I sometimes wonder how I would see my marriage if I were no longer in it."

I pretended we had not gotten into a new uncomfortable area. "Well, I have to say, that was her idea too. I never thought about it before it happened."

"Really?" He looked at me speculatively, and then the waitress came up and he ordered a steak sandwich and I ordered a hamburger. We didn't say anything more until she was gone. Then Marcus said, "You know, Linda and I are very alike. We like the house to be the same way, we like the same sorts of clothes and books. We agree on how to raise the kids. I mean, lots of times couples say they've known each other so long they finish each other's sentences, and they usually think of that as a bad thing, but I think of it as a good thing. I guess you will have noticed that I have an exacting side myself. Well, I prefer to call it meticulous. No, I prefer to call it a sense of style. Anyway, it's something Linda and I share completely, and that's valuable, and for a long time—I mean, until we moved here—I thought that was everything. But I see the move has brought out other sides of both of us, and it's been kind of a surprise."

"Meaning?"

"Oh, you're being very cagey, aren't you? But let's put it this way. Have you noticed anything about Felicity Ornquist?"

"I guess I've noticed a lot of things about Felicity over the years." I said it, and I said it casually, but the sudden intrusion of her name into the conversation electrified me to the roots of my hair. "I'm not quite sure which thing you mean."

"Well, she's ready for anything, but he isn't, you know? Hank's not ready for anything."

"He's very outdoorsy."

"And he doesn't like our project at all, at all."

"No, he's mentioned that to me."

"I don't think he's as much against our project as he's just against anything new, and she's just the opposite. She's very game." I didn't say anything about what Felicity had said to me about the project, but I did feel a sharp retrospective pang. "Anyway. Let me put it this way. I hope being game is either learned or contagious, and that Felicity manages to communicate some of it to my wife." The food was set on the table. By then, I hadn't seen Felicity in a month and a half. I couldn't help issuing a sigh, which Marcus didn't seem to notice.

Marcus was a big talker but now he fell silent, and I have to say that the silence was companionable. I thought for a moment there about a strange thing: I couldn't really say that I had ever had a male friend, even a buddy. My best friend in high school was Sally, I didn't last long enough in college for anyone to make an impression, and I had been in business since I passed the exam for my broker's license when I was twenty-two. My business didn't really promote friendships—Realtors are likely to be loners. There was Gordon, too fatherly, there was Bobby, too goofy. I wasn't a sports fan, I didn't play golf or hunt or fish. It was odd to think of myself, a sociable guy, as someone without a real friend, but right then it didn't upset me, because I felt I now had a friend, Marcus. He had slipped under the fence and into the compound and guess what? I liked him. I thought he was smart and interesting and imaginative. He laughed at jokes I made that I was used to laughing at by myself. He had a trick of laughing and glancing at me sharply, looking right into my face, that made me feel like I was actually communicating with him. I wasn't surprised he had noticed Felicity's gameness. I valued that about her too. If we were friends, then we would notice the same things about people. I ate my hamburger; then I said, "You know, Hank thinks I'm the brains behind this operation."

"Who told you that?"

"He did, a few weeks ago, when he was try-ing to dissuade me from going forward. He hates golf courses."

"What's there to hate about a golf course?"

"Fertilizer, I suppose. Or maybe social privi-lege."

"What did you say to him?"

"I said what else are we going to do with the place, let it go to seed?"

"What did he say?"

"He didn't have an answer."

He ate a few french fries; then he said, "It's good that he thinks you're the brains." But he didn't say why. After that we chatted idly about golf courses and made plans to see four more. He promised me that after those four we would know all we needed to know about golf courses.

I said, "I still know nothing about golf courses."

"Just wait. I guarantee you've taken in more than you think, just driving around."

"Well, I'm glad there are only four more, be-cause I have to get back to selling houses."

"Oh," he said, "we'll just see about that."

N<small>O MATTER WHAT SIZE</small> your
project is, the first person you pay is the
town engineer and the second person
you pay is your own engineer, so I called up Marcus when the bills came in and told him to pay
them right away. Our start-up money, which had
looked like not enough but at least respectable,
had dwindled considerably. The imminent
merger between Portsmouth Savings and the S
and L from the western part of the state, after
which we were planning to roll in money, had hit
a snag and wouldn't be complete until at least the
late summer. In the meantime, Marcus had hired
an architect to refurbish the house and a firm of
golf course designers from North Carolina who
were not famous but better than famous, because

they were absolutely guaranteed by the insidest of the insiders to be the next great thing, to design the golf course. As long as I had known him, Gordon had engaged in robbing Peter to pay Paul, as did most developers, and I didn't know who all the Peters were.

Marcus told me he had it all in his head. "I keep telling you that my mind works like an adding machine."

"All right," I said. If he wanted to take care of it, so be it. Just organizing the paperwork for the township was plenty of work for me.

Gordon called me early in May. "You know that farm on the interstate north of Portsmouth? You got to go over there."

"Why?"

"You got to see it, that's all."

"Why?"

"What are you doing right now?"

"Some paperwork. Then I'm showing a house in Farmington."

"Forget the paperwork. You meet me there." He hung up. I put on my coat.

Gordon had owned the Portsmouth farm for years, ever since he bought it from a farmer whose house had been separated from the rest of the farm when they rerouted the interstate in the early fifties. He had sold the lot with the house on it back to the farmer. Then he had leased the rest of the property to another farmer, who kept some of his own cows and some of Gordon's cows there. I wasn't too knowledgeable about that business, except that the cows had started out black-and-white and then become all black and now they had disappeared.

The farm had two pieces, a front piece of some twenty acres and a back piece of some forty-five acres, joined at a narrow waist where a grove of trees crossed the property and hid the back part from the road. The forty-five acres was a hilly pasture that was too steep ever to be cropped. You could just see the barn from the highway, I had thought, but on the day I met Gordon there, I couldn't see it anymore.

"Tore it down!" exclaimed Gordon. "Sold the cows, too, but that isn't the brilliant part. Follow me!"

I followed him to the back part of the property, where I saw ten large dump trucks idling in a line, maybe four hundred yards from the old house, and a large earthmoving machine and a large backhoe picking up topsoil and pouring it into the first truck bed. I got out of the car. "Look at that!" said Gordon. "You know that crazy intersection up by Fox Mountain where they used to have that three-lane highway and they made it four-lane with the median, but regular intersections? Terrible stretch of highway. People killed there all the time. Well, the state highway department called me and said they're finally building a regular interchange, but it's all clay soils up there and they want all this alluvial soil I've got here, so there it goes. They've been carting it away for two weeks."

And they had made something of a dent in the hill, which now looked like a cliff, with the machines working away at its face. It was nice loose soil, full of tiny pebbles, not great loam or anything like that, but perfect for draining the highway. I said, "The township is letting you remove part of itself and send it to Fox Mountain?"

"The value of the whole property will be enhanced when it's leveled off, and it will. And the state, you know, they want what they want. Otherwise, they'd have to go another hundred miles for the right gravel. I love it. Look at it! Those cows hardly even paid the taxes, but finally this place is coming into its own. It's going to be flat as a pancake in another month or two."

"Free money," I said.

"Free money," said Gordon.

• • •

A few days later, Marcus called me up and asked me to come over to the office. He wanted to have a meeting with all the partners.

"Who are all the partners? You mean me and Gordon?"

"And Jane."

But when I got there, there was quite a crowd. Not only Gordon and me, but Bobby and someone I vaguely recognized but didn't know from where. Marcus introduced me. "Hey. Joe. This is Mike Lovell. You know, Mike's garage?"

I nodded. At that point, all I remembered about the February meeting (which had been succeeded by two more) was that it had been really cold. Marcus said, "We took out and replaced that tank at Mike's garage last week."

"I will never understand that bitch," said Mike.

Marcus grinned at me and said soothingly to Mike, "Well, it's done now."

"Thanks to you," said Mike. He sat down in Jane's office and picked up a magazine. As we went into the conference room, Marcus whispered, "That guy is going to come in handy. He knows the township like the back of his hand."

Marcus sat at the head of the table and motioned me to the foot. Gordon and Bobby sat to my right and Jane sat across from them. She was smiling as if something amused her. Marcus was in a good mood. He shut the door and said, "All right."

It was a nice table, cherry or maybe a dark-stained hickory with a handsome grain in the wood, and stylish comfortable chairs. The carpet was a deep green plush with a white fleck in it. They had painted the walls cream above the chair rail and green below it, not unlike the hallways in the rest of the building. There were pictures. Jane looked rich, and Marcus did too. I wasn't quite sure why Bobby was there—whether at the invitation of Gordon or of Marcus, or whether he had just barged in—but he ran his hand over the surface of the table and smiled appreciatively.

Marcus said, "Well, thanks for coming over. Jane and I were talking the other day, and we thought that since things are beginning to roll, we should stop doing things by rumor and gossip and start holding meetings and agreeing on things as a group. I had a moment of—oh, I don't know, fear or just maybe anxiety the other day—when Bart over at the savings and loan told me he heard the golf course designer had designed a course up in Buffalo, New York, and I knew that wasn't true. I'm sure he's never been to Buffalo, and it wouldn't matter if he had, but talk is talk."

"Oh, that was me," said Bobby. "Gordon said the guy had worked somewhere, but I couldn't remember where, so when Bart asked me I said

Buffalo because that was the first city that popped into my head." He continued to smile.

Marcus's smile flickered, but only for a moment. He said, "You know, this is something I was thinking about. We don't really want a lot of extraneous information floating around. We need to all know the same things, but even more important than that, we need to all agree on what is to be divulged and what isn't. With a development like this, especially with the sort of financing Jane and I are working on, even the tiniest thing can put off a potential investor or lender. Let's say I wine-and-dine some guy until I'm full to the back teeth, and he hears the golf course designer is in the habit of designing courses in Buffalo and West Nowheresville. Then in comparison to someone whose designer is designing courses in Houston or Palm Springs, we don't look serious. So I think the best thing is, if one of us doesn't know the true answer to a question, he just refers that questioner to me, and I will answer."

We all nodded. Seemed reasonable to me.

"Now," said Marcus, with a look at Jane. "Joe can correct me, but it's my understanding that the permit procedures are proceeding fairly deliberately, or even glacially, so this puts us in something of a bind."

"No more slowly than I expected all along," I said.

"I was more optimistic," said Marcus. "I really was. I really thought we would be building by now, and we aren't, so I think that it would be wise, Joe, if you closed up your business and came over here to work and just devoted all of your time to getting these things through. Potential investors have to know there's a full-court press here."

The group became very quiet. I wasn't sure why. It was as if Marcus had said something embarrassing, but it didn't embarrass me. I just laughed. I thought he was joking. "I can't afford to do that, Marcus."

"You can if I pay your bills. You just change all their addresses, send them to me, and I'll pay them."

"What bills?"

"Oh, I don't know. Lights, heat, car payment, gas for the car. The partnership will just pay them, and then you can devote your time to getting all of this going. You've got some savings. You can pay your beer bill out of those." He grinned. Maybe because this was such an unexpected idea, inserted into my brain without any preparation on my part, it rather blossomed there for a moment. I saw myself driving around the countryside, everything paid for, in some sense, everything free. No more getting and spending, which suddenly seemed tedious and repetitive to contemplate. I knew how to get projects moving, at least small projects, and there would be none of that conflict between doing my own business and doing Salt Key business that had come up from time to time—several times I had had to choose between showing a house and making appointments with one engineer or the other. If I did this, I would have no one to please but Marcus, and, as I knew, Marcus was easily pleased.

And, of course, no taxes to pay.

Jane said, "That's ridiculous, Marcus. I told you you can't ask that." She looked at me. "Marcus was always terribly spoiled, you know. He would sit down at the table, and there would be eight pork chops for the dad and the mom and the six kids, and Marcus would look right at our mother and say, 'Can I have two?' and more often than not she'd say yes and give him hers! The rest of us considered him such a brat."

I said, "Actually, it makes some sense. Not complete sense, but some sense."

"This project isn't a part-time job," said Marcus. "You know, there's always a point with every big project where the people doing the work have to make the commitment or not. This is what I do all day every day. It's not like you're going to do this, make millions of bucks—"

"Billions," I said.

"And go back to being Joe Stratford Realty. I mean, is this a part-time job for everyone but me?"

I looked at Gordon. For Gordon, everything was a part-time job. Not putting all your eggs of any kind—financial eggs, job eggs, recreational eggs—in one basket was a life principle with him. And Gordon was looking at Marcus with a Gordonish look on his face, irritable but not resistant. It meant that he didn't like the discussion, but he did agree with the point. I did too. I thought Jane was implying that we couldn't really do this, couldn't really do what it took to make this go. I thought this was a relic of Jane's former corporate life, where the size of the company did a lot to carry you forward, so you could pay attention to the difference between your life and its life. But when you were starting something, you had to accept, and even to embrace, the fact that there was no difference between your life and it. That was the way it had been when I started out as a real estate broker. What about all the times I had gotten up from dinner with Sherry, or left a party, or even gotten out of bed to go show someone a house? All those times I had said, "If I want to get this going, I have to do what it takes." Now I said, "I'll think about it." But I didn't really mean that. What I meant was that I would exit my little company as gracefully as I could and do what had to be done. Marcus cocked his head and cleared his throat. He was satisfied. I knew he knew exactly what I meant.

Bobby, who had been quiet, said, "What about me? Are you going to pay my bills too?"

Marcus turned to him. "How much did you clear last year after taxes?"

"I don't know."

"You should know."

"I could figure it out."

"Why don't you? You're almost thirty years old, Bobby. It's time you got it together and grew up, and the first step in that direction is sorting out your financial situation instead of coasting along hoping your dad will give you a new car and find you something to do and talk your girlfriend into marrying you. You could start by calling yourself Bob."

Bobby said, in a deep voice, "Hey, *Bob*!"

"I'm not kidding. You talk too much. You don't take responsibility for yourself in any way. You act like a baby. You don't take care of anything, and you require lots of care. You're a hindrance rather than a help. You don't have to break this and sprain that and come down with the other thing. You don't have to live like you do."

Jane said, "Good Lord, Marcus!"

"If no one else is going to do you a favor and furnish you with a good swift kick in the ass, I will. The others care about you, but not enough to show you how to be a man. I care about the partnership and the project, and I care about it enough to care about what *you're* doing. You can't be fired, so you've got to be fixed. So get your financial stuff together and bring it over here tomorrow and we'll start there." He spoke energetically, even indignantly, but it was more like he had to do it than that he really felt something. Bobby looked startled but, let's say, invigorated. He nodded.

Jane said to Marcus, "May I speak with you out in the hall, just for a moment?"

He replied, in a congenial tone of voice, I thought, "Not right now." Then he took a deep breath and looked around the table. "It isn't comfortable for me to talk like this. You know"—he looked at Gordon—"maybe I rely more than I should on charm and indirection and I suppose what you, Gordon, would call a good line of bullshit. But I'll be honest with you. I'm a little scared right now because I've quit my other job, the one that brought me here in the first place, and my wife doesn't have a job other than the house and the kids, and I'm a little overextended." He looked at me. "I didn't tell you that a branch came down on the roof a couple of weeks ago and made a hole and guess what? We can't afford to have it fixed."

"Homeowners' insurance," I said.

"Deductible," he said. "Anyway, we'll get it fixed. I think I'm just afraid of the idea that Gottfried would find out that something has been damaged and take the house away from me. But I didn't mean to get off on that track. What I'm saying is, indirection and all of that has led to a little meandering here. That's what I feel. We aren't progressing. We can't let things develop because we can't afford to let things develop. We have to develop them. This brings me to a touchy point." He glanced at Gordon. Gordon met his gaze, and Marcus looked back at the pad in front of him, on which he had written a couple of things, and then he looked at Gordon again. This time their gaze held. He said, "The fact is, we need more funds to tide us over, and I know there is a source of income, and I know it is producing right now, and I would like to tap that source of income for some of the funds we need."

Bobby said, "You mean the gravel?"

Gordon winced and said, "It's not that much money." Then there was silence.

Finally, Marcus turned to Bobby and said, in a mild, instructive voice, "Now, see, that's just what I mean. Do you realize that it was indiscreet of you to blurt that out? You should have learned years ago just to keep quiet and wait to see what I was getting at. What if that isn't what I meant? What if that were a secret?" He glanced at me with a grin and said, "Though it's a pretty noisy secret. But why should you reveal what you know before the other guy reveals what he knows? Right, Gordon? Gordon knows how to bluff, how to keep quiet. Your mom, too. I've watched her. She never lets out any information that she doesn't want to let out."

At last Bobby looked abashed.

"I mean, it's a kindness to lay this stuff on the line for you. You can't go on for your whole life playing the fool."

Jane was really squirming by now. She muttered, "Marcus—" and suddenly he turned right toward her. "Jane, what? Do you disagree with anything I've said? In twenty years of banking, haven't you learned the same lessons? Why should everyone know how to grow up except Bob here?"

Jane nodded.

Bobby said, in a guilty voice, "I know you're right. Fern says the same thing. She says I never should have talked to you in that bar in the first place."

"Well"—Marcus leaned across the table— "she's right."

"It seemed like an opportunity at the time."

"It did to me too. But I'm sure everyone in the entire world would tell you to be more cautious, don't you think, Gordon?"

Gordon nodded, but he didn't say that he'd been telling Bobby to pay more attention for thirty years without effect.

Marcus went on. "I guess that's really the point of this whole meeting. We have to keep our mouths shut. Joe, I trust. Gordon, I trust for a different reason, just because Gordon always keeps his mouth shut. Jane knows what there is to be gained and lost from information management. I trust myself most of all. But you, Bobby, you I don't trust, because you are not trustworthy. And I don't think your dad trusts you, either, do you, Gordon?"

Gordon said, "Depends." I considered that reply pretty loyal, actually.

"Okay," said Marcus. "Enough of that. Here's what we all know, here's what we all can talk about." He named the names of the architects and designers and where they were from. Further information about their credentials was to be had from him. Several firms were interested in bidding on the waste plant. Those names were confidential until we had decided on one. I didn't point out that we hadn't decided on the architects and designers as a group. Certain bills had priority. We would all have input on which those would be, especially me, since I would be at the office and working with him on a daily basis as of—? He looked at me.

I shrugged and said, "June first?" This was two and a half weeks away. He nodded. After that, I didn't remember the rest. I didn't plan to talk about anything anyway. I was musing about how quickly I had come around to the idea of closing my business and devoting myself to this project, when I had always thought I would keep my business as my ace in the hole. I had planned every day to be cautious, to make sure I knew what I was doing, to reserve something, to be smart. . . .

Marcus broke in on my reverie. He was looking at me and talking. He said, "Every guy I ever met who made a million bucks only did it by going for broke." I nodded. It was exciting, going for broke. After a while, the meeting broke up. As we stood up from the table, Marcus turned to me and said, "How about lunch?"

We passed up the Italian place and the French place. Instead, we walked across the parking lot and across the street, then walked down a block and turned the corner. Lo and behold, here was the Portsmouth I remembered, a little run-down. Halfway down the block was a café.

Marcus said, "You won't believe the onion rings." In his linen slacks and his open-collared shirt with a subtle windowpane check, he was the best-dressed guy in the place, but in fact they all greeted him when he came in—the two waitresses and the busboy, even the cook behind the barrier. He sat down in what appeared to be an accustomed place. All the smiles and waves gave way to a big sigh. He rubbed his face in his hands and looked across the table at me. He said, "So tell me something."

"What sort of thing?"

"Something not about the project or the business. Just something interesting."

"I heard a joke at the Realtors' weekly lunch the other day."

"All right."

"One of those thirty-five-year-old women— you know, the ones who are less likely to get married than to be killed in a terrorist attack—is sitting in a bar. A guy comes in and sits next to her. He orders a beer. He's looking around furtively, won't make eye contact with the bartender. When he glances at her he immediately looks away. She goes to the john and comes back, orders herself another drink. She sees that everyone else who was sitting even remotely close to the guy has moved away. She glances at him. He finishes his drink and orders another one, but now he looks really scared. She happens to catch his eye. He looks away, then looks back. Finally, he moves over into the seat next to her and sits there for a second. She takes a sip of her drink. He leans toward her and says, 'I just did a terrible thing.'

" 'What's that?'

" 'I killed my wife and children.'

"She looks at him for a moment, then says, 'So you're single?' "

Marcus smiled. The waitress brought a plate of onion rings. Marcus pushed a five toward her, gave her a smile, then waved her off. I said, "What's up? Or maybe I should say, what's the matter?"

"What would you say if I told you all of this is too much for me? I'm in over my head."

"Why do you think that?"

"Does Gordon sleep?"

"Well, sure. I mean, they're all night owls and they play poker all night from time to time, though not as much anymore as they used to—"

"I admire that. That's cold-blooded. You know, I think I've underestimated him. When you see a guy who owes that much in back taxes and has never dealt with it at all, you think he's kind of a schlemiel, but now I see it differently. I mean, when I first met him and talked to him, I really liked Betty more than Gordon. I thought it was Betty who kept things going over the years, who was putting out fires all the time while Gordon fucked up this and fucked up that."

"You saw them like that? I always saw Betty as kind of a jewel in a box. The box is a little beat-up, but the jewel sits in its little nest, safe as can be."

"I see that now. I see that Gordon really has kind of an outlaw mentality. When I was first talking to him about his tax problem, it seemed like he just didn't understand it, and if he were to understand it, then he would be amazed and terrified. But now I think he did understand it all along. He was just playing out his hand. What I thought was lack of understanding was really nerve."

"Maybe."

"That's what I feel like I don't have."

"Let me close down my business, then, and put all my eggs in your basket."

"Well—"

"When is it you feel this nerve is missing?"

"In the middle of the night, mostly."

"It didn't sound like you were missing any nerve during the meeting."

"What's the difference between nerve and desperation?"

"Probably nothing. I don't know. My small-time life hasn't exposed me to any risks, remember?"

He laughed louder this time, but then he took an onion ring and ate it thoughtfully. Another.

At last, he said, "You know, I used to sit around the office and look at my co-workers and wonder what working for the IRS was doing to us. I don't know what it's like. Maybe being a doctor in the sense that lots of people's lives pass across your desk in the course of a week, so no one seems unique or special. Everyone falls into a category. And you also have the power of life and death. I'm sure when people come in for an audit, they are just like guys going into the doctor's office after a test and getting the bad news, except they know that the agent has discretion, and so they are always polite, always trying to please. I liked that part. At first, I was just interested in it—I used to go home and tell Linda and we would laugh—but then I got to like it. You'd have to be a saint not to. Some guys' whole personalities would change for an audit. Somebody would be standing around the office, telling a fart joke, and then he'd go have a meeting with a taxpayer and he was the pope." He shook his head.

I was eating onion rings too. They were definitely good. I said, "One thing I like about you, Marcus, is that you not only always want the best, you actually find it. Everyone wants the best, but not everyone knows what it is even after they've found it."

He ignored me. "Anyway, it's easy to have a very high opinion of yourself if you work for the IRS. Talk about a rising tide lifting all boats. The tide of ego in an IRS office is very high. And outside the office—well. Just try going to a party where everyone is having a great time, and mentioning that you work for the IRS. It's a social death knell. I'm sure you've been warned, yourself."

"By Norton, yes. He thinks you're doing an undercover investigation and that you will eventually bust everyone for tax fraud."

Marcus rolled his eyes and ate a french fry. I agreed that Norton didn't bear further discussion. He said, "Yeah, well, the other thing is, you can see the mistakes people are making, right there, written down in black and white. You start to think if you had that kind of money to invest, you wouldn't make the same kinds of mistakes. I can't tell you how many times I've lain awake at night, concocting some plan. No capital! That was my only problem. But now there's the capital and there's the project and there's the vision, and hey! I'm still lying awake at night, only now it's a cold sweat. I never thought I would lack nerve! I was a tough kid from a tough neighborhood. And I was the *smart* tough kid, not like the dumb fucks I grew up with. You want me to inventory my talents? I do it every night. I know the numbers, not like Gordon. I have the taste and sense of style, not like most people, say Donald Trump. I have a sense of the big picture—"

"Not like me."

He shrugged, nodded. "I have a perfect knowledge not only of the theory of the tax code but of the actuality of the IRS structure. I have the contacts now. If there's one thing I really have, it's the persuasive ability. That goes with the contacts."

"So what *don't* you have?"

He put his hands around his neck, and made a wide, silent face like he was choking himself to death. "So many contacts! So much persuading! And then they get right to the verge and walk away!"

I laughed. "That's the Realtor experience. Or the missionary experience. When I was a kid, the missionaries always complained when they visited that everyone was ready to come to dinner, but no one was ready to come to Jesus." I took another onion ring and said, "I'm not worried."

And I wasn't.

We talked and ate. Marcus said, after a while, "Did I tell you about the woman I met on the plane a couple of weeks ago?"

"I didn't realize you were out of town."

"Just for a few days. Anyway, I was sitting next to this beautiful chick, tall and very elegant. Dark hair. Designer clothes. Every time she would sneeze, she would open her handbag, take out a tissue, and fold it neatly, then she would discreetly put her hand under her skirt. Then she would fold up the tissue and put it in the air-sickness bag. I didn't think she realized I was watching her, but I couldn't help myself; it was driving me crazy. So anyway, after I watched her do this—oh, I don't know—half a dozen times, I finally said, 'Excuse me, ma'am, I don't mean to be watching you, but I can't help it. This is really awkward, but I have to know. How come every time you sneeze, you fold up a tissue and put it under your skirt?' She blushed, and she leaned toward me and whispered, 'I have this very strange condition. Every time I sneeze I—um, have an orgasm.' I guess I wasn't really surprised, but I wanted to keep the conversational ball rolling, you know, so I said, 'Do you take anything for it?' She looked at me, and then she whispered, 'Pepper.'"

We roared. I thought how much I liked Marcus.

When we got back to the office, Jane said, "Well, aren't you two thick as thieves."

CHAPTER

19

I T WAS A LONGER DRIVE to the new office, but I didn't go there every day. Some days I went out to the farm, some days I went to the township or the county, some days I went to engineers of one sort or another. I was called upon to make various arguments and promote various plans, so I did. I just opened my mouth and out it came. Afterward I hardly remembered what I had said, only what to report to Marcus, more success or less success. Every report was greeted with a grin. He was always happy to see me, and I enjoyed going there. Always I had this sense of the money draining away, sometimes more slowly, sometimes more quickly, but inexorably nonetheless. That's what motivated me. It was like a constant tickle, and it worked more to jazz me up than to frighten me.

As for my business, it was easy enough to get rid of. I called the Realtors I liked the most from the Tuesday lunch crowd and made introductions. Only Gottfried Nuelle was different. Fortunately, he was between sales. I told him I was moving his business into the Salt Key Corporation and closing up shop on everything else. He stared at me, not in disbelief but because he wanted to figure out exactly what I meant and what it meant to him. I didn't say anything, just let his mind work on its own. Finally, he said, "I'm not going to have anything on the market for at least another five months."

Now he expected me to tell him that after that he would be at the farm. I gave him a friendly smile because I wanted him to think that. And after all the years I had spent listening to the ranting and raving, I didn't mind reading his mind one bit and knowing that I was misleading him. I said, "This place is nice."

"Dale wanted to try a California-style bungalow: you know, that front-to-back roofline, lots of woodwork, and sort of Art Deco feel. Mullioned windows, the whole deal. He wanted to get into the twentieth century for a while. Nothing boxy, though. I hate that boxy shit. Metal window frames." He spat out the words. Things were okay with Gottfried.

When I asked Marcus what to say to engineers, supervisors, secretaries, Bart, Jim Crosbie, the stray investor or two, inspectors, and bureaucrats, he told me to try and figure out what they needed to know, what they were looking for, and then tell them that. The overall plan, he said, was a kind of beautiful dream—a vision of a place not to buy a house but to live in a certain way, a better way than most people were used to but a way that everyone understood without even trying. The immediate objective was only a step to the overall plan. Each person I talked to was to be a stepping-stone to the overall plan. It was my job to educate them so they would take their natural places in the plan. I should consider myself a kind of fortune-teller. Had I ever been to a fortune-teller? If I ever had, I would notice that the fortune-teller always looks you right in the face, looks at you in a searching and interested way that no one else ever does. While you are having your fortune told, you think that the fortune-teller is fascinated by you and your fate, and maybe he is, but he is also watching the feelings and thoughts pass across your face, and that is how he knows your fortune. Your fortune, said Marcus, is what you *want* to happen, and if you go to the fortune-teller and he divines what you want to happen and agrees with you that it will happen, then it will. *You* will make it happen because the fortune-teller told you it would. It was this sort of influence I was to exert over everyone—even receptionists, even the women at the board of records whose only job was to retrieve surveys and plats. It was global.

That was why, I realized, I wasn't allowed to be a Realtor any longer. A Realtor finds people more or less the house they want, then does the paperwork so they can get it but leaves the decision to the people themselves. I was no longer in the business of leaving the choice to others. I was in the business of inspiring them.

I would come home and watch a little TV or read a magazine and laugh at this bullshit idea, and then I would go out the next day and inspire people. One by one, all that summer and into the fall, everyone I dealt with got very enthusiastic.

Marcus called me and asked me to take some clients out to Salt Key Farm and show them around because he had to go to the doctor.

The three investors were two brothers and their cousin. They didn't precisely have the look of investors, if you thought of investors as darksuited older men with ties. These guys were about my age, and shortly after I met them at the property and buzzed in their new black Caddy, they let me know that they were close to Donald Trump. After that, I recognized them, because they dressed in that Trumpish style and bragged in that Trumpish manner. They had made their money in meat distribution—sausages, salamis, sliced Italian beef, pastrami, corned beef. They supplied every deli chain on the whole East Coast and down to Florida with slicing meats.

Marcus had told me not to talk about money, either expenses or expectations. Earnings were for Jane and costs were for Marcus. My job was class. And the place looked great. It was June and summer was right on time. We had retained a couple of the Thorpes' gardeners, who had duly fertilized the shrubs and the roses and raked back the mulch so the flowers could come up. The color of the grass was blinding, the first rosebuds were opening, and it was still cool under the spreading, leafy maples. It wasn't hard at all to produce class for these guys. All I had to do was walk behind them with my hands clasped behind my back and speak when spoken to. They more or less sold themselves. Their names were Terry, Tommy, and Donnie. Inside the house they kept their hands in their pockets as if they had no right to touch anything. They stood back in the center of the rooms and cocked their heads and said, "Hey, look at this. This is nice. Real nice. Look at these floors, man. You don't see floors like this every day. It won't be hard to turn this place into a club, it's made for it. Can you believe one family lived in this place all those years? How many kids did you say these folks had?"

"Two."

"Shit, man."

And then we went outside.

Even though Marcus had called them investors, we quickly fell into a Realtor/buyer mode. I showed them where the golf course designer (who had been there once by that point) had tentatively located the golf course, and I speculated knowledgeably about where the houses would go and what they would look like, three to five bedrooms, four to six baths, of course a few special houses might be a little bigger, depending on special needs, but we all agreed that families were smaller now, and that what people really wanted were amenities. It turned out that Terry grew up in Chicago, the sixth of ten children, and the house he grew up in had three bedrooms, one for the parents, one for the girls, and one for the boys. Two bathrooms. I expressed appreciation. All the men agreed that when they had lived like that as a kid, no one had known any better and it hadn't really mattered. Tommy said, "I had three sisters, and you know, every night they'd stand in front of the same little bathroom mirror, rolling up their hair for school and fighting over bobby pins. My sister Mary used to wait until the other two were asleep and then take all the bobby pins she could reach out of their rollers."

"Did she grow up to be a pickpocket?" I asked. There was a laugh.

"Nah. But she doesn't have seven kids, like my mother did. She stopped at two."

The meat business was unbelievable, according to them. "You don't have to run the delis themselves, that's a nightmare with all the health regulations; you just make sure there's lots of variety and that it's real authentic, and you paint the delivery trucks so they make people hungry." Tommy looked at me. "It's like stealing money," he said. The three of them confided that they liked a certain lifestyle—they themselves would never live all the way out in the sticks like this—but none of their wives really liked urban life, and that was the way with most wives, when you came down to it. So even though it was doubtful they would ever live in a place like this, in their considered opinion, this was the wave of the future, because this was what women wanted.

I was smooth. "We do think the club will be a social center, with debuts and parties and weddings for the members and the residents."

"Yeah. That's a good idea. My opinion is, hotels are out, clubs are in. This place is perfect for that."

All in all, everyone was satisfied.

Jane called me the next day and thanked me; the showing was just right. I said, "Should I plan for more of that sort of thing?"

"Not really. Showing the place off is Marcus's favorite part. These guys, frankly, have been investing most of their excess funds in sports bets. I suggested that a steadier return from a legitimate enterprise might persuade the IRS not to scrutinize them so frequently." She laughed.

"Do they really know Donald Trump?"

"Not through developing. Maybe through boxing or something like that."

"You're a bold woman, Jane."

"Some of our investors are the height of respectability."

"I'm not objecting."

"I know."

Jane was friendly to me. Over the years she had perfected a way of getting on with men at the office that was comfortable, circumspect, and teasing, absolutely guaranteed to disarm any and every personal thought. Every time I came into the office, she said, "Oh, Joey! How are you today? What have you been doing?" She would push her chair back from whatever she was doing and turn right to me and give me a big smile. If she had a pencil in her hand, she set it down. If she was typing something or calculating something, she stopped what she was doing. If she was on the phone, she waved at me and gave me a big grin. I began to feel that she liked me. If I asked where Marcus was, she always said, "Making mischief," then grinned and rolled her eyes. Other times, she would say, "Joe! I am getting! Are you spending?"

"Always!"

"Spend more!"

"Can't help that!"

When I expressed admiration and friendship toward Marcus, Jane would always grin, as if this were especially amusing, but when he was in the office and telling her what he wanted her to do, she was serious and attentive, eager to please him. Her manner toward him was a combination of secretary, older sister, ally, and tease. Finally one day I said to her, "Jane, who's the boss around here, you or him?"

"I thought you were the boss, Joe."

"No, really."

"Marcus and I have a strange relationship."

"Because—"

"Because I have a hard time taking him seriously, whereas he listens to everything I say. On the other hand, he never does anything I tell him he should, and I do everything he tells me in spite of myself. I'm starting to think it's a kind of enchantment."

"Sounds like my marriage."

"Really? My marriage was not enchanting at all. We were best friends. It wasn't till the end that I found out he had a romantic side. Now he has a baby. I can't imagine it."

"Why not?"

"I could swear I never saw him look at a baby in twenty years. Not once. But he would swear that he was obsessed with babies. So it was like we didn't live the same life after all. But at least splitting the property wasn't hard. He had his, I had mine. We never even had a joint checking account. Each of us was very self-sufficient. I thought that was our strength. But then it turned out he didn't even like the dog. I thought he loved the dog, and I thought the dog was impossible not to love, so I'm not quite sure what to make of that." She shrugged.

"Marcus thinks my former wife was a little on the commanding side. He went to her restaurant, and she forced him to eat his salad. I just saw her as more firm in her desires than I was."

"But Joey, you don't mind being commanded, do you?" She picked up a pencil and tapped it on her desk. She was smiling, though.

"Am I being insulted, Jane?"

"That's what he's going to kill us with, you know." She set the pencil down.

"Who?"

"Marcus. He doesn't mind conflict and we do, so in the end he's going to win."

I didn't know what she was getting at.

Although I was unattached and Jane was unattached, there seemed to be no possibility that we would connect away from the office, so we got to be something like friends, but always between us there was Marcus, with whom we both were allied, but whom we did not seem to see in the same way. I finally decided that working with a brother and sister was almost like hanging out with some married couple. In the end, your best bet is to stop noticing their relationship altogether.

We were happy as could be, it seemed. One day, I saw a check on Jane's desk from Gordon, for twenty thousand dollars. The gravel, I thought, an interesting and amazing turn of events, in its way, and the next day Gordon called me and told me that Marlborough County, where Portsmouth was, had decided that the project was amazing in its way, also, because they had sent him a letter telling him that he was required to get a mining permit, and that the removal of county soils had to cease immediately, pending the implementation of required permitting procedures.

"When is the letter dated?"

"Well, let me put on my glasses here. Let's see, May tenth."

"Gordon, that's over a month ago. Was it lost in the mail?"

"It got into the seat of Betty's car and we didn't find it until she was cleaning up a Popsicle that one of the kids had that melted in there yesterday."

"A mining permit? That could be expensive."

"I'm thinking the state and the township are going to want to get in on this too, but really, you better meet me out there and take a look, because things have changed since you were out there before." I took this as an emergency request.

The earthmoving machine and the line of dump trucks were now considerably closer to the old farmhouse. In fact, the house, which must have still been inhabited because an old pickup was parked beside the door, now sat on what looked like a mushroom. They had dug away the former hillside for about 300 degrees around the house. As I pulled my car up next to Gordon's, I saw the door of the house open and something fly out. I said to Gordon a moment later, "Is someone still living there?"

"Uh, Gerhardt, the old guy, is moving to the

old folks' home on the first of the month. It's gonna be interesting to get into there. He's got newspapers back to the birth of Jesus in there. That stuff is valuable in some quarters. Well, maybe not to the birth of Jesus. But the First World War, anyway." He handed me a Popsicle-sticky paper from the county.

I said, "You don't seem worried about this." It was a very official letter from an office I hadn't ever dealt with in a building in Portsmouth I had never been to, the Commercial Land Use and Mineral Rights Inspection Board. Among other things, the letter declared that recipient *may be charged a penalty in addition to the normal permitting fee, and a fine for every cubic yard mined . . . which shall be assessed according to . . . please contact this office as soon as . . . ordered to desist.*

Gordon shrugged. "We'll go talk to them. So what? We're recontouring is all."

"Gordon, you're taking down the whole hill."

"There's as much as we've already taken out still in there. The road-building guy said it was the best he's ever seen. You know, I always thought the drainage on this farm was perfect. Those cows were never slogging through mud."

The next morning we went to the Marlborough County Auxiliary Building, which was a former high school. The official we saw, named Sherwin Dorsett, turned out to be a young woman, maybe thirty years old. She took the letter in her hand, read it over, and then looked at me. She said, "You're Mr. Baldwin?"

"This is Mr. Baldwin."

"You his lawyer?"

"His Realtor, actually. I'm Joe Stratford, Salt Key Corporation."

"I drove past that site on the way to work. I drive past that site every morning. Mr. Baldwin, you've got twenty trucks passing in and out of there on a steady basis. The mining regulations are very clear in this county. If you export more than the specified cubic yardage of ore or rock or soils, you have to have a mining permit."

Gordon twinkled at her. "We're not exporting anything. It's staying right in the state."

"This is a county agency, Mr. Baldwin. I work for the county."

"If I didn't supply the state highway commission with this gravel, they'd have to go another hundred miles to get it. That would be quite an expense, they told me."

"I'm sure it would. County regulations are clear, though."

"I'm recontouring that property. I've done it all over the county. If you're going to build fifty houses somewhere, you've got to have level ground. The front section of that farm is level, right along the highway. The back section you couldn't do a thing with. It was too steep. Now it isn't, thanks to me."

"Have you applied for a building permit?"

"Not yet, but—"

"May I say something?" I piped up.

She led us into her office. I thought about Marcus and said, "Maybe you could tell me precisely what it is you would like us to do?" I smiled and smiled.

"You should have applied for a mining permit six months before beginning the project. That's how long it usually takes to consider the various documents that would inform the county about whether or not the proposed mining is in the county's best interest."

"I don't think Mr. Baldwin knew in November or October that the state would be needing the gravel. He was really responding to an appeal by them, because, you know, they have to do the roadbuilding now, in the summer, when the soil is stable so they can lay a good roadbed."

"There are no filings on this project at all, so, as I said in the letter, the project is ordered to desist and all monies received are to be put in escrow until the project is approved."

I reached out my hand for the letter and

looked it over. I said, but oh, so pleasantly, "I'm sorry. I don't see anything here about putting money in escrow."

"Well, that is the next step with a noncompliance of this kind. How much have you received so far?"

Gordon stared at her. It was as if she, a girl, a blond girl, a blond girl younger than his daughters, was asking him to show her his poker hand. I leaned forward, shook my head regretfully. I said, "You know, I do think we need to talk about this further between ourselves before we decide what to do."

"Mr. Stratford, there is no deciding, really. The rules are the rules." She coughed. "The mining has to cease as of this afternoon. You may begin the permitting process as soon as you put together your impact statements and your soil analysis statements. The company doing the roadbuilding will have to be contacted so they can submit documents about the relative value of material from this site."

I took out a pen and a little notebook, and I said, "Why don't you give me the list of documents that you need?"

She softened slightly, I thought with relief, which showed me right there that she was more nervous than she appeared. Her voice strengthened. She gave me the list. I numbered each one. The last one was number fourteen. Fourteen applications and statements and authorizations required to move some gravel, including the "precious metals statement," which was a soil analysis to be done by some expert from somewhere stating that we were not mining for gold, silver, or platinum and therefore not seeking a "premium" mining permit. I said, "Has gold ever been discovered in Marlborough County?"

"Not so far." She spoke gravely.

I gave her a friendly look. I stood up. I said, "Thanks for your time." I patted her on the shoulder. Marcus couldn't have done a better job. Gordon was coughing and clearing his throat as we went out, as if he were choking to death. I poked him in the ribs and pushed him toward the exit. Out in the parking lot, he said, "It's my property. I've had that piece for twenty years. It just sits there for twenty years, and finally they come to me, and I make a little something off it! Nathan knows a guy, a lawyer."

I said, "Gordon, you've got a better idea than a lawyer."

"What's that?"

"Think about it. Think about that time six or seven years ago when they weren't going to let you put those houses at Rookwood Crossing on quarter-acre lots."

"I went to the township board of supervisors

and asked where they were going to put in the mandated low-income housing. Oh, they approved those quarter-acre lots so fast! That's a nice neighborhood now, you know. I went past there last week. It's a regular town. Let's go see Ivan Kruger."

We got into his BMW.

"How much money have you made on that gravel?"

Gordon shrugged.

"Do you not know, or are you not telling?"

"I loaned some to Norton. He's got a guest house he wants to buy. Betty's putting down new carpets at the shop. You know, it comes in. I gave some to Marcus, but you know, Joe, you've got to hold something back with him. I'm not saying I'm not committed to the farm and all, but there's a difference between paying top dollar when you have to and paying top dollar because that's what you are in the habit of doing. Marcus doesn't know the difference, you ask me, but he's persuasive. That's why I stay out of the office. Limited contact."

"Well, yeah," I said.

Gordon said, "Let's go for a drive."

The drive took us east of Portsmouth, to an area I didn't often visit, a flat, not very pretty area where the farms still prospered—cattle, corn, tomatoes in the summer, onions, a few hogs, you name it. We turned down a dirt road and ended up at the Krugers'. Ivan Kruger had been a county supervisor since before the county had supervisors. He generally ran unopposed. He farmed about two hundred acres or so. When we pulled up next to his barn, he was standing there, holding a baby pig nose-down, his fist around one of its back feet.

Gordon brought the car to a halt beside him; we got out of the car; we came around the car. He did not greet us; Gordon did not greet him. I guessed they had known each other for almost forty years. The pig squealed and arched itself, then hung there for a moment, its ear twitching. Ivan was wearing greasy old overalls, a long-sleeved shirt with an elbow out, and an old fedora, against the sun, but it was a mistake to think he never got off the farm, because he said, "You got all those folks out there up in arms, Gordon. Those trucks are going in and out day and night."

"That shouldn't last much longer. A few weeks, maybe."

The pig tried to stretch down and put its front feet on the ground. It squealed again.

Gordon said, "It was about time that place was recontoured. If old Gerhardt had done that years ago, he might have had a farm." He nodded toward the barn.

"Might have." Ivan tightened his grip on the pig but didn't look at it. He cleared his throat, then said, "You're making some money on that gravel."

"One-time deal. Once the land is recontoured, it's done. It's not like it's going to be a gravel pit out there."

"I suppose," allowed Ivan. With the hand not holding the pig, he hitched up his pants.

"Would have had to do it anyway, to put a neighborhood in. It's just opportune that the state needed the gravel at the same time. You know there was four high school kids killed at that intersection up there last Christmas."

"Folks drive too fast, that's for sure." The pig swung back and forth. "But they do. You know, we used to think, well, if there was part of the road that was interstate, then there was part of the road that wasn't, well, people would notice that, but they don't. It's like those three-lane highways we used to have. Seemed like a good idea at the time, but it was the worst idea in the world." I stared at the pig's face, and I thought it caught my eye. Ivan said, "This is going to come up at the next supervisors' meeting. You know it is."

"Well, sure," said Gordan.

"But if you do something for the county, I don't see any reason to go through all the rigamarole they want."

"If I shut down the project now, it's going to look like hell," said Gordon, "and the state isn't going to hold off on that overpass till next year."

"Nope."

"Well, I got men who aren't doing anything right now for a while. You know we're getting ready to do a big project in Plymouth Township."

"I did hear about that. Say, there's a lot of kids in Rookwood now. The school bus won't go in there. They have to come out and wait by the side of the road. I get complaints about that, too."

"The school bus ought to be able to pull right off the road there."

"I've always thought so."

"Let me go look at that on my way back to Portsmouth."

"You should."

Suddenly, the pig began screaming and squealing, and behind Ivan some other pigs, it seemed like, began squealing in response. It writhed and jerked its foot. Ivan grabbed the other foot. Now he had the pig hanging down in front of him. He tossed his head at us, then turned away. We got into Gordon's car. As we drove away, I said, "So what was he going to do with that pig?"

"Believe me, you don't want to know. The thing about farm animals is, when one gets sick, they just put it down before it infects the whole herd. You don't even have time to get the vet out, because all he's going to do is tell you what you already know."

"I guess you're going to put in a school-bus stop."

"My bet is, we won't hear from Miss Sherwin whatever-her-name-is anymore."

"I doubt it," I said.

"But I'll tell you another thing."

"What's that?"

"Ivan isn't going to run for election again, so she's the future, not him."

"Her and Marcus."

"You got it."

CHAPTER 20

A FEW DAYS AFTER our visit to Ivan Kruger, I saw some papers on Jane's desk, and since no one was in the office I glanced through them. They were Bobby's financial papers, such as they were. Things noted here, slips there, old pay stubs from me. The only thing that prevented them from being a disaster was that the sums were so small. I kept my eyes open, and not long after I saw a folder labeled R. BALDWIN, 1981–82. I opened it when I had the chance. I only looked at the top page. There, in Marcus's neat and extremely legible handwriting, was a spreadsheet detailing Bobby's financial condition, and underneath that was his amended tax return, also in Marcus's writing. It was twenty-six pages long and earned Bobby a refund of $236. One schedule after another detailed this write-off and that. I was impressed that he would take the time, and also at how neat it all was—chaos reduced to order.

When I got home, I took out my own books and opened them up. I was not as disorganized as Bobby—I did have everything entered into an actual set of books, and I brought it all up to date every month, but I usually did so in a hurried way and didn't often look at the big picture. Some months I paid my rent and my condo mortgage and my utility bills and not much else. Like Gordon, if I knew there was enough—more than enough—I often let it go at that for months at a time. Once a year I took everything to my tax accountant and then sent in a check for what he told me I owed. I had a couple of savings accounts. I was single and had few expenses. Now, under the influence of Marcus Burns, I suddenly got interested in my net worth. I took out the box I had brought from my office (which Gordon was renting to some crony of his month by month on the understanding that Bobby could keep his space and I might need to return, so we didn't have to move the furniture or clean out the closets) and opened it up. Pretty soon I had spread it all out on my kitchen table. It was interesting reading. For example, as of my divorce from Sherry, a little over two years previously, I had owned my condo

($10,000 equity with a $35,000 mortgage); my car, worth about $9,000 or $10,000; my savings account (about $17,000); and the two pieces of ground, one worth maybe $40,000 and the other worth maybe $38,000. After two years selling real estate, one of them bad and one of them good, I had $20,000 equity in a condo worth $65,000 on the market; a new $20,000 car; and savings of $51,000. The pieces of property I had sold for $100,000 altogether, which I had put into the corporation along with my share of the Phase Four commission. In other words, without my even really noticing, I had gotten to be a third of a millionaire.

I can't say that I had ever felt the presence of that kind of money so close to home. Certainly, the word *millionaire* had never, could have never, occurred in connection with my parents. In the first place, their financial life was entirely bounded by a little display on the kitchen table that I had seen every Saturday night as a child— ones, fives, tens, twenties, so much to the store rent and inventory, so much to the mortgage, so much to the church, and then small amounts to the tangible needs of clothing, food, and transportation for the family. There was another stack—the funeral account—right there on the table with everything else, sometimes getting more and sometimes getting less, depending on the requirements of the other stacks. If there was a surplus, it was divided between *savings* and *church*, and if there had been a real surplus, no doubt most of it would have gone to the church, since the church's state of repair and sightliness was as important to my mother as that of her own house. Nor, for all I knew of Gordon's way of life—much more lavish than my parents'—had I ever viewed him as a man with money. He was more a man who made use of money as it flowed past, as if he had been born lucky enough to live right beside a sweet and brimming stream. Out of that natural bounty he had made a comfortable life that also was bountiful, but the bounty ebbed and flowed—there was no cistern, only activity and good luck. And then there was Marcus. I had seen his tax returns. By the evidence of those as well as of what he said, he was living on the come more than anything else. Billions there well could be, but he hadn't actually made contact with them yet. I had more money than he did, and he probably knew it.

My new status at first only intrigued me. I left the books and papers out on the table for a few days, though neatly stacked, to remind myself that there was something about me—I had made it. I was forty-one now and, by any measure, several of those American words you heard all the time—successful, comfortable, well-off—

applied to me. And respected. Marcus had mentioned that one himself. When people heard he
was my partner, they breathed a sigh of relief. I
was to be trusted. Of course, I was no longer
married and I didn't have any children. I had no
family sitting solidly on some square of ground
like a pyramid, the way most men my age seemed
to have, but I didn't mind about that really. So
many families were odd and suffocating in reality that I wasn't impressed by either the ideal
or my own capacity to realize it. For a couple of
days, I wondered whether I should forgo Marcus's offer to pay my bills—I had already had
them all addressed to that office—but upon reflection I decided that there really was no telling
when Salt Key Farm would get off the ground,
and after all I had put my equity in. The commissions, for one thing, but also those farms I had
bought for under fifty and sold for a hundred,
those farms I had been making payments on of a
couple hundred dollars a month and could never
decide what to do with, had been turned into
something more elegant and profitable. My
other funds, I thought, ought to be held in reserve until we really saw what was in store. And
while I wasn't using them, they would appreciate. So I drove about on my appointed rounds
with a greater sense of self-confidence. I was a
successful Realtor and small-time developer.

GOOD FAITH

That I should build on this solid base wasn't surprising, it was natural, the almost automatic effect of normal ambition. I had lived, without understanding it, the proper American trajectory, rising and rising, dropping off the first-stage rocket, then the second stage, then shooting into space, destined to orbit the earth for some uncounted number of times before splashing into the ocean off Florida, retired in the far-off twenty-first century.

A month later, when I went into our conference room, I saw a Xerox machine. It was large—you couldn't miss it—and it looked brand-new. It didn't quite fit in with the décor. I hadn't had one in my real estate office, and it seemed like a luxury. I went out into Jane's office. I said, "You'll never guess what's in the conference room."

She grinned. "I haven't felt this good since I bought my first washer and dryer."

"We bought it? They're awfully expensive, aren't they?"

"No. Leased it. Actually, I took over Mary's lease because she wanted something smaller."

"Mary King?"

"Well, sure."

"Are you friends with her?"

"Sisters in free enterprise. There's a number of us. We have a lunch group. Every couple of weeks."

"What do you talk about?"

"Xerox machines. IBM typewriters. Whether, if you have daughters, you should let them learn to type."

"Is this group based on shared feelings of resentment?"

"Shared ambition."

"Hunh. Whose job do you want?"

"That's one of the things we talk about. What to aim for."

"Did Marcus tell you about the billion dollars?"

She laughed happily.

A few days later, I was making use of the Xerox machine to copy a letter I had written to the Plymouth Township Planning Commission. When I lifted the top lid, I saw that someone had left a sheet of paper facedown underneath it. It was a property description of a thousand-acre ranch in western Kansas. It belonged to Jane. I looked at it for a long moment. I thought she must have gotten it in her divorce settlement and was now selling it. I took the description and put it on her desk. A week or so after that, I got a letter from Bart telling me that the appraisers in Kansas had put the value of the ranch at a million dollars and advising me that my application for an 80 percent loan on the property was approved. I looked again at the top of the letter. It was addressed to Marcus but put into an envelope to me by mistake. I put the letter on Jane's desk too. Funds were good. I was happy to see funds, and I was happy to see that Jane, who must have been holding off from really committing herself to our project, was committed now.

An 80 percent loan on collateral of a million dollars was eight hundred thousand dollars. I knew the merger hadn't gone through yet, so I was especially impressed that Bart and Crosbie were working other options. Whatever their source of income, they seemed to want to throw money at us.

I ran into the Davids. They were standing next to the weathervane display at the lumberyard and saw me immediately. David John exclaimed, "Ask Joe. I told you he would show up eventually."

"He's definitely going to be in favor of the cock," said David Pollock.

"Where are you putting a weathervane?" I said. Their roofline was simple and straight, a gable at each end. "With the pitch you've got, it's hardly worth—"

"Have you not seen our cupola? It's the talk of Deacon."

"I hate to ask."

"It's got a widow in it," said David John. "Gazing forlornly out to sea."

"Sea is a hundred miles from here."

"Oh, God! No wonder she's so upset!" David John turned to David Pollock. "You never told me that."

"Who's the widow?"

David Pollock looked right at me. He said, "Well, of course we've named her Felicity. But really she's a mannequin from a Woolworth's they were tearing down in the city. We found her abandoned on the street, naked as a jaybird. She's happy, though." He lifted his arms in a pose of exaggerated delight. "Come over. You can see her carmine lips from the sidewalk. She needs a cock swinging around above her."

"I prefer the trotting horse," said David John.

"We have this argument every weekend. But do come over and we'll tell you everything."

"About the widow," said David John.

"I want to hear. But I have a better idea."

"Oh, God, what's that?"

"I have to go out to the farm we're developing, and I think you guys should see it. It's not something you would pass in the normal course of things. You might want to invest."

"We might?"

"Or you might have friends who would."

"We have friends with scads of dough," said David John.

"So you've said."

We went out to the parking lot without buying anything, and I opened the passenger door to my car. David Pollock said, "Should we drive with you? What about Marlin and Doris?"

"Bring them along."

We piled into my Lincoln and headed out of Deacon. As soon as we were in the country, David Pollock said, "Joey, you notice you haven't asked us why we named our widow *Felicity*."

"Yes, I noticed that. I suppose you had better tell me."

"You've been very naughty, we're told."

"I have?"

"Dropping her like a hot potato and all."

Even though I was heading down the road at sixty-five miles an hour, I turned and stared.

"I think he's genuinely surprised," said David John.

"I tend to agree," said David Pollock. "Maybe we should hear your side of the story after all. But only if you promise to stay on the road."

"We've got plenty of time," said David John.

My mind had been full of the farm—I had

stopped into the hardware store to buy ant traps for my condo, but what I was really doing was wondering what my share of the payment would be when our first payment was due, on the first of October, more than two months away, but still worrying, as I estimated we were a year away from selling off the first lots and getting some income. That was why I had brought up taking them out there—these real estate investment trusts of Jane's seemed to have appeal for a surprising number of people, but they had to be people with excess tax liability, according to Marcus. Anyway, shifting the farm out of my mind all of a sudden and bringing Felicity in seemed disorienting. I had not asked about the "widow" not because I was afraid to, but because I hadn't gotten the point of the name.

I tried to think of something to say about myself, not precisely an excuse or a reason, but something true, something that would originate a way of talking about Felicity, but not only was my mind a blank on that, I was a blank. I had no way of talking about Felicity other than saying I loved her, and I could not say that. I don't know if I couldn't say it to them or if I couldn't say it at all. We kept driving.

"He's not answering," said David John.

"I was surprised. I guess I don't have an answer except that. I mean, are you telling me the truth, that Felicity thinks I dropped her like a hot potato? The last time I saw her I had the distinct feeling I had fatally trespassed. And she never called me again or came by."

"I told you on the phone that night that there was stepped-up surveillance."

"I took that to mean I should be careful."

"I meant *she* was being careful. You were supposed to become assertive, I believe it was."

"I guess I didn't get the hint."

"No," said David Pollock. A silence settled over the car, as of a subject that was closed—only of historical interest now. After a moment, I said, "So, what is she doing lately?"

"We haven't seen her in over a month. Hank likes us, you know. He approves of everything we do, because we scavenge and improve and add value, and we are exotic all at the same time. He stares at us. He calls me *Dave* and him *David.*" David John, who was speaking, sighed. He said, "Once we got approval, she stopped coming over. Now *he* comes over."

"He's a very well-meaning person," said David Pollock.

"Probably a saint," said David John.

We arrived at the gate of the farm. "She'll never leave him," said David Pollock.

"That's what I thought," I said. I looked at each

of them and each of them looked at me. All three of us nodded slightly. We were agreed, then.

We had gotten the permit for the golf course, and we were very close to getting the permit for the clubhouse and the waste-treatment facility (pending ironing out some provisions about community access to it after a certain date, or in case certain things did or did not happen—there was a definite feeling that everything had to fall into place in order for anything to fall into place). Most days I put one foot in front of the other and left the larger issues for Marcus and Jane. The farm still looked the same, though, as when the Thorpes had lived there. But it was the wrong time of year to begin contouring the golf course. Marcus had told me that once they came in I would be surprised how quickly it went. I told him I had seen that over and over; it seems like you're not getting anywhere and then, all of a sudden, there you are. As we drove through the gate and under the overhanging trees, the Davids were quiet, staring out the windows. In midsummer, it was like driving back to the thirties or the twenties, down the green-gold hillside to the creek. The bright flat sky beyond looked eternal. Simultaneously, they opened the windows of the car, and I turned off the air-conditioning. I halted beside the front entry. A grassy fragrance passed through, and the rat terrier stood up, stuck her nose out of the window, and sniffed. Then she jumped out the window onto the driveway.

We wandered around the grounds. We hadn't planted any annuals, but the perennials were taken care of by the gardener and his assistant, who were still living on the property, keeping an eye on it. Nothing delicate or springlike, everything happy in the heat, hardy in the breeze. We walked down the slope a ways and looked back at the house, then came up and stood on the porch and looked down the slope. David John said, "I think it's more than we can take on as a weekend job." We all laughed.

"We're looking for investors. This is going to be the clubhouse; the golf course runs along there. And then we're going to put up fancy houses."

"Whatever happened to buy low, sell high?"

"Come inside."

We wandered through the house without saying anything. The rooms were entirely empty now: hall, library, two sitting rooms, sunroom, formal living room, dining room, kitchen. Up the carved walnut staircase. At the landing, you could turn either way below the bank of windows that looked out on the formal garden; then there were six bedrooms, two of which were suites; and then, above that, storage, servants' rooms, two more bathrooms. Much woodwork, many windows, many doors. "It's going to cost a mint to furnish this place," said David John. "I don't think a few throw rugs here and there are going to do it, honey."

"That's why we need investors."

"You know," said David Pollock, "we have a friend of a friend who's got the furniture. You know Martin, with the costumes?"

"Thank you for that tip."

"He knows James, with the furniture."

"He knows," said David John, "Yves, with the money."

"Yes, he does," said David Pollock. "We've only met Yves once, but he's a designer. He's so hot right now. People bow to him. I'm sure he's looking for a sinkhole, a very beautiful sinkhole, just like this one, to throw his extra money down."

We wandered around for another couple of hours, looking, chatting, naming names. I kept a list. I thought Marcus and Jane would be pleased. When we were driving back to the hardware store in Deacon, I said, "So, what should I do about Felicity?"

"She's not going to leave him," said David John again.

"Her real problem is that she doesn't have a

vocation. Or even a job," said David Pollock. "I think she's stuck here. Her only salvation is to travel back in time and do it all over differently."

The three of us nodded together.

On Monday, I gave Jane the list of names. She looked it over, and then I said, "Do tell me, Jane, what the point of these real estate investment trusts is."

"Well, I think the real point is cash flow."

"Yes, but, pardon me for asking, what do the investors get for their money?"

"I'm sure, in the end, some of them hope to profit."

"In the end?"

"Well, think of it as a sort of junk bond. High risk, big payoff. Most people who have plenty of money to invest understand that. Believe me, we are not going after little old ladies on widows' pensions. That's a game for the S and Ls."

"Excuse me?"

"Oh, you know, bundling passbook savings accounts and selling them to other institutions that are paying a quarter of a point higher interest. Or less than that. I'm sure that's what Crosbie is doing. That merger hasn't gone through yet, but they're rolling in dough. Not just investments, either, but a flood of deposits. I guess they raised payouts by a quarter of a point or something, and some deposit brokers started sending them more deposits than they can have on the books and still look good. Crosbie came to Marcus just the other day and asked if we have any other properties anywhere." She shrugged. "And what else did he say? Something about how Portsmouth Savings was thinking of getting into T-bill futures or even junk bonds. It's a new world, that's for sure."

"I'm not sure Bart is ready for the new world, Jane."

"Who *is*? I've been doing finance and investment for fifteen years, and I'm not ready for other people's junk bonds. Most junk bonds are pure roulette, is what I told Marcus. There's no way to judge their value except by some kind of intuition. Marcus says they have no real value, only market value, and I understand that in principle, but I don't know. I suppose I'm lucky to find myself here in this little office in a little town with a tangible asset on my hands."

"It's a good asset."

"I know you think that, Joe, and when I wake up in the night, I remember that you think that and I can actually get back to sleep."

I stared at her.

"Anyway, Bart doesn't have to deal with that end of the business. As long as they keep doing a few residential mortgages, he'll have something to do. But listen. These trust people aren't like buyers. You know, I know a woman who went into the horse business. She bought two miniature horses. You know what they look like? About the size of Great Danes, or even golden retrievers, if you're lucky. Anyway, they graze out on her lawn, and she deducts everything—part of her mortgage payment, her lawn maintenance costs, her house maintenance costs. I mean, she's in the horse business. She doesn't have to make a profit for seven years. By that time she will have saved a small fortune in taxes."

"I hope we make a profit before seven years is out."

"Me, too, but these guys"—she gestured at the list of investors—"they don't care one way or the other. They have to have losses too. So we can do that for them. Profit and loss; both are services in the end." She smiled.

She seemed in a good mood, so I hazarded a question. "Did you know Marcus was leaving the IRS, or was it sudden?"

"Oh, God, Marcus complained about working there so much, it was me who told him he had to get out. It took him a year to make up his mind. Between you and me, I don't think he ever would have left if he thought he could get promoted, but after the election, he bet me that there would be cutbacks, and sure enough there were, and that was it for him." She grinned. "Marcus is always ready to sell himself to the highest bidder, even if the bid isn't very high."

"You have a very jaded view, Jane."

"Yes. I'm so smart, why aren't I rich?"

We laughed.

A couple of days later, I ran into Bart. He was coming out of a travel agency right next to the drugstore I was going into. He waved his tickets in my face and said, "Whatcha doing?"

"Buying some Pepto-Bismol for my mother. What are *you* doing?"

"Going to France. Everyone. The whole family. Two weeks. We leave tomorrow, and we're flying first class. It was Crosbie's suggestion. I mean, he said, you know, time to give the place a little style. No more bow ties."

"Are you taking my money with you?"

Bart laughed. "You won't believe this, but no. Crosbie gave me a little bonus. Well, not only

me. All the vice presidents. We had some investments that paid off."

"What were they?"

"Let's see. Oh, yeah. T-bill futures. See you in
a couple of weeks!" He jumped in his car and
drove off.

SOMETIME IN MID-SEPTEMBER, Marcus and I were driving out to the farm to have a look at the progress of the golf course. It was a blank sort of day—hot but hazy, humid. I had the air-conditioning on high, but it wasn't making much of a difference in my mood. I had a Rolling Stones tape in the tape deck. Marcus hadn't said much since we got in the car, but I was used to his moods by now and didn't pay any attention. The scenery looked tired and uninteresting, the dusty end of summer. I passed the intersection of Felicity's road and thought of her, and Marcus said, "You need a date."

"What gives you that idea?"

"I was in your office the other day looking for a copy of the site plan, and I think you're aging prematurely."

"Why do you say that?"

"Well, it looks like you dust, for one thing."

"I do dust."

"And everything has a place and everything is in its place."

"This is true. I'm a well-brought-up boy."

"I moved a few things out of their places."

"I thought something funny—"

"And when I let myself in this morning, you had moved them all back and straightened things up a little bit."

I stared at him.

He said, "That's very codgerlike behavior."

"I've always been that way. I'm supposed to justify being a little meticulous because you went into my office on the sly?"

"You need kids."

"I've never needed kids."

"You're spiraling inward. I told Linda about this test I gave you, and she said, 'He's spiraling inward.'"

"I am not spiraling inward."

He ignored me. He continued, "Come to dinner Saturday night. Linda has a friend for you to meet."

"I don't want to meet any friends. I don't want to come to dinner."

"She's making a standing rib roast with roast potatoes and a chocolate cake."

"I'll come for the food." But not really. Really, I was coming because I had never been invited before and I wanted to see what their family was like. Others had been invited. Until that very moment, I hadn't even realized I was jealous of them.

He said, "Think about it. What kind of life do you have? No girlfriend or wife, no kids, no hobbies." He shook his head.

I said, "My hobby is making a billion dollars. After I have it, my hobby will be spending it." A few moments later, I said, a bit defensively, "I like to travel. Sherry and I went to someplace exotic every year."

We drove on. We were almost to the farm when he said, "Do you think Jane is interested in you?"

"No. Why?"

"Because I think she's interested in someone, but I can't figure out who."

"Well, what difference does it make?"

"She's my sister."

The coincidence was that about halfway through the dinner Linda cooked for us a few nights later, I realized that the woman I was there to meet was the same woman Betty and Felicity had discussed introducing me to on

some previous occasion that I couldn't quite remember—I could only remember the feeling I
had had that Felicity had been courting me and
teasing me in that unique way she had, and as
soon as I realized that this was that woman, she
began to look better to me—she got to be in-
fused with Felicity's playfulness and subterfuge.
I won't say that I got interested, but I did get
looser, and I began to think of things to say.

Susan Webster was blond and pretty. She had
made the appetizers, which were a selection of
tapas that we ate with the wine she brought.
She talked nicely about her life in Spain, in
Granada, where the Alhambra was. She
painted tiles and wrote occasional articles for
local newspapers. She was thinking of going
back to school, maybe art school. What she
really liked to do was decorate bathrooms to
be very bright and cheerful, with Mexican and
Spanish tiles. Marcus assured her that you
could, indeed, have a whole bathroom designing business, if you were creative enough.
Linda said she wished she were creative. The
ten-year-old, Amanda, offered comments from
time to time. At one point, she said that if she
were allowed, she would paint her room completely black—floors, walls, and ceiling, and
then put those kind of stars all over it that lit
up when you turned on one of those purple

lights, and then you could lie on the bed and feel like you were out in space and there was no such thing as up or down. This seemed quite charming to me, until I saw her glare at her mother after this comment, as if this were a realistic plan that her mother had unreasonably balked. Justin, who seemed more than just a year younger, occupied himself with eating the food on his plate in some kind of pattern or sequence that was more complicated than I could figure out by simply observing him. It was disconcerting. But he was polite and cleaned his plate and I thought that my mother would have been happy to have him as her grandson.

The house looked good, but I wouldn't have brought Gottfried around. The Burnses' taste was excellent, and the furniture was expensive but not quite right for the house. The house was American, their taste was European—a little too deluxe. Susan Webster kept oohing and aahing at what they had done, and the *touches* they had added, and Linda nodded and smiled, more as if she were relieved than pleased. The children adjourned to the TV room, and we went into the living room. I wondered if they expected the fix-up to take immediately, or if I had some time to make up my mind.

GOOD FAITH

· · ·

Marcus called me the next day. He said, "She's a good choice for you. She's well traveled and sophisticated without being hard or intimidating. She's petite. Petite is good, I mean generally good. There are specific petite women you wouldn't want to get involved with and specific tall women that you would, but in general petite is a better category than tall."

"What am I looking for, Marcus?"

"A wife."

"Oh. Why?"

"Because if it's been too long since your divorce, people start wondering about you."

"Why?"

"Because men are better off married. Single men die much sooner than married men, and you don't want to look like you're queer."

"I don't, that's true."

"Investors don't like it."

"Some do." I was thinking of the Davids. He ignored me.

"Didn't you like her?"

"I could hardly tell. It was too much like our parents were arranging an engagement and we were on our best behavior. Frankly, I like to meet women in bars and assess them primarily on their ability to throw off their inhibitions with grace."

I thought of Felicity. "Especially bars at the shore."

"So take her to a bar at the shore and try her out. But remember, she's auditioning for wife, not girlfriend. This is a public relationship, not a private one."

"Excuse me?"

"I wish I were in your position. You know, most guys get married in their twenties, before they really know what their careers are going to look like, and most of the time they pick someone they're comfortable with, which means someone from the neighborhood or from college—always someone from the place where they happen to have been *most* comfortable. But if they have any ambition, their lives change and that person may not want, or be able, to go along with those changes. I just think I'm lucky. Linda and I are so much alike we can more or less do it together. But I'm telling you, if you look at the first wives of most self-made men, you have to say, '*that's* a picture of who he once thought he was.' But you—through no fault of your own you can now design your marriage to fit your future."

"I hardly know this woman. What if I don't happen to fall in love with her?"

"Every successful businessman is married. If his wife can't stand him and lives a long-suffering existence, that's all to the good, because it gives him something to bond with his golf buddies about, and it shows that even though he isn't very nice to her, he's got something she's willing to stick around for, at least until he leaves her for someone younger and more beautiful."

"I never thought of it like that."

"Whereas if the younger woman subsequently treats him badly, he doesn't lose any points. I mean, he *gains* points if the younger woman caters to him and makes a big deal of him, but if she's a bitch he's still even. And he might even *lose* points if he sticks with the first wife, depending on whether the guys he associates with have stuck with theirs."

"How did you figure—"

"Big money is like the army or the priesthood or the Senate. It's about being a guy among guys. You have to be very careful of the appearance you project, or you don't look right as a guy."

"Why do I always end one of these conversations with you with the feeling that I should stick with what I know?"

He ignored this. "You can't tell this, but my instinct is, she's right for you." He hung up. Hadn't Betty said something like that when she spoke to me about her?

I spent that day, Sunday, cleaning my condo and thinking about Susan Webster. It was certainly possible to conjure up a fantasy about her. She had a nice neck and a nice smile. She wore sexy shoes. She had a soft voice. She was young. And it was certainly possible to look around my abode and watch what I was doing and wonder what my fate would be if someone like Marcus didn't intervene. Here was my list of jobs for the day:

Wash windows inside and out
Wash windowsills
Pull out refrigerator, mop floor, change
    refrigerator filter
Change furnace filters
Vacuum hot air registers
Clean carpets

Was that a guy's sort of list, apart from the furnace filters? It occurred to me that my guy-ness might rise if I just hired a cleaning lady, but as soon as I thought of that, I thought instantly that she might not do the sort of meticulous job I would do myself. Then I wondered if that was a tycoonish sort of thought (no, of course not) and what a tycoon would do about that, and then I thought, Well, he would probably yell at someone. And say I did marry Susan Webster and she did move into my place, or we found a place together. She painted tiles and wrote, and possibly she wasn't very good at cleaning up after herself, so that would be a whole new can of worms I would have to deal with. I imagined myself down on my hands and knees, a rag in my hand and some turpentine beside me, cleaning up stray dots and dabs of Susan Webster's paints. It was a great antidote to romance, in spite of the sexy shoes.

So I went outside and washed the car inside and out, including removing and vacuuming the floor mats and under the seats, and wiping down the plush upholstery with upholstery cleaner; then I soaped the car with detergent and polished it with carnauba wax and it looked great, and no one would accuse a guy who washed his car of being anything other than a guy. But when I came inside, as I was going to the bathroom to take a shower, I noticed that the tops of the drapes were dusty, and the whole time I was taking my shower and washing my hair and half thinking about where I was going to go that evening—out to eat? to a movie? down to the Viceroy?—that dust niggled in my mind and I just could not help myself; when I was dressed and ready to go out, I got out the vacuum cleaner and put the long wand on it and vacuumed the tops of the drapes, and then I put the vacuum cleaner away, everything having a place and everything being in its place, and after I got into the car I thought about my father, who had taught me these sorts of habits and led me to think, possibly incorrectly, that these were the ways of men, but my father was, if anything, the opposite of a tycoon or an executive, or even a self-made man in the American sense. My father's idea of an important thing to do was to preach submission to the will of God at Sunday service.

By the time I had gone out to dinner and to the movies and come home again and parked my car away from the trees so nothing would drop on it in the night, and in general by the time I had observed myself being careful and persnickety, as my mother would have said, I thought maybe Marcus was right, I needed to find someone. It had been too long since Felicity. I could spend the next however many years lamenting and marveling at the fact that she was married to Hank, or I could get on with it.

The next day when I was at the office, I said, "So, Jane, how did you and your former husband meet, if you don't mind my asking?"

She smiled. "I'll tell you the truth, if you don't tell Marcus."

"What?"

"We met in a hot tub in California. We were both naked."

"You're kidding me."

"Nope. The first words he ever said to me were"—she mimed drawing in her breath and pinching a joint between her thumb and forefinger—"'want a hit?'" She laughed merrily. "And the first words I ever said to him were, 'Is it good shit?' I'd like to say it was all bravado, but it wasn't. I smoked a lot of dope in those days."

"Which days?"

"Late sixties. Some of my girlfriends were in school in Lawrence, so I would go over there from KC every weekend and hang out with them. One August, we drove out to San Francisco and stayed with some friends of theirs for a week. We went down to Big Sur. That's where I met Howie."

"Marcus always makes him out to be Mr. Corporate America."

"Well, he got to be that way. His father was an executive at Boeing. In the end that's what he felt comfortable with. Here I was, this naked chick with long hair and a way with a joint, who had a job at a bank. He loved that combination."

"Why did you get married?"

"Why not? Doesn't everyone?"

"That's what my wife thought. I'm not sure anymore, because we didn't have kids and were never going to have kids." Remembering what Marcus had told me about Jane's divorce, I glanced at her. She was still smiling. "She was—is—a little high-strung."

Jane laughed. "And now you're wondering if I was a little high-strung too."

"I wasn't, but I *could* wonder that."

"Not at all. But guess who took care of darling Marcus and darling Katie and darling Mary Rose when they were infants? I knew how to change a diaper when I was six. So did my mother. I'm sure *her* mother did, too. I thought it was a tradition that needed to end in my generation. Marcus is the only one of us with kids. The girls all ran screaming in the other direction. But the others are young yet."

"What do they do?"

"Well, Katie is actually a nun, but she's radical nun; she's always getting into trouble. Mary Rose is a social worker in White Plains, and Johnny is up to no good in Anchorage, Alaska. No one's seen him in eight years. He used to call my mother every year at Christmas, but when she died, that ended, and we all breathed a sigh of relief. He's a year older than I. You heard the expression Irish twins?"

I nodded.

"He was born at the end of January and I was born the following Christmas. They didn't make *that* mistake again."

"I think *my* problem was that when I was growing up I never actually knew a baby. My cousins were all older, and I was an only child. No one younger ever came into my area. Maybe I didn't think it was possible."

"You sound regretful."

"Well, I never think I might have lived my life differently. But I sometimes wonder if I would have enjoyed someone else's life more than mine."

She laughed.

I said, "Would you do it now?"

"What, have kids?"

"Yeah."

"No. Frankly, I would rather raise dogs. Train dogs. Seeing-eye dogs or tracking dogs. That's my fantasy. You should have seen me eyeballing the pink kennel lady when we were at that meeting last winter. I thought about calling her afterward, but in the end, she didn't project an image I trusted. Would *you* do it now?"

"I'm wondering about that."

"Ah. Well, you know, don't act out of desperation. At least, not yet." She gave me an amused smile.

· · ·

I was still turning these things over a few days later when I was crossing the Cheltenham Park lot between my car and the front door, and I saw, only for a moment, Marcus and the landlady, Mary King. They weren't doing anything suggestive—no kissing or touching or possibly even smiling—I only saw them for a moment, and I didn't register their facial expressions, but I knew instantly that they were having an affair. I kept walking, and I did not turn my head to try and catch another glance. My main thought was that they should not realize I had noticed them or that anything at all had been communicated from them to me.

I went upstairs and sat down in my office. It was late in the day, and Jane had gone home. Marcus's office door was closed and the lights were off. Perhaps he was done for the day too. I sat behind my desk, which was clear, and I set my briefcase on top of it and straightened it so that it aligned with the edge of the desk. I put my hands behind my head and leaned back in my chair so that my hands were against the wall, and I looked out my window at the alley behind Cheltenham Park. There was nothing natural or scenic to see back there. I missed my old office, which at least looked out on traffic and a planted field and my own fence and strip of lawn.

I wondered how naïve I was that I should find this eventuality so surprising. Nothing Marcus actually said about himself implied that he disapproved of or condemned adultery. If he had failed to talk about it, or to reveal through implication or demonstration that he could, would, or had done such a thing, wasn't that discretion? And wasn't Marcus a master of discretion first and foremost? And if I were married to Linda, wouldn't I be tempted to refresh myself elsewhere? And if he was otherwise a good and attentive husband, which I had reason to believe he was, did it make any difference? Not to me, of course, but to her? How was I to know? Maybe, in fact, they had an arrangement. Maybe that was the reason she had said various things to Felicity, who had, after all, told me Linda was an unhappy woman. Marcus sleeping with Mary King. Was that the effect of the unhappiness or the cause?

But it rattled me. I sat there for a long time not exactly liking Marcus or respecting him—I, Joe, who had thought nothing of sleeping with Felicity whenever I could manage it, and who had no feelings about Hank at all except a desire not to get caught. I fiddled around my office, putting things away, then I noticed I was putting things away and I stopped. I told myself it was not a guy thing to care who your friends were sleeping with, and then I put it out of my mind. I did not empty my wastebasket. Instead, I turned out the light, locked my door, and went to my car. Of course, I stared at the Cheltenham Court management office as I walked past it, and then I had a reaction I recognized. I was turned on.

That night I called Susan Webster. She had a soft, melodious voice; I noticed it the moment she answered her phone. She seemed pleasantly surprised to hear from me, and she thought a Saturday-night movie would be fun. Something about her manner on the phone was a relief. Perhaps she had been doing something, painting something, and I had disturbed her briefly. Perhaps she had a busy life and perhaps she was happy no matter whether someone called her or not. Perhaps she wasn't looking for any kind of change, only to expand the life she already had, friend by friend. We laughed a couple of times for no reason. She had a cheerful laugh, too.

When Marcus heard I was taking Susan Webster to a movie, he came into my office and leaned against the edge of a table I had beside the window. He crossed his arms over his chest and grinned at me. "She called Linda, you know. She called—before you ever called her—and said you were cute."

"I am cute. They've been saying I am cute for years. Cute but untrustworthy. Skittish. It's a good thing Susan Webster was living in Spain for ten years, because maybe she doesn't realize what a known quantity I am in these parts." Was this true? I hadn't thought of it before, but it seemed true as I said it. "And there's a whole group of Sherry's friends who have really got my number."

"But I'm telling you—I've been telling you all along—no man is a hero in his own hometown. This is a turning point for you. This girl is a really unusual combination of sophistication and sweetness. It's like she turned twenty and then got put away for ten years. She's behind the times, but she knows lots of things. She's a prize."

"I'm not disagreeing with you, Marcus. But what about the humble shortcomings of yours truly?"

"That's the beauty part. She tried the exotic and it was wrong. She tried someone her own age, and it didn't work out. Now she's looking for something homegrown and more mature."

"We'll see. We haven't even gone out. I've never been alone with her."

"I don't know that you should be alone with her. You know, arranged marriages in Japan and places like that work out fine. Just as well as American marriages, in general, or better. It's a marriage, for God's sake! It's a formal arrangement for which there are numerous models. It's like any other contract. You follow the rules, and it works well enough."

I thought of Mary King.

"And the difference between well enough and great isn't very much, in the end. When kids come along, they take so much of your attention, you can't really tell the difference, and when they're gone you have to start over anyway. I think myself that people take all of this much too seriously. Life is too short. That's what rules are for, so you don't have to reinvent everything."

"Easy for you to talk."

"Do you doubt what I'm saying? You know, I do want to meet your parents, because they must be really good parents or you wouldn't have such a romantic idea about marriage at this point in your life."

"My parents are the perfect example of the idea that you can live up to your ideals every single day of your life, absolutely follow the book, and still get the wrong child."

He laughed. Then he looked at me and laughed again. He said, "Well, look at Jane and me and my sisters. My parents broke every rule in the book and got four bonus babies—no drunks, no shirkers, no ne'er-do-wells." He shook his head.

I said, "Jane said you have a brother."

His grin vanished and he stared at me, then broke his gaze and said, "Sorry. Yes, of course we do. I've pretended for so long that he's just another one of my father's brothers that I let myself forget about him. He was a scary one. Animal torturer and all. Jane says he wasn't that bad, but he was frightening to me." Marcus sighed. "I was so glad Amanda was a girl. And then I was even gladder that Justin was a sweet-natured kid. Still is. Anyway—"

"Anyway, if I follow the marital rules, every-thing will be fine."

"As long as you make a rational choice, and, provisionally, Susan Webster looks like a rational choice. I also don't hold with deciding yes or no early on. Some people, they go out with some-one once and they already know whether they're going to marry that person or not. Very dumb. Not only are you likely to say yes unwisely, you're even more likely to exclude good candi-dates before you've really gotten to know them. So I'm not urging you to decide prematurely—just to recognize that, for now, Susan Webster looks very very good." And then the phone rang and Marcus left and it was Betty calling. She said, "I hear you're finally going out with Susan Webster."

"Who did you hear that from?"

"Felicity heard it from Linda Burns."

"I should have known."

"It's about time, dear. That's such a nice family. Very interesting, all of them. Not just your run-of-the-mill landowners and lawyers. You'll like her."

"I will?"

"Oh, of course you will. She's a very kind person. Original mind. Kind of a sly quality underneath it all that's very appealing. She's one of the ones that grow on you, I think. Starts out good and gets better."

"What about me, Betty? What sort of references am *I* getting?"

"What do you think, dear? Sterling ones, of course. Everyone is very prejudiced in your favor, you know that. Apart from my granddaughter Peachie, who was going to keep you to herself. She told Susan's mother you have a black fungus between your toes that is very contagious and Susan should stay away from you. Then she confessed to me that she had read about that in a comic book and was just trying it out to see if it would scare them off."

GOOD FAITH

So, in short, my first date with Susan Webster was as public as possible.

All of this was on my mind when I picked up my phone to call Susan to tell her I was going to be ten minutes late and discovered that my phone was dead. It was Saturday night, very inconvenient, but I didn't think about it again. When I got to her place, she was sitting on her front stoop, lit by her porch light, smoking a cigarette. She had her elbow on her knee and was gazing pensively up at the cigarette. Smoke rose in a lazy curl toward the light. She was wearing a hat. Her hair, which she had worn up for our dinner with Marcus and Linda, spread out from under her hat along the angle of her neck and down her back almost to her waist. She saw me when I pulled up, and took another luxurious drag on her cigarette before stubbing it out and standing up. She dropped the butt into a flowerpot sitting on the concrete banister of the porch and approached the car with a smile. She opened the passenger door and leaned into the car. "Is that you?"

"It is."

Her hair fell forward in a graceful mass, and

she pushed it back. I was impressed. She had a sensuous quality I had forgotten, or possibly missed. I wondered why I had been so reluctant. She got into the car and closed her door. I said, "I used to smoke. Watching you take that last drag made me wish I still did."

"Did it? I just started when I got back to the States. I only smoke a pack a week. But my mother is scandalized. It took her years to quit."

We drove along. She said, "It's very nice, isn't it? I see that people do it for a reason. I never realized that before." She fell silent for a moment, then said, "How are you?"

"I'm fine."

"I've noticed there's a kind of hushed, anticipatory quality about this date. I can only attribute that to the fact that my mother and aunts have been praying steadily since you called, and they've succeeded in changing the weather this time."

I laughed and said, "What are they praying for?"

"I suppose that I will be rescued at the last minute from a life they can't imagine—or, rather, *another* life they can't imagine. The first one was bad enough. When I got home from Spain, I was just sort of pulling myself together and trying to remember words for things like *bread* and *won't you please sit down?* and my Aunt Nona came up to me and said, 'Oh, Susan! What can I say? Your mother was so upset when you got married, and then, my land, you got divorced! You know, it broke her heart, but don't tell her I told you!' And now I'm single!" She threw up her hands and grinned at me.

"Me too."

"They know that. They prayed for that, and their prayers were answered, and so they are praying harder than ever."

Her tone was lighthearted, casual. We passed under a streetlamp and I glanced at her. The expression on her face fit her tone. Once again I thought she was more interesting than I expected. Why wouldn't Marcus and Betty be right?

It went like that for the rest of the evening, unexpectedly enjoyable and relaxed, and then something additional that was even more unexpected behind that. She had a self-assured and self-reliant sensuousness that become more evident when she talked about the art she liked to do. I liked that especially. It was like being shown a secret. We went to dinner. She ate heartily. We went to the movie. She laughed readily. We went for a drink, not at the Viceroy but at a fancier place in Deacon. She asked me in some detail about the project, looked right at me when I told her about the houses and the golf course and Marcus and Gordon. She had a kind of slow nod followed by a quick smile that indicated to me that she was interested or, at least, interested enough. I took her home about two. She didn't invite me in. She didn't even think about it, as far as I could tell. I liked that too. I said I would call her. She pushed her hair back and said in a low, musical voice, "I would like that."

CHAPTER 22

SUNDAY AFTERNOON, when I picked up the phone to call Susan, the line was still dead, so I put on my clothes and a jacket and went outside to see if I could figure out the problem. One time before, a branch had fallen behind the condo unit, where there were some large trees, and severed the line. I had fixed it myself.

But out behind the condos, everything was fine. I knocked on my neighbors' door. The wife answered and I asked her if her phone was working.

"Oh, yes, I was just talking to my daughter. Are some of the phones out?"

"Mine is."

"Oh, I know. I saw them Thursday. They

were here turning it off for nonpayment." She looked carefully nonjudgmental.

"They were?"

"They were right out there. Nick, here, saw them, and I went out and talked to them." She shook her head and closed the door.

I hadn't seen a phone bill in four months.

On Monday, Jane told me I had better talk to Marcus. Marcus didn't come in until late in the afternoon. By that time, I had ascertained that I owed the phone company a hundred and forty-six dollars, that my bill was owing from July, and that they had sent me two cancellation notices. I told them I would be passing their office toward the end of the day and would bring a check. Marcus was standing in the door to my office, listening. I hung up and said, "Why didn't you pay my phone bill?"

"When did you notice it was off?"

"Saturday evening."

"See? It was off for two days and you didn't even realize it. What does that tell you? You aren't using that phone. It's an unnecessary expense."

"A phone is necessary. What if there's a fire or something?"

"Leave the house."

I took my checkbook out of the drawer and

began to write a check. Marcus said, "Are you paying that out of your own pocket?"

"Well, you didn't pay it. Or Jane didn't. My neighbor was very disapproving. The phone guy told her all about it."

"We let it go a little too long, I admit."

"I always pay my bills on time."

"Why?"

"Why? Why do I always pay my bills on time?"

"That's a very bad habit."

"Pardon me?"

"You train them to consider you a patsy. You can't believe how the collection agencies treat the ones who always pay on time and then get a little behind. Brutal." He came into my office and closed the door. "I can see that you and I need to have a little talk."

"About what?"

"About what we need to do here. Now, Joe, we're trying to eke our funds out as long as we can, right?"

"I suppose." I thought of that eight hundred thousand dollars coming in for Jane's Kansas farm, but I didn't say anything just then.

"The permitting process isn't going as fast as we thought it would, right?"

"Well—"

"Be that as it may, and I'm not blaming you or

anyone, things go as they go and you have to accept that. Right? Right. Anyway, look, here's the deal. Here's the main life lesson I learned at the IRS. As long as you keep in touch, you're fine."

"What does that mean?"

"This is something everyone does. No one has enough money to follow his vision and also pay all his bills. That's the point of a windfall. A windfall is like an overnight success. You work hard for it and sweat and then, all of a sudden, there's plenty of money—more than you ever expected—and that's when you pay all those bills you let accumulate. No one really cares that you let them accumulate. They say they do, and they yell and scream and even try to bully you, but everyone knows the same thing— they'll get it eventually. So you string them along, pay them a little now and then so they don't cut you off, and when your ship comes in you settle up. You know how they feel?"

"How?"

"Grateful. They feel grateful that you paid your bill. You know how they feel when you pay up every month, right on time?"

"How?"

"They feel as though they have a right to your money."

"Don't they?"

"Do they? Wouldn't you rather they felt grateful?"

I looked down at the checkbook, in which I had written out a check to the phone company. I said, "I prefer having a phone, and believe me I can still afford to pay the bill."

"Make it out for half and order a couple of new services. Whatever they have, then make out a separate check for those services. That way, they see that you're going to be an even bigger customer, so they'll extend you more credit. You could even get yourself a couple of more lines."

"I don't need any more lines."

"Joe. I don't think you get the point. Here's another accounting tip. It's important always for a business to grow, especially a business like the phone company, where they already have the whole market. So they focus a lot of corporate attention on growth. Collection isn't as important, because they always have a certain amount of bad debt; it's written off or sold and is, at any rate, a part of doing business. But they don't want to look like they're not growing. So you pay enough of your debt so they'll turn the phone back on and then place an order. They have more to gain by accepting your business than by turning it away, especially if you talk to a supervisor about the number of phone lines you expect that we're going to install in our development, with the clubhouse and all, and you ask a few questions about state-of-the-art and what's coming."

"Collections isn't the same department as new service. It might not even be in the same building."

"If you go far enough up the chain of command, the branches will cross, and some guy will make a deal with you. Why not? It works with other businesses. Try it with the phone company." He shrugged.

"I take it that you've never tried this with the phone company."

"Not around here. Worked like a charm on Long Island. If you can't get a peon to turn it on, keep going up the chain of command and talking about what you need, and eventually someone will do it. If you want my help, let me know." He went out.

I remembered how my mother used to carry her payments around on the streetcar, always careful to pay up on time, as if electrical service and telephone service and everything else were a privilege. Maybe she felt that they were.

Even though I was perfectly willing to pay my bill, I decided to try Marcus's idea, just to see how far I could go—and, I admit, to see if I could show Marcus up for once. Long Island wasn't the same as Marlborough County. I pretended I was Marcus and took on his smooth, friendly tone. I chatted up everyone I could reach. Martin Cranston, the supervisor I ended up working with, was only too happy to oblige. I almost offered to pay my phone bill at the last minute, but in the end I played it out. It was interestingly different from a real estate negotiation in that there was no tension. I was indeed trying to put something over on him, and he knew it, but he didn't seem to care. Real estate negotiations were more often than not edgy because even though the property in question was there for everyone to see, and quite often the buyers and their representatives had seen it over and over and found nothing really wrong with it, buyers were often worried that something was missing, or something would be taken away, or something would be left behind (toxic waste, for example). Sellers, on the other hand, didn't like to feel that their honesty—or even worse, their taste—was being denigrated. But for Martin Cranston and me, the problem was only money, and not even his money at that. We parted very warmly, and I promised to call him as soon as we were ready to install phone service for Salt Key Farm, and he promised to keep me posted about the latest developments in telecommunications, which were about to change in unprecedented ways, Martin confided in me, and, frankly, I felt very executive when I had hung up the phone.

• • •

Once the phone was turned on again, I started calling Susan Webster. I would tell myself that I wasn't going to, and I would plan to be doing something else before going to bed, but then I would call her anyway, in spite of my anxiety that I was being a pest. The problem was her melodious voice with just that hint of an accent. She often paused while talking, which she told me was because she was trying to think of English words when she could only think of Spanish ones. One time she said, "You know, I was terribly shy in English, but I was never shy in Spanish. My in-laws thought I was a tremendously forward young woman. It didn't even have to do with fluency, I was just a completely different person in Spanish. I thought it was unusual until I met a woman who had been married to a South African man. In English he was very harsh and hard to get along with, but he could be very affectionate and kind in Zulu, because that was the language his nurse spoke when he was a child." This seemed marvelously exotic to me. But maybe I called her because I could. All those times I had thought of Felicity and known not to call her, and the only time I *had* called her Hank had answered. Now I could just pick up the phone and she would answer and say, "Oh! Hi! Is it you?" It was a luxury I tried out over and over.

We went out again a couple of times. She came

to my place. I went to hers. No towels or T-shirts were hanging over railings. Her house (a small rental in Roaring Falls) was bright and idiosyncratic. It didn't look blank and even empty, like mine, or uncared for, like Felicity's and Hank's place. It looked like only she could have made it the way it was and that she paid attention to it. Without saying so, I decided that must be what was termed *artistic*. That was exciting too. I compared her favorably to Felicity, and in my comparison I discovered a hidden and heretofore unrealized resentment. I had thought Felicity was perfect, that our arrangement was perfect, that I had let our arrangement go because I had known all along it was temporary. But now I was glad, even to the point of getting a repetitive little thrill every time I thought of it, that Susan Webster had so much more to offer than Felicity. Felicity, you might say—I came to think—had been lucky to find me, since I went along with whatever she wanted, but it was me who was lucky to find Susan Webster, who was, as Marcus had told me all along, a superior model.

And I was in no hurry to sleep with her, contrary to my usual MO. What I really wanted to do more than anything was to call her on the phone late in the evening and hear her talk. Given the inevitability of our future together, I thought, I was happy to prolong the preliminary stages as much as possible.

I paid more attention to Marcus and Mary King. I was waiting for two things from Marcus. One of them was a single undeniable sign that he knew that I knew that he and Mary King were having an affair, and the other was news about the eight hundred thousand dollars that was winging its way toward us.

Instead, he came into my office every day and lamented the ineptitude of Jim Crosbie and his attempts to get his savings-and-loan sold to some big buyer or other.

"The problem," he would say, "is so obvious. It makes me crazy. I could walk right in there and make it go. I mean, I know what it sounds like to say that, but Jim Crosbie is the wrong person for this job. He's basically a sad sack combined with a tough guy. He doesn't know how to give them what they want when they want it. That's a timing thing and a personality thing. You have to be able to read the other guy and know what's going to turn him on. But Jim is a turf protector. He has no instincts. I mean, I know they installed him as an administrator because the joint was falling apart, but you know what kind of guy this is at heart? He's the kind of guy who goes out to lunch and then divides up the bill down to the penny, and then all the way out of the restaurant, he's saying, 'Now, Fred, you owe another ninety-seven cents on the tip, and George, I think you owe extra because you had a side of fries.' Makes me want to wring his neck. But another thing about those kinds of guys is they're very sensitive to slights and they have radar. If you disapprove of something they're doing, they just back off."

I said, "They've got plenty of money from something. I told you I ran into Bart in August, and he was waving his tickets to France around and saying they were making a killing in T-bill futures."

"Very iffy. And Crosbie doesn't have the mind of a real investment genius. I mean, I'm sure things are running his way right now, but—"

He went out. He came back in.

"Bart is better. You know, Bart could do this merger, but he's so impressed with Crosbie that he doesn't do a thing. Crosbie makes him stupid. I can see it going through his mind. 'I don't agree with this guy, but he's a big shot and I'm not, so he must be right; we'll do it his way.' That's so local. That's how local guys just fail to break out, you know?"

He went out. He came back in.

"So what if this big S and L from out West looks like it's expanded too fast? Looks are deceiving. If they'd just ask me, I could tell you in an hour or two what was up with the books. But it's like empresses meeting, or the negotiations at the end of the Vietnam War. It's all about the shape of the table and who's going to sit where. If they would put that through, I wouldn't have to spend all my time beating the bushes for investors with ten thousand dollars to spend."

I decided to bring up the eight hundred thousand dollars, which I hadn't heard a single word about in weeks, not since Marcus's letter came to me.

"Oh, that! That's another thing. Where is that money? Is it just incompetence over there? I mean, you saw how they sent the letter to the wrong person. Or don't they really want to give it to us? You know what? You should call Bart, or even go to lunch with him, and feel him out about all of this. I thought I was in Crosbie's complete confidence, and maybe I am, but the closer I get to him, the more I think his mind works like some sort of labyrinth. I think he spends more time thinking about rugs and paintings than actual business."

"I didn't know Jane had that kind of property out West."

"Jane?"

"The thousand-acre ranch?"

"Oh, that." He laughed and looked at me for a

moment, then said, "Well, it would be a tragedy if she'd been out in the godforsaken plains all those years and had nothing to show for it."

"I guess."

"But on the other hand, there's real estate and then there's unreal estate, as they say." He walked out. My phone rang. I spent fifteen minutes talking to my mother about where my father might be, and by the time my father walked in and relieved her fears, Marcus was gone.

In the course of the day, Marcus called me four times. First to urge me to have lunch with Bart, and then to coach me on what I was going to say to him. Finally I said, "You have a lot of trouble delegating, don't you, Marcus?"

He replied, "You know God? How God is omnipotent, omniscient, and omnipresent?"

"Sure."

"Which one would you like if you could just have one?"

"With my upbringing, if I think a thought like that, I will die."

He laughed, then said, "Omnipresent for me. My greatest frustration is that I can only be in one place at a time." He hung up.

I bullied Bart into having breakfast with me the next morning, and he didn't seem happy about it.

He was willing to meet me at a Denny's near Portsmouth Savings' new offices, but when I got there I saw he was much different from the way he had been before his trip. He ordered melon and Special K with skim milk, black coffee, and grapefruit juice. I ordered eggs, bacon, and home fries. He stared at my meal and shook his head, but all he said was, "You ought to come over and look at the plans for our new building. You've never seen anything like it."

"You sound glum about it."

"Do I? I don't mean to. It's nice."

Marcus had told me not to seem curious but just let him talk. If the conversation failed, so much the better, because then he would say more when he started up again. "Order a big meal, and then if you can't resist opening your mouth, just put something in it." I thought maybe the new offices were a safe topic, though. "I bet they're pretty posh."

"I'm telling you, the home owner isn't who we're aiming at anymore. When the home owners come in, they'll be intimidated." Bart spooned up his melon until it was just a thin bowl-shaped skin. He took a sip of his coffee. "You've got to be thankful, though, that things aren't the way they were a couple of years ago. Now we've got a chance, anyway."

"A chance?"

GOOD FAITH

"Two years ago, you know, I was looking for another job. I thought the place was going to go under. My daughter Ginger and I were all set to go into the physical training business. We had the plans, and we were going to build a gym. Well, not that grand, but a fitness center. Fitness, weight training, aerobics classes. That Jane Fonda thing."

"That sounds like a good idea. But I always thought you guys were doing fine over there."

He said, "Ha!" and shrugged, then, "Good thing interest rates went down and the S and L picture changed. I said to Ginger, 'I don't want to get out at the bottom.' And we could still do the fitness center. She's taking some classes over at the junior college in the recreation department, just in case. How to keep old people going is what she's taking this fall. That should come in handy, no matter what." He laughed, suddenly a little brighter.

Now was when the conversation died. I was tempted to push about two years ago, but in accordance with Marcus's instructions, I kept eating and eating. He sighed. I ate. He sighed again and put his napkin in his lap, then motioned to the waitress for another cup of coffee. She came over, gave him a smile, and said, "So, how's tricks in the money business?"

"Tricky," he said. She left and he took a sip of coffee. He said, "So, what's up?"

"Not much. It looks like we're going to have the preliminary building permits by the first of the year. Marcus is looking at builders now." I leaned forward. "Not to hire them, but to raid their crews. Gottfried keeps telling me he's about to finish those houses he started in the spring, but he doesn't ask me to market them. I think he's using them as bargaining chips."

"Gottfried isn't your man." We looked at each other for a long moment.

I said, "I know that. We could hire him to refurbish the clubhouse, though. I suggested that to Marcus. He could do that through the winter. It's not going to take much that I can see, though I'm sure the wiring and the plumbing have to be brought up to code."

"Can't cut any corners with this place, that's for sure. Crosbie was saying just yesterday that—well, frankly, that Gordon Baldwin is the wrong name to have on this project. His name is not a byword for quality, Joe."

I shrugged. "Too bad, because he's in it up to his hairline."

"Tell me about it. Every property he's got is cross-collateralized. Even the house."

"Even the house?"

"All the farms, the store, everything. The weekly poker game is cross-collateralized." Bart chuckled at his own joke. Then he said, "Even so, I think he's going to be a PR problem."

"We'll see. Anyway, so no fitness center?"

"Not here, at any rate."

"Somewhere else?"

He shrugged. "Look around. Do you see any joggers? Most of the times I go to the gym, there's me and three guys I've known since college. But it's big business in other places."

"What places?"

I listened closely. He said, "Well, Denver. Colorado's the fittest state in the union. Minneapolis. Lots of outdoor sports there too. Seattle. Run on the treadmill and read a book at the same time. That's what they do in Seattle. No sunshine, of course."

"Hmm." I thought about the eight hundred thousand, but I didn't have the gumption to ask about it.

That was all I got out of him. When I reported this conversation back to Marcus, he said, "Big, big S and Ls in Denver, Minneapolis, and Seattle. They could merge now, since deregulation, but who's doing it? Who's making it happen? That's what's driving me crazy, because I don't trust Crosbie to make it happen. Business is about relationships. Marriage is about contracts and business is about relationships. Remember that talk we had about marriage? Well, this is the other side, the other paradox. Business is much more exacting in terms of the demands made on your relationship skills than marriage. And Crosbie has no relationship skills at all that I can see. It drives me crazy."

No one said anything to me about the payments we now owed every month on the farm. I would wake up in the night sometimes and think about them, think about my name on the note, and the next day I would call around that much more industriously to keep the permitting process going forward. When the permits were granted, then the great sell-off of lots would begin, and we would all be okay. Better than okay. I told myself this wasn't that different from anything else. There was always a touchy middle period to any project, where you'd sunk a lot into it, too much to walk away, and you had to keep sinking more into it, more than you'd planned, in order to get to the place where the returns would begin. That was almost a rule of projects, I knew, whether the project was adding a room onto your house or, let's say, building a space program or making a movie. Cost overruns. Thoroughly routine. Nothing to get excited about.

Mike Lovell, who was in and out of the office all the time, viewed me with suspicion. At first I didn't wonder why, since I viewed him with suspicion and it seemed natural that he would reciprocate my feelings. I especially viewed him with suspicion when he began dressing in suits rather than work clothes. This happened as the fall got colder—jeans and T-shirts gave way to khakis and jackets which, sometime after Halloween, gave way to a gray suit, with a green shirt and a dark red tie. He sat in the office sometimes for hours at a time, reading magazines that he brought with him. Those changed too, from *Field and Stream* and *Popular Mechanics* to *Money* and *Consumer Reports*. Sometimes he would go into Marcus's office and be in there for an hour or more. Finally, I said to Jane, "What is Mike's job?"

"That's an interesting question."

"Do you know the answer?"

"Well, his job used to be general lackey. I mean, he said to me last spring that he wanted to make something of himself, and now was the time, and he was going to sit around the office and wait until Marcus would take him on, and I said why, and he said that he'd been to a self-help seminar and the guy who ran it said everyone should find a mentor and more or less wear the guy out until the guy agreed to teach him three different things."

"So that was what he was doing around here after we switched the tanks? Waiting for Marcus to teach him three different things?"

"More or less."

"And now."

"He's very helpful."

"I hadn't noticed."

"Helpful to Marcus. He hasn't yet generalized his interest to the rest of us."

"I still don't know what he does."

"He gathers information."

"Excuse me?"

"Well, it started last spring, when he was first coming in. Marcus would get him to gossip about everyone out in Plymouth Township. He knew a lot of gossip. Marcus wanted to know everything: who was sleeping with whom, who was paying their bills and who wasn't, what properties might come on the market, who was related to whom, all that sort of thing."

"Why?"

"Just to know. Just because he's interested. Some fact might turn up. For example, you know the bottled water idea?"

"Yeah."

"Well, he kind of dropped that with regard to the farm, but it stayed in his mind. You know the place out there; it's farther back in the county, almost to the state park, what's the name—oh, the Underwood Farm on May Hill Road."

"Yeah. I've been by there, years ago. My dad knew Frank Underwood."

"Tremendous spring on that farm. It was famous a hundred years ago. It was called Saint Lucy's Spring, or something like that. Anyway, Mike knew all about it. Marcus has been out there three or four times. I can't say the Underwoods are interested in selling it to him, but they don't mind him coming out there. That was one thing he learned from Mike. And there's a quarry somewhere out there too, an old slate quarry. Slate roofs all over that area."

"The clubhouse has a slate roof."

"Bingo. And the ownership of that quarry is very complex. Lots of heirs who didn't even know they owned a quarry, things like that. I think Marcus is negotiating with someone in Alaska who's never even been to this part of the country. But it would be great to have a source of slate just like the slate on the roof of the clubhouse. Not for every house, mind you, but a few."

"A few expensive ones." I smiled. Once again, Marcus impressed me. He just didn't think like everyone else. Once again, I felt lucky he'd come along. "What three things did Marcus teach Mike?"

533

"So far?" She rolled her eyes discreetly toward the ceiling. "Let's see. How to dress." She paused. "Almost. How to read what rich people read rather than what garage mechanics read. It's kind of a *My Fair Lady* thing, really. And how to play the commodities market."

"How to do what?"

"Oh, you know. Pork bellies. Wheat. Soybeans. Mike went out to Chicago a couple of months ago. Didn't you notice?"

"I noticed he wasn't around at one point."

"That's where he was. He was having a field trip."

"What do you think about this, Jane?"

"I don't agree with it. But you know how Marcus takes people up. He gets infatuated. You must have noticed that he fancies himself a great teacher. He told Linda, who told me, that Mike was the perfect sow's ear. He goes over there all the time. Linda can't stand him." Jane shrugged.

"Marcus told me that after the billion comes in, he's going to quit business and write books."

"Or endow a business school. Did he mention that?"

"Why doesn't he teach the guy some manners?"

"Why indeed?" said Jane.

I was on my way out of the office, and what she had said started me ruminating. I wondered how I fit in with Marcus's idea of himself. Had he just taken me up in order to show me something? Our friendship did have that side. Wasn't that a side I was grateful for? And hadn't I agreed when he showed Bobby how to get himself together? Bobby had had a little more on the ball, at least around the office, ever since his dressing-down by Marcus. He looked better, he seemed to be less goofy, and he hadn't injured himself in months. And he was an even bigger fan of Marcus, though at the same time he more or less stayed out of his way. At the Baldwins' Labor Day picnic, I'd asked him if he'd ever sorted out his books, and he grinned a big wide grin. He said, "God! Marcus sent in a twenty-five- or thirty-page tax return! You couldn't understand a thing on it. He said those IRS guys get paid by the unit, so if there's lots of pages and it doesn't look like there's going to be a big payoff, they just ignore it. My personal opinion, Joe, is that this guy is the best thing that ever happened to us, but I'm not saying he isn't irritable. I'm not saying that at all." And then I passed Mary King's office. She wasn't there, but the light was on. Her office had changed too, in the last year. It was decorated with more taste and comfort. The whole building was full now, no unleased space. Was that owing to Marcus too?

My mother had always said to think about something nice before going to sleep, so that night, on the phone, I told Susan Webster about the old slate quarry. She said, rather sleepily, "Where is that, out past Plymouth Village? Not far from the state park?"

"I'm not sure exactly, but somewhere around there."

"Who owns that is the Burmeister family. There was this kid in my class in high school, Mickey Burmeister." She went on. "So, have you and Marcus Burns been friends for a long time?"

"Friends, maybe a year. He only moved into the area about a year and a half ago. I sold him his house."

"I can't figure him out."

"How so?"

"Well, it has to do with that kid of his, Justin. He's such a fearful kid. If you come up behind him and make a noise, he jumps. I've had that happen twice, both times when I thought he knew I was right there. I mean, I wasn't sneaking up or anything. I thought the kid was going to shriek."

"What would that have to do with Marcus? Maybe he's just a fearful kid."

"Maybe."

"Or he could take after Linda. She strikes me as kind of on the fearful side."

"But why should they be fearful? Do they have something to be afraid of?"

"Oh, I doubt it." But what about Mary King? "He always talks about them with affection and respect. He's crazy about Justin." I kept thinking of Mary King. Even a little kid could sense if his home life wasn't quite as secure as it had been, as he would like it to be. "I'm an only child, so I don't know much about it, but it's the sister who strikes me as fearsome. Amanda. Maybe Justin thought you were Amanda and you were going to—"

"Rake my sharpened fingernails down his back?" She laughed. "Actually, I did that once, when I was eleven and my brother John was nine. I got my mother's nail file and sharpened all my fingernails to points so I could draw blood the next time I caught him in my room." She laughed again. "If I had to judge by my own experience, it isn't good to have the girl first."

That night I woke up for about the tenth time in a couple of weeks, worrying about the unheard-of farm payment. I rolled around for about half an hour, got up and read for a while, then went back to sleep and dreamt I was driving around looking for Felicity. I drove into a long driveway and found Sherry. She was doing some kind of construction—I could see excavations. I explained to her in a panicky way that I was looking for Felicity and drove off. Then it got dark, and I could see Felicity down the street, almost invisible, except that she was wearing a white sweater. When I came up to her, she leaned in the window of my car, smiling and very beautiful, and she put her hand on my face. She was loving and reassuring—not as energetic as the real Felicity, but softer and more soothing. She comforted me, and when I woke up, I felt well and truly comforted, comforted without any resistance, comforted as you could only be comforted in a dream. I turned over and went back to sleep. When I woke up the next morning, it seemed to me that I had experienced some kind of bona fide miracle, a visitation. I remembered that dream for days, a sign of how happy and how reassured it was possible to be.

CHAPTER 23

A FEW DAYS AFTER my conversation with Jane about Mike, I pulled into a parking place at Cheltenham Park, and when I got out of the car I saw that Mike Lovell was leaning against a car—his car, no doubt—a few spaces down. When he saw me open my door, he came toward me. He said, "Trouble up there."

"How do you mean?"

"When I got here this morning, the two of them were having a screaming fight. I could hear it all the way down the hallway. When I got to the door, I waited for a couple of minutes, but they were really going at it, so I just turned around and came back out. I been up there one time since, about twenty minutes ago. They were still going at it."

"Could you make out what it was about?"

"Nope. She was calling him six kinds of a bastard, was all I heard, and he kept saying, 'Goddammit, Jane! Goddammit, Jane!' I don't know if you want to go up there."

"Well, why not? At least we can maybe see what's going on. Or pull them apart if we have to."

But when we got to the office, all was quiet. I opened the door as if I had no idea that there was anything wrong, and there was Jane, sitting at her desk. She caroled, "Good morning, Joey!" No bruises, anyway. Mike and I glanced at each other. The door to Marcus's office was closed. Mike said, "He got anything for me?"

"You'd have to ask him that. I wouldn't know," said Jane.

"Okay," said Mike. But instead of knocking on Marcus's door, he went over to the mail basket and picked it up. He said, "I guess I'll mail these things, since I have to go to the PO, anyway."

"That's fine," said Jane.

Mike departed. I went into my office. I was preparing final instructions for the engineer, which involved writing up some things that we had been talking about—mostly heating and wiring changes in the clubhouse that would bring it up to code. I was also getting ready to call Gottfried and give him the job. We had been leaving each other messages for about two weeks. If we really wanted to talk to one another, we both knew how—I could go to his job site or he could call me at 6 A.M.—but we didn't really want to talk to each other at this point, so we left messages with each other's services, saying that we did, during business hours. I put a piece of paper in my typewriter. Everything was quiet. After a bit, I heard the outer office door open and close; then, a moment after that, my office door opened and Marcus came in. He closed the door behind him.

I sat back in my chair. "Was that Jane leaving?"

"Yeah."

"Are you and Jane having a disagreement?"

"A misunderstanding."

"Was she leaving for good, by any chance?"

"Oh, God, no. She was going out to get her hair cut. She'll be back in a hour and a half. What's that?"

"I had a meeting with Ralph Hokanson yesterday about retrofitting the kitchen area. I'm just writing that up. He and Gottfried are going to meet with Jerry on Monday. Then Gottfried can get started. Say."

"Say."

"Say, do we have enough to pay those big payments on the farm that started to be due the first of this month?"

"We don't have to pay yet."

"How'd you manage that?"

"Crosbie got Bernie Wrightsman to reappraise the property, and they loaned us more money. They're covering the payments themselves for an additional six months out of the loan amount. Until we're in a position to sell some lots." He said this as if it were routine, but two years before, or even a year, such a thing would have been unheard of. I was relieved, if a little suspicious. But Marcus had said from the beginning that it was a new world, and every time he turned out to be right. I said, "What did they appraise it at?"

"Five."

"Five what?" I sat back and looked at him. He was smiling.

"Five million."

"I don't see how it's doubled in value in a year, even with what we've done. Real estate around here's only gone up about sixteen–eighteen percent. And that's close to Deacon. Out by Plymouth—"

"Well, you know, I had a talk with Bernie about that, and he agreed with Crosbie that we're so close to the permits that it really doesn't make a lot of difference. A month or two, right?"

"That's the best case; but, you know, the best case can—"

"Now, Joe. You have to be the positive thinker. You're the one who meets with these people and does this sort of thing. If you look like you're willing to wait, they'll make you wait. I'm not talking about getting angry or irritable. It's something different. It's more like pulling them along in your wake. See what I mean?"

But he didn't have his usual verve and fire. I nodded. I said, "You want to talk about the thing with Jane?"

"Oh, it was nothing, really. Family spat, not business. It's amazing we haven't done it before, really. What's it been, almost a year since she got here? Anyway, we're older, but we still have to blow off steam once in a while. That's all." I nodded. I was relieved about the payment, really relieved. And my relief felt exactly like it had after my dream of Felicity.

It took me about a day to realize that Jane and Marcus weren't speaking, and by that time it was Friday. But they still weren't speaking on Monday and on Tuesday. Jane sat at her desk in a state of high chill toward Marcus. When he came in or went out, she turned her back on him but glanced at him out of the corner of her eye. His demeanor was more interesting—he was never smoother, but not in the least abashed or embarrassed. It was impossible to tell from their behavior who owed whom an apology.

On Tuesday, standing in front of Jane's desk, knowing Marcus was in his office with the door ajar, I said in a somewhat loud voice, "Well, I'm going to go find Gottfried and put him on this job."

Jane nodded.

I said, "I have to go to his job site. I can't find him any other way and I'm ready to commit."

Jane glanced toward Marcus's office. We waited. Normally, Jane would have called out "Marcus? That all right with you?" or "Marcus, you want to come in here?" but she didn't say a word. We waited for another moment. I said, "Okay, I'm going. Time and materials. I guess we're all agreed." And I thought we were; we'd talked about this several times among the four of us, Marcus, Gordon, Jane, and myself. I looked at Jane. We shrugged and I turned and went out of the office.

As I was unlocking the door of my car, Marcus trotted up behind me. "Hey," I said.

"Yeah. Everything's fine about Gottfried. I guess we've got to think of something about the office, though, because Jane is really digging her heels in. Frankly, if it weren't you and Mike, I'd be a little embarrassed, but I figure we're good enough friends by this time that a little frost in the air isn't really a problem. I mean, other than practical."

"No big deal," I said.

"To tell you the truth, it kind of puts a spoke in my theoretical wheel, because you know I kind of pride myself on making things go, greasing the skids, all that. You're not supposed to say this, but women in the office can be a problem, just because of the way they do things. Frankly, I didn't expect this sort of thing from Jane. It's very capricious, but hell, what can you say?"

"What happened in the first place?"

He glanced at me. "It started with Linda. She said something and then Jane said something and then Linda said something back, and you know how that goes. Linda felt judged by Jane, and Jane felt offended by Linda. Well, *that* went on for two days. You know how women are. And then I thought I had to get in on it. Really, I was just kind of playing the mediator. But mediation is something I consider myself good at, so I was thinking just how great I was going to do with them, and now neither one of them is speaking to me, because they *both* think I'm on the other one's side."

"It's been almost a week, Marcus."

"Is that all? I thought it was three lifetimes. Now my strategy is to just keep my mouth shut."

"Do you want to go with me to find Gottfried?"

He shook his head. I got in my car and pulled out of my spot.

The weather was dampish and brown. All the leaves were off the trees, and the countryside had a look about it that I liked, that made me think of the word *Umbria*. I'd had been in Italy during November once, with Sherry, and I'd enjoyed it—driving through the small towns, seeing game birds, rabbits, and deer hanging everywhere, along with piles of autumn vegetables and flowers. It had seemed very exotic and alluring to me, the raw materials of savory hot meals, provisions for the winter gathered everywhere. Sherry had liked it too, not being at all squeamish, and we had enjoyed those few days quite a bit. Once in a while, only for a day or two in the year, the color of my plain old American countryside was *Umbrian*.

I found Gottfried at the site of his second house, the one that was a little less finished. I hadn't seen it since it was in the framing stage. This one was also in Blue Valley, maybe a mile from Marcus's house. It was a beautiful place—a rambling American farmhouse style, white with a black peaked roof, with a porch that wrapped around three sides of the one-story section and a taller two-story section, white-accented with black shutters, that rose above that. It was sited on its lot in a very welcoming way. If I'd had the wife and the kids, I would have bought it from him right then. I had a single happy thought of Susan Webster as I turned into the driveway.

Gottfried and Dale were in the kitchen. As soon as Gottfried saw me, he charged. "Have you been up there?"

"Where?"

"To my house I built, the beautiful Queen Anne you sold to that asshole."

"Marcus?"

"That's the one."

"I was there for dinner a few weeks—"

"Did you see what they did?"

I thought of several things but didn't dare name any one of them. I held my peace.

"Did you?"

"I don't know."

"They put up a *red* roof! Why did they put on a red roof?"

"I think they had some tree damage from a storm—"

"But red! That house had a perfectly good black roof, the absolutely right black roof!

They could have repaired it! I would have sent a roofer, but they reroofed the whole thing in this shitty red color."

"It's their house, Gottfried."

"I never trusted that guy. He's too sharp."

"Taste isn't a moral question, Gottfried."

"Oh, you don't think so?" He said this so pugnaciously I stepped back and looked at Dale, who gave me a maybe-yes-maybe-no sort of shrug. "I'm finished."

I glanced at Dale again, who by this time wasn't looking at me. I said, "What do you mean, Gottfried?"

"I've had it."

"Had what?"

"I can't work with you people. I can't do the house at the farm. I can't renovate it. That guy is going to be in my face all the time, telling me to change this and change that and try this and try that and this thing, whatever it is, won't be so bad. I can tell you right now I won't have a free hand, and between us all we're going to screw it up. That house is a work of art. I won't wreck it."

"No, you won't. You're about the only person who won't."

"Who's paying?" He almost shouted this.

"We are."

"So I've got to do it *your* way. That's the way

it works. The guy who pays has the say. That's the way it works. I can't do that."

I looked at him, then looked around the room. They had put up plain pine cabinets with black wrought-iron pulls in the shape of oak leaves. The cabinets had lots of knots in the wood and were a rich yellow color. The floorboards were of differing widths, also pine. Gottfried had laid the interesting knots in the middle where they could be appreciated. I said, "Well, you've never done that, that's true, but you're always complaining about the carrying costs of taking your own loans and building on spec. This is a way out of that. You finished these houses. I'll sell them over the winter, and you just do this job. It won't take long, and in the spring you'll have plenty of money to go on to something you'd rather do."

"I can't do it. I knew you were coming out today. I told Marie you'd be coming out today, and I said, 'He's going to ask me and I'm going to have to turn him down, so be ready, because it might be a hard winter.' I already told Dale I might have to let him go for a few months."

"Gottfried, you know, I've been putting up with you for years. One crazy thing after another. But this is the craziest thing you've ever said to me."

"You think you can insult me and maybe it will change my mind, but—"

"You know what, Gottfried? I'm not insulting you. I'm telling you the truth. Anyone in the world would agree that it is crazy to turn down an indoor job in the winter and lay off your favorite co-worker and refuse to work in a place that you love and get lots of money for it just because someone else is paying for it, especially after complaining for years that you always have to front all the money and take all the risk yourself."

Dale cleared his throat. I looked at him. He said, "I don't like to say anything."

"I know," I said.

"Especially since, you know, I don't want to seem like I'm trying to save my job and all."

"Why not, Dale? It's okay to try and save your job."

"Okay. Well, then. Here's what I think."

We waited for a long moment while he looked out the window.

"You can't always pick the guy you want to work for. I was reading about this artist: Poussin. I saw some of his paintings one day at a museum. Anyway, he was in Italy, minding his own business, and the king of France got him to come back to Paris and gave him lots of things to do that he had never done before, and he had a terrible time getting paid to boot, and then when he managed to get back to Italy and be his own boss again, he died."

"I can't tell whose side you're on, Dale," I said.

"Well, it just made me think of that."

"I can't compromise certain things," asserted Gottfried.

I turned back to him. I opened my mouth. I started yelling. "Who says, Gottfried? Who says you can't compromise? Who do you think you are? You're a builder! You're a small-time builder in a small place! You do good work, but you're not Rembrandt! You're not even this guy Poussin, who I've never heard of! You're not rich! You're not Frank Lloyd Wright! You build in a traditional style that is pleasing to people! So what? Get off your high horse and live in the real world!"

I turned on my heel and stomped out.

He really was the only one capable of remodeling the clubhouse and making the new work disappear into the old, but I was fed up with him. As I drove back to the office, I tried this idea out in several ways. Fed up. Fed up with Gottfried. Not kidding. Who did he think he was. And so on. Maybe I could get Dale by himself.

Marcus was gone. It was after lunch by now, and when I walked into the office, Jane was just hanging up her coat. I said, "Where did you have lunch?"

"Laguna."

"Very high class."

"I just had an appetizer-size plate of tortellini with pesto sauce."

I went into my office a little abruptly, still annoyed with Gottfried. Jane followed me. She stood in the doorway. She said, "So. Did you find Gottfried?"

"I did, unfortunately."

"Did you finalize the deal?"

"I did not."

"You seem—uh, pissed off."

"I am."

"I've never seen you pissed off before."

"Frankly, Jane, I think this process is getting to everyone." I straightened the folders on my desk.

She stood there with her arms crossed over her chest. She said, "It's taxing, I admit. I mean, for me, the hardest part is that there's always something more to do. I focus on something, like fitting some investors to a particular deal or putting together loan papers, and it's a tremendous effort to get that one thing done, and as soon as it's done, there's this moment when I realize that that one thing, as hard as it was, wasn't even the point."

"Like getting the permits."

"We haven't even started building yet. The thought of that terrifies me."

"Or selling. Try thinking about that. These

houses are as expensive as one of Gottfried's houses. He builds and sells at the most two or three of those a year. I've had a couple of his houses on the market for six months or more. Who says there're buyers for a hundred of those houses?"

"Marcus," she said.

We stared at each other.

She said, "Don't listen to me."

"What?"

"I don't want to say it."

"Say what?"

"Say anything negative."

"Then don't say anything negative."

"Okay."

We looked at each other again, both knowing that she was going to say something negative. She said, "Marcus was a stranger when you all took him in here."

"Yeah."

"I mean, think about that." She looked at me soberly, giving me a moment to think about it.

"I have."

"I'm going to say something." She was still looking at me, and without her customary air of faint amusement.

"Say it."

"Okay, I will. No one who knew Marcus before would have ever taken him in like you all did."

"Is he a crook? Is there something we should know?"

"Well, it's not that. It's more like he's a crackpot. He's always had big ideas, but no one ever listened to them before."

"No one is a hero in his own hometown, Jane. You know that as well as I do. The people who know you are used to pooh-poohing you."

"Maybe. But I remember when Marcus first met Gordon and everyone. He called me and told me about it, and he was so excited, and I had no idea who anyone was, and I thought, Someone has to warn these people."

"Of what? Are there things he's done in the past that I should know?"

"No. But I'll tell you why. No one ever gave him a chance before."

Together we let this sink in.

"Are you saying we're the biggest suckers ever?"

"Maybe. Of course, that makes me a sucker too. I mean, when I told my sister I was working for Marcus and had put some of my assets in, she told me I needed my head examined."

"Gordon is cross-collateralized up the butt."

"I know that."

I sat down in my desk chair. I said, "You're right. I'm sorry you said anything. I'm sorry I listened."

"I should tell you something else."

"What?"

"We haven't paid your electric bill, and they're going to cut you off."

"You mean in the condo?"

She nodded.

"When?"

"Next couple of days."

"Why didn't you tell me that until now? Were you going to tell me, or just wait until they cut me off like before?"

"Well, actually, since I haven't spoke to Marcus in a few days, I don't know what the plan is now. I got the warning last week, and I told him about it, and he said he was going to negotiate it but then we had that argument so I lost track of what he's done. It may be okay, but maybe not."

"Why don't I just pay it?"

"You could do that."

"Have we reached some kind of a crisis, Jane? I don't know what's going on. Do you? Is there something you argued about that you haven't told me about?"

She gave me what I would have to say was a

calculating stare, went to the door of my office, looked out into the other office, and came back in. I said, "He's not here."

"He said not to tell you what we were arguing about because it was too embarrassing. Anyway, how did you know we were arguing?"

"Mike heard you from outside the door and went back out into the parking lot to wait things out. When I pulled in, he told me. What he heard didn't sound exactly like an argument, Jane, it sounded more like a knock-down drag-out fight."

She burst into tears. "He's seeing someone."

"Who?"

"Someone I know. A friend of mine."

"Mary King."

She looked at me in surprise.

"I figured that one out a few weeks ago."

"I'm not going to say yes and I'm not going to say no."

I took this as a yes. I said, "But why should that cause a knock-down drag-out fight?"

"I hate it. I'm caught in the middle, for one thing. Linda has no idea. She comes over to my place and she says to me, 'What's going on, Jane? Why is he acting so strange? Do you know anything? Does he need to go to a therapist or anything?' and then—uh, this other person comes over and says, 'Does he love me? Is he going to leave her?' And of course he's stringing both of them along. I've been going crazy."

"What is he going to do?"

"What do you think? What would he do?"

"I have no idea."

"He's going to play it by ear. At this point he's still planning to have it both ways. But this other person, I know she isn't going to stand for that. She's not that type. That's what we were arguing about. He said it was my job to help him keep things going, that that was what the project needed, and if it all blew up right now we'd lose everything we've put into it."

"Why would that happen?"

"It would just fall apart. I know it would. I can't say why." She heaved a deep sigh.

I said, "I don't see how Mary King would jeopardize the whole project, but maybe it's a psychological thing. She's not an investor or anything, is she?"

Jane shook her head. After a moment, she said, "Joey, Marcus has a heart about the size of a pea. Once I said to him, 'Watch out, Marcus, your heart is going to swell to the size of a walnut, and then it will burst,' and he just laughed. He doesn't care about anyone else."

"Oh, Jane." I thought this was typical of a

woman, to realize that a guy wasn't putting her first and so taking that to mean that he was heartless. My experience of Marcus wasn't like that at all. I said, "I'm sure it's not that bad. I'm not saying there's nothing to worry about, but I think when you don't talk to someone for a week and you spend that time brooding about the things you hold against them, that makes everything look worse. Make up with him, go along with him for now. What is there to be gained by blowing his cover? Nothing. He could get over Mary King. Does he love her?"

"I don't know. It's not—"

"Does he know?"

She shrugged.

"So just go along with him. Make up with him. See what happens."

She nodded and went out of my office. Marcus came in about ten minutes later, and after five minutes or so, I heard her say something to him, and I heard him reply. Their voices were too low for me to make out, but the conversation went on and seemed amicable. In about five minutes, Jane came in and put an envelope on my desk, addressed to the electric company, bearing a stamp. She said, "You mail it, just so you know it's paid."

Later that day I went out to find Gottfried, who was also in a better mood, and he said as I walked up to him on the porch of the house he was building, "All right. Dale and I talked about this. You're right. You sell these houses and I'll take that job, and in the spring I start work on that lot I got in Deacon. Wait till you see what I'm planning to build there."

I HAD A DATE with Susan Webster. It was
a real date, not a casual getting together. I
put on a jacket and a tie, and when I
picked her up she had her hair done up on her
head with wispy curled tendrils floating down
on the sides and the back, and she had a black
dress with a wide neckline that showed off her
collarbone and a tight-fitting beaded top. When
she turned around for a moment, I saw that instead of a zipper up the back there was a row of
small buttons, maybe forty of them. I said,
"How did you button all those?"

She laughed. "I had my neighbor's sixteen-
year-old daughter come over. I said if she but-
toned all these buttons, I would loan her this
dress for the prom. It's an antique."

GOOD FAITH

I didn't ask who was going to unbutton her, because I knew.

I took her to the Rochester Hotel, a resort across the river from Roaring Falls, kind of a famous resort from before the Second World War that had revived in the last couple of years and become a luxurious spa and supper club. They had upscale food with a chef from California and a band and dancing. I knew how to dance, though I hadn't danced since my marriage, but I had come up with this plan when I was looking at my ads for Gottfried's houses and right on the facing page was a picture of a couple dancing in an ad for the Rochester. Dinner and dancing seemed suddenly exotic and fun and elegant and completely nonlocal.

I liked the way Susan got out of the car and stood looking at the Rochester Hotel while I handed the keys to the parking valet. She was relaxed. She surveyed the façade of the hotel and waited for me; then we ambled up the steps. She smiled at people we passed, in a gracious way, but didn't look at them as if she were curious about them. When the maître d' showed us a table not far from the door to the kitchen, she smiled at him and said, easy as you please, "Oh, do you mind? I'd rather sit over there." She gestured toward a banquette under the windows. He showed us very smoothly to the banquette, and she said, "Thank you. This is much better, don't you think, Joe?" She paused just for a moment, and the maître d' pulled out her chair and she sat down. When he spread her napkin over her lap, she had just the proper degree of nonchalance about it. She glanced around the room. She said, "They've done a nice job refurbishing the room. Look at the faux marble woodwork. I can do that. Do you like it?"

"This is the first time I've seen it."

"It's lots of fun. Do you know, I met a woman from New York. They have a big apartment on Park Avenue. She had the whole place marbleized." She leaned forward. "She paid twenty thousand dollars just for paint." She laughed merrily. "I mean, it's time-consuming, but it's not six months' work! I did it to my bathroom last weekend. You'll have to come up and see it. It's very funny. This tiny bathroom from the thirties, very utilitarian, with faux marble around the doorway and along the baseboards."

"It sounds great."

"Well, it is, but don't tell anyone you caught me being immodest."

She picked up the menu. I appreciated how seriously she looked at it—not like a person who was hungry but like a person who meant to enjoy herself. The food was Italian, but not the usual sort of Italian you found in our neighborhood, just pasta and plenty of red sauce and sausage.

"I love risotto," she said. "I thought I would order the saffron risotto with truffles and slivers of fennel, and maybe the salad of greens with olive oil and balsamic vinegar."

"I eat Italian all the time, and I've never heard of half of those things."

"I make risotto. And gnocchi. I much prefer them to pasta."

"What do you recommend?"

She looked the menu up and down.

"I would try the bruschetta." That was pieces of toast with chopped tomatoes on top. "Then the crab tortelloni with the light chanterelle sauce. There's only three of those, they should be nice. And then, are you hungry?"

I nodded, but really I was horny. She went on. "Hmm. I would have a bite if you tried the chicken, prosciutto, and spinach roulade. I don't think the chef would put that on the menu if he didn't enjoy making it. It's rather delicate."

"Have you made that too?"

"Something like it, but I like to use chard. It has a brighter flavor, if you're careful not to cook it too long."

"I'll have all those things."

She smiled and fingered one of the pale ten-drils of hair that curled around her ear. Her smile got wider. She said, "Now you have to tell me what's gotten back to you about me. I mean, about what I've said about you."

"I haven't heard a thing."

"You're kidding me."

"No."

"I thought the grapevine was working all the time around here. I mean, they practically prom-ised me that if I liked you and found you attrac-tive, you'd know within days." She was grinning.

"Who promised?"

"Well, my mother and her sister, but they promised on behalf of all the intermediate con-tacts."

"Everyone has been very quiet, so you'll have to tell me yourself."

The waiter came and Susan ordered, not for-getting the wine, which was some sort of Ital-ian white. When he was gone, she said, "Well, I am in a spot now."

"I think you can handle it."

"Maybe. Let me see. I said you were cute."

"Everyone thinks I'm cute."

"Oh. Well, I said you had a very melodious deep voice and that I enjoyed talking to you before bedtime."

"That's rather suspicious."

"Yes, isn't it? And I said you have very appealing hands." She reached across the table and took one of my hands. She looked at it for a long moment, then said, "Yes, I was right about that. And grace. You are graceful."

"*You* are graceful."

She smiled again. I was enjoying myself very much. There was something about the way she said things that made replies easy. I didn't have the sense I had often had with Felicity that there was no answer possible because what she said was unexpected and a little challenging. I thought I knew Felicity, but she perplexed me. I didn't think I knew Susan, but she was comfortable. She took my uneasiness upon herself and made it go away. My mother would have called that *manners*. My mother was going to like her very much, I thought, but for the time being Susan Webster was mine alone.

We talked and then we didn't talk. The food came, and it was delicious, especially the bruschetta, which for some reason was far more tasty than I expected chopped tomatoes on toast could be. The tortelloni, which were large envelopes of pasta shaped like hats, had a light, delicate filling, and the spinach rolls were a bit more pedestrian but still good. I said, "The only thing is that I'm still hungry." She looked up and signaled the waiter. When he came over, very eager to serve us—her—she ordered again, this time thin slices of veal in a lemon-artichoke sauce, and we shared that. It was a perfect meal, and as soon as I had finished the last of the bread and the sauce, I moved around the table until I was next to her on the banquette, and I put my hand behind her neck and leaned toward her and kissed her. When her lips softened and she bent into me, I put my arm around her and deepened my kiss and our embrace. She put both her arms around me. We kissed for a long time, and when we opened our eyes, the waiter was standing there with a bottle of champagne. He said, "We have this excellent Chandon. It's really very very good."

I said, "Let's have it."

Susan said, "Oh, let's do!"

After the champagne, which the waiter poured with a great flourish and a conspiratorial look at me, we went into the next room and danced. Then we went back to our table and drank more champagne and ate crème brûlée with pears, and then we danced some more. Of course she was a good dancer, and of course I was a good dancer, because that was her great talent, to bring out the talents of those around her. She made requests of the band. The band members said, "Oh! That's a good one. We know that one," and then played the numbers perfectly. The waiter set dishes in front of us with pleasure and in anticipation of our pleasure, and after watching us dance, other couples got up and danced, too, and laughed and joked with us. At midnight, we were still dancing, and the band was still playing, and I said, "I don't think I've ever had so much fun."

She said, "Let's go back to my place," and kissed me. I paid the check and we went out to the car. The valet had gone home. The car was far away. I held her tightly under my arm, almost smothering her, but she hung on to me and turned her nose into the wool of my coat, and the air was full of tiny bright prickles of snow that swirled and fluttered in the veranda lights and the lights of the parking lot, and I felt as if Susan Webster had designed this night for this purpose, for my enjoyment, like the meal and the conversation and the dancing.

All of this was joyously expected. I had prolonged our courtship, retarded my wishes and expectations, and now, driving toward her little house, the moments were especially sweet and smooth. I didn't know how she would be making love, but I did know how she was, and so it was a perfect combination of familiar and exotic, known and new. She seemed to understand this and feel the same way, because she welcomed me into her house with a kind of decorum. She took my coat and hung it in the closet. She offered me something hot to drink. She showed me where to set my shoes and gave me a towel to wipe them off. The place was familiar to me, but I appreciated the way she had left certain lights on and turned off others, to make the progress to the bedroom inviting and easy.

In her bedroom, where one lamp was lit, she sat on the bed. One by one, I undid the forty buttons. Then she went into her closet and, as naturally as you please, took out a pale silk nightgown that looked more like a slip and put it on. I undressed down to my shorts and laid my clothes over the back of a chair. She came over to me and rested her head against my chest. We were quite sober in spite of the champagne, what with the food and the exercise. She sighed, then said, "I'll be right back," and went into the bathroom.

I stood at the foot of her bed, looking at a large picture of a tree branch hung with oranges and orange blossoms and shiny green leaves, all very realistic and lacquered-looking but much larger than life. When she came out of the bathroom, I said, "You can almost smell these."

"Aren't they great? My friend in Spain painted that. Her name is Lupe. That's her signature. She doesn't use her last name. Have you ever tried cocaine?"

I turned to look at her. She was holding a thick

greenish piece of glass, about the size of a small windowpane, and on it was a razor blade and a little white hill of what I recognized as cocaine but had never actually seen before. I said, "No."

"Do you mind?"

"In what sense?"

"Do you mind if we snort some? Or if I snort some? It's fun."

"What's it like?"

"It's *compelling*. It's not dangerous. We aren't going to go anywhere. It's not like LSD or mescaline or that sort of thing, where something can go wrong unexpectedly."

"Except a drug bust."

"Except a drug bust, but there isn't going to be a drug bust. I don't sell cocaine. I am not a suspicious character. Am I?"

She smiled winningly, and I said, "Not in that sense, no."

She sat down on the bed with the pane of glass on her knees and arranged the white powder with her customary grace and ease. In a moment or two, she had set up two lines and pushed the rest off to the side. I had seen it all in the movies, but in the movies there was a charged air about it: danger, anticipation. Here it was very cozy. The room was warmly lit. The bed looked inviting. I had a little buzz from the champagne still. Above our heads, the beautiful branch of orange blossom threw off a glow. She reached into a bedside drawer and took out a short straw. She said, "In the movies they do it with money, like a hundred-dollar bill, but it always seems to me that some of it is going to get caught. Money isn't smooth, and money has a lot of germs on it, doesn't it? It's very show-offy to do it with a hundred-dollar bill."

"Somehow I think that a hundred has fewer germs on it than a one. Or maybe they are just a better class of germs."

She leaned forward and drew the line of white powder into her nose, snorted a couple of times, and smiled at me. I said, "Do you do this often?"

"Are we good enough friends for me to answer that question?"

"That would be for you to decide."

"There we go," she said, and grinned. She looked at me for a long moment, very friendly and intent, and then she kissed me. There was a faint acrid odor that was more than an odor on her lips. It was almost an electrical sensation. I could not help but notice that her kiss was softer and more intense than her earlier kisses had been. My desire, which had vanished as soon as I said the words *drug bust,* flooded back, and I gently stretched her backward against the pillows. She continued to kiss me. There was something odd about it, as if she was so involved in kissing me that a part of me, the part that wasn't kissing her but was noticing the bed and the room and her body, was alone. She kissed me and kissed me, and I went in and out of the kiss, alternately absorbed in what my lips and tongue were feeling and what I was thinking, which was that the evening had taken an unexpected turn and I wasn't sure what I thought about it. She broke away and murmured, "Oh, that was good. You should try it. It can't hurt to try a line. It's not like heroin. One line doesn't make you an addict. I promise."

I looked at her. She didn't look odd or overexcited or drugged. She looked like she was having a good time kissing me. So I sat up. She sat up and put the glass on my knees and handed me the straw. I remembered what I had seen in the movies and snorted up the line. It burned and I rubbed my nose; then I looked at Susan's face. While I was looking at it, it got brighter and bigger, not as if it had changed shape, but as if everything else around her face had dropped away. The only way to describe it is to say that her face got remarkably important. After a moment, she laughed; then she started kissing me again.

Of course I noticed a difference between after the snort and before, but it wasn't like any difference I had ever noticed in the past. It wasn't like getting drunk; it wasn't like smoking marijuana; I don't think it was like taking a psychedelic drug, but I had never done that, so I didn't know.

It was just like having more. It was like having reached the limits of your capacity for enjoying something or eating something or engaging in any good thing, and suddenly finding your appetite expand. We kissed and kissed. If she hadn't said "Breathe" from time to time, I might have forgotten to. And then it wore off, and she did another line, and then it wore off for me, and I did another line, and after that line we had sex. In the course of that, I noticed that my cock was huge and hard, and then I became somehow tremendously absorbed in my cock. It astonished and delighted me. Just as, when I was looking at her face or kissing her or stroking her body, that got to be the only thing in the world I was thinking about or doing, so when I saw my cock and put my hand around it, that got to be the only thing in the world, just the perfection of my own member, rigid and silky, beautiful and enormous. I started to laugh; it was so wonderful that it was mine. I saw that Susan was looking at it, too, and I watched her stare at it, then I looked back at it and forgot that she was looking at it, too. It did not seem to be possible that my hard-on would go away.

Susan whispered in my ear, "Let's do it."

"Do what?"

"Make love."

"Oh, yes. Let's." And then we did. I had to

consciously close my eyes, though, so that I could stop looking at my cock. It was a good thing I did, because the inner life was at least as involving as the outer life. I became lost in the sensations of penetration, accompanied by the secondary feeling in the palms of my hands where I was gripping Susan around the hips. I could feel her skin against my palms and her vagina around my dick and I could feel my own thrusts and it went on and on, no shifting of position or change of any kind. Change seemed irrelevant and impossible until our balance shifted and the old way was completely gone and a new way was installed. It was entirely strange and involving and then the sensations began to fade and I opened my eyes. She said, "You're coming down from the high."

"I suppose."

"There's more."

"Can I ask a stupid question?"

"There are no stupid questions. There are only stupid assumptions."

"Oh. Well, am I going to come?"

"Nothing is going to stop you from doing that, though it could be awhile."

"Well, judging by this, am I going to live through it?"

"Maybe not in this form." She laughed.

"I can believe that."

"This is nice, isn't it?" She removed herself from me. I was still hard, as hard as I had been however long ago that was. It was wonderful but it wasn't quite as riveting as it had been. I was noticing that, as she lay down beside me on the bed and snuggled against me. She said, "Let's have a little rest. What is it? Oh, about three. Three-o-nine. That's not all that late."

"What time did we get here?"

"Twelve-fifteen, maybe. Coke kind of makes the hours disappear. It is nice. Very nice. Sherlock Holmes was a coke addict."

"I thought Sherlock Holmes was a fictional character."

"Well, Sigmund Freud, then. He was too. My boyfriend used to say it was the drug of intellectuals and artists."

"Really?"

"I would think, Then why are you taking it, Billy?"

"He was not an intellectual or an artist?"

"He was a coke dealer. That was as close as he came. A purveyor to the stars, as it were. I met him on the plane home from Spain. He lives in New York. They prayed that we would break up."

"They?"

"Mother and the aunts."

"Oh, them."

"Their prayers are often answered, I have to say." She snuggled closer. I felt the texture of the room slowly return to something I recognized. "The danger is that you'll just get worn out, but if you are organized and careful, it's not at all like the addictive drugs."

"If you say so."

"I do. I've had lots of experience, no problems." She hoisted herself on her elbows and looked at me. She went on, "It's just a thing, you know. It's nice but it's not great. It's fun, but it's not art or religion or a baby."

I looked at her. She smiled prettily and self-confidently. It was all the same thing, I thought, the pictures and the tiles and the décor and the neatness and the hair and the clothes and the general savoir faire and grace. It was all the same thing as the cocaine. She was the first woman I had ever met who was universally competent. I saw that my hard-on was subsiding. I pulled a sheet, a very delightful sheet, smooth and cool, up over us. She said, "I don't think I've known anyone quite like you, Joe." The fact was that sometime later we fell asleep, and in the end, I didn't come. But afterward, I was kind of glad of it, because it seemed like that would have been almost too much, almost too dramatic. It was a pleasure to be saved for later.

A ND SO GOTTFRIED FINISHED the two houses he was building and I put them on the market, and the money I used for the advertising was my own, because I didn't want to involve Marcus and Gordon. The day the ads came out in the paper, I was actually a little nervous, as if I had done something and now I was going to be found out, especially since they were good-sized display ads with several views of each house. HOME FOR THE HOLIDAYS was the title of the ad, and both properties looked terrific. I planned to run the ads through Christmas, which was expensive, but they were perfect houses to show during the holidays, and I managed to get Dale and Gottfried's wife to trim them out a bit with some wreaths and some lights. One early snow and they would look like Hallmark cards, I thought.

Marcus stayed mum.

Gottfried moved his trucks and tools and crew (two other guys named Jim and Jack) out to the farm, and Marcus went out there at least every other day. When he told me he was going out the first time, I stopped him before he walked out the door. I said, "You know Gottfried can't stand you, right?"

"I knew he was miffed about the fence, but—"

"And the color of your new roof. Don't try to win him over. Don't make suggestions. He's got the plans. He's gone over the plans three times with all of us. Let him follow the plans."

"What if we want to make a change, or there's something that doesn't look quite—"

"My first choice would be that you not make any changes at all. But if there's really something, let me suggest it. You keep your mouth shut. Just stand around and admire, if you have to be there, which I don't really buy."

"It's our project."

"Don't think of it that way for the next four or five months. Think of it as his project."

"But what if—"

"I'm telling you. If he walks away, he won't come back, and there isn't a single other builder we can get in the area or at the price. The houses will be different. Now we're talking about the clubhouse."

"I don't think money is the real object here. We want it to be exactly right."

"He will do it exactly right, but he's very touchy. Imagine the touchiest person you've ever met."

"Linda?"

"Whoever. Now, imagine someone ten times touchier."

"Gottfried?"

"Yeah. Now, if you make one inadvertent mistake, or maybe two, I can work through the wife, but that's all the rope you've got, so don't waste it and don't use it up."

Marcus laughed, which I didn't think was a good sign, but at the end of the first week I still hadn't heard from Gottfried, so I began to relax a little, though I did say to Jane, "Give him as much work to do as possible to keep him away from there." Jane understood. I was coming to like Jane.

One day not long after this, I was pulling into the parking lot at about the same time as Marcus, and when he saw me he jumped out of his car and sprinted over to my spot. As soon as I had gotten out, he said, "Come with me. I've got something to show you."

"Don't tell me that."

"No, really. You'll love this." He slapped me

on the back. He was in a better mood than I had seen him in weeks. He stepped behind me and hustled me toward the door. He didn't even turn his head to look at Mary King, sitting behind her desk, though I saw her eyes follow us. Good, I thought.

When we got into the building, he turned me right instead of pushing me straight ahead, and in a moment we were standing outside of the South African Gold Trading Exchange. Marcus reached around me and opened the door. I had never been in here before.

But Marcus had. The receptionist said, "Hey, Marcus!" with a grin, and Marcus said, "Hey, Dawn!" and then a door to one of the offices opened and out came George Sloan. He was dressed in a black funereal-type suit and a very white shirt, but he didn't have a mournful air. Rather, he was grinning, and he had large yellow-gold cuff links. He too said, "Hey, Marcus! I was hoping you'd come in."

"How's it going?"

"Great! Say, Joe! Long time no see!"

It was as if our most recent interaction hadn't ever happened. In fact, it was as if all our interactions hadn't happened. The George Sloan I had taken around to house after house, the faintly exasperated, suspicious middle-aged guy who had transformed into the lovelorn trespasser had now

transformed again into a chuckling, hearty, welcoming, even good-looking man. I said, "George!
I thought you'd disappeared."

"You thought I'd gone to jail, I'll bet!" He
guffawed.

"Well, they didn't say anything in the paper—"

"Oh, I paid a fine." He waved his hand. "But
come into my office. I want to show Marcus
something."

He ushered us into a nice hard-edged office
with severe black and gray décor, except that
everything had bright gold accents. I said, "So,
how long have you been in the gold business,
George? I thought you were in business supplies or something like that."

"I'll tell you what happened. I came into
some money, I won't say how much, but
enough to have redone that house if those
restaurant people hadn't bought it and gutted
the downstairs to build the kitchens, so I was
looking around for an investment, and I came
over here—just a little research—and I got to
talking to one of the partners, Simon Lever, you
know him? And a couple of weeks later, here I
was, and Simon said he'd teach me the business,
and of course Marcus was in on it." He glanced
at Marcus. "But look."

There was a lighted computer screen in one

corner of the office, and numbers were scrolling across it.

"This is like minting money. The trade I made this morning has already earned four percent, and it's only been—what?—a couple of hours. If it keeps going like this, I'll be ready to buy a piece of land." He looked at the computer screen admiringly.

"And I'll be ready to buy an ingot of gold," said Marcus.

"I keep telling you to get in."

Marcus shrugged. "Simon Lever is a good prospect for us."

"Look at me. I'm an idiot," said George. "What have I been doing all my life? Glorified inventory. But this is making me rich. This is making *me* rich. All you need is a stake. Doesn't even have to be a big stake. What I do is retire a certain percentage of everything I earn. I learned that from watching my father-in-law play blackjack in Vegas. He'd go out there with a stake, absolutely ironclad. If he was losing, well, so be it, but if he was winning he put money into his left pocket every winning hand, and he never took it out. Over the years, he's one of the few guys I ever saw who made money gambling."

"And paid his taxes," said Marcus.

"Yes, he did. I told you that."

"So he wasn't as smart as he looked."

We all laughed.

George put his hands in his pockets. "Fellas," he said, "it's lying around on the floor here, waiting for you guys to stoop down and pick up."

"Everything I got is tied up." Marcus glanced at me. "I don't know about Joe."

I shook my head noncommittally.

"You know where I am," said George Sloan.

As we went up the stairs to our office, I said, "Between you and me, it is quite a transformation. Like a personality transplant."

"He got rich."

"Well—"

"George Sloan is the first guy I've met around here who can take a dare."

"You could've fooled me."

I went to bed before ten Sunday night. I thought I heard the phone ring; I was sleeping so soundly I couldn't even begin to wake up and answer it, but when I got to work in the morning, Marcus was waiting in the parking lot for me again. The weather had turned especially cold overnight, below zero, and he was bundled up to the eyebrows. I almost didn't recognize him. But he opened the door to my car as soon as I turned off the ignition, and said, "So, what do you think? Did you think about it over the weekend? I tried to call you last night but you didn't answer."

"I fell asleep early."

"It's fucking cold out here. Let's go for a drive. Let's drive out to the farm."

"Okay. I'd like to see how Gottfried's getting on, anyway."

"He hasn't done a thing except set up. It's taking him forever to set up."

"When were you out there?"

"Saturday. He wasn't there. I didn't touch anything. I wore gloves. I didn't leave finger-prints. But he seems slow."

"He isn't fast, and he also takes a long time to set up and scope out the job. He always says, *Well begun is half done.* Believe me, you won't see Gottfried running to the lumberyard for three two-by-fours and a package of screws he forgot to account for. Don't worry about it." We turned out of the parking lot and headed down the street. The car was warm, and Marcus unwound his scarf. After a moment, he unbut-toned the top button of his overcoat. He stared out the windshield. I could recognize that stare now. It was the worried stare, the what's-going-to-happen-to-us stare. I didn't say anything. I let Susan Webster come into my mind, the way she looked when we were dancing, bright and happy and pretty, just a little disheveled, pinning her hair up after a fast dance, then putting her head against my chest for the next slow dance.

Marcus said, "I think we have to do something on the side, something that the others aren't involved in. I think we have to diversify."

"What do you mean?"

"This thing George Sloan is into is a great thing. I hate to see it get away from us."

"I don't know anything about that."

He looked at me. "Neither does George." We laughed.

"How much do you think he's made?"

"Well, actually, I can tell you that, because he's another one who can't keep his mouth shut. His mother or someone left him about a hundred and twenty-five. He's turned that into something like seven."

"Seven hundred thousand dollars?"

"As of Friday."

"This time last year, he was griping about how he was going to meet his sixteen-thousand-dollar down payment for his mortgage. Of course he was also stalking that hillside house, so I don't know what was really going on with him. Maybe he was just griping in front of his wife, as a cover."

"Well, I didn't know him then, but I feel like

the chance of a lifetime is getting away from me."

"What about Jane?"

"Jane doesn't have any money either. At least, not what she calls poker money. You know, my authority with Jane only goes so far and no farther."

"I know that."

"If I had fifty thousand bucks I could turn it into three in no time."

"Three thousand?"

"Three hundred thousand, you idiot!" He started laughing. "And get this. Mike put two thousand with George. You might ask yourself where Mike got two thousand? Well, he's saved it in a tin all these years. In a tin! When I met Mike, he thought a financial instrument was a money clip. They ran the two up to fifteen, and he went and bought some futures in soybeans, got it up to nineteen, then sold those and decided to try the currency market. He's turned that two into twenty-three thousand dollars, and now he wants to buy a house. By the way, I meant to tell you to look for a house for Mike out there in Plymouth Township somewhere. First a suit, then a house. But, shit, they're leaving me behind."

"I'm feeling a little stodgy myself."

"I am in a dangerous mood."

"In what sense?" I looked him up and down.

"Well, I'm not going to do you any bodily harm. But I'm sort of in a let's-plunder-the-children's-college-fund mood. I was the guy who got these guys into this! It's driving me crazy, but I am so overextended!"

I thought of the eight hundred thousand but I didn't mention it, not wanting to tempt him, if he was indeed in that sort of dangerous mood. I thought it was probably a good thing that the eight hundred thousand was still safely at the savings and loan. Moods tended to pass, didn't they?

"I've got to get some money."

I looked at him. We were on the highway now, and it wasn't very crowded, so I looked at him for a long moment. Then I said, "I don't know that I've ever seen you—I don't know, desperate like this. Is this thing with George Sloan really the problem, or is it something I should know about but don't really want to?"

"Like what?"

"Like something with the project."

"Nah. The project is fine. I mean, fine enough. Slow. It's so fucking slow. I didn't realize it would be so fucking slow. But it's still a sure thing. This is how I look at it. It's 1983. My best guess is that 1985, or even 1986 are going to be the best times to be selling luxury homes.

GOOD FAITH

The longer we can hold on, the better off we'll be. We don't want to panic and sell and see our investment turn into gravy for the buyer. That's the worst thing in life, to be on the buy-low end of the equation. My parents owned a house once, for about three years at the end of the sixties. All the kids were pretty much on their own, so they bought a brownstone pretty cheap. My mother was beside herself, she was so happy. She felt like she'd achieved a lifelong dream, but then my dad lost his job, and they were late with the mortgage payment, and she didn't say anything to the kids because she was embarrassed. So anyway, someone offered her the same price they'd paid for the place three years before, and she took it, because she was afraid, even though the two of them had fixed the place up pretty well in the meantime. She said it was just too nerve-racking, worrying about the mortgage every month. Anyway, a couple of years later, when property values began to shoot up in New York, the guy who bought it sold it for twice what he'd given her. My father, who was the reason she sold in the first place, raged at her for months for being such a sucker. All he could think about was that free money he could have had if she hadn't let the other guy get the best of her."

We were silent.

He said, "So anyway. What was her mortgage payment? Maybe two hundred fifty a month or something like that. I always thought that was the worst thing that ever happened to her in a long life of bad things. Because it was the most unnecessary."

I didn't know what to say, so I kept my mouth shut and kept driving.

"You know what the rich have?"

"What?"

"Staying power. That's all. They aren't smarter or even better organized or morally superior or more ruthless or whatever. They just have the wherewithal to last longer."

"How do you get that?"

"I was going to say luck, but really it's just recognizing that that's what you need. And I recognize that." He sighed.

I admit that all through this conversation I had been thinking of my own savings account and my net worth. Did I have any "poker money"? Did I care that George Sloan and Mike Lovell, two guys I had no respect for, were busy making money hand over fist while I was playing it safe? I didn't know, and since I didn't know I didn't say anything about my funds, but the temptation was full and pressing. Some natural caution held me back, but its hold on my tongue was slight, and driving through the countryside with Marcus came suddenly to seem like an unexpected dilemma or test. I knew this was true: that if I said anything at all, made even the slightest or most distant reference to my reserve funds, Marcus would have them out of me as he had had everything out of Gordon, out of Bobby, out of Jane. I was the only holdout.

The landscape was bare and cold. Even the entrance to the farm was uninviting—a chilly wall and an icy gate, a leaf-strewn driveway and all the trees bare and the vegetation dead. It was therefore especially nice to drive up to the house, see the lights on and the big doors cozily shut, and hear the sounds of hammering and drilling coming from within. Gottfried had gotten things set up and gotten to work. I said, "Gottfried is completely reliable and completely competent. He's an asshole, but he's an oasis of know-how in a world of idiots, and when he's finished in the spring we'll be on our way."

"Do you think so?"

"You know what? I do, I really do. The worst is over—or at least it will be over by early next year, when the permitting process is complete, the golf course is showable, and the clubhouse is done."

"That *is* something, isn't it?"

"Yes, it is."

"Yes, it is. Let's go find something to eat."

"Don't you want to go in?" I was pulled up in front of the door.

"Nah. The sound of hammering is enough for me."

After our amazing date, it seemed obvious that I would take Susan to a big party that a developer we knew was giving to show off the house he had built for himself about ten miles south of Portsmouth—not exactly in our area, but worth seeing nonetheless. The guy's name was Mack Morton. He had worked for a long time for the local branch of a big national outfit from Atlanta, then taken his crew and gone out on his own. He put up subdivisions of houses on the south side of Portsmouth that were fancier and bigger than Gordon's, but not one of a kind, like Gottfried's houses. I had had some good luck selling the Morton properties, but he had never used me as a listing agent and we weren't particular friends. Nevertheless, I usually got invited to big Morton Land Company parties, and sometimes I went. This time the invitation said to bring swimming suits. I thought this was interesting. Not many people in our area had indoor pools.

GOOD FAITH

Marcus had been hot to go. "If he wants to show off the house," he pointed out, "and he's inviting all his builder friends, it must be something special and we can get some ideas. Even if we can't get any ideas, everyone will be there, and I for one am keeping my eye out for ways to put our crew together." It did seem that we were going to have to raid other local contractors for building crews if we were going to put up a hundred houses, or four hundred, or six hundred, or however many.

The house must have been six thousand square feet. It was built on top of a hill, and you couldn't help staring at it from at least half a mile away. Susan, sitting beside me, said, "Do you really think that's it?"

I really did. The style was French country provincial, but expanded, as if built for exceptionally large people. It was basically L-shaped from the front, with a steeply pitched red-tile roof and stonework all along the façade to about five feet. Also leaded windows (which I later found out had come from a house in the Hudson Valley that was being torn down). The most charming or most ridiculous element, depending on your taste, was the three-story round tower that nestled into the crook of the L and formed the entry and the stairwell to the upper floors. We drove up the circular drive, and Mack's sixteen-year-old son slouched over and stood outside my window. I rolled it down. He said, "I'm supposed to park all the cars? I'm being real careful, sir." I handed him my keys.

The wind was pouring over the top of the hillside like a waterfall, and I realized as soon as I got out of the car why the kid looked blue. "My God!" said Susan, and huddled up against me. But the view was miles and miles in all directions. I had wondered why the party was starting so early, but now I could understand. Off to the northwest, you could see where the Nut River met the Blue. Off to the northeast, Portsmouth was just beginning to light up for the evening, and off to the south, the interstate came out of our hilly, woodsy region and entered a wider, more open landscape.

I said, "I wonder if you could see the farm on a clear day."

"You can see where the mountains get higher. The farm is before that. But jeez. You need a lot of body fat to enjoy the view."

"Got your suit?"

She nodded. Her hair was up, wrapped around what looked like a pair of elegant chopsticks, and I knew from when I picked her up that she was wearing a green silk dress with a vaguely oriental style to it—not like anything I had seen lately, but very chic. I was proud to be seen with her. She said, "I can't believe we could swim!"

But the house and the pool room—with a full view of Portsmouth, which looked terrific from a distance—were plenty warm and, judging by the lighting and the trays of food and the buckets of wine and beer and the twenty or thirty people jumping around in the water, the conspicuous consumption on display was just exactly to the taste of everyone there, including Marcus and Linda, Bobby and Fern, Gordon and Betty (who I saw was diving off the high dive as soon as I came in), Jim Crosbie, Bart and his wife, and everyone else I knew, slightly or well. Laughter and shouting and splashing filled the space, bouncing off the surface of the pool and the windows and the tile pool deck. A few teenagers were standing by, rather quizzically gazing at the grown-ups' antics.

"It's a nice facility," said Susan, with a smile.

I thought how cool she was, not cool in the popular sense, but in the sense of temperate, smooth, agreeable. I gave her a squeeze around the shoulders and we walked into the pool area. Mack Morton came up to me immediately and handed me a beer. He had a beaming smile on his face. I slapped him on the back. I said, "Hey, you're supposed to sell this one, not keep it for yourself."

"Shit, man," he said. "Look at this fucking tile. It's slate. See how it isn't slippery? You can get a grip when it's wet. I got these tiles from a place out in California! In spring and fall, they soak up the sunshine and heat the place up, but in the summer, the sun's too far to the west to shine in here. And anyway"—he gestured over his head—"we put the skylights on electric openers and closers"—Susan and I looked up at the bank of skylights—"and when we open them up, they suck hot air out of *here* and bring in a northerly breeze from over *there*. It's like a fucking flue!"

I sensed that Mack had had a few. "It's a fabulous place, Mack, it really is!" I exclaimed.

"I never fucking imagined—"

His wife, Jolene, came up with an apologetic smile, and said, "Sorry, Joe. Say, honey—" and led him away.

As he went, he shouted over his shoulder, "I'm going to show you around myself later! Don't forget!"

I waved him off in a friendly way. Susan said, "I guess he's kind of excited, huh?"

"I guess." I kissed her on the hair. She was so unfrumpy.

I began to feel warm and damp in my clothes, and Susan reached up and pulled the sticks out of her hair. It fell down over her coat in a shining stream. A couple came out of a sliding glass door into the pool area, wearing suits and carrying towels, and I steered her in that direction.

I never thought you should have your own swimming pool—too much work after the novelty wore off—but it was tremendous fun to run out of Mack's office, throw down our towels, and jump into the water with the other swimmers. It was not lost on me that Susan was the youngest woman there and was unconsciously and naturally beautiful in her bikini, whereas the other women were a little defiant in their rather more sedate swimwear. Here, as in every other facet of her personality, was just that touch of the exotic that thrilled me—her bikini was an old one but that meant she had bought it in Europe, and it was cut just a little more stylishly than everyone else's Cole of California bathing suits. I leapt into the pool with a shout, cannonballing off the low dive, and as soon as I came up out of the water and looked around, Betty was on me, smiling, kissing my cheek, and holding my shoulder. She said, "You seem very excited, Joey."

"I am. Look at this place."

"So deluxe. I love it. I've been diving for an hour. I can't get enough. The pool is so warm."

"Did you see Susan?"

"She looks lovely, dear. Are you progressing?"

"Well, yes."

She kissed me again on the cheek and patted me on the head before swimming off. When she got out of the pool, it was obvious that she was sixty, but she was laughing and she carried herself with such athletic grace that I couldn't help watching her climb the ladder and dive again, a perfect jackknife that bent the board nearly in two and made a big booming sound in the space of the pool room. Then I watched Susan dive off the low board, a nice swan dive, neat and clean. I treaded water, and she swam over to me underwater, grabbed my leg, and came up and kissed me smack on the lips.

The party went on like this, people in and out of the water, drinking beers and eating hors d'oeuvres and talking talking talking about money.

The guests were divided about equally between developers and bankers, and everyone was turned on by the grandeur of the setting. Once it was fully dark, Mack turned down the lights and his wife and the caterer lit candles on the food tables, so that we swam by dim and flickering light, which seemed sybaritic. Or you could walk to the expanse of window glass and wipe away the steam, and see the light and glow of Portsmouth spread before you, a wide lake of yellow against the dark backdrop of the hills beyond, and then, above that natural darkness, the constellations spread out and returning light back to you. It was intimidating and delightful to see all that and to be inside this warmth with all this money talk. Mack had this place, but we had the farm, and once the potential of the farm was realized, we would all have something like this, not like this exactly but something equally wonderful, to be created later. Dripping, holding canapés and glasses of wine, I listened in on conversations between virtually naked men I usually didn't ever see in anything but suits and work clothes. And every naked man was excited.

I heard Crosbie say, "We are so close! This outfit from Texas sends more money out every night, looking for a few extra basis points, than most S and Ls send out in a year. They've got the whole place computerized, up and running, and they can really handle it. You know, that's our next project, get a computer expert in, or ten of them, whatever it takes, make everything so much more efficient. No more paper, nothing but big numbers!" He guffawed in delight.

I heard Marcus say, "He tells me that *Golf Digest* contacted him about a piece on up-and-coming designers and he's getting three pages, and he's going to put our spread first—"

I heard Gordon say, "Yes, Gottfried Nuelle is doing the clubhouse. Have you seen this kid he has doing the detail work? No one else like him around here that I've ever seen. They offered him I don't know what kind of money to come up to New York and do some repairs at the Morgan Library, but he said he didn't like cities—"

I heard Bart say, "The whole business is changing so fast my head is spinning. But with these new investment advisors we've got, we're right on top of it. Those kids, they're maybe twenty-eight and they look twenty-two, but that's the wave of the future. You ask me where the money's coming from, and frankly I don't know, but hey! Who's asking?" And he grinned right at me.

And I kept diving in and swimming around and kissing Susan and admiring her.

At eight or so, Jolene came to the doorway of the pool area and called out, "Dinner in twenty minutes!" and it seemed impossible that there could be more of everything that was so luxuriant already.

In groups of twos and threes, people got out of the pool, took their towels, and went into Mack's office to change. He had set up a clothing rack in there where we had hung our clothes, so well-dressed folks emerged rather quickly, their hair still damp but nicely put together again, smiling the way kids do when they've been in the water and forgotten all about whatever was bothering them before submersion. Susan and I had been last in, so we waited until everyone else was dressed and heading for the dining room before leaving the pool.

Mack's office was large, with sliding doors on two sides—one set opened into the pool area and the other set to the outdoor patio. There was a French door into the kitchen and another door, too, probably into a corridor or the foyer. I could hear guests on the other side of the French door, but its blinds were closed for privacy, as were the drapes between the office and the pool area. The slider to the outside was uncovered, but there was nothing out there but space and stars. The furnishings were spare, either for the party or because they hadn't completely moved in—only a bare desk, a big leather chair on casters, and the clothing rack. I said, "I guess we should hurry if we want to get some food," but Susan pulled off her bikini and dropped it to the floor, sat down in the leather chair, smiled at me, and turned it away from the desk. Then she lay back in it and lifted her hair out from behind herself, so that it draped over her shoulder and covered her right breast. Her nipples were erect and her skin was flushed. I walked around the desk and took hold of the brown arms of the chair and begin kissing her. She turned her face up to meet mine. As we kissed the chair reclined suddenly, so that I stumbled and found myself nearly on top of her, so the obvious thing seemed to be that we would make love, and I was certainly ready. I yanked off my trunks. She laughed. On the first thrust, the chair rolled backward and hit the wall with a thud. We laughed, but it wasn't easy to get leverage on her, and the chair kept rolling around. I would pull it toward me, thrust into her, the chair would rebound, and the next thing we knew, we were running into some-thing and laughing. I was drunk enough so that I thought this was a very intriguing way to be making love, and anyway, we had waited long enough, and it did seem imperative, no matter what the deal with the chair was, to keep at it. Finally, we were laughing so hard that I pulled out of her, picked her up out of the chair, and laid her out on the carpet. I went down on top of her, then into her, and she lifted her legs and folded them around my waist. She was little and athletic and there was a startling wildness about her, quite in contrast to how I had come to think of her. I kept having to tell myself that she was thirty and had been married. It was like making love to a very wild and willful and you might say naughty kid. When we were done, I fell back on the carpet, but she jumped up laughing, grabbed her towel off the floor, and ran out of the slider toward the pool. By the time I was on my feet, I heard the splash she made as she jumped into the pool. I wrapped my towel around my waist.

The pool area was empty, and the door to the rest of the house was half closed. Susan was jumping up and down in the middle of the pool, going under and then leaping out with her arms in the air, then going under again. She was shouting, "Yes! Yes! Yes!" each time she emerged. I laughed, threw down my towel, and jumped in after her. Just then, the door to the rest of the house opened and Mack peered in. He said, "You guys all right?" just as Susan emerged naked from the water up to at least her waist. I called out, "We're fine! We'll be there in a moment!" The door closed. She jumped out again. She looked beautiful—firm-breasted, her hair flowing in a watery stream down her back, her fingers spread and her arms wide, as kidlike as when we had been making love, and in fact, I felt a little old and a little on the spot, as if she were my responsibility and I didn't quite know how to manage her.

Just then, the door opened and Mack came

in again. He was dressed in khaki slacks and a sport jacket. He was very drunk by this time, and he walked right over to the middle of the pool and squatted down, staring at Susan. He said, "You need anything? Is there anything I can get you?"

Susan stopped jumping and began to tread water rather modestly. She said, "No, thanks. We really should get dressed. I'm sorry."

And then the door opened again, and one of the other builders, Sam Reading, wandered in, too. He said, "Everything okay in here?" He went up behind Mack. Mack stood up. They stood there.

Within five minutes, they were joined by five other guys, very casually, who were all concerned that Susan might need help of some sort. They milled around for at least another five minutes, until Betty swept in, laughing, and shooed them out, caroling, "Give the poor girl a chance to get out of the pool, you-all; good Lord, this prime rib is gettting cold! Joey! Dinner!"

When Susan and I got back to Mack's office and began changing again, we started to laugh and could hardly stop.

CHAPTER
26

BUT OVER BREAKFAST the following Monday morning, Marcus was not
laughing at all.

I said, "The whole party was a little wild. I
mean, there was food in the pool."

"You offended the wives."

"*I* did?"

"We could hear you two in the office.
Crosbie's wife was standing right next to me.
She said, 'I think that sort of behavior is just
awful.' The chair was banging against the
wall."

"Once or twice, maybe."

"Enough for people to know what you were
doing and start talking more loudly."

I scratched my ear for a second and then ate

some more of my hash browns, but I really didn't know what to say, since I had been very much enjoying doing what everyone knew I was doing. "All the men—well, some of the men—came out into the pool area. That was—"

"Very awkward. And don't you think that offended their wives even more? I mean, don't you?"

"I suppose."

"Thank God for Betty. I mean, she got the whole party started again, and she was laughing and making light of it, but the whole stark deal of a bunch of forty- and fifty-year-old men filing out to have a look at someone the age of their daughters—"

"She's thirty. Almost thirty-one."

"—the age of their *daughters,* I'm telling you, was not to the taste of any of those wives, and will certainly lead to guilt on the part of the men and a rather disapproving attitude toward *you,* who's the one they may end up working with."

"I'm sorry. I—"

"I think you should write some notes of apology."

"Oh, Marcus! Who do you think you are? I've been around here forever. I knew everyone at that party."

"Who do you think *you* are? This is not 1969

anymore, and we're not in our twenties. Don't you understand that?"

I scraped my fork around my plate. Even though I didn't like being talked to like a child, I saw his point. And then for some reason, maybe just to hear him go on about this sort of thing, maybe because it was still bothering me, I said, "A couple of weeks ago, she gave me some—uh, coke."

Marcus looked at me, a forkful of hash browns right in front of his mouth, for a long second, then he opened his mouth and put them in it. He chewed. He said coolly, "Ever try that before?"

"No."

"What did you think?"

"It was okay."

"What did you really think?"

"It was fine."

"I'm not kidding. I want to know what you really thought."

"Well, I guess my feelings were complicated. It wasn't like anything else I've ever tried."

"It wouldn't be."

"Have you ever tried it?"

"Yes." That would be why he was calmer about this than about the other.

"What did you think?"

"Well, my thinking changed over time, and I'll tell you how. There are only a couple kinds of luxuries. Some kinds have a chance to profit you in the end—fine art, say, or racehorses. Others profit you right now, because they get you in contact with people you want to know, like golf, or even boats, but boats are so time-consuming that the people you meet who also have boats usually aren't in the market for anything. Some kinds of luxuries just make your wife feel better, like fancy clothes, but that's okay. That's what you owe her. I guess I would put charity, which I consider a luxury, in that category. But myself, I don't see how that particular luxury you are talking about has any profit potential at all."

"Well, I wasn't—"

"I have to say I have second thoughts about Susan. This is a perfect example of what I was talking about."

"When was that?"

"About caution. You aren't in love with her, are you?" He leveled a suspicious look at me.

"I like her."

"These are red flags."

"Oh, lighten up."

"I'm not kidding. I mean, everyone is innocent until proven guilty, but if I am your partner and I see something going on that's a threat to the partnership or a threat to you, then I have to speak up, right?"

"Of course."

"You're not the Lone Ranger anymore, with the faithful Bobby at your side. You're part of a team."

"I don't think these two little things have such far-reaching implications."

"Well, be careful and pay attention."

I thought of Jane's outburst and, a little ticked off at his self-righteous tone, I asserted, "I don't know that your recent behavior has worked entirely to the benefit of the partnership."

He knew exactly what I was talking about. He said, "Whatever Jane has been telling you, she is wrong and she knows it. If she were a guy, I would give her the poke in the nose that she deserves. You know, I haven't told you this because I thought I could keep her under control, but Jane is a pathological liar. Always has been. I mean, I don't blame her. My older brother John is the reason. He was always getting her in trouble and leaving her to pick up the pieces, and kids who have fathers like ours have to lie to survive, but I said to her when she first got here that I was on to her and that part of going to work with this deal was playing it straight. I only believe what Jane tells me if I have independent supporting evidence. It's so much a habit with me that I don't even think about it, but if she's coming to you with lies about me, I think my loyalty to her on this score is misplaced, and I am giving you fair warning."

"You and Jane seem pretty close. I mean, apart from the odd argument or two."

"We are close." He leaned across the table. He said, "Your parents are so upright and sincere that you think moral failings in a person are a reason not to love them or commit yourself to them. You think character matters. Well, in the larger scheme of things, of course it does. But what I found out growing up is that it doesn't matter what shits your parents are, you love them anyway. That's your burden. Brothers, sisters. They drink and they steal from one another and they embarrass you and they lie and they commit every single one of the seven deadly sins, and you still love them. Ask me why, I don't know. So I don't even think about what it means if Jane lies through her teeth. She lies because she lies and I'm close to her because she's Jane. That's the way it is, but I'm not stupid. I still think it's my responsibility to make sure that her lies don't hurt me or the partnership and that my own kids know that lying isn't right or acceptable." He scraped up the last bits of food on his plate and ate them.

• • •

GOOD FAITH

And then it was Thanksgiving again. By the time I got to Gordon's, I was in a very good mood. For one thing, it was a beautiful day. Bright blue and cool, every winding country road bordered with crisp leaves. The road, the tree trunks, the barns, the fences were wet and vivid, and so was the grass, which was that last rich green of the year. Bushes by the side of the road were hung with brilliant red berries. I was pretty much alone in the landscape, but expected, welcomed, a guy with places to go and people to see.

My parents were especially jovial, I think for the sake of the two elderly sisters they had invited to share our meal. One was a widow and one was a spinster. My mother whispered to me when we were dishing up food in the kitchen that the younger one had decided to go to a nursing home, and both of them were worried about it. "You know," she said, "Selma doesn't drive, so they just won't see each other unless someone takes her over there. It's a shame. I only pray to the Lord she can stay home through Christmas. At least they can have that." She shook her head sadly.

But in the dining room and the living room, she was very lively and bright, and she had done an especially good job with the dinner. The turkey was moist and the gravy was dark and savory and the mashed potatoes were delicious, and the two women ate heartily, even though they had been talking about not having much of an appetite and nothing agreeing with them lately. After we ate, I did the dishes while my mother sat down at the piano and played hymns and my father sang. The ladies sang along, quavery but happy, and the house was warm and bright and I could hear them from the kitchen without having to join in. My parents harmonized very prettily, and the songs they sang, I suppose to keep everyone's minds off the future, were happy and hopeful. As I was leaving to go to Susan's, their minister was pulling up to the curb, and I waved at him, knowing they would all feel especially blessed that he had stopped by for coffee.

The ride through the misty twilight, cool and solitary for a few minutes before the onslaught of Baldwin activity, was very refreshing. I thought I was living a good life, and I looked forward to making a home someday myself, a place where future single guys who lived in condos would feel happy to come.

All the BMWs were lined up in the driveway, and several other cars as well. I looked for Marcus's Caddy, but I didn't see it. The house was ablaze with light and the front door was open. I parked and walked toward it, and who should be coming out, a dark figure in the light of the doorway that

I recognized immediately, but Felicity. I came up the steps and said, "Hey!" and she barreled toward me and threw her arms around me and pressed her head against my chest. I put my arms around her. Then she looked up at me, her hair dark and unruly around her head, and she said, "Oh, God, I miss you, Joey." She lifted her face and kissed me on the lips. All of this was hurriedly done, and when she stepped away, I was still startled. She turned back into the house, calling, "Here's Joey! I'm leaving now!" And she ran down the steps.

Betty was standing in the entryway, a dish towel in her hand. She stepped toward me and put her arm in mine. I said, "Where's she going?"

"I'm not sure. I was in the kitchen, and then I heard the sound of a quarrel, and when I came out here Felicity was putting on her coat, and she looked upset, but she waved me off when I asked her if there was a problem, and ran out the door. Did she say anything to you?"

"Just—uh, hi." I heard the sound of one of the BMWs starting up and zooming out the driveway.

"Well, she's been very prickly all fall. Just not herself at all. I don't know." She shrugged. "But she's a grown-up, and if she isn't voluntarily going to say anything to me or to Leslie, there's not much I can do." She turned and led me down the hall toward the family room. She said,

"You know, when Sally was killed, the one I worried the most about was Felicity. I just couldn't imagine how Felicity was going to make a life without Sally, but she picked herself up and went on, and all these years I've been a little relieved that she had the strength to do that. So always when she acts a little funny, or desperate, or unhappy, I go back to that worry, and I think—oh, here it is at last. This is what I've been waiting for." She stopped me and whispered in my ear, "And Hank is the wrong man for her. It's not his fault, but they are in different universes."

"I've kind of thought that too."

She continued to whisper. "You should have—" But then she thought better of her remark. We glanced at each other. Then she said, "You were very badly behaved the other night. Very devil-may-care." She leaned over and kissed me on the cheek. "Nothing wrong with a little of that, dear."

"Do you think I should send notes of apology?"

She laughed in her Bettyish way and we came into the family room, where the football game was ending and several other things were going on too, including a game of Monopoly around the coffee table that was a chaos of grandchildren and game pieces and beer bottles and chip bowls. She whispered, "Apologies are never a mistake, dear," then said, "Turkey in ten minutes! I need some helpers!"

I greeted Gordon and Hank and Norton and Bobby and Fern, and then Bobby and I followed Betty into the kitchen, where Leslie was making the gravy and Norton's wife, Margaret, was browning almonds in butter. Betty had a huge restaurant-style gas stove, and every burner had a simmering pan on it. The turkey was already on its platter, twenty or more pounds. Betty said, "Joey, you can carry that to the table. It took three of us to get it out of the roasting pan."

"And we dropped it twice," said Leslie, "but don't tell anyone. We kind of pushed it back into shape with big spoons." She glanced at Betty. "Was that Felicity?"

"It was. She left."

"Where did she go?"

"I don't even know who she was arguing with. There wasn't anyone around," said Betty.

"I told you, Mom. She's so touchy lately."

She glanced at me, obviously weighing whether to go on. I said, "Don't mind me, I'll just be picking up the bird here."

"It's okay. Mom, I think you should take Hank aside and ask him what is going on. Maybe he knows."

I said, "Maybe he doesn't."

Betty gave a rueful smile and said, "Joey's right. Maybe Hank doesn't know anything."

Leslie sighed.

Betty said, "Oh, I'm sure it's nothing. And it's her own fault if she misses dinner, because everything's ready, and we can't wait for her. She'll snap out of it. You remember the Cushings? They lived at the end of the street when, until about seven years ago? Frank Cushing had two sisters, and they came to Thanksgiving and Christmas at his house every year—oh, for twenty years or so. And you know what? The sisters weren't speaking to each other that whole time! What were their names? Oh, Edith and Letitia. Caroline Cushing didn't dare invite one and not the other one, so they would just come and glare at each other! Frank said a couple of his uncles were the same way. There we go." She laughed, tossing off this example of human strangeness as if it could have nothing to do with her or her family, I thought.

All this time, she had been dishing things into serving bowls and garnishing them with parsley and chives and sprigs of mint, and now the dishes were ready to be carried into the dining room, and so we did, me leading the way with a very heavy turkey on a very big platter, which I set in front of Gordon, who said, "Didn't I tell you we should go out? A nice buffet at the

Hollister Cafeteria? The kids would have loved it, the way they always have the desserts first."

Betty laughed and everyone pulled out their chairs. The mothers began setting the children up at a card table in the living room, and it was warm and comfortable. Gordon was smiling, so I knew he didn't mean it.

It wasn't until dinner was over, right through the coffee and the After Eight mints, and Norton and Hank and Gordon and I were sitting at one end of the table, next to an open window, having a smoke and gazing down upon the frozen pond and the piled-up, covered lawn chairs that the mood changed. As usual, the changer of the mood was Norton, who said, "I'm telling you, Gordon, now is not the time to be plowing a lot of money into high-end residential property. You look where I am. Now, my area has generations of history as a luxury destination. Ups and downs, maybe, in terms of this group coming in and that group going away, but we got the shore, we got the roads, we got the entertainment infrastructure. A hundred and fifty years, and it's a barometer. Some years, you can rent out a postage stamp for whatever price you want; other years you got to give away a mansion. Investment flows in and out, almost like the tide; that's what I say. And when rents are up and money flows in—well, eighteen months down the road everybody's rich, and when money flows out, eighteen months down the road everybody's poor. It's as simple as that. It's flowing out. Take this summer. I had a place on the market all summer, not a bad place, my worst place but not a bad place taken all in all, and I thought, Norton, the canary is dying here. Everything else was rented, but that one place got me to thinking."

"So you're saying that eighteen months down the road—"

"Whatever you have, you won't be able to give it away."

Gordon, who was smoking a cigar, took it out of his mouth and looked at the tip.

I said, "But it's a long-term thing. If there's a long-term rise, there're bound to be dips along the way. The vacation rental business always goes up and down. That's like the car business. But real estate doesn't lose value just because it isn't producing income."

Gordon looked at me.

"What I'm saying," said Norton, "is that the tide is always high enough to make business in my area, because we've got the proximity. Where you-all have that farm, the tide is only high enough to make business once in a while. It's in the boonies. That's why those people bought it in the first place. Because they had places in New York and Paris and wherever, and they needed a place to get away."

"Mind if I say something?" said Hank, who had moved his seat closer to the window and was not smoking.

"Go ahead," said Gordon.

"Preserving wild spaces is where the thinking is now. The Nature Conservancy is very big and getting bigger."

"What's that?" said Gordon.

"It's a nonprofit. They buy property and easements in wild areas or preservation areas, and they maintain the integrity of the area for future generations."

"They don't pay top dollar," I said. "And Norton, even though of course you're right in a lot of ways"—I hadn't known Norton for twenty-five years without learning that if you disagreed with him you had to placate him— "I don't think you're reckoning on the population explosion and the way people want to have something special. Nobody wants to get on the train and go to the shore and stay in a boardinghouse anymore. They want to have a place. I mean, why would they? There's no hassle like the hassle of having a house two or three hours away that you have to look after. I mean, do you really want to get in the car after every storm and drive to the shore and repair broken windows and water damage? No. But they do it. Why? Because shore property is limited and they aren't making any more of it. Same with our clubhouse. Places like the farm are few and far between, beautiful and classy and not something you can buy into every day. I mean, whatever you say, Hank—and we've had this conversation before—what we're doing *is* preservation, because say the farm went to this Nature Conservancy or whatever, or even the state. Are they really going to take care of it? Or won't it kind of get dusty and old and damp pretty quick? And as soon as a place like that gets old-seeming and loses its feeling of warmth—well, people don't want to go there and the whole thing deteriorates further."

"It's just too far away," said Norton.

"Well, I beg to differ on that one too, because traffic makes a difference. Suppose you zip out of town and drive for three hours and go two hundred miles, so what? Or you crawl out of town and spend three hours in traffic and get fifty miles—and even when you're there you've got cars and people everywhere. What's more desirable?"

"It's a gamble," said Gordon.

I said, "Look at someplace like Pebble Beach, out in California, or one of those golf resorts in North Carolina. That's our analogy, not the shore.

GOOD FAITH

The people we're trying to attract want amenities, and we're planning to give them what they want. A golf course, a swimming pool, a clubhouse restaurant, maybe even a riding center, right by the house. This is a place where people can live together in luxury in a beautiful spot."

Norton kept shaking his head, and Gordon had gone back to inspecting the tip of his cigar. Norton said unpleasantly, "Look, Gordon. Why don't you admit you're in it with Burns up to your ass? This advantage, that advantage, so what? Are you really going to back out of a deal with a guy from the IRS? A guy from the IRS who *got you off*? At least be honest!"

But Gordon ignored this. After a few moments, he looked out the window and said, "You know, I'm not saying I haven't had second thoughts, Norton. I'm not saying I haven't had the feeling from time to time that we've bitten off more than we can chew, but every project is a gamble and the property has intrinsic value from its uniqueness."

"That's right," I said, addressing myself to Norton more than anyone else. "Portsmouth Savings has had a tremendous amount of faith in the project. And they're just giving money away."

Gordon nodded. "I never asked for so much before, and they didn't bat an eye. Most of the time, the savings and loan makes sure you know they're doing you a favor when they make you a loan, but not this time, Norton, not this time. Bart and Crosbie both, they were hot to do it, hot to make this their baby. I remember thinking, They must know something we don't know. My feeling is, if they could get this merger through, there would be even more dough lying around waiting to be put to good use. Bart keeps calling me and saying how these things take time and everything's on track and all."

"Well, Gordon, what does your famous gut tell you?" pressed Norton.

Gordon put the cigar back in his mouth and drew a long breath through it, lighting up the tip. Then he blew out the smoke. He said, "I'll tell you what. My gut tells me something different every day. Your mother said she didn't want to hear about it anymore for two days at least, so I guess that's why *you're* hearing about it."

I said, "You've had big projects before, Gordon. You had that development up on the hill for fifteen years, and there was a time last year when I told you those higher-priced garden apartments wouldn't go, and in the end they went like hot dogs at a picnic. Everything Marcus said was true turned out to be true. You said it yourself to me—people want to live like they do on TV."

"But do they want to pay for it?" Norton was beginning to sound irritated.

GOOD FAITH

"I think they do," I said. "What else are they going to spend their money on? Real estate is still the—"

"Well, I guess we'll find out," said Norton, and he pushed back his chair and walked out of the room. On the way out, he muttered, "I give the fuck up."

"Is he mad?" I asked. "We were just having a discussion."

Gordon shrugged, then smiled at me. "That's what I've always said about you, Joe."

"What's that?"

"You have a great ability to just keep negotiating. You keep coming back and coming back and you never get mad. It's a rare quality."

"I'm glad you've noticed."

Hank said, "You can be very persistent." Whereas Norton had walked out in a huff, Hank looked defeated. What had it been, a year since my time with Felicity? And I had found someone new and all, but I still resented his relationship to her. He stood up. "I wonder if Felicity ever showed up."

"You concerned?" I said this cautiously.

Hank looked me right in the eye. After a moment, he said, "I don't know. The other day I told Felicity that I didn't understand her anymore, and then on my way to work I have to say I began to wonder whether I've ever understood her. I certainly don't know what in the hell she's after these days, and maybe I never knew what she was after. So, yes, I'm concerned, but I don't know what to do about my concern, either." Something Felicity had once said crossed my mind—that she felt like she was living in a frat house.

Gordon sighed. I felt a sense of alarm suddenly jolt awake. Felicity! This time last year I would have known everything about what was going on with Felicity. I took a deep breath and said very carefully, "I don't know Felicity all that well, but she's always struck me as someone who was able to take care of herself."

"Really?" said Hank.

"Sure." I glanced at Gordon to see if he was agreeing with me. He glanced back and gave a little shrug. "Maybe I'm wrong," I said.

"I wish I knew," said Hank. "I really wish I knew." He turned and went out of the room.

Gordon said, "Well, if *he* doesn't know, how are the rest of us to know? They *are* a strange pair, Joey, that's for sure. Betty and I were talking the other night. Between you and me, we don't know how we got these kids. We don't know how any of the folks we know got the kids they got. It's a mystery to me, that's what I say." He put his hands on his knees and stood up. Then he bent down and looked into my face. "What if you put the farm on the market right now?"

"I don't know. I have to do some comps, look at sales in the last six months. I'm not that up to date right at this minute."

"Well, let me know."

I nodded. He turned away from me, but I said, "Hey, Gordon. You know, about Felicity. I've always thought she had a kind of ready-for-anything quality. I thought she got it from you."

"Betty says she's more like me than the boys are. I don't know. There's a lot of women's lib around these days. Maybe that's what Felicity needs."

"Are you worried about her?"

"Nah. Well, yeah, in this sense. I used to not worry about anything. Something always turned up, for one thing. I began with luck and I went along being lucky, and I depended on going along being lucky. Then we bought that farm. I thought I was being lucky again. But when I think about old man Thorpe—well, he was never lucky. With all his money, when something had to go one way or another, chances were it went against him rather than for him, all the way to the end, to the way he died on Friday the thirteenth."

"Well, the stringer from my fence didn't impale him."

Gordon laughed. "No, it didn't. But the kind of luck I want is not the avoiding–disaster kind but the winning–the–jackpot kind."

"Well, yeah."

"Anyway, here's hoping we didn't buy into his bad luck, you know?"

"I know."

"Let's go see what the kids are doing."

I went home late that night. Felicity never came back.

CHAPTER 27

GOTTFRIED DIDN'T MIND me
coming over, especially since his two
good houses were getting a lot of
lookers, and the lookers were doing a lot of admiring. Over the week of Thanksgiving, four
Realtors let me know I could expect to see offers on the one—the farmhouse-style with the
huge kitchen—shortly after the holiday was
over, and so on the Wednesday after Thanksgiving I called Gottfried and said, "Meet me at the
Hopewell Road house at ten to one." Of
course I no longer had an office. And I didn't
have to have Gottfried along, but I wanted him
to appreciate what I was doing for him.

When we got there, three cars were already
parked across the street, and as I unlocked the

front door, another pulled up. It was a beautiful sunny day, and even though the kitchen was heated only to fifty-five, solar gain made it warm, almost tropical.

At one, the doorbell rang.

Each of the four Realtors presented an offer. I thanked each one, said that we would get back to them in twenty-four hours, and closed the door. Gottfried and I went into the kitchen and laid the offers out on the kitchen counter. One was easy to throw out. The buyers' financial statement showed it would be a stretch for them to qualify and they were borrowing part of the down payment from her parents. We set that aside.

I said, "Here's one. Twenty thousand more than the asking price."

"What do they want?" he asked suspiciously.

"Well, they'd like you to replace the refrigerator with a Sub-Zero."

"What else?"

I read down the list of contingencies. Best to get the toughest one out of the way first. "They want you to build a wine cellar in the basement in the same style as the kitchen cabinetry."

"Stupid. Get rid of it." He put that one underneath the other one.

The last two, both for the full price, were almost identical. The buyers had plenty of money and qualified easily. Their contingencies were mostly about time and financing. One wanted a forty-five-day closing—after Christmas—and the other wanted to be sure he got a mortgage. I said, "We don't have to respond until tomorrow. I expect I'll be hearing from all four Realtors tonight, now that they've seen the competition."

"Yeah." He didn't crack a smile.

"Aren't you happy? Look how this is going! I'm going to have an offer on that other house pretty soon too."

"I'm happy."

"Then smile."

"I'm not *that* happy."

He meant it. He said, "We done here? I got to get back to the farm." He left. Someday, I thought. Someday I will get used to him.

That evening, the four Realtors, who had of course seen one another, called me to sweeten the deals they were trying to make. By the end of the evening, Gottfried's wife and I had accepted an offer for the house in question—fifteen-day closing, no mortgage contingency—and had generated tremendous enthusiasm in the breast of the losing buyer for the other house, a Queen Anne not unlike Marcus's house but on a bigger lot. That buyer had seen the Queen Anne once. The next day he and his wife would be seeing it again. I expected I would be making a deal on that one within days. Closing on the first house meant over sixteen thousand in commission for me, before Christmas, and after I called Susan and then got into bed, I lay awake for a while, spinning a fantasy of short-term riches. There was, on the one hand, the future billion, but perhaps even more interesting than that, there was the immediate, say, fifty thousand. I could build a nice house for that in a spot that Susan would like, maybe on one of those south-facing hills near Roaring Falls, not so far from Deacon, up on high ground. Gottfried could build it.

In the morning, I got to work ten minutes early, and I went into the gold trader's office, and there I found George Sloan, still with that permanent grin on his face, and I said, "Am I going to be priced out of the gold market by Christmas?"

"It goes up and down. I've made a bundle in the last week. But I've been tracking it pretty closely." He shrugged.

"Well, I'm coming into a couple of unexpected commissions. Well, not unexpected, but unexpectedly early. I thought I might gamble a little."

"I think that's a good idea, Joe."

"Don't tell Marcus."

"How come?"

"Well, I want to try this once without him breathing down my neck. If it works, I'll tell him."

"I've got you. Boy, if ever there was a guy with a theory, he's the one. I sit here for hours, just listening to him."

"What do you think?"

"About his theories?"

"Yeah."

George looked at me, then said, "Shit, Joe, I haven't got one hell of a clue!" We laughed. "But I do listen to him about any tax thing. I figure if he does it, it's okay to do."

"Don't we all? But what's your theory about the gold market?"

"I don't have a theory. I do it by feel."

"And that works?"

"Works so far. But I told you my rule. I define my stake ahead of time and then I put a certain percentage of my winnings away and never touch them."

"I'll call you when I get the money."

"I'll be here."

That was Thursday. The next day, the buyers who had lost the first house of Gottfried's made a good offer on the second house and Gottfried accepted it Saturday morning. They offered to close between Christmas and New Year's. Gottfried said that was fine with him. Then he got off the phone and put his wife on, and I said, "Is he smiling yet?"

"Kind of."

"This is the quickest we've ever sold any of his houses, and these are the most expensive."

"You do a good job, Joe. I bet he doesn't tell you that."

I thanked her.

When I saw Susan over the weekend, I had a strong sense of having a delightful secret, and there was no repeat of the cocaine. We went for a walk on Saturday afternoon, then got a bite to eat and went to a movie, and somehow that evolved, and we were still together Sunday morning, reading the paper and making toast at my place, which was nothing at all like her place, and she said, "You keep telling me how sterile your condo is, Joe, but I find it soothing."

"Bland."

"I don't judge it like that. It's clean. It's neat. The surfaces are clear. You know what my mother says? If you're depressed, you should always clear the surfaces in your house and put things away, and then you'll feel genuinely better."

"What if that doesn't work?"

"Then you do three small things that you've been putting off."

"And then?"

"Well, then you pray."

GOOD FAITH

We laughed and went back to bed.

I took her home around dusk and drove back to my condo, thinking about what sort of dog we would have and how he would go out and about with me, lying on a blanket on the backseat.

Marcus was at my condo when I got home, peering at the numbered doorbells. He'd never been there before. When I pulled up, he turned on the headlights and waved to me, then came over and opened my car door. He said, "I was trying to call you all day."

"You came all the way over here because I had the phone unplugged? I guess you've forgotten what it means to be single, huh?"

"That's an understatement. Listen, what do you have stashed away?"

"What do you mean, like dope?" But I knew what he meant.

"No, not like dope. Say, do you remember that old question, is it better to have money and no dope or dope and no money?"

"No."

"Oh. Well, it was the great existential dilemma when I was in college."

He seemed in high spirits. I said, "Come on up."

When we got inside, he looked around, wandering from room to room for four or five minutes. I occupied myself by putting things away. He came out into the kitchen. He said, "So, you had a woman here last night."

"Yes, Dad, I did. Is that why you came over?"

"No. Was it Susan?"

"Seemed like it."

"Well, best not to progress too fast. But I've said all I have to say on that score." He sat down on the couch. He still hadn't taken off his coat. His demeanor changed. He rubbed his hands together for a moment, then looked at me. He said, "You know, Joe, I didn't want to come to you, because I've honored your wish to keep a little separate from the project. I think that was a natural wish, and you've certainly worked hard—as hard as anyone, or harder, frankly. I said to Jane that your circumstances were a little different, but she's been after me for weeks to talk to you. Last night, she said she was going to talk to you herself if I didn't, so I figured I'd better get to it."

"About—"

"About some bills we've got to pay. Those last engineer's bills, for one thing, and some materials for Gottfried, and the last design fee for the golf course guy. I've put off the architect who did the drawings of the clubhouse."

"I thought you paid all the engineer's bills."

"I thought I had, but another one came in, and Jane argued with him about it for two weeks, but they went all through everything, and yes we do owe him and he wants it before New Year's."

"How much?"

"Well, everything together comes to about ten."

"Ten what?"

He smiled at my evasion. "Ten grand. Well, that covers everything, including this month's rent for the office. I'm thinking the big check will be here by the first of the year, so it's just a little year-end crunch."

I said, "I can do ten grand." Actually, I was surprised we had gone this far without him asking me.

"I'm glad, because no one else can. If this big check doesn't come in, it's going to be very hard to segue into February, let me put it that way. But what's that saying? 'Sufficient unto the day the evils thereof.'"

"What does that mean?"

"That means, if it doesn't work out we'll eat shit at the time."

"How about my mortgage payment and all that stuff?"

"Well, you ought to pay that, actually. And whatever other bills you think are essential."

"You know, Marcus, I have the feeling you're giving me some bad news."

"Not really. Nothing has changed, we're just

waiting and waiting. Things are always hard around the holidays."

I said, "The squeeze will be over once spring rolls around."

"Yeah. Did I tell you the article is coming out in the golf magazine in March?"

"That's the key."

"I think so too."

He looked at me expectantly. Finally, I said, "Oh. I guess you want a check."

"Well, yeah."

I stood up and went over to my desk and wrote a check out to the company for ten thousand dollars. I handed it to him and he looked at it. I said, "Thousands in, billions out." He laughed. Only then did he stand up and take off his coat, which he draped neatly over the arm of the couch. He sat down again, put the folded check in his breast pocket. He leaned back and put his hands behind his head. He sighed. I couldn't tell if he was relaxing or worrying. I sat down again without offering him a beer. I only had one in the fridge, and I was saving that for myself. He said, "You know, it about kills me to ask you for money."

"Why is that? I'm a partner."

"I don't know."

"You've been pretty straightforward with everyone else."

"I have—I *was,* maybe is what I should say. I'm not quite as sure of myself now, so I can't summon up the same self-righteous attitude."

"That's interesting, Marcus, because from my perspective, things are progressing and we're getting closer and closer to actually turning up some buyers."

"I know that."

"So what's the problem?"

"Probably marriage."

"How so?"

"Imagine this. Every night you go to sleep, and a couple of hours later you wake up, and right next to you in bed someone is sighing and muttering. So you lie there quietly. You can feel her shaking her head, then lying quietly, then there's a little sigh, then there's a sniff. Then her head turns, and she looks at you for a long moment; then she sighs and lies flat on her back."

"Yeah, I can imagine that."

"Well, I can read her mind. This is what she's thinking. 'Oh, God. I don't know what's going to happen. I've got to get this out of my mind. I believe Marcus, but what if Marcus is wrong? He's been wrong before. He's been wrong more times than he's been right, hasn't he? Well, in some ways yes and in some ways no. Of course, there were reasons why things didn't go the way he said they would. I've got to forget this and go to sleep. Is he awake? No, I don't think so. I hope not. If he were awake, we would talk about this for the millionth time, and that wouldn't do any good. You just can't predict the future. Everyone knows that. I don't know if I can stand this.' So eventually she goes back to sleep. But then, in the morning, when the children are getting dressed for school, she says quietly to me, 'What's the plan for today?' as if I'm going to tell her something the children shouldn't hear. The plan for the day is the same as every other day—to get on with it. But she wants there to be a breakthrough, some event that will make her feel safe, except that nothing makes her feel safe."

"My mother is kind of like that."

"Is she? Anyway, for the last week, she's been saying, oh, so respectfully and casually, that maybe she would like to get a job. She misses teaching. But I know it's not about that. She didn't like teaching very much and was glad to stop. She thought she was going to write children's books. That was the plan when we moved here. She set up that fourth bedroom as a study so she could write a series of young adult mysteries. But she hardly goes in there. Anyway, it isn't about missing teaching, it's about putting her finger in the dike." He sighed. "The worst thing is, Justin is taking her mood. He's sensitive, you know. You saw that, I'm sure. And even though she doesn't talk about it in front of the kids, Justin understands that she's on edge. Actually, I think for him not talking about it is worse, because he knows something's going on, but no one tells him how big it is. Or isn't." He got up and walked around the room, stopping for a moment to look at an old picture I had of woman with her hand in a muff. "So, he thinks it's really big and getting bigger."

"So talk to him about it."

"Oh, I think we're past that point. I've thought about that, but if she doesn't agree with me about talking, then things could get out of hand. I don't know." He turned away from the picture and looked at me. "Look. I'm going to be up front with you. George Sloan told me you were in there asking questions Friday."

"He did?"

"Well, I asked him when we went out to dinner Friday night if he'd seen you and he said that as a matter of fact he had, but he didn't volunteer the information. I was a little hurt that you talked to him without—well, behind my back."

"I didn't." I felt a little alarmed.

"I feel like you're holding out on me, when I haven't held out on you at all."

"Holding out on you?"

"Caution is understandable, I suppose, though I still think it shows a lack of commitment, but that's your business. I'm not going to question your commitment because you work as hard as anyone, and if—when—this project goes it will owe a lot to you and your knowledge and hard work. But"—he sat down again and stared right at me—"I can't help feel that you're holding out on *me*. That you don't trust *me*."

I didn't say anything.

"I knew that would be a danger when I brought Jane in. I thought about it for weeks, balancing the likelihood that she would undermine me against her abilities and expertise, and finally I decided to give her the benefit of the doubt, and maybe, to tell you the truth, I didn't have a choice, because once Jane makes up her mind to do something, she generally does it, and she made up her mind that she wanted a piece of all of this, so maybe I'm kidding myself, but anyway, you were the person I worried about. I knew all along you had reservations about the whole project from the beginning, you were the one I had to win over, because your influence with Gordon was greater than anyone else's. So I was careful with you, and I spent time with you, and I told you things I didn't tell anyone else, and when you then decided to maintain your distance—well, I honored that, because you're smart and I respect you. But still, when I was talking to George, I got kind of upset, because I felt betrayed. I thought, Well, the project is one thing, and Joe can do whatever he wants with regard to the project, but this gold thing—well, that is my thing. Those are my marbles, and he's trying to get at my marbles without telling me."

"Marcus, I don't—"

"Of course it doesn't look that way to you. I see your point of view. I don't have a stake and all. But it was my *idea*." He looked at me. I looked at him. He said, "Pretty childish, huh?"

I licked my lips and said, "Well, Marcus. I understand your point of view too. I guess that's why I told George not to tell you about me coming in. Maybe I was being a little—I don't know—sneaky. But it really isn't that. I don't know what it is. I was kind of up about these commissions I'm getting from Gottfried. We sold the houses fast, and they were expensive, and I was having a get-rich-quick fantasy."

"So what's wrong with that?"

"I know you want me to put more money into the project—"

"Do I? I don't. Getting rich quick is my fa

vorite fantasy. There's nothing wrong with it. I want to do it too. Shit, man! Of course I do! Here's Mike, getting rich without me. Here's George, getting rich without me. Here's you, getting rich without me." He laughed.

I said, "Look. Let's do it together."

He said, "Nah. Nah, you don't want to do that. When all is said and done, and we've talked about marbles and friendship and everything, really it *is* every man for himself. I know that. I wouldn't even let you get me in on this deal, and that's because you're about the only friend I've ever had."

"Excuse me?"

"Doesn't that make you want to puke? I mean, that whole expression? It's very corny, and I apologize, but if I had to be honest, I would have to say, Where am I going to get a friend? My brother is a shit. My father and his uncles were shits. I went to college and all, but I spent most of that time and my time in the army in a fog of dope, so even though we were great friends, we didn't actually know one another's names. And then there was the IRS. Do you know how suspicious IRS agents are? It's a way of life. You think you aren't bringing it home from the office and all, and you do get together with the other guys, but if all day long every day you're looking for cheaters, then what you do is think the world is full of cheaters. I didn't even realize I didn't have any friends until just a while ago, like a few months ago, when we started to be friends, and it wasn't like anything I knew before, and I wondered what the hell was going on."

"Well, Marcus, I don't have a lot of friends either."

"Here's what I learned about having a friend. The fact is, I actually care about your welfare. And you aren't a member of my family. I mean, you can tell that, can't you? That I care about your welfare?"

"I can tell that. I mean, all that talk about marriage and everything. And the advice you give. I can see that."

"So, let's not talk about it anymore."

"That's probably good."

"Yeah."

So we sat back in our chairs and didn't talk about it anymore. We were silent. He looked at his watch. He said, "I guess I'd better get home. It's almost dinnertime." He reached for his coat, but he didn't stand up. Finally, he said, "Look, there's something else."

"I hope it's not about feelings."

"It's not." He laughed. "It's about my last adventure in the gold market."

"When was that?"

"Eight or nine years ago. Remember I told you about a guy from my neighborhood who went to Yale?"

"I think so."

"Well, he was a go-getter, and he had a friend there whose family owned an oil shipping company. I mean, this guy he knew was rich, and the wealth went very deep, so he always had a lot of money to play around with. And my buddy had gone to work for a Wall Street firm and was making plenty. I still had some money from before I was married, that I'd saved—not much, just a couple of thousand bucks—but I put that in, and the three of us played the gold market for four months. We put in twenty thousand to begin with—two from me, six from my friend, and twelve from the rich guy, whose name I won't tell you right now but maybe someday. Anyway, we turned over a hundred thousand bucks. At the end of that time, we split our money and went our separate ways, and I had ten thousand, my old neighbor had thirty, and the rich guy had sixty. I think he went and bought a yacht. It was so easy, it was like finding it in the street; they decided they had a license to blow it on anything they pleased. Not me, though. This was my big chance. So, I did what they do on the racetrack— and believe me I know all about the racetrack, because next to the local bar, Belmont Park was my father's favorite place. An Irishman always thinks of the racetrack as a steady job. Anyway, I parlayed my bets, and six months later I had four hundred thousand dollars."

"You did?"

"Yep. I turned two thousand bucks into four hundred thousand in ten months. And then I ponied up the taxes on it. Capital gains. I mean, I worked for the IRS, right? So I filled out my tax forms, and on the fifteenth of April, 1975, I wrote a check to the Internal Revenue Service for a hundred and sixty thousand dollars. I put about fifty into my house—you know, fixing it up and everything. My mom was dead by that time, or I would have put some money down on a house for her, but anyway." He sighed and leaned back. He looked up at the ceiling. "You want to hear what happened to the rest of it?"

"Sure."

"I got out of the gold market because I thought my luck was changing. I'd gone to Atlantic City for the weekend and lost five hundred bucks playing blackjack, and that convinced me it was time to take the rest of my money and put it into some good investments. So I knew a guy who was starting a jazz club on the Upper West Side. He borrowed fifty thousand to do the place over, and it did look great; I advised him on how to fix it up, but he never actually got his liquor license, so that was that. I invested forty thousand in a recording studio, but the manager was more interested in shooting heroin than recording anything, so that never got off the ground. And, let's see, a car, some clothes, ten each in college funds for the kids, which have grown nicely, I'll admit. And, oh, yeah. I bankrolled a friend in the wilds of New Jersey who was growing marijuana, and the field got burned to the ground right before harvest. No one got arrested, though. Did you ever invest in a dope deal?"

"No."

"I had a girlfriend in college who gave a thousand dollars to a guy who was going to import camel saddles from Morocco that were stuffed with hashish. I'll never forget how happy she was when she came up to my apartment after giving him the money. She was sure she was going to be rich."

"That's quite a story."

"Well—and I'm speaking as a bureaucrat when I say this—the only part I regretted was the check I sent to the IRS. I was very naïve. That's why I prefer living on borrowed money. I mean, you pay the interest, that's kind of like paying taxes in a way, but it's not as high a rate, even these days, and when you pay it, you know it's going to a person or at least to support the bank, and not disappearing altogether into the maw of the Pentagon."

"I guess."

"But the moral of the tale, Joey boy, is that I never lost a penny in the gold market or, for that matter, the real estate market, and I can do it this time too." He looked at his watch again, and it was now very dark. I got up and went around the room, turning on some lights. He stood up. "And now I'm late for dinner, but, hey, fuck 'em if they can't take a joke." He grinned at me, patted his pocket where he had my ten-thousand-dollar check, and walked toward the door. He turned. He said, "I'll tell you one thing."

"What's that?"

"If I'd had a good-sized stake in the gold market the day Reagan was shot, I wouldn't be busting my ass with real estate right now."

I laughed. He opened the door, and a moment later I heard him trotting down the stairs.

CHAPTER 28

I HAVE TO SAY that after that point Jane
and I were a little distant. I was annoyed
with her for not telling me I had to pay
my own bills. I didn't know what was up with
her. But the next day, when I said, "Why don't
you give me my bills that I have to pay, and I'll
pay them?" and she got them out of the file
drawer and pushed them across the desk without a word, I didn't say, *Were you just going to let
these go?* But I certainly thought it. It was one
thing for Marcus to let payments slide because
he thought some money was coming in, but it
was quite another, I thought, for Jane not to tell
me about it. Paying the bills was her job. I leafed
through them, then looked at her and said,
"I would like to talk to you, Jane, about what

is going on and exactly what is required of me."

She nodded.

"But I have an appointment and I have to pay these bills, so we can do that later this afternoon." In fact, though, what with the discomfort between us and my sense that Marcus wanted me to stay away from her, I didn't press for the meeting that afternoon, and I let it slide for the next few days, as well. Wasn't she the one who had pointed out that neither of us liked conflict?

But I watched her covertly. She was far less busy than she had been in the spring and summer. On the phone much less, writing up fewer prospectuses, talking more to Mike and to Mary King, who was in and out and seemed to be openly waiting for Marcus as well as very chummy with Jane. Mary was friendly with me too, frequently taking the opportunity to touch my elbow or put her hand on my shoulder, the way, I couldn't help thinking, that women do when they aren't exactly flirting but have an excess of sexual energy that keeps overflowing onto those around them. She was friendly and pretty, maybe six or seven years younger than Jane and better dressed. Most of the times I overheard them, she was asking Jane for advice: What kind of car should she buy? Was she really ready for something sexy, like a BMW? Wasn't it a good idea to move out of her house into an apartment? In her house she felt like an ex-wife but in an apartment she might feel more truly single. And the downstairs corridor in Building Two had suffered water damage, and it really did seem so dull to go with the same carpeting; would Jane look over some samples with her? And had Jane ever done needlepoint? Jane was tall, Mary was short; Jane gave advice, Mary took it. She was in and out of the office five or six times a day (always with her eye out for Marcus, I thought, though when he came in, they were very discreet). It was very much as if the two women hadn't a thing to do in the world. If I had been on good terms with Jane, of course, I would have pried into the Relationship a little—whether it was a live thing still or petering out—but I wasn't and I didn't. I knew we were in a holding pattern until Christmas, that it was Gottfried who was doing the real work, and the rest of us were more or less waiting for the permitting process to be over (I could see the end of it, I thought), and the clubhouse to be finished, and the golf course to be shaped and planted, and the first house lots to be surveyed and staked and sold, and, of course, for the money, the beginning of the billion, to come rolling in. And when it did, I would propose to Susan and my life would begin after what my parents certainly considered to be a very long preparatory period.

Even though I was in a very good mood, what I had seen of Felicity at Thanksgiving niggled at me every day. I would wake up in the night and think I had to call her, and then in the morning it wouldn't seem that important. Or I would drive past the Davids' house during the week, when they were in New York, and make a plan to stop when they were there over the weekend, but then not go even a block out of my way on Saturday or Sunday. I would see Gordon, but not ask about her. I began to feel very cowardly, and I wondered what I was afraid of. Just my way, Sherry would have said, to avoid any potential can of worms, but really, it was no longer my can of worms, was it? That was what I must have decided, after all. I must have had some instinctive reluctance to take on more than I could handle, and events had proved me right. But on the other hand, Felicity had called me "kind" and I wasn't acting kind.

The compromise I made was to call the Davids, at last. David Pollock answered, and as soon as I asked whether they were having a Christmas party this year, I could tell by the sound of his voice that they weren't. He sounded depressed. He said, "I guess we're spending Christmas in the city. I just came down here to drain the pipes and pour antifreeze in the bottom of the dishwasher."

"Are you guys all right?"

"Oh, I guess so. Marlin Perkins, you know. We had to put her down. She got in a tremendous fight with a pair of Australian shepherds. Her small intestine was perforated in eight places. Septicemia. Oh, it was too awful. She lingered for a week and a half. I thought it was going to kill us."

"I'm so sorry."

"We don't have quite our usual joie de vivre this year."

"I can tell."

"I think we need to hibernate and return in the spring. Sacrifice of the sun god at the winter solstice, blood and bone meal on the garden. Resurrection of the blighted earth. All that sort of thing."

"Oh. Say—"

"Be forthright, Joey."

"What's up with Felicity?"

"Something, that is for sure."

"Why do you say that?"

"She's got that look of desperation. And when I called her and told her about Marlin, she told me later she cried for twenty-four hours. She couldn't stop. And I didn't even detail the injuries, because I didn't have the heart." He sighed, then said, "Personally, Joe, I don't feel that things in general are on the upswing right at the moment, so what can I say?"

So what I did was, I put Felicity out of my mind.

I saw George Sloan in the hall, and I said, "Say, Marcus said to me the other day that he sure wished he'd had money in the gold market the day Reagan was shot. What did he mean by that?"

George laughed and motioned me into his office. He greeted an old man who was just leaving, and said, "Look at him. He *did* have money in the market the day Reagan was shot. Now he has krugerrands stashed all over his house. He's waiting for the world to end. I guess he thinks he'll be the richest man in the county then."

"Do I have to buy coins and keep them?"

"Oh, God, no. There's funds and securities and futures and options. It's just like any other commodity. Or you can buy one-ounce coins. I have some. It's just a hedge."

"Against—"

"Inflation, really. Apocalypse, too."

"I thought your hedge against that was prayer."

George glanced at me, then laughed again. We went into his office. He said, "God knows how long speculation in gold is going to be fun, but it's fun now and has been for the last several years, because no one knows when inflation is going to end or how high it will go."

"Limited supply, like oceanfront property."

"In a way. If you don't have to get a mortgage. And it's portable. Fleeing dictators buy a lot of gold. The Shah of Iran had a lot of gold with him. Gold speculators like civilization to be tottering but not toppling. Oceanfront-property people like there to be plenty of services, so they're different in that way."

"I understand that."

"But for your purposes, just a little inflation is fine, or some social disruption here and there. The gold market is sensitive to current events, so one thing I do is read the paper, especially the international news, and if it looks like something is about to happen somewhere, I buy a little, or if it looks like things are getting better, I sell. It's not especially sensitive to production rates, like some of the other commodities markets are. I don't like to listen to farm reports, so I stay out of things like pork bellies and beans. Mike likes that sort of thing. Seems boring to me." He hummed a little tune.

I couldn't help saying, "You're so different,

George, from the way you were last year. I would never have expected this of you. Everything about you is different. You were so cautious."

"That house changed my life, I guess."

"You didn't even buy it."

"And I'm glad I didn't, now. Everything you said about it was exactly right. It would have been a nightmare and I wouldn't have known where to turn about the repairs it needed. But after the cops found me and brought me home, my wife said to me, 'George, don't you realize you've had an affair? When someone has an affair it's a sign that their old life has to change or they're going to die.' Oh, she went on about it for weeks, and I was too depressed to listen to her for a while, but she kept after me, about how we'd always been so careful and so worried about everything, not just me but her, too, and the kids. We never allowed the kids to do anything. No skiing, no horseback riding. If they wanted to ride their bikes, we watched them out the window to make sure they didn't fall down. If they wanted to go over to a friend's house, we'd take them over and get ourselves invited in, and we'd spy out the potential dangers while we were leaving them off. One time, I saw a locked gun case in the father's study, and I made an excuse and took my little boy home. I guess you could say with that house, I had a nervous breakdown and I decided something had to change. And then, when you're rolling up and down with the gold market, even if you are mostly doing okay, that pretty much roots out any lingering shreds of caution you might be feeling."

"I'm amazed."

"We do lots of things now. I even go to bed at night without going down to the basement and checking the pilot light on the furnace." He guffawed. "But I'm good at this because I used to be that way, and so I know how these gold types think. I know in my gut when they're nervous—that means they're going to buy—and when they feel like they can relax a little—that means they're going to sell."

"Wow," I said.

"Oh, yeah," he said. "Oh, yeah. Marcus is pretty shrewd too. I don't know what it is. He's not like me at all, but he's got an instinct. Sometimes, he'll just call me up and say *up* or *down,* and he'll be right. And I'll say, 'So did you see the paper?' and he'll say, 'What was in the paper?' I don't know where he gets it, but he's got it."

"He told me he has second sight."

"Well, he's Irish, so maybe he does, but normally that sort of thing—well." He shrugged.

"Like I said before, he's got a lot of theories. And every single one of them could be dead wrong and he'd still have a feel for it."

No doubt about it, I was interested. So I walked past the gold trading office sometimes when it wasn't actually on my way to my car or our office. But our office was dead and Jane and I weren't getting along, and the gold office was lively. A couple of days later, I was passing the office, and one of the women I had seen in there, whom I now knew as Dawn, opened the door and called out to me. "Mr. Stratford? Are you Mr. Stratford?"

"Yes."

"They want you to come in. Mr. Sloan saw you passing." She stepped out of my way with a smile and I went in. George was standing in the door to his office with a grin on his face. He said, "Just in time. Come here."

Marcus was sitting at a screen in George's office, staring intently at some numbers. I said, "Hey, Marcus."

Without looking away from the screen, he said, "Hey!" Then, "There! There. Okay, it's topping out. I'm selling." What seemed like ribbons of numbers streamed across the screen. Marcus glanced at me and pointed at one of them. A little symbol that looked rather like an A was followed by the number 464.23. George Sloan picked up a black telephone and after a moment said, "Yeah. Okay, Fred, sell at 464.23. Yeah, right. Thanks." We continued to watch. The next time the symbol went across, it was at 464.75, then 464.90, then 464.12, then 462.43. I couldn't have said how long it took, but maybe ten or fifteen minutes later, the phone rang and George said, "Yeah. Okay. 464.36. Great." He turned to Marcus. "464.36."

"Look at it now," said Marcus, without turning away from the screen. 459.92. 458.23. 457.11. 455.20. 453.45. He said, "What time is it? About one-twenty? You know, I bet it gets below 425, anyway. Where did it open this morning, George?"

"Four-ten."

"Oh, that's good," said Marcus. "That's good. That means, Joe"—he turned to look at me—"that you earned about thirteen hundred bucks today."

"I did?"

"Yeah. You know that check you gave me?"

"The bill-paying check?"

"Yeah. Well, Jane hasn't seen it yet, but now she has eleven-three to pay bills rather than ten. She's going to be very happy."

"I gave you that check Sunday."

"Well, Monday and Tuesday weren't really very good days to play. I didn't get a good feeling, so I held on to our stake. But that's enough. Time to pay some people." He pushed back the chair and stood up. I stepped out of his way. He said, "You going upstairs?"

"I was going out."

"Well, I'll walk you to your car."

We didn't say anything, because I didn't know what to say, and Marcus didn't seem to think anything needed to be said. Finally, though, I said, "So, why are we developing property when we could be bankrolling your golden touch?"

"Because I never trade commodities on margin. You can do real estate on margin and no one ever says boo. The banks are happy, you're happy, and the buyers are happy. It's a system that's in place and that more or less works. If I put ten thousand dollars into a property and get a ninety-thousand-dollar mortgage and rent the place out so the interest is covered, and the place appreciates at ten percent a year, which isn't unusual in these times, then my ten thousand is appreciating at a hundred percent the first year alone. In seven years, when the place is worth two hundred thousand, and I sell it and pay off the mortgage, I'll get—what, say a hundred and twenty thousand? My ten thousand will have grown much faster than it would have in the stock market, without all that watching and worrying. I mean, I want a *life*. I don't want to watch a stock ticker all the time. Day trading is for people who don't have any other interests." I nodded. He put me into my car with a grin and waved me away.

I knew perfectly well not to mention Marcus's speculating, and my temptations, to Jane, but all the time I was driving around, taking my parents Christmas shopping, helping them get their lights up and their tree and then shoveling their driveway and front walk after the first heavy snowfall, I thought only about Marcus and George. Or rather, I had lots of thoughts about Christmas and Susan and houses and a future with children and cozy prosperity and comfort of a not entirely material sort, but they all spiraled back to the thought of Marcus staring at the trading screen and then picking just the exact moment when the price began to drop, and George calling the broker and telling him to sell.

Not long before Christmas, in fact, I found myself in the neighborhood where, the year before, I had sold the Sloans the house they finally bought, and I detoured off the main road and drove past it. It was one of Gordon's nicer houses, the Mendocino, I think, and when they bought it, it had been much like it was when it was first built, except the trees and shrubs were grown up. Now, in the late afternoon twilight of mid-December, I drove toward it. The street was slippery and I drove slowly. All the houses looked good: maybe four inches of snow on the roofs and porch railings, white caps on bushes, tree limbs a filigree of black and white. Not many people were out; it was a little early for the men to be coming home and a little cold for children to be playing. The Sloan place had been re-painted—once brown, now cream—and it looked like they had added on to the deck and built an elaborate playhouse in the back; I couldn't see very well as I passed. And then all of a sudden the whole place lit up—lines of Christmas lights along the eaves and spidering up into leafless tree branches. The front porch was outlined in white, and a Christmas tree suddenly appeared in the front window. Obviously, Mrs. Sloan had happened to turn on the lights as I was going past, but it seemed less mundane than that, more as though I had witnessed a sign. I felt good all evening.

The next day, I stopped in and saw George again. He was doing some trades but was happy to talk to me while keeping his eye on the screen. I said, "George, I just want to ask you one question."

"What's that?"

"Well, you know, that house you bought last Christmas. It's rather a modest house for your present circumstances."

"Oh, yeah," said George. "But we like it. Marcus has been talking to me about your new places, though."

"Good."

"But I don't know. We like that neighborhood. The kids have lots of friends there. There's enough room. I just don't know. Personally, I don't like this idea that as you get more and more money, you've got to get yourself a more and more luxurious house. Why bother? A house is a house. What you could do, and I think would be fun, would be to live at home just like you always did, but then go to France, say, and have a château there. It would be like a joke, sort of."

"What kind of a joke?" A joke on Realtors, I thought.

"Oh, you know. An I'm-not-who-you-think-I-am sort of joke. What we think is that we'll just enjoy our freedom these days. If we commit ourselves to any particular course of action, we won't have this kind of freedom again."

"That seems smart, George."

He shrugged. He said, "Got to get back to work!"

The first of Gottfried's houses closed. He was mild-mannered at the closing and hardly made any fuss at all. Maybe that was because we held it at the end of the day and he had already finished his day's work at the farm. The only thing he said to me was, "You got a check for me? I was supposed to be paid Thursday. Thursday was the fifteenth."

"I don't have it. I'll find out when I get back to the office tomorrow. I thought they were paying everyone at the end of last week."

That night I went to the movies with Susan. She wore silk, and I spent the night at her place. The next day I looked at the check I had gotten for my commission in Gottfried's house. Seventy-eight hundred dollars. I sat and looked at it for a long time, sitting in my office with the door closed. I could hear Jane and Marcus outside, chatting about what Marcus was getting Justin for Christmas. Their voices were pleasant; it sounded like they were getting along. After a while, their voices quieted and a door closed. The phone rang. I looked at my phone, but it did not light up. Not for me. I looked at the check again. I didn't know exactly why I was looking at the check. I had gotten nice commissions in the past, and I certainly expected to get plenty more of them in the future, but this check had some significance that I wanted to fix on, something like those pictures you would see in delis or antiques shops, of the first dollar the shop ever took in. I set the check down on my desk, then put it back into my wallet. A few minutes later, I got up and went down to the gold traders and walked in. Dawn was sitting at her desk. She was wearing a brilliant purple blouse. I said, "George in?"

"Oh, no, Mr. Stratford. He went home early. He had a terrible sore throat. I told him strep."

"Oh."

"My bet is, he won't be in now till after Christmas. You just can't fool around with strep."

"No, you can't."

When I left the traders, I didn't know if I was disappointed or relieved.

CHAPTER

29

ON CHRISTMAS EVE, early in the day, I went to the dry cleaners to pick up my mother's tablecloth, which had been there since Thanksgiving and which I had been promising to pick up for three weeks. I felt harried and pressed all of a sudden, because the night before, Jane and Marcus had left two Christmas presents on my desk, which I had opened at home that morning—a red cashmere scarf from Marcus and Linda and a bottle of Grand Marnier from Jane. I had nothing for them and no ideas. My plan after the dry cleaners was to go to Deacon and walk around until something presented itself. For my parents, I had bought and installed a new exterior lighting fixture with a vague coaching theme that cast more light on the steps. For Susan,

I had agonized and finally decided on a purple bathrobe that had both a sensuous feel and a sensuous look, but I had also looked at pearl earrings and copper pots and a polar bear rug with a head (I hadn't looked at that very long).

While I was standing at the counter of the dry cleaners, waiting for the tablecloth, turning gift ideas over in my mind and worrying about the purple robe, arms came around my waist from the back and a head pressed itself between my shoulder blades. I didn't have to be told it was Felicity. I didn't have to look down, even, and see her hands and the sleeves of her coat. I didn't even have to think that it could only be Felicity. I sensed her presence as readily as I ever had. I turned around. Her face was flushed and her eyes were bright. She said, "Let's have some coffee. There's a place two doors down."

I received my tablecloth, paid for it, and followed her out the door. She waited for me and took my available hand in her gloved one. As we entered the coffee shop, she kissed me on the cheek. She seemed happy, normal, the way she had always seemed. "I'll buy," she said. "You look very handsome and good. Whose tablecloth is that?"

"My mother's."

"How innocent!" She laughed.

"Well, sort of. She's been asking me to pick it up for three weeks."

"Oh, I'm so happy to see you!"

"Me, too. You look good. Your hair is bigger than ever."

"I know. I thought I might cut it all off. My head has a very nice shape, you know."

"I know. You look good, Felicity. David Pollock said that you—uh, had a look of desperation."

"Did he?" Her face fell. "It's them who are in a bad way. And the dog! That was so sad I cried and cried. But I'm perfectly all right. Better than ever, darling." She made a kiss and winked at me. It turned me on. I had forgotten she was like this, so free and so bright. Susan was not like this.

She grabbed my hand, then sought my face with hers. She said, "Well, I should have come over. Things would be different now if I had, I think. But after you closed your office, I knew there wouldn't be any privacy, and going to your new place seemed like too big a deal, so time just kept passing. I'm sorry you closed your office. I loved that building. It was fun there."

"I thought so, too." The waitress came over to us, and we ordered two cups of coffee. Felicity ordered an apple Danish. The waitress said, "You two look happy."

Without missing a beat, Felicity said, "He just got back from the Bahamas. He's been gone for six years." Then she laughed.

The waitress said to me, "What did you do, stay inside the whole time? If I went to the Bahamas, I would at least come back with a tan."

Felicity and I spoke at the same time. I said, "She's putting you on," and she said, "I meant the Bahamas, New York, not the Bahamas, Atlantic Ocean." The waitress walked away. I said, "The Bahamas, New York?"

"Do you think there is one?"

"You're very playful, miss."

"Yes, I am. It's Christmas Eve. And I miss you. You're the one that got away. My whole family thinks of you as the one that got away, first from Sally, then from me."

"Sally broke up with me."

"Well, that's a form of the one that got away. The one that wasn't sufficiently appreciated." Then, as if it weren't a serious question at all, she said, "Do you think I should have left Hank for you last year?"

"It didn't seem like you would."

"Did you want me to?"

"I didn't want to be married. I thought what we had was superior to marriage."

"Explain that to me."

"Well, I would overhear people in the grocery

store, and I would know they were married because of the tone of their voices. Even if there was
nothing really wrong with how they were speaking to each other, there was something too public about it. I enjoyed our secrecy. It was very
exciting. But on the other hand, I'd known you
for a long time, so it was familiar."

"Best of both worlds."

"I thought so."

"So why did we let it go?"

"Well, I don't know about you, but I guess I
was afraid that private things were about to become public. It gave me a feeling sort of like
setting off a bomb at the family reunion."

She looked at me thoughtfully, then said,
"Well, yes. I guess I thought of it as, What am I
going to say to my mother when she finds out
about *this*?"

"So, we were agreed, I suppose."

She nodded, then said, "I heard you were dating Susan Webster pretty heavily."

"I guess I am."

"So do you want to be married?"

Looking at her, I could honestly say, "I don't
know."

"I know people look at me and Hank and
say, 'Why did they get married?' I look at us and
say, 'Why do people get married?' I just don't
understand it. I mean, he hasn't changed. I

haven't changed. That's the weird part. I just think we thought, Well, everyone is married. Our parents are married. The alternative to marriage must be death, since the only grown-ups we know who aren't married are dead." She laughed. I laughed with her. She went on, "That was so 1962, wasn't it? Nobody thinks like that anymore. But, anyway, do you think I should have left Hank for you last year?"

"Well, it's been about a minute and a half since you last asked me that question, and I still don't know. But you are very—you were very—well, every time I saw you, it was like the sun coming out. I guess I would have to say I didn't feel like it was possible to possess that, so it didn't cross my mind to try."

"That's a very sweet thing to say. It might be my most favorite compliment that I've ever gotten."

"Well, it's true."

The waitress brought our coffee, set it in front of us, and returned with the Danish, which Felicity picked at for a moment. Her face became calm, and she looked at me more seriously. She said, "That's a problem you have, Joey. You forget to claim what might be yours. I don't know why that is, but between you and me, it's better to claim it, even if it isn't quite right in some way, than not have any life at all, because that's what happens. I know lots of women nowadays who are just so indecisive, and then they turn around, and really, twenty years have gone by and they don't have anything except maybe a few well-chosen objets d'art and some nice dishes." She scowled.

I laughed.

"It's not a joke." But then she laughed. She finished her Danish. "Anyway, don't let that happen to you: just because Sally and I got away—which will always be a source of regret for Betty Baldwin, who is a great believer in marriage but only to the right person."

"Okay."

"Gotta go."

She jumped up and left. When I followed a few moments later with my tablecloth, which had gotten entangled in some chairs, I saw her car pulling out of the parking lot and heading west.

Christmas went by. The whole time I thought about Marcus and George. On Christmas afternoon, I pulled out my last bank statement and had a long look at it. There was plenty of money in my savings account, even though I had given Marcus that check for ten thousand dollars and I hadn't had much of an income for the last six months.

And there was eight thousand in my wallet and another eight thousand, more or less, coming in a day or two. I added everything up and wrote down the number. It was sixty-two thousand dollars. Nothing about that sum fooled me. I knew it was a lot of money, more than a 20 percent down payment on a house that you couldn't even buy in our area. With that sum, I could have gotten a good mortgage on an apartment in Manhattan, a place in San Francisco, maybe even London—any stratospheric city in the world. I didn't tell myself anything about what I was going to do with that number, I just looked at it.

The morning after Christmas, I got up, put on my clothes, and drove to the office. George was right there, fit as a fiddle and ready to trade. I showed him my check from the real estate closing and he said, "Let's call Marcus."

Marcus came down from our office in five minutes. He sat down at the screen and stared at it. I saw that little sign, the A-like thing. The number after it was 434.23. I was disappointed. Marcus said, "How much do you have to play with?"

"Eight thousand."

"More would be better."

"More is always better," said George.

We stared at the screen for a while, but the

price stayed in the same region, 430–438, without varying very much. Marcus said, "How about silver?"

George pointed to another little symbol. The number beside it was 52. Marcus looked at it for a few moments, then said, "Oh, I don't know. Let me think about this. You got a paper?"

"Dawn has one."

I went and got it and handed it to Marcus. Marcus grinned at me, perhaps an acknowledgment that I had caved at last, but he didn't say anything. For Christmas, I had given him a Waterman pen and I had given Jane a pair of black fur-lined calfskin gloves to go with a red coat she wore. I had given Linda a plant, an orchid. It was expensive and it came with detailed instructions. I had given Justin a baseball glove and Amanda an elaborate set of art materials. Right there at the last minute, probably because I'd run into Felicity and we'd talked so congenially about love, I had gotten into the Christmas spirit.

Marcus was looking at the paper, but George was looking at the screen, and just then George said, "There we go." The price after the little symbol was now 431.76, and soon after that, 427.76. I said, "Why does it do that?"

"Ah," said George. "If only I knew."

"It does that because some big player decided to park his millions somewhere else," said

Marcus. "Maybe he had a good lunch and felt better about life. Maybe shares in Philip Morris went down. At any rate, he's convinced a lot of his friends. Look at that." The price continued to fall. Soon it was at 416 and change. The skin on my arms began to tingle, and then Marcus said, "Let's go out and get a cup of coffee and come back."

I wanted to do that too.

When we came back half an hour later, the price was at 397. Marcus said, "Okay, George, buy what you can." George picked up the phone.

We sat there through the rest of the morning, through lunch, and through the early afternoon. After bottoming out at about 395, the price rose all the rest of the day. We laughed and joked and jumped up and down from time to time. I went out into the parking lot once and smoked an imaginary cigarette to ease the tension, sure the price had dropped in my absence. But it hadn't. When I came back in, without any supervision on my part, it had risen another three dollars. Sometimes the three of us stared at the screen and shouted, "*Up! Up!*" and it went up. We tried that three times, and got to feel we had an intoxicating power. We shouted a lot, actually, making big loud noises and stomping around. It was fun, like being at a football game where your team was scoring one touchdown after another. At two-fifteen, even though it hadn't yet dipped, Marcus said to George, "Okay. Take the profit." George placed the call. We sold at 436, only two points above where the market had begun that morning, but I had made seven hundred fifty dollars or so, less the broker's commission. It was nice. It was my mortgage payment for a couple of months. It didn't take me long to figure out that if I had put all $62,000 dollars of my savings into the gamble I would have made six thousand on the deal instead of seven hundred and fifty. Ten percent in a few hours. It was very interesting.

As we went up to the office, Marcus at first didn't say anything, but then he said, "Don't be seduced. I'm not kidding. Not every day is like this."

"Well, obviously not."

"Some days are better!" He guffawed, and I did too.

The next day was Tuesday, and then it was Wednesday, the last Wednesday in the year. I hemmed and hawed and hemmed and hawed. I was to go to Gottfried's second closing at eleven, so rather than going to the office first, I hemmed and hawed around my apartment. Just before leaving, though, I got out my checkbook and wrote a check for $60,000. The closing was uneventful, or maybe I just didn't care about the events, because whatever they were, they did not stick in my mind. Just before one that afternoon, the last Wednesday afternoon in the year, I got to the office. Marcus's car was in the parking lot. So was George's. So was Jane's. Everything normal. I got out and walked across the ice, which was pretty slippery, though sanded and salted. My knees were knocking. I passed the gold traders' offices without looking in and walked up the stairs. I opened the door. Jane was at her desk. She smiled at me. Mike was changing the supply on the water cooler. He said, "Hey, Joe. How's it going, man?" I gestured toward Marcus's office. His door was closed. Jane nodded. I knocked and went in. Marcus was leaning back in his chair, reading some paper, but he looked up with a grin when he saw me and his chair fell forward toward the desk. "Hey, man," he said.

I had my hand in my pocket on the check. I fingered it and brought it out and laid it in front of him. I said, "Let's try this. Let's try it together. I've got the capital and you've got the instincts." It seemed the obvious thing to do, nothing more obvious.

He looked at the check and then at me and

then back at the check. He was no longer grinning. He said, "You mean it?"

"Yeah."

"Okay, then. But don't tell Jane. This is private."

"I think so too."

He came around the desk and we opened the door and went out into the office. I felt like we were running, but really we were acting very cool. If anything, Marcus was even more good-natured than usual. Jane said, "Are you leaving? I thought you were going to be around all afternoon."

"Joe and I are going out to the farm. Gottfried has run into some problem."

"Can I go?" said Mike. "I'd like to see how it's coming."

"No," I said. "Gottfried will be much less receptive if there're too many people around."

We closed the door behind us before he could reply.

But when we got down to the gold traders' offices, George was out. Then he came back and Marcus sat down in front of the screen and said, "I don't like it today."

"I haven't traded a thing today," said George. "Market's way up. You never can tell what it's going to be like at the end of the year."

"That's true," said Marcus. We sat around the

office, idly checking the numbers for a while, but then Marcus said, "Well, some of us have to actually do some work," and he got up. I followed him out of the office. In the hallway, he said to me, "George is right. The end of the year can be a bad time. We'll wait and see. And, of course, people who have profited over the year often take their offsetting losses. When we should have done this was around the tenth–twelfth of the month." He shrugged. "But, you know, when we do do it, it will be fun."

I nodded. He said, "You got that check?"

"Yeah." I patted my wallet.

"A personal check is going to take some time to clear. If we want to do this this week, you have to go to the bank and get a bank draft made out to me, like this one. I'll put it into an account at George's office. I have an account in my own name, with nothing in it. But I'll change that into both of our names. Here." He handed me a card. "Put your social security number on there."

I wrote my number on the back of one of his business cards.

He said, "We'll see how it goes over the next couple of days."

"I still think that was a helluva day Monday."

"Oh, yeah. Oh, yeah. Say, do you want to really go out to the farm?"

"I was out there yesterday. Gottfried is doing fine, but you know, he hasn't been paid."

"I'll go up and get Jane on it right now."

"All right. I'll go to the bank." At the end of the day, I handed him the bank draft. He looked at it and put it into his wallet.

Thursday was no better, according to both George and Marcus, and when I looked at the screen myself, I could see that they were right—prices declined over the course of the day. Marcus left to do an errand. George said to me, "You don't have to stay in for just a few hours. You can go more long-term than that."

"Yeah, I know."

"But the price is high, compared to what it's been over the year. I just put everything away myself, all in cash for the time being. But I hate having things in cash. Cash loses value so fast when you've got this kind of inflation. I had this funny dream this year. I'll never forget it. I had this wad of cash in my pocket, in a money clip, the way my grandfather used to carry his money, and I took it out and laid it out in my hand, and you could barely see the printing, and even as I watched, the green just faded to white. I was terrified! I woke up and said to my wife, 'I've just had this dream about inflation!' Oh, we laughed!"

Friday was December 30. We went down to the gold traders' office early, before nine. When the market opened, the price was still up, though not quite as high as it had been the afternoon before. Marcus seemed depressed and George seemed distracted. I said, "We aren't very psyched for the game, guys."

"Oh, Linda and I had another go-round this morning, and I guess you've seen Jane."

"I didn't notice anything with Jane."

"That's because you have dollar signs in your eyes. Do you ever feel surrounded by women?"

"No."

But George nodded.

"Jane. Linda. Amanda. All cut from the same cloth."

"Which cloth is that?"

"Well, the female cloth. 'I'm mad.' 'What about?' 'You don't know?' 'No, I don't.' 'Think about it.' And then you're sitting there inventorying your possible sins, and you know there are plenty of them. The only question is, which ones does she know about and which ones doesn't she? So you decide that the problem is you were lying in bed last night right next to her and, very quietly, you beat off, and she must have been awake rather than asleep, so *that's* the one. But it's very important to be cautious, so you say, 'Really, I can't think of anything. I want to know, I really want to know,' and she says, 'You really don't remember yesterday when I was bringing all those groceries in from the car, and you just sat there in front of the TV even though I asked you twice to help me?' Oh, yeah! That! Don't remember a thing about it. So, I said, 'Oh, I am sorry, dear, I guess I was preoccupied and didn't hear you' and she says, 'You were? You were *that* preoccupied? What about . . . ? Is something wrong I should know about?' That sort of thing. And then Amanda comes in and says, 'Justin is picking his nose and eating it! Aren't you going to stop him?'"

"Glad I got boys," said George.

Marcus said, "At least Jane is going to go to our sister's house without me this year. Linda and the kids and I are going to her family. They live near a ski area, so I'm going to spend the whole time on the slopes."

"When will you be back?"

"Monday evening. Monday afternoon if the weather looks bad. Believe me, I want to be right here first thing Tuesday morning."

We watched the screen. It was as if the numbers didn't know how to change. After about half an hour, Marcus said to me, "Let's do this Monday. First trading day of the New Year. I bet things will be quite up and down and we can turn it over a little."

Actually, I was relieved to put it off. We went up to the office. Jane seemed fine to me. She was wearing an especially attractive outfit, a sort of rose-colored suit, but not too bright, very flattering to her skin tone, which I told her. She laughed and said in a friendly, pleased way, "Well, I just bought this at an after-Christmas sale. Maybe I'll wear it every day. I love it." And she reached up and tweaked me affectionately on the cheek. I said, "Marcus says you're going away for the weekend."

She glanced at Marcus, then nodded. "How about you?"

"I'll be right here."

"You should go somewhere."

"I'm waiting for that billion, I guess."

She laughed.

Marcus came out of his office about five minutes later. It was maybe ten-thirty. He said, "I'm off then."

I said, "Have fun skiing." Jane's eyebrows rose, then she composed her face again. Marcus nodded and went out, letting the door slam behind him. I said, "Don't Linda's folks live near a ski area?"

"Oh, yeah. But Marcus is a terrible skier. I'm surprised that's what he's planning to do all weekend. I hope he gets back here in one piece. Say, Joe, you aren't getting into any deal with him, are you?"

"I'm already in a deal with him, as you know."

"But other than that?"

I definitely didn't want a third party in on this. I said, "No, of course not."

She said, "Well, good. Have a Happy New Year."

Her tone seemed unusually warm, which I found a little embarrassing, so I just thanked her and went into my office. A few minutes later, I heard the outer door open and close, and I was alone in the office. Our business for the year was done, and, I thought, it hadn't been easy, had it?

CHAPTER 30

SUSAN AND I WENT OUT for New Year's Eve with some of her friends. They were younger than I was by about ten years. We went to a couple of clubs and danced, then back to her place. We went quietly and affectionately to bed. It was cold, and she wore a light blue flannel nightgown and socks. When I was unable to fall asleep, I thought because of the food we'd eaten late, she said, "Let me do this," and she stroked my forehead. I thought of Marcus as I fell asleep with my arms around her. I was planning to tell him that his first instinct about her had been right, and we didn't need to worry about the other stuff after all. I suppose it took me until about noon to wake up and get moving. Susan and I lolled in bed, a lazy Sunday in front of us. We ate some muffins she had baked, with dried cranberries and orange peel in them, another something I had never tasted that tasted good. And her coffee wasn't Maxwell House, either, but ground fresh beans she'd ordered from New York.

It was a bright, sunny, cold day, and I got into my car at Susan's and I drove through the brilliant countryside. I was ruminating pleasantly on how rich I was going to be. Later in the afternoon, I dropped by my parents' house and cleaned their furnace filters and changed the element on their electric hot-water heater. I swept their walk. We hadn't had any snow in over a week.

For dinner, I made myself a ham sandwich and a bowl of tomato soup. When the phone rang, I looked at the clock. It was seven forty-two. I picked it up. On the other end of the line was Betty, whom I was not expecting. She said, "Joey."

"Yes. Hi, Betty."

"Joey. Have you seen Felicity?"

"No. I mean, I saw her Christmas Eve day, but I haven't seen her since."

"How did she seem?"

"Fine. I actually thought how fine she seemed."

"Well, no one has seen her since Friday morning. She didn't come home last night or call. Hank is worried. I'm a little worried myself."

That was a thought I could not get past, so I just said, "I don't know, Betty. Keep me informed."

Patience was the only option. I went to a movie by myself. There was something about this Felicity thing I couldn't discuss with Susan. She was too cool. She would point out some detail in a way that would be both insightful and irrefutable. I was sorry Marcus wasn't around, because I knew he would have plenty to say.

By the time I went to bed that night, I had more or less reassured myself, but I lay awake anyway. I thought two things. One was that she was too smart to get into trouble and the other was just an image of her face, ready and accepting, the sort of face that might tempt someone to give her trouble.

Monday night, Betty called me again. She said, "You'll never guess. They found her car parked at JFK."

"JFK airport?"

"Yes. The parking ticket was in it. Stuck behind the visor."

"So she went somewhere?"

"Somewhere. The car is fine. It was locked.

"Felicity seems like she can take care of herself."

She said, "I think it's over with Hank."

"Well, Betty, when I talked to her last, she said that not only didn't she understand why she was married to Hank, she didn't understand why anyone was married at all."

"She said that to me too."

"What did you say?"

"Well, I think I said something very unhelpful and obtuse, like, 'Oh, Felicity, for goodness' sake.'"

"What does Leslie say?"

"She hasn't heard from her either."

"Where's her car?"

"Gordon says we should call the state police and have them look for her car."

"What about Hank?"

"Hank knows she's left him, but he isn't willing to admit it yet."

"I'm sure she'll get in touch by morning, Betty. I don't feel like anything has happened to her." That was right, wasn't it?

"Oh, of course," said Betty. "But it makes me nervous, because we went through this with Sally. We didn't hear anything for two days, and then we heard from the police. Felicity knows that. She would surely avoid worrying us if she could."

Maybe she just wanted to get away. Gordon says she'll come back. The police don't really want to pursue the matter any further, and Hank doesn't either. I guess he doesn't want to hound her into saying that she's leaving him until she makes up her mind, if that's what's going on."

"I think that *is* what's going on, Betty. I really do. She went somewhere to make up her mind. We should just be patient."

"I keep feeling that if she had married you, she wouldn't be doing this."

"There's no way to know that, Betty."

"I knew you were seeing each other last year."

"Was it that obvious?"

"Not to anyone else. But, yes, to me."

"She was afraid of what you might say."

"Then maybe she underestimated me." She sighed. Then she said, "Okay. Well, okay. I won't worry."

"I'm sure when Marcus gets home, he'll have some idea about what to do, or a connection somewhere that will lead right to her."

"Where is he?"

"They all went skiing."

"I hope so. I mean, obviously what's needed

is patience more than anything else, but that's the hard part."

"I know she's fine, Betty."

At 2 A.M. Tuesday morning, my phone started ringing and ringing. I thought of Felicity and woke right up. But it wasn't Felicity, or Betty either. It was Linda Burns. She said, "Joey. Joe. Where is Marcus?"

"I have no idea. I haven't seen him since you guys got back."

"Back from where?"

"Back from your trip. Didn't you go to see your folks?"

"Yes. But Marcus didn't come along. He stayed here to do work."

"He did?" Maybe I was still asleep, I thought, because I sounded very dumb. I said, evenly, "He told me all of you were going and would be back tonight."

Her voice got more penetrating. "His clothes are gone. About half his clothes from the closet in our room. And there's just a note that says *I'll call you and call Joe.*"

"Did you call Jane?"

"Yes. There's no answer at her place. The kids and I went over. It's dark there and the dog is gone."

"Wouldn't she take the dog to her sister's?"

"Jane didn't go to Mary Rose's house or to Katie's. I saw both of them this weekend. I drove down with the kids. That was part of my agenda, so they could see the kids. I was fit to be tied with Marcus because I was supposed to do all this relatives stuff on my own." Now, she sounded conversational, matter-of-fact, almost cool.

"Jane told me she was going to see her sister."

"She did?"

I tried to remember more clearly. Then I said, "Well, I suppose it was Marcus who told me that."

"Joe."

"Yeah?"

"Joe, I'm going to say this while I'm still kind of sane."

"What's that?"

"I think they've left. I think they've walked out and left and Marcus knew if I talked to you, you would tell me. Did they leave? Marcus and Jane? Did they go off together? You can tell me."

"I can't tell you. I don't know."

"You told me that Marcus told you that he was going with me, and Jane was going to Mary Rose's. Why would he tell you that? You're sure he told you that?"

GOOD FAITH

"I'm sure."

She hung up.

By eight o'clock I was in the office, looking through all the drawers in both Marcus's desk and Jane's and through the file cabinets too. I kept looking at my watch. At 8:05, I began calling downstairs to the gold trading company and asking for George. George called me back at 8:36, casual and relaxed from a ski weekend. I said, "Say, George, did Marcus deposit a check with you, in a gold trading account, in both of our names, his and mine, last Thursday?"

"What would that be, the twenty-ninth? Let's see. How much would it have been for?"

"Sixty grand."

"Oh, goodness, no. Marcus owed me about three thousand at that point, so I would have noticed that for sure. Is he around? The market is jumping today already."

"Marcus is not around."

"When do you expect him?"

"You know, I'm not sure of the details of what's going on, but I feel certain it's some simple thing and we'll all look back on this and laugh."

"Laugh at what?"

"Oh, laugh at how worried we were."

"What do you mean?"

"I'll call you back."

I called Betty. Gordon answered. I said, "Hey. Any word from Felicity?"

"No," he said. "It's been four days now. I hired a guy."

"What sort of guy?"

"The sort of guy who looks into things. Nathan knows him."

"How's everyone over there?"

"Not sleeping. I don't know, Joey. I don't know. It's a bad deal that Marcus Burns is—"

"Do we feel like Marcus Burns is—"

"Is gone? Yes. I think Marcus Burns is gone. Betty doesn't agree with me. Linda Burns was over here."

"I'm sure there's some explanation, Gordon."

"What would a good explanation be, Joe? I mean, an explanation that we would like?"

"Did she take any money with her?"

"Hank says about ten grand."

"That's a good sign."

"It's a good sign if you're worried she's dead."

"Well, yes."

"So, it's a good sign."

He hung up.

What was missing from Marcus's desk were the financial records of our partnership. That, I thought, was a bad sign. Just as I thought that thought, the phone rang and it was Bart from the savings and loan. He said, "Is this Joe?"

"Yeah."

"Joe, I took your name off the loan."

"Which loan?"

"The last loan, the loan on the farms in the Midwest. Where was that, Kansas? Nebraska."

"My name wasn't on that loan."

"That's why I took your name off it."

"Excuse me?"

"I have to make this quick. There's a lot going on."

"Yes, there is. But I never even saw the paperwork on that loan."

"Well, after thinking about it I decided probably that was the case, so however your signature got on that loan, and your condo—well, I removed them."

"Marcus and Jane forged my signature on that loan?"

"That's what it looked like to me after I thought about it for a while, yes. I thought that rather than going down that road, since there are going to be plenty of other roads to go down, we would just—you know. Less said the better."

"We've been waiting for that money for months."

"It did take awhile. Lot of money, in some

ways. But I'm sorry to say that it was paid out ten days ago, and we understand from Mr. Nuelle, to whom I spoke this morning, that none of it has been paid to him, and none of it has been paid to the engineers, and so, I have to say, that's a loan that is going to be scrutinized very closely in the near future."

"Ten days ago?"

"Let's see, yes, more than that now. Paid out on December seventeenth. I'll call you back." And he hung up.

That's the exact moment I realized that Marcus and Jane and Felicity had taken at least eight hundred thousand dollars, plus my sixty, which would make it eight hundred and sixty thousand dollars, which was a lot of money in 1984, and left the country.

In the newspapers, the reports and the investigations centered on Jim Crosbie, and for a long time the collapse of Portsmouth Savings and Loan, which became official on the fifteenth of January, was considered to be an example of malfeasance on the part of Crosbie and only Crosbie. It was Bart, it turned out, who alerted the FSLIC and supplied the government with notes he had been keeping since Crosbie's arrival. Apparently, Portsmouth Savings had been hiding losses since the late seventies, and hiding their diminishing net worth from the regulators by inflating loan appraisals and cooking the books. Crosbie's job had been to make risky investments and apply the proceeds to Portsmouth's net worth, and he had risked millions of dollars in deposits on T-bill futures and junk bonds. When the regulators had a look in November, just by chance, there had been plenty of money in the coffers, but three big losses after New Year's had wrecked that—and when Crosbie had to cover margin calls with almost all the deposits, Bart had phoned the regulators. The government sent in eleven accountants, and it took them months to figure out all the details. In fact, that chaos was part of Crosbie's defense—what with the slow transition to computers, the unfamiliarity of the staff with the new system, and the huge new variety of transactions the S and L had been engaged in, he more or less didn't know what was going on. The *Portsmouth Herald* supported Crosbie at first, if you consider calling him *an incompetent boob* support. He lost a good deal of credibility, or maybe it was sympathy, though, when he happened to shrug on the local news and say, "All the deposits are insured, aren't they?" There was a considerable outcry about how he didn't seem to care, and, in fact, he didn't. When the *Portsmouth Herald* did a story about all the falsified loan documents found in the files, with appraisals from guys named *Joe Blow* and *Roger Roe*, things got more serious, and eventually Crosbie was sent to federal prison for fraud. After a while, the FSLIC sucked up all our firm's collateral—Gordon's properties and farms, Salt Key Farm, Bobby's little house that he had bought with Fernie, and Marcus's house—and everything was sold for what it might bring. For a long time, until the Resolution Trust period, the $800,000 that Marcus and Jane took with them to the Bahamas was listed as an asset. Then the debt was sold off, Marcus and Jane were indicted in absentia, and I didn't have the heart to follow the money, wherever it had gone. Bobby Baldwin said it was in Switzerland somewhere. Perhaps that was true. Marcus also took our books, so we never figured out how much of our original stake he had with him, but what with all the bills left unpaid, my guess was about $200,000.

Susan Webster was very cool when she ended our friendship. It was maybe ten or twelve days after my conversation with Bart. We were sitting on her bed, and I was looking at the picture of the glossy oranges across the room and saying, "I think I would be satisfied in some way if I just knew when he made up his mind. I mean, was it all the way from the beginning? Was it some kind of panic deal at the end? Did he, or all of them for that matter, just look at that money and say—"

Susan said, "Joe." She removed her hand from mine, and I realized that I had been rubbing her thumb a little hard, and I kissed the spot that I had been rubbing. She took it back anyway. She went on. "I have to say that I really don't want to go on with this."

"With what?"

"With this thing that happened to you. Or that you did. Or, anyway, it's going to take a long time to sort this out, you said so yourself, and I don't want to go through it with you. I like you, but I thought about what sort of thing this is going to be, and I have to be honest. It's not for me." She smiled quietly and with complete conviction. Then she glanced into my face and shrugged slightly. She said, "But it's late. I wasn't going to say this until tomorrow, but, you know, I just don't want to talk about it. You can stay if you want to. I don't mind."

I got off the bed and left. At that moment, I was mostly annoyed with her for not letting me finish my question about Marcus and for not giving me her opinion. She could have allowed me at least that. Afterward, though, I was more surprised that I didn't miss her, and surprised that I had been thinking I was going to marry someone I didn't actually miss when she was gone. But this was what she was like—she was like those oranges. Like holding a cool, perfect, fragrant orange in the palm of your hand, and putting it to your cheek, and being glad you have it, because it is perfect and strange, but then, after all, it's not important. That was the first good thing that happened to me, but I have to admit I didn't realize it was good until long after I saw Felicity's picture in the paper.

We all knew when Felicity got back in the country, because her picture was in the paper. When I opened it that day, which was just as the forsythia was coming out, the first thing I noticed was that she had cut her hair after all, and that her head was beautifully shaped, just as she'd said, and her eyes and mouth looked bigger, though she wasn't smiling and she was looking down, and a man in a uniform had his hand on her arm.

I heard from Betty within a couple of days of Felicity's return. She said, "She hasn't been with Marcus. She hasn't been with him since the end of January."

"Where is Marcus?"

"When Felicity left them, they were in the Bahamas. She doesn't know where they are now."

"Really?" I loved Betty, but I knew I sounded hostile, suspicious.

"Really. She's been in France. I mean, she was in France until she ran out of money. We had to send her a ticket."

"She ran through ten thousand dollars?"

Now there was a long silence for which I wanted to apologize but couldn't. Finally, Betty said, "They can't link her to Crosbie in any way, so they've kind of lost interest in her, I gather. She's staying here while she and Hank work things out."

"What about Marcus? Aren't they interested in Marcus?"

"Not very, I gather. I mean, the bird in the hand at the savings and loan is so big, the bird in the bush in the Bahamas is small by comparison."

We were silent again. She said, "She would like to talk to you."

"Why wouldn't I talk to her?"

"She thought they were going on a vacation. She thought they were going to run off for two weeks and decide if they had a future. She thought it was her idea, even, and her money. Marcus told her he couldn't afford a vacation, but she wanted to do it. She didn't realize there was anything else going on until they got to the hotel and Jane was there."

"Do you believe that, Betty?"

"I think when a woman has been married for twenty years and is crazy to leave her husband, she thinks anything is plausible. Now she realizes she was an idiot."

I admitted that Marcus was good at getting you to think that his ideas were your ideas.

"You see?" said Betty.

But then I couldn't stand to talk about it any longer.

I have to say that Betty was persistent, though to what end I didn't understand. One day I ran into her at the shopping village, and it took her less than a minute to get back on the subject. She put her finger on my arm and drew me into a corner. She said, "She never realized that Marcus had our money or your money or the money from the savings and loan until she got home. Norton told her. When she was with Marcus and Jane, the only person who bought anything or paid any bills was Felicity."

"Was that why she left?"

"That was the catalyst, I guess. I mean, when she realized they were living off her, she knew she had to get out of there. But she said they started bickering almost as soon as they got there. Marcus would leave her in their room, and go to say something to Jane, and then he would be gone for hours, and Felicity could hear them through the wall. Joey, you should see her. She wants to see you."

"I will. I really will."

But I never went over, not as long as I knew she was staying there. One time, I even saw her at the end of the aisle in the grocery store and turned around and walked out the door and got into my car and drove home.

I asked Betty, "Why did he take my money?"

She said, "I think it was Jane's idea, myself. I liked Marcus. I think he was committed to the project, and then Jane saw it wasn't going to work and she cooked it up. You never really noticed Jane, did you? I mean, she was plain. Men like you are friendly towards plain women, but you never really *observe* them, do you?"

"But why did he take *my* money?"

"Why not?" said Betty. She smiled. She smiled genuinely. I never understood that about Betty, how she never lost her equanimity. She and Gordon moved into one of the townhouses we had built, and Betty continued to run her antiques shop. The lease had been in her name all along, ever since Gordon bought those pink silk chairs. Bobby went to work for her, and he and Fern got married, but they never had any children. Gordon found himself a truckload of antique-furniture-making planes, and then a traincar load of brick paving stones from some-where in Connecticut, which he sold to Columbus, Ohio, for repairing the brick streets of some quaint neighborhood they were trying to preserve. We didn't see much of each other, and so I don't know what was really behind how he and Betty went from land baron and patriarch to an elderly couple in a townhouse. His lawyer was Martin Jenkins, and then he got Sol Bernstein, who after a while joined the poker game. Betty's voice always sounded light and good-natured. When I didn't want to talk about Felicity, she told me stories about her grandchildren. She asked me if I was seeing anyone. I said I wasn't. I said I wanted to see her, but I didn't. It was odd the way that friend-ship dissipated, or at least I thought it was odd until I woke up in the middle of the night and realized how I had betrayed them, bit by bit—first for Felicity and then for Marcus.

I had lunch with George Sloan every so often. He was very philosophical about Marcus. I would sit quietly while he would expound his theories. He was on a low-fat diet, eating his salad and waving his fork around. "What you've got to ask yourself about Marcus," he would say, "is when exactly did he know what he was going to do? I mean, if we could talk to him now, what would he say? Maybe he would say that it was *us* who tempted *him*. We—I mean you-all, really, since I only let him have about five grand in all. You just handed it over. Maybe he was planning to go right down the straight-and-narrow but how could he, because here was the land and here was the estate and here were the guys, and, eventually, here was the girl, and so why not? Sure his wife thinks he's the devil incarnate and so do you, probably, but who's the tempter and who's the tempted here?" He would chuckle at this point. He was an investment genius, making money hand over fist. "So, that place. They redid the roof and fixed it up, and now they're out of business. Look into it for me, okay?"

George Sloan was the only person I could talk to about it. My lawyer kept saying, "Look, don't speculate. Every motive you attribute to the guy, every story you make up, it compromises you. And I don't just mean legally. Put your life back together. You've got your real estate license, and you've got some listings. If you keep turning this over in your head, pretty soon you're going to be fifty and you'll still be sitting on square one. Between you and me, be grateful you aren't the wife and get on with it." Linda *was* in a pickle; eventually she got a ruling that divorced her from Marcus and went back to New York.

The prosecutors and the auditors and the federal officials and the state officials breathed on me, and their breath was hot, but in the end the flame from the throat of the federal dragon burned others. They would send me notices and call me up and have me come in and talk to them, or they would subpoena me, but there was never a trial except for Crosbie. I read about that in the paper. People from North Carolina and even New York had more important things to say about him than we did.

Of course, my parents were getting older. In the fall of '84, I sold their house and my condo and found a duplex, three bedrooms downstairs and two up. They had almost a hundred thousand dollars in equity. We were moved in by the first snowfall. I kept the walks shoveled and salted. My dad parked his car in the garage and never drove it again after that, but we weren't far from the center of Deacon, and they went for walks in the spring, two or three blocks and home again. My father discovered gourmet coffee. Every morning, he would walk down to the Larkspur Café and have some roast or other—Blue Mountain, from Jamaica, or Kona, or dark Sumatra—and he would read a newspaper from a different town or a different continent. My mother would lament to me, "I know he thinks we should have traveled more. I know he's sorry now that we didn't even get to New Orleans." But my father said, "This is enough for me, just the papers and what things are called and the different flavors. I never was much for leaving home." In my spare time, which sometimes was quite plentiful, I fixed the place up. It was soothing.

The hotel division of Avery Development bought the farm for a million. They paid off the lien Gottfried had put on the place, brought in a big construction firm from Florida, and added on to the house to the west and the south. Ten suites and a hundred rooms; another dining room, which made two gourmet restaurants; eight tennis courts plus the golf course; gift shops that were auxiliary to the fanciest ones in the shopping village; and an ice rink and hot tubs and saunas for the winter, when guests came to eat steamed vegetables and slim down. No horses. When it opened in 1988, they called it THE SPA AND RESORT AT SALT KEY.

By 1988, Gottfried's houses were selling for half a million dollars. He was using Carla King as his Realtor. The only thing he ever said to me about Marcus was, "I told you you should have listened to me about that asshole. If you'd listened to me, you would still be selling my houses." That I wasn't selling his houses was my one relief.

They wanted more for the former restaurant than it would have cost George Sloan when we first saw it, but not as much more as the improvements were worth, and anyway George had a lot more money now, and he could buy it without deciding, for the moment, what he wanted to do with it. What had happened at the farm, what had happened with the restaurant, perfectly illustrated his theory of value, which he expounded to me more than once— "In the end, you know, there's a premium to be paid for starting something yourself. The deal is, tempting as it is to start it yourself, it costs more. You got to get in there after the building's done but before they've got anything to show for it, and you can get yourself a deal. That's what I think anyway. I mean, this restaurant is a case in point. It was a good idea. Who says it might not still be a good idea, but not every good idea is a profitable idea, if you know what I mean. Now, your friend Marcus, I always thought he was full of good ideas, I'll say that for him."

I did call Marcus my friend. I would say, "He was my best friend. I don't understand it." But, really, I hadn't called him my best friend when he was still around. Calling him my best friend was a bad idea, an expensive idea, too. During the period that I was referring to him as my best friend, I had shooting pains in my knees, constant migraine headaches, and a persistent pain on the right side of my neck. I spent a lot of money at the chiropractor, who took X rays and decided that my atlas was completely out of alignment, and then I went there and had my atlas aligned six times, which cost plenty of money with all the doctors I was seeing as well, but the pains didn't go away until I stopped referring to Marcus as my best friend and started referring to him as Marcus-Burns-Oh-I-had-a-run-in-with-him-too.

George Sloan would go over to the house on the hill and sit in a chair in the front room and gaze out over the valley and the trees and the deepening twilight until the earth was dark and the entire dome of the sky was a fountain of stars: "As good as a movie, as far as I'm concerned." He was right. The time I went with him, it was quite spectacular. We sat in a couple of plastic chairs, with beers, and for once George was quiet and I was the one who talked. I looked out at the cosmic display, and I said, "But why did he have to take all my money too? It was like he was waiting around just to screw me. He got the bank's money on December seventeenth, but he waited around an extra two weeks for me to clean out my bank account and give it to him. Why did he

want my money? My own money? Was it revenge for me holding out on him somehow? Did
he see it like that? I mean, I gave it to him of my
own accord, but he acted as if he was my friend.
He *said* he was my friend."

"Every word Marcus Burns ever spoke was a
lie," said George, "even when it was factually
correct."

"Yes, but—"

"Think about that. Just think about it."

We were sitting entirely in the dark. I was
quiet for a moment; then I said, "But George.
Listen. You could say he just decided to steal the
money at the end, or you could say he looked
at us right from the beginning and saw us as
patsies, or you could say the plan kind of grew
as things went along. I feel like it's killing me
not to know. He was my best friend."

"He *was* your best friend."

"What?"

"I mean that when he stole your money he
distanced himself from you, and for all you know
that's the one thing that's kept you out of jail.
Look at that Milky Way, how it cuts across the
sky. You know, I bring the kids over here, and
they say, 'Yeah, Dad, stars. They're nice, Dad.'" He
laughed affectionately. "Marcus Burns made out
like he knew the ins and outs of everything.
Maybe he did. So who's to say he didn't know

what was up with Crosbie? Who's to say he didn't know everything that was going to happen with Portsmouth Savings and all of that? Who's to say?" He settled comfortably in his chair. He said, "You know, that's a nice window. I love a mullioned window."

"He told me he had second sight."

"He had a good instinct about the market, I'll go that far." He opened the cooler and offered me another beer. I showed him I wasn't finished with the one I had. He took out a handkerchief and blew his nose. Finally he said, "Here's what I thought about Nixon. It's the same thing I thought about that guy, Lee Harvey Oswald. They were making it up as they went along. That's what I think about Marcus. That's *all* I think about Marcus."

And that was the last time we talked about Marcus.

Felicity was divorced from Hank and both of them left the area. Hank went out West somewhere, maybe Montana, and Felicity moved to New York City after the younger boy went to college. I was working for a big national real estate firm by that time, and one of the first good sales I had was of the Davids' house in Deacon. True to form, they tripled their investment and found a place in North Carolina. I had paid back the ten thousand dollars I'd borrowed from my parents when Marcus stole my money, and no one ever talked about Marcus Burns or Jane anymore. I no longer saw anyone who had known them.

Of course I had been a sucker. One thing about it all was how easy it went down. Day after day, driving around, thinking of this billion and that billion, the seasons rolling by. It was Marcus who made it easy, smiling, talking, persuading, telling me what to do. By contrast, everything I'd done before him and everything I did after was an effort. As much as I knew I was a sucker, though, it was almost impossible to accept the fact that I was likely never to hear anything from Marcus, never to know from his own lips what his story was. I felt like I wanted a very small thing—not my money back, not to do everything all over again differently, not to be a big American success, not even to exact revenge, after a while, but only to know what really happened. Everyone seemed to agree that Marcus was a liar, though, so what would he have told me? A lie, I suppose. Anyway, most people blamed Jane. It all changed when Jane came. It was Jane who cooked up the idea of the fake farmland in Kansas, Jane who put together the paperwork, Jane who knew that Portsmouth Savings was so awash in paperwork of all kinds and so eager to cook the books they would never check on anything as far away as Nebraska. Everyone said they had never liked Jane to begin with. Mike Lovell, who went back to running his gas station, swore that the big fight he heard between Marcus and Jane was all about that. "She had something over him, I guarantee it," was Mike's line. "She blackmailed him. I had her number from the first time I saw her, but you couldn't say anything bad about her to Marcus." Even so, I didn't think that Jane wanted to steal my money. I thought that was Marcus's own idea. That's what I was really interested in.

I thought maybe Marcus and Jane would eventually come to trial and it would all come out, under oath: the truth at last. But Marcus and Jane disappeared. If there was a truth to be known, I was not, and probably would never be, in a position to know it. For a while, the thought that made me angriest was the thought of myself coming upon Marcus on a beach somewhere, of recognizing him instantly from afar and going up to him, and him not remembering who I was.

I came to feel that no one was interested in our particular events as long as I was. I came to think I was the last holdout, the one who couldn't move on. Even my parents had a theory that reassured them—the workings of Satan in the world. They shook their heads regretfully when they discussed their theory, but it was something they understood.

In the winter of 1990, I went skiing at Hunter Mountain, north of New York City. I had been skiing a lot for about three years at that point, always by myself, sometimes every weekend for two or three months, at least for a day. I was getting pretty good. But I was fifty now, or as good as fifty, and, yes, my lawyer's prophecy had come to pass. I was still at square one. Still living in my parents' duplex, still selling houses, still spending a fair amount of time at the Viceroy. This was one of those sharp, clear, very cold days. I think it was below zero. I had on some new goggles and was making my third run of the day. The first two had been fast and exhilarating and I was in a good mood, so when it happened it didn't at all surprise me that the woman who got into the chairlift with me and pulled off her hat and mask turned out to be Felicity, laughing. Nor did it surprise me that she exclaimed, "Oh, Joey! It's you at last!" and put her free arm around me.

The feeling of amazement grew from there, though, and most of the way up the mountain I was speechless. Her hair was long again, and her curls were edged with gray. Her face was thin. She looked beautiful. She said, "We're all poor now. Isn't that funny?" She laughed. Then I laughed. She said, "Don't you ever think about that? That this is what it's like not having to pay taxes ever again?" And then she kissed me on the lips and we got to the top of the mountain and got off the lift. We stood there for a moment, putting our hats and goggles back on, adjusting our poles and stamping our skis, left, right, and then she stepped over the edge, down the mountain, and for once I recognized something my parents had talked about all my life, and that was the operation of grace in the material world, and I followed her, as fast as she could go.

ACKNOWLEDGMENTS

Several lawyers advised me on this project, but they preferred not to be mentioned by name. I thank them anyway.

A NOTE ABOUT THE AUTHOR

Jane Smiley is the author of many novels, including *A Thousand Acres,* which won the Pulitzer Prize, and *Horse Heaven.* She lives in Northern California. In 2001, she was inducted into the American Academy of Arts and Letters.